PRAISE FOR

First Comes Love

Praise for Emily Giffin

The One & Only

"A poignant, entertaining novel." —*People*

"Giffin scores again by bringing her discerning understanding of matters of the heart." —*Family Circle*

"Deep, beautifully written . . . [Giffin's] latest focuses on a forbidden love of sorts, but in a new setting: a fictional small college town in Texas." —*Marie Claire*

"Giffin's playful prose will draw you in." —*Chatelaine*

Where We Belong

"Emily Giffin ranks as a grand master. Over the course of five bestselling novels, she has traversed the slippery slopes of true love, lost love, marriage, motherhood, betrayal, forgiveness, and redemption that have led her to be called 'a modern-day Jane Austen.' With Giffin's use of humor, honesty, originality, and, like Austen, a biting social commentary, this modern-day 'woman's novel' sits easily on nightstands and in beach bags. Even Austen would find it hard to put down." —*Chicago Sun-Times*

"In another surefire hit, [Giffin] serves up pathos, humor, and one doozy of a twist." —*Entertainment Weekly*

"Book clubs will have a field day with this one. Thorny mother-daughter relationships and secrets we keep from loved ones burn up the pages." —*USA Today*

Heart of the Matter

"Giffin displays her trademark ability to capture the complexities of human emotions while telling a rip-roaring tale."
—*The Washington Post*

"Giffin's latest opens with one of the more haunting . . . scenes in recent memory [and] toward the end things are so tense that the pages pop with each turn." —*People*

"Giffin beautifully shows how quickly need becomes love [and her] chronicle of fluid, almost casual marital disconnect is a powerful cautionary tale." —*The Boston Globe*

Love the One You're With

"Giffin's talent lies in taking relatable situations and injecting enough wit and suspense to make them feel fresh. The cat-and-mouse game between Ellen and Leo lights up these pages, their flirtation as dangerously addictive as a high-speed car chase."
—*People*

"Giffin excels at creating complex characters and quick-to-read stories that ask us to explore what we really want from our lives. *Love the One You're With* skillfully explores the secret workings of a young woman's heart, and the often painful consequences of one's actions." —*The Atlanta Journal-Constitution*

"Giffin is a dependably down-to-earth, girlfriendly storyteller."
—*The New York Times*

Baby Proof

"Giffin's writing is true, smart, and heartfelt. Claudia is both flawed and achingly real." —*Entertainment Weekly*

"When it comes to writing stories that resonate with real women, best-selling author Emily Giffin has hit her stride. . . . [*Baby Proof*] examines the great lengths people go for each other, and is filled with well-developed female characters."

—*San Francisco Chronicle*

"One of the sharpest writers out there . . . profound, humorous, and reveals layers about a woman's deepest desires."

—*The Arizona Republic*

Something Blue

"Giffin's writing is warm and engaging; readers will find themselves cheering for Darcy as she proves people can change in this captivating tale."

—*Booklist* (starred review)

"Giffin's plotting and prose are so engaging that she quickly becomes a fun, friendly presence in your reading life."

—*Chicago Sun-Times*

"Highly entertaining."

—*Boston Globe*

Something Borrowed

"Hilarious and thoughtfully written, resisting the frequent tendency of first-time novelists to make their characters and situations a little too black-and-white. . . . You may never think of friendships—their duties, the oblique dances of power and their give-and-take—quite the same way again."

—*The Seattle Times*

"A thrill to read."

—*The Washington Post*

"This page-turning, heartbreakingly honest debut deftly depicts the hopeful hearts behind an unsympathetic situation."

—*Entertainment Weekly*

BY EMILY GIFFIN

Something Borrowed
Something Blue
Baby Proof
Love the One You're With
Heart of the Matter
Where We Belong
The One & Only
First Comes Love

First Comes Love

First Comes Love

A NOVEL

EMILY GIFFIN

ANCHOR CANADA

Library and Archives Canada Cataloguing in Publication

Giffin, Emily, author
First comes love / Emily Giffin.

ISBN 978-0-385-68047-9 (paperback)
ISBN 978-0-385-68046-2 (ebook)

I. Title.

PS3607.I28F57 2017   813'.6   C2016-901019-8

This book is a work of fiction. Names, characters, places and incidents are
products of the author's imagination or are used fictitiously. Any resemblance
to actual events or locales or persons, living or dead, is entirely coincidental.

Text design: Victoria Wong
Cover design: Belina Huey
Cover images: Leah Reena Goren (bird), Marlene Silveira (birdhouse)

Printed and bound in the USA

Published in Canada by Anchor Canada,
a division of Random House of Canada Limited,
a Penguin Random House company

www.penguinrandomhouse.ca

10 9 8 7 6 5 4 3 2

Penguin
Random House
ANCHOR CANADA

For Suzy, with love
And in memory of Bob Gipe

First Comes Love

PROLOGUE

Time is a tricky thing, Daniel said to his mother when he was still very young. When you wanted to savor something, it would speed by in a blur. When you wanted to get past something, it would drag on forever. Elaine Garland recorded the quote in her journal, because it was such an astute observation for an eight-year-old.

Much later, she would go back and read the entry, and think to herself that memories were that way, too. When you wanted to forget, everything would return in raw, brutal focus. When you wanted to remember, the details would slip away like a dream at dawn. It was that way for all of them now, though it was something they seldom discussed, at least not with one another. Nearly fifteen years had passed, both slowly and suddenly.

It happened the day after Daniel's twenty-fifth birthday, and three days before Christmas. He was halfway through his third year of medical school at Yale, and had just returned home for the holidays following his clinical neuroscience rotation, bringing with him his girlfriend, Sophie, a beautiful, upper-crust Brit whom Daniel once called the most charming woman he'd ever met. The two had been dating for more than a year, but this was her first visit to Atlanta, as well as the first time meeting his parents and sisters. Everyone felt varying degrees of anxious, eager, hopeful. Elaine worried the most, both because she was the worrying kind and because Daniel didn't have the best track record when it came to girls. His high school sweetheart had been clingy, his college girlfriend controlling.

But within seconds of their arrival, she felt enormous relief, taking to Sophie at once. *A keeper,* Rob called her, clearly proud that his son not only was in medical school but also could land such an exquisite creature. Daniel's sisters approved as well, Josie dazzled by Sophie's style and beauty, openly admiring her expensive European clothes and shoes, while Meredith, who often accused her sister of being shallow, liked Sophie in spite of those trappings. Most important, they could all tell that she brought out the best in Daniel—which was saying a lot. He was, without a doubt, the shining star of their family.

Sophie earned more points the following morning when she insisted that Daniel and Rob keep their long-standing father-son birthday-breakfast Waffle House tradition. She kissed him goodbye, pushed him out the door, then helped Elaine bake a chocolate cake from scratch, another Garland tradition.

"What was Daniel like as a child?" she asked as she awkwardly stirred the batter, after confessing she was clueless in the kitchen.

Elaine thought for a moment, then said he was exactly the same now as he'd always been. The classic, driven firstborn. A perfectionist. But also sensitive and sentimental, quirky and kind. "The only real difference is his temper," she added with a laugh. "Thank goodness he grew out of that."

"Oh? He used to have a temper, did he?" Sophie asked.

Elaine nodded, then told her favorite tantrum tale—the time Daniel hit his bedroom wall with a wooden bat after Josie scribbled pink crayon graffiti on his treasured Hank Aaron card. "You can still see the plaster where it was patched," she said fondly.

"Wait. Is this the baseball card he still carries in his wallet?"

Sophie asked, her accent making everything she said sound so earnest.

"That's the one," Elaine said, then went on to tell her about the home run Daniel hit the day after the incident—and how he had christened the card his good-luck charm.

THAT EVENING, THEY all went to Blue Ridge Grill for Daniel's birthday dinner. Looking Ivy League sophisticated, Daniel wore a jacket, silver knot cuff links (his gift from Sophie), and sleek black loafers with a long European toe that were unlike anything in Rob's preppy wardrobe. The two teased each other as they got out of the car at the valet stand: *Where the hell did you get those, Danny boy? . . . Lose the old-man tassels, Dad. . . . You're wearing enough hair gel to choke a horse. . . . At least I have hair.*

Elaine knew their banter was a sign of their closeness, and her heart swelled with affection and gratitude as they were escorted to the round table near the fireplace that Rob always requested. She wasn't sure when it had happened exactly, but her son was now a man, and very nearly a doctor, the first in their family. And it wasn't just Daniel who was thriving. They were *all* in a good place, she thought. Rob was doing well at work, and hadn't had a drink in three years. Their marriage wasn't perfect, but it felt solid. Josie and Meredith were works in progress, one a little too wild, the other far too moody; yet each was following her passion, studying to be a teacher and an actress, respectively.

The conversation that night was smart and lively, heavy on current events. September 11 was still a fresh wound. The war in Afghanistan was under way. Enron had just filed for bankruptcy, and Winona Ryder had shoplifted. And in news that seemed to interest only Daniel and Sophie: the Earth's record high barometric pressure had just been recorded in Mongolia—over a thousand hectopascals, a measurement that meant absolutely nothing to the rest of them but would remain lodged in Elaine's brain for years to come.

"You're such a nerd," Josie ribbed her brother at one point, though she secretly admired his intelligence. She had always relied on the force of her personality, but a girl like Sophie made her re-think things, and she vowed to get more serious about her studies in her final, fifth-year stretch of college.

Meredith, too, reflected on her life that evening. She was as dili-gent and hardworking as her brother, but she was more of a loner than he, and often felt a void she could never quite pinpoint. Maybe it was love, she thought that night, watching Daniel with Sophie. Maybe that was what was missing.

After dinner, they went home to have cake in the dining room, Elaine pulling the good china and silver from the butler's pantry. Rob lit twenty-five candles, then they all sang off-key (except for Sophie, who had a clear soprano voice) and watched Daniel close his eyes for several seconds before blowing out the flames in just one try.

"What did you wish for?" Josie asked, the way someone always did.

Of course Daniel wouldn't say. He just smiled a secretive smile before Rob cut the cake and he opened his family presents—a leather briefcase from his parents, flannel pajamas from Josie, a coffee-table book about baseball from Meredith. They all retired a short time later, Elaine pretending that she didn't hear the creaky floorboard outside the guest room.

The next morning she awoke early to the sound of rain on the roof and Rob packing for a quick trip to Memphis, his last-ditch effort to settle a case before year-end. She got up to make him coffee and send him on his way, then went to the gym with her daughters, all of them wishing to lose five pounds, especially knowing that after the holidays, it would be ten. They came home, showered, and spent the rest of that day shopping, fighting gridlock traffic and Lenox Square mall crowds, and getting into occasional squabbles with one another.

They returned home at dusk, just as Daniel was leaving to take Sophie to the airport for her red-eye back to London. The rain had finally cleared, but the temperatures had plummeted, and they stood in the driveway, shivering as they hugged and kissed and wished one another a very merry Christmas. As they got in the car, Sophie said a final thank you.

"We'll see you soon," Elaine replied, because she'd never liked saying goodbye.

ABOUT AN HOUR later, as Elaine wrapped presents at the kitchen table, Daniel burst in the side door with a gust of cold and a trace of Sophie's perfume. Elaine quickly drew a piece of wrapping paper over the slippers she was giving him and told him not to peek.

"I won't," Daniel said, shaking his head. He had never been one to peek, unlike his sisters, who prided themselves on finding the most cleverly hidden presents.

He sat at the table and sighed, looking wistful, clearly missing Sophie already. "Where are the girls?" he asked—the way he always referred to Josie and Meredith.

"Meredith's up in her room. . . . Josie went out . . . somewhere."

He nodded, then helped her wrap, handing her pieces of tape or holding ribbon in place with his thumb while she tied. He wasn't a big talker but was unusually chatty that night, and couldn't stop gushing about Sophie. He confided that they were serious, committed to doing their surgical residencies together.

"You think she's 'The One'?" Elaine asked.

"I do," he said, looking starry-eyed. "She's so *amazing* . . . and I couldn't imagine a better mother for my children."

Elaine smiled at her son, thinking that as young and ambitious as he was, he seemed to understand what really mattered most in life. She wondered whether she and Rob deserved credit, or if he'd simply been born this way. She decided it was a little of both and kissed Daniel's forehead before he went upstairs to shower.

On his way to his room, he passed by Meredith's open door. She looked up and asked if she could borrow his Macy Gray CD. He went and got it for her, telling her to be careful, not to scratch it.

"I'm not Josie. I don't trash things," she said. She knew her expression was morose, but she couldn't change it, blaming PMS, the weather, and her older sister, who had pissed her off before she left the house in jeans too tight and a top too small.

"You okay?" Daniel asked her.

"What do you mean?"

"You seem sad."

"This is just my face," she said.

He sat on the edge of her bed and asked her a few more questions about her acting classes and whether she liked anyone. As in a boy. She hesitated, very nearly telling him how lonely she'd lately felt, but decided against it. So he gave up and went to take his shower. After he left, she felt guilty that she hadn't said anything about Sophie, how much she liked her. She would do that tomorrow. She would be nicer to everyone tomorrow, she told herself, closing her eyes and listening to Macy Gray singing, "I believe that fate has brought us here."

About an hour later, after his shower, Daniel reemerged in the kitchen, his mother still busy putting ribbons on the tins of home-made cheese straws she always delivered to their neighbors.

"I'm running out for a quick burger," he announced.

She glanced up at him and frowned. "With a wet head? You'll catch a cold."

He grabbed his Yale baseball cap and green plaid scarf from a hook by the door, put both on. Satisfied, she nodded, then returned her gaze to a big red bow.

"Be right back," he told her as he opened the door.

"All righty," she said, this time not looking up, not knowing that it would be the last thing she'd ever say to her son.

AT DANIEL'S FUNERAL, Rob talked about those final days, what a good son he had been, how much he had loved his family and friends and Sophie. He talked about how proud he and his wife were of all that Daniel had accomplished, but how that paled in comparison to their pride in his character and compassion.

"He never once, in twenty-five years, let us down," Rob said, his voice shaking, his pauses painfully long as he tried to keep it together. "Not once."

Later, Elaine would wonder how many in that church thought her husband was exaggerating. Of *course* a father is going to speak in superlatives about his dead son. Of *course* he's going to paint his child as extraordinary. Yet Daniel really *was* extraordinary, and sometimes it actually, illogically, seemed to her that being so special had made him more susceptible to tragedy. That if Daniel had been deeply flawed, or simply a more typical, aimless, inconsiderate twenty-something, off getting drunk or having meaningless sex with forgettable girls, then maybe he'd still be alive. But he was a golden child, too good for the world.

Sometimes she even asked herself if she'd make that trade—one of the endless variations of the pointless and cruel what-if game. *What if Daniel hadn't gone out to get that burger? What if she had insisted that she scramble him eggs instead? What if she had stalled him just long enough to tie the plaid olive-green scarf dangling around his neck, one side longer than the other? What if she had simply gone to him, kissed his unshaven cheek, said something, anything, more than* all righty?

She knows the answers. She knows that's all it would have taken for Daniel to miss the Denali sliding on a patch of ice at the intersection of Moores Mill and Northside, less than two miles from home. And that she would never have laid eyes on that soft-spoken, gray-haired officer who appeared in their doorway some thirty minutes later, his patrol lights casting eerie red and blue flashes across the front lawn. She wouldn't have called Rob, frantically hitting redial, redial, redial until he finally answered from the airport in Memphis. She wouldn't have had to say those words aloud to him, or to awaken Meredith moments later, repeating the news for the second time. She wouldn't have tried in vain to track down Josie, before she drove to Grady Hospital with one of her three children, selfishly praying for a case of mistaken identity, hoping that it was *anyone* but Daniel. She wouldn't have the horrifying memory of watching her now ex-husband, when he arrived later that night, clinging to their dead son, sobbing his name, again and again and again.

Instead, in an alternate universe, the one they all futilely imagined, Daniel would be happily married to Sophie, the father of two or three children. He would be practicing medicine somewhere, likely right here in Atlanta, making a real difference, saving lives. He would be turning forty at the end of this year, an older, wiser version of the young man he had been. The kind of person who understands that nothing is as important as family. That love comes first.

They tried to remind themselves of this—of what Daniel stood for and what he would have wanted for them. Sometimes they even made choices in his memory or imagined him watching from above. But that was just something they did, and it never really eased their pain. Instead, nearly fifteen years later, he would remain gone, and they were still right there where they'd always been. Still reeling, regretting, wondering *what if*.

chapter one

JOSIE

It is the first day of school, a symbolic and hopeful fresh start, at least that's what I tell myself as I stand before my captive, well-scrubbed audience of ten boys and eleven girls in my J.Crew finest—gold ballet flats, gray pants, and a pink, sequined sweater set. Sitting cross-legged on the braided rug, some children beam back at me, while others wear blank expressions, waiting without judging. It is the beauty of first graders. They are guileless, not a jaded one among them.

Odds are good that they'd heard that they'd scored in the great, mysterious teacher lottery before they even walked through my classroom door, adorned with a construction-paper maple tree, cut-outs of twenty-one personalized bluebirds, and a banner swinging from the boughs that exclaims: WELCOME TO MISS JOSIE'S NEST!

After fourteen years teaching at the same elementary school, I have a reputation as fun, energetic, and creative. I am not considered strict, but not a pushover, either. Incidentally, I am also known as the "pretty teacher," which some parents (fathers and mothers alike) seem to value as much as anything else, including straight-up intelligence, a sentiment that has always confounded and vaguely annoyed me. I mean, I know I'm not teaching quantum calculus, but I *am* instilling critical survival skills in children, teaching them how to add and subtract, tell time, count money, and most important, really *read,* unlocking the mystery of consonant combinations and abstract sounds, blended and pronounced as words, strung together in sentences, filling the pages of books, whether with or without pictures. It might seem like *Groundhog Day* to some, including a few of my colleagues who really need to change professions, but I am passionate about what I do, thrilled to watch things click for a new crop of children every year.

Yet amid the anticipation is always a melancholy feeling that the summer is over, coupled with a familiar prickling of self-doubt and anxiety that has marked all my first days of school, both as a teacher and as a student before that. I consider the many potential obstacles ahead, wondering how many of my kids will have ADHD or dyslexia or other garden-variety learning issues. Who will become frustrated or disheartened when they fall behind their peers? Which children will have impossible-to-please parents who will bombard me with emails and calls, make outlandish suggestions for our curriculum, or point out grammatical errors in my newsletters under the guise of constructive criticism? (No matter how many times I proofread my correspondence, it is inevitable that at some point during the year I will misspell a word or misplace an apostrophe, mistakes that somehow seem more egregious from a teacher than, say, a lawyer or doctor.)

Then there is the disturbing matter of Edie Carlisle, the firstborn of my most significant ex, Will Carlisle. Will and I broke up years ago—eight to be exact—but I'm not yet over him, at least not completely. And I simply can't believe that his little girl has been assigned to *my* class, a fact I try in vain to forget as I launch into my script, a variation of what I say every year.

Hello, boys and girls! My name is Miss Josie! I grew up right here in Atlanta and graduated from the University of Georgia. Go Dawgs! I love animals and have a rescue dog named Revis. I have one sister and a beautiful four-year-old niece named Harper. My favorite color is pink, like my sweater. My hobbies include swimming, reading, baking cookies, dancing, and playing board games. I'm good at keeping secrets and being a trustworthy friend. I hope you will all be good friends to one another this year. I'm so excited to get to know each and every one of you and I feel very lucky to be your teacher!

It sounded pretty good, the exuberant delivery elevating it to a solid A, even though I could hear the annotated version in my head, which went something like this:

Every time I say "Miss Josie" I think it sounds like a stripper—a job I fleetingly considered taking one summer in college because strippers make a hell of a lot more money than waitresses. And teachers, for that matter. I have a dog, and a sister named Meredith. She drives me nuts, and I would mostly avoid her altogether if it weren't for my niece, Harper. I used to have an older brother, but he died in a car accident a long time ago, something I don't like to talk about, especially to my students. I think the subject of one's favorite color is supremely boring because it really doesn't tell you much of anything (color for what—a car or a purse or your bedroom walls?), but for some inexplicable reason, you all seem hyperfocused on it, so I'm going to say pink because roughly half of you will be pleased with my choice and at least a third of you will marvel over the coincidence of sharing the same favorite hue. Swimming isn't really a hobby, just a thing I sometimes do at the Y in an attempt to keep off the weight that I'm prone to gaining around my midsection (from all the cookies I bake, then eat), something you seem not to notice or at least not to judge. I do enjoy board games, but I'd rather play drinking games with my friends—or go dancing with them (did I mention I could have been a stripper fifteen pounds ago?). I can keep secrets, especially my own, which is a good thing, because if your parents knew some of my skeletons, they might send around a petition to have me fired. Friendship means everything to me because I'm thirty-seven and can't find a decent man to marry, which is depressing both because I don't want to be alone and because I adore children more than anything else in the world. I know I'm running out of time, at least to birth my own. Please be nice to one another this year because the one thing I will not tolerate on my watch is mean girl (or boy) escapades—though fortunately those dynamics don't really kick in until next year, yet another reason to teach the first grade. I'm so excited to get to know each and every one of you, and that includes you, Edie Carlisle. Did your father tell you that he dumped me right before he married your mother and had you? I will do my best not to hold this against you, but please show a little mercy and keep your happy-home anecdotes to a minimum.

I smile down at their eager, shining faces and say, "So? Do you have any questions for me?"

Four hands shoot into the air, and as I consider who is the least likely to ask the one query I have come to loathe, a fidgety boy with messy hair and ruddy cheeks blurts it out: *Do you have a husband?*

Three seconds flat. A new record. *Congrats, Wesley,* I think, glancing at his laminated name tag which I made over the weekend, and making a mental note to work into the curriculum that a bare left ring finger means *please do not ask questions on the topic of marriage.* Perhaps I could squeeze it in between our weather unit and the introduction to the metric system.

I force a bigger, brighter smile, doing my best to ignore the knot in my chest. "No, Wesley. I'm not married. Maybe one day! And let's try to remember to raise our hands before we call out. Like this," I say, raising my hand for a visual demonstration. "Okay?"

Wesley's head bobs up and down while I reassure myself that

surely Edie knows nothing about my relationship with her father. After all, any knowledge of his romantic past would indicate inappropriate mothering—and I'm sure that Andrea (pronounced on-DRAY-ah) Carlisle has immaculate judgment to go along with her impeccable taste, which I've gleaned from stalking her Pinterest page. *Gluten-free snacks! Homemade Halloween costumes! Postpregnancy workouts you can do with your child! Paint colors for a serene master suite!* Thank God the woman's Instagram and Facebook profiles are set to private—a small blessing from the social media gods.

As if on cue, Edie raises her hand as high as it will go, elbow straight, fingers erect and skyward. She is holding her breath, her little chest puffed out, her bright blue eyes wide and unblinking. I look right past her, though she is seated front and center, and field a question from the back of the rug about my favorite food (pizza, unfortunately) and then my second favorite color (yawn).

"Hmmm. Maybe blue. Or green. Or orange. Orange is good," I stall while doing a quick scan of Edie's features, searching for a resemblance to Will. She has his olive complexion and his mouth, her lower lip significantly fuller than the upper one, but the rest of her features belong to her mother, who often appears in the pages of *The Atlantan,* either cozied up to Will or expertly posing, hand at her waist, elbow jutting out, with one of her couture-clad gal pals. I've only seen her in person once, about four years ago, as she strolled down the cereal aisle of Whole Foods, pushing her precious Lilly Pulitzer–clad toddler in her well-organized, produce-rich cart. (Even back then, I knew from the usual two degrees of Buckhead separation that her child's name was Edie, short for Eden, Andrea's maiden name.) Wearing black Lululemon workout gear and flip-flops, Andrea looked effortlessly chic. Her skin glowed from a recent workout or facial (perhaps both); her limbs were long and toned; her thick, wavy blond ponytail was threaded through a Tel-luride baseball cap. I covertly trailed her for three aisles, torturing myself with her self-possessed air, graceful gait, and the deliberate way she checked labels while murmuring nurturing commentary to her daughter. I hated myself for being so mesmerized with her every move, and felt something approaching shame when I plucked her truffle oil of choice from the shelf, as if that single overpriced ingre-dient might bring me one step closer to the life she had, the one I so coveted.

Not much has changed since that day, other than the addition of Edie's little brother, Owen (with whom Andrea was actually five weeks pregnant at the time, I later calculated). I catch myself star-ing now at Edie, who is propping her raised hand up with the other, demonstrating that she has as much staying power as her mother. Reminding myself that it isn't Edie's fault that her father left me, or that I never learned what to do with that damn truffle oil and really had no business shopping at Whole Foods, aka Whole Paycheck, in the first place, I force myself to acknowledge her. "Yes? Edie?"

"Um," she says, her expression blank, her eyes darting around the room as her hand falls limply to her lap. "Umm . . . I forgot what I was going to say."

"That's okay. Take your time," I say, smiling, a portrait of pa-tience.

Her face lights up as it comes to her. "Oh, yeah! Um, do you have a boyfriend?" Edie asks, throwing salt on my wounds.

I stare back at her for a paranoid beat, then make the sick split-second decision to lie.

"Yes! Yes, I *do* have a boyfriend," I announce, lifting my chin a few inches, clasping my hands together. "And he's amazing. Just amazing."

"What's his name?" Edie fires back.

"Jack," I say; it has been my favorite boy name since I first watched *Titanic*. I am also a sucker for all things Kennedy, choosing to focus on the Camelot version of JFK rather than the sordid Marilyn Monroe side.

"What's his last name?" Edie presses.

"Prince. Jack Prince," I say, then add a wistful footnote. "Unfortunately, Jack doesn't live in Atlanta."

"Where does he live?" asks a girl named Fiona, whose brutally short bangs do not take into account her cowlick. An oversize bow perches atop her head, seeming to mock the unfortunate back-to-school cut.

"Africa," I say. "Kenya to be exact. He's a doctor in the Peace Corps. Working at a refugee camp."

The lie feels therapeutic, as does my silent afterthought: *Take that, Edie. Your daddy's in wealth management, a euphemism for playing golf with his blue-blood friends while occasionally shuffling around family money they never earned.*

"Has Jack ever seen a lion?" asks a miniature boy named Frederick with a soft voice but perfect diction. I feel instantly protective of wee Freddie, projecting that he will become a favorite. (No matter what they tell you, all teachers have pets.)

"I'm not sure, Frederick. I'll ask Jack that question later when we Skype—which we do every day—and get back to you tomorrow," I say.

Because after all, it is *way* tougher to answer a yes-no question about lion spotting than it is to manufacture an entire transcontinental relationship.

A barrage of frantic questions ensues about whether Jack has had any run-ins with tigers or alligators, hippos or monkeys. First graders love a good tangent. So do I, actually, and as tempting as it is to keep talking about my do-gooding beau, I know it's time to take control of the situation and actually teach.

THE REST OF the day hums along smoothly, as I memorize my students' names and get to know their personalities. I even mostly manage to forget about Will until Edie loses her bottom left front tooth while eating her carrots and hummus at snack time. She's already missing her bottom right, yet she is as jubilant as a tooth virgin as her classmates gather around to examine the bloody trophy. A veteran at loose and missing teeth, both in the actual pulling and in the recovery and storage, I help her rinse out the gap in her gum, then clean the tiny tooth, stowing it safely in one of the Ziploc baggies that I keep in my desk for such occasions. I pull out a pink Post-it note from another drawer and write "for the Tooth Fairy," then draw a heart and slide the note into the baggie, sealing it.

"What do you think she'll bring you?" I ask, gazing down at my plump heart, then looking right into Edie's pretty eyes.

"Same thing she brought me for this tooth," Edie says, pointing to the inside of her mouth as she thrusts her tongue into the hole. Her voice is low and raspy—the kind that will one day drive guys crazy.

"And what was that?" I ask, wondering about her mother's voice, knowing that I'll be unable to resist gathering intelligence all year long. I have already asked several questions about her little brother, learning that Owen's nickname is O, that he has an airplane-motif bedroom, and that he "goes to time-out a lot."

"She brought me a dollar coin," Edie replies, which gives me a fresh pang, along with a wave of disappointment that I can't paint Will and Andrea as overindulgent parents. Most Buckhead tooth fairies *vastly* overpay, but a dollar coin is both an appropriate amount and more satisfying than a crumpled bill. *Damn.*

As I hand the baggie to Edie, I regret my heart on the Post-it, worried that her parents will read into the artwork. But it is too late for a re-do, as Edie is already gripping it with a proud smile. She then marches over to her cubby and stows it in the back pocket of her monogrammed pink butterfly backpack. I tell myself that it's no big deal, that Andrea and Will are likely too busy and too happy to scrutinize something so trivial. More important, I tell myself that I am a good teacher and a good person—and that sweet Edie deserves that heart even though her father shattered mine.

chapter two

MEREDITH

"Well, today sucked," Josie announces as she waltzes into my kitchen and interrupts a rare moment of peace.

It is Thursday, my one day off every week, and I've just parked Harper in front of the television so I can go through my email. In other words, I don't want company, and if my sister had, say, phoned first, I would have told her as much.

"Oh, hi, Kimmy," I say over my shoulder, referencing the annoying neighbor on *Full House* who regularly barged into the Tanner house without knocking.

Josie, who still watches reruns of the show, a sign of her overall maturity, laughs and says, "Do you really expect me to ring the doorbell of my childhood home?"

I resist the urge to say *yes because it's no longer your home, Nolan and I bought it, fair and square*—or I could point out that my husband and I need privacy and could have been having sex in the foyer, at least theoretically. Instead I take the high ground and leave it as a rhetorical question while I continue to click through my inbox.

"I mean—it *really* sucked," Josie adds, hovering over me.

"What happened?" I ask, remembering that today was her first day of school, and positive that her answer involves her ex-boyfriend Will or his wife or their daughter, who was assigned to Josie's class.

She has talked about little else since receiving the class roster this summer, pretending to be outraged by circumstances that I know, deep down, delight her. Josie relishes drama that involves her stable of men, past or present.

She sighs, leaning on my desk. "Where do I begin?" she says, as I eye her scuffed gold flats and remind her that we are a shoeless-indoors household.

"C'mon, Mere," she says as if this is the first time we've had this discussion. "You act as if I just walked through a field of feces. You really need to take some medicine for your OCD—I hear Zoloft is good for that."

I cut her off, wondering if she somehow knows I *am* taking Zoloft. It would be just like her to snoop through my medicine cabinet. "First of all, you absolutely *could* have unwittingly stepped in something that isn't welcome in rooms in which we live and eat. Besides, it's our house and our rule. So . . . *there*."

She stares at me a beat, then haphazardly kicks off her flats, one sliding under my chair. "Just so you know, I read an etiquette column that said it's the 'height of tacky to invite people into your home and then require that they remove anything other than their coat,'" Josie says, making air quotes as I picture her Googling the query and memorizing the answer that suits her while ignoring all other opinions, such as the ones that point out just how filthy a practice it is to wear shoes indoors.

"Well, I didn't 'invite you into my home,' now, did I?" I say, making air quotes back.

I know there is a fifty-fifty chance that she will turn and storm out, and I'm okay with those odds. But because Josie's skin has always been selectively thin, and she clearly is in need of some kind of free therapy, she simply shrugs and goes for the last word. "Well, I think I may have a foot fungus. Don't say I didn't warn you."

"We'll take our chances," I say, then cut to the chase. The sooner

I let her obsess over Will, the sooner she will be on her way to her happy hour or whatever mindless activity she has planned from here. "So what's she like? Will's kid?"

"Her name is Edie. Short for Eden. Andrea's maiden name," she says, pausing for effect as she walks barefoot over to the refrigerator, then opens the door. "And as much as I'd love to tell you she is a precocious brat . . . I actually really like her. She is sweet, engaging, and generally adorable."

"That's great," I say.

"*Great?* It's far from great. It's painful. A daily reminder of what I don't have," she says, as she plucks one of Nolan's Bud Lights from the bottom shelf, then twists off the top and takes a long drink. "And I bet you anything that Mrs. Will Carlisle volunteers to be room mom. You watch."

"You're the teacher. Don't you get to pick your own room mom?" I say, as I RSVP no to an Evite for a birthday party at one of those inflatable play venues where kids are more likely to get a concussion or skin disease than they are to actually have fun.

"Ultimately. But it's based on volunteers. Which mother checks the little box on the form I sent home. So if she's the only volunteer . . ." Josie sighs, leaving her sentence unfinished.

"First of all, you'll get at least five volunteers," I say, thinking of all the eager-beaver mothers of children in Harper's preschool class. "And even if you don't, you could just ask another mother and hope it doesn't get back to Andrea."

Despite Josie's insistence that teaching is one of the most emotionally, physically, and mentally draining professions, I always feel like I'm missing something. I just don't see her job as all that complicated, at least not in comparison to the politics and pressures at my law firm, and especially given her twelve weeks of vacation every year.

"Oh, it would get back to her," she says. "That kind of thing always gets back."

I nod, granting her this much. Mothers always talk. In fact, unless Will's wife is amazingly tactful or shockingly in the dark about her husband's past, I feel sure that half the moms have already heard the gossip about their child's first-grade teacher. "Well, I *told* you that you should have intervened," I say, remembering how I scripted the phone call with her headmaster boss weeks ago, requesting that said child be moved to another first-grade classroom due to a "personal situation."

"By the time I got the class list, it was too late," she says. "It had already gone out to the parents."

"So?" I say.

"So they would know that I made the switch."

"So?" I say again.

Josie stares at me, then takes a long drink of beer. "So the opposite of love is indifference. And switching a kid out of my class is not an indifferent move."

"Well, neither is stalking," I say at my own peril. "And that's never stopped you."

Josie grins, apparently wearing stalking as some sort of badge of honor. "I haven't stalked Will in years. Until recent developments. Besides, you can't really count an innocent drive-by as stalking. It's not like I egged his house. I just wanted to see where they lived."

"Right," I say, thinking that Will and his wife might not characterize the late-night maneuver as entirely innocent. Creepily worrisome is probably closer to the mark.

"Did I tell you what she drives?" Josie asks with a note of glee.

"You mentioned a minivan," I say, thinking that her victory is pretty hollow. "Maybe it's *his* car," I add.

"Nope. It had a College of Charleston bumper sticker," she

says. "Her school. Her car. Please shoot me if I ever drive a mini-van."

"Are you forgetting that *I* drive a minivan?" I say, wondering if she's intentionally *trying* to offend me—or if it just comes that natu-rally to her.

"How could I forget such a thing?" she says. "No offense. I mean—you and I are clearly very different."

"Clearly," I say, marveling that we actually share the same par-ents and upbringing. In the next instant, I think of the only other person in the world who shared our genes and childhood. I glance at the clock—5:50—an ingrained habit whenever I remember my brother. For a long time, Daniel was my very first thought of the day, even before my eyes opened or my head lifted from the pillow. Now, all these years later, I sometimes make it until midmorn-ing—or even later in the day—though I'm never quite sure if this is a sign of progress or a source of guilt. To mitigate the latter, I clear my throat and say his name aloud. "I bet Daniel would have driven a minivan."

Josie's face clouds the way it always does when I mention our brother. Then she shakes her head and says, "Hell, no. Surgeons don't drive minivans."

"Practical ones with small children do," I reply, thinking there are few things in life as satisfying as that little button that auto-matically opens a sliding door before you buckle or unbuckle your helpless offspring.

"Practical ones with small children *and* taste . . . do *not*," she says.

"Thank you very little," I say with a glare.

"You're welcome," she says with a smile, confirming my con-stant suspicion that on some level, she enjoys conflict, especially conflict with me.

I push my luck. "Speaking of Daniel, Mom called yesterday. . . ."

"Daniel and Mom are interchangeable now?"

"Can I finish?"

She shrugs, then corrects me the way she would her students. "Yes, you *may* finish."

"She was talking about the fifteen-year anniversary," I begin, choosing my words carefully, and feeling resentful for having to do so. If I could change one thing about Josie—and there are many, *many* things I'd change—it would be the way she has handled our loss of Daniel. The impenetrable wall she's built around him and his memory.

"Anniversary?" she says, picking up her beer, then putting it back on the counter without taking a sip. "I'd hardly call it an anniversary."

"It actually *is* an anniversary."

She shakes her head. "Anniversaries connote celebration. Years you've been married . . . good stuff . . . not accidents and *death*."

It is the most she's said about Daniel in ages, and in some sick way, the words *accidents* and *death*, spoken aloud, feel like a small victory to me. "An anniversary is the date on which something occurred in the past. Good or bad," I say, keeping my voice soft. I almost stand up to put my arm around her, but we aren't a hugging family. At least we haven't been in years. So I stay put at my desk and watch her from a comfortable distance.

Josie swallows, staring down at her toes, painted a bright orange hue. I remember the time I told her that people with chubby toes should stick to neutral polish. It was a little rude, I guess, but I'd only been kidding. She still freaked, then stated for the record that she'd rather have chubby toes than stubby legs, and I swear her toes have been neon ever since.

When she doesn't look back up, I say her name. "Josie? Did you hear what I said?"

She says yeah, she heard me.

"So Mom wants us to do something. The three of us. Maybe even invite Dad."

"She'd have to talk to him first," Josie snaps. "Besides, he has a new girlfriend."

"He does?" I ask, feeling a stab of resentment, but also jealousy that she has a closer relationship with our father. "Since when?"

"Since . . . I don't know . . . months ago."

"Do I know her?" I ask, thinking they can't be that serious—there was no sign of her on Facebook and it was something his girlfriends always did: post photos, often on trips or at his Lake Burton house, then tag him so they show up in his feed.

She shrugs and says, "Her name's Marcia. . . . She's a court reporter." She then proceeds to type on an imaginary keyboard as I picture a girl with a lot of cleavage and red acrylic nails.

"How old is she?"

"Why do you always ask that?"

"Why not?"

"I don't know . . . mid-forties . . . divorced . . . two sons. . . . So what does Mom have in mind for this awkward 'anniversary,' anyway? A fancy dinner? A little spin with the Ouija board?"

"Josie!" I cringe.

"What?" she asks. "You know Mom believes in that weird shit."

"She doesn't believe in *Ouija* boards. . . . She believes in *signs*."

"Well, it's ridiculous. There are no *signs*. Daniel's not making rainbows appear or dropping pennies on the sidewalk," Josie says with a disdainful look on her face. "And you still haven't answered my question. What does she have in mind to commemorate the anniversary of a tragic car accident?"

"I don't know," I say. "Maybe take a trip."

"Does that seem right to you?" Josie says, lifting her gaze to meet mine. "Taking some tropical vacation—"

I cut her off before she can really get rolling on her rant and say, "I don't think it's a question of *right* and *wrong*. And I didn't say tropical *or* vacation. She mentioned New York, actually."

"Why New York?"

"Because of Sophie."

"Sophie who?"

"C'mon, Josie . . . you know *who*. . . . Daniel's Sophie."

She shakes her head and says, "It's weird that she still thinks about her. It's unhealthy."

"Maybe," I say. "Maybe that's why she wants to visit. To get closure."

"Closure? Daniel died *fifteen* years ago, Meredith," she says, her gaze steely.

"I *know* that," I say.

She stares at me a beat before replying. "And you know what else?" Before I can answer, she continues, "They would have broken up. She would have broken his heart—or vice versa. And in either event, Mom would have hated her and held a grudge the way she does with all of our exes, and she would have long forgotten Sophie by now. And instead—"

"Instead Daniel died," I say, thinking that that sums it all up, really. Daniel died and that changed everything, forever. And *that* is the part Josie always seems to be missing.

Josie's face goes blank before she announces that she's going to talk to Harper.

I sigh and watch her walk out of the room. Seconds later, I hear her and Harper squealing with laughter, corroborating one of two theories I've always had about my sister. That either (a) she uses children to hide her real adult emotions, or (b) she is still a child herself.

Thirty minutes of gaiety later, Josie returns to the kitchen with Harper in tow. She retrieves her shoes and says, "All right. It's been real. But I'm out."

"Where're you headed?" I ask, though I'm really not all that interested.

"I'm meeting Gabe for dinner," she says, tossing her empty beer bottle into the recycling bin.

"Don't you see him enough as your roommate?" I ask, wondering when that situation will finally implode. No matter what they say, I firmly believe that men and women can't be "just friends," at least not when they're cohabiting.

"You'd be surprised. We both have very busy social lives," she says. "That's what happens when you have friends."

She's directing the statement at me, having always believed in quantity over quality of friendships. The more photos you post with the more people in them means, of course, that you are having more fun. She is a thirty-seven-year-old woman who has never outgrown the concept of popularity. "Right," I say. "Well, have fun."

"I will. Thanks," she says, throwing her tote over her shoulder. Meanwhile, Harper pulls on her arm and begs her not to go. I can't help feeling irritated, noting that my daughter never objects to my departure quite so vehemently. Then again, it's a little bit harder to be a mother than it is to roll in and play the fun aunt for an hour here and there.

"I have to go, sweetie," Josie says, kneeling down to kiss Harper's cheek before standing and making her way to the foyer.

"Bye, Josie," I say, suddenly and bizarrely wishing she weren't leaving. That it were the two of us headed to dinner together.

"See ya," she says, without looking up from her phone as she heads out the door and down the front path.

I watch her for a few seconds, then call out her name. She turns back to look at me, her long blond hair blowing across her face.

"Yeah?"

"Will you at least *think* about what we discussed?" I say. "Please?"

"Oh, yeah. Sure thing," she says in a flippant way that makes it clear she not only is lying but wants me to *know* she is lying. "I'll get right on that."

chapter three

JOSIE

"Perfect timing," I say to Gabe as he joins me at the bar at Local Three, one of our regular hangouts. I point to the pan-roasted monkfish and chilled watermelon soup, which I bribed him with after he told me he was too tired to get off the sofa. A foodie verging on food evangelist, Gabe can always be motivated by his next meal, especially when I promise to pay—which I did tonight.

"What'd she do this time?" he asks. I haven't yet given him any details about our conversation, only that I needed him to reverse the "Meredith effect"—my shorthand for the mix of bad feelings my sister so often gives me.

"I'll get to her in a second," I say. "But first things first."

I hand him my phone and watch him read the email I received just as I was parking.

From: Andrea Carlisle
Sent: August 18
To: Josephine Garland
Subject: Room Mom

Dear Josephine (aka Miss Josie)—

Thank you for a great first day of the first grade. Edie came home so excited and I know you had much to do with that.

Thanks, too, for sending E's tooth home safely. I'm sure the Tooth Fairy will also be grateful for your care. ☺

I'm returning the volunteer form via Edie's book bag tomorrow, but wanted to give you the heads-up that I'm putting my name in the hat for room mom. I feel certain that I could do a good job as your liaison to the other parents.

Either way, I look forward to meeting you face-to-face on Open House night. I've heard a lot of nice things about you (and your family) from Will. Small world, isn't it?!

Best,

Andrea

"Interesting," Gabe deadpans, putting my phone down on the bar in front of me. "What do you think?"

I love this about Gabe. He consistently asks what *I* think before he tells me what *he* thinks—the opposite of Meredith's approach, and really most people's.

"I'm not sure," I say. "Maybe it's a keep-your-friends-close-and-your-enemies-closer type thing?"

"Maybe," he says. "But I'm not getting an ulterior-motive vibe here. Other than the obvious brownnose-the-teacher angle, I suppose."

"What vibe *are* you getting?" I say, eager for his no-frills analysis.

"I'm kind of just getting a *nice* vibe, actually."

I nod reluctantly. It was so much easier to hate Will's wife than to deal with the possibility that she could actually be a likable person.

"Have you written her back?" he asks, sipping the draft beer that I also had waiting for him.

"Not yet."

"But you will?"

"Yeah. I have to," I say. "It's policy to reply to all parent emails."

"And you always follow policy," he quips.

"I do, actually. At school, anyway . . . Think I should pick her for room mom?"

"What does room mom entail?"

"As Andrea so eloquently put it, she'd be the *liaison* to the other mothers," I say, maximizing my sarcasm and exaggerating my French accent, though I'm not sure what point I'm making other than to charge her with using a pretentious noun.

"So throw her a bone," Gabe says. "It would be a good-faith gesture."

I make a face.

"Jeez, Jo. You really gotta relax about this Will thing. He's ancient history."

"I know," I say, thinking that I've had at least a half dozen breakups since Will.

"In fact, I don't think you ever really loved him," Gabe says.

I've heard this theory of his before, and want to believe it, but never quite can, especially now that I know Will's little girl. I think of the gap in her gum and feel a wistful pang that borders on actual pain.

"That's ridiculous," I say. "Of course I loved him."

Gabe shrugs. "Your actions would indicate otherwise. You sabotaged that relationship."

"Did not," I say, thinking that he, of all people, knew that it was a lot more complicated than that.

"Did, too," he says. "And now look at you."

"What do you mean?"

"You're stuck eating pork sliders with *me*," he says, the king of self-deprecation.

"What's wrong with pork sliders?" I say with a smile, already in a better mood.

. . .

GABE HAS BEEN my best guy friend for a long time now. It's always the way I refer to him, although I don't know why I include the gender qualifier when he's really just my straight-up best friend. He grew up in Atlanta, too, but went to North Atlanta High after getting kicked out of Lovett for tapping into the computer systems and changing his friends' grades (even though he did not need to change his *own* grades). So aside from some attenuated social overlap, we really didn't know each other until my final year at the University of Georgia, just after Daniel died. Gabe came to the funeral, along with his whole family, but that alone didn't stand out to me, as literally hundreds turned out for the service and the whole thing was a blur anyway. It was the handwritten note he sent me later that really registered. He didn't say anything that profound, just how sorry he was, and that he had always looked up to my brother "in pretty much all respects." A lot of people did—Daniel was that kind of all-around great guy—but the fact that Gabe actually took the time to spell out his admiration meant a lot. So when I saw him a few weeks later at East West Bistro in Athens, I went up to him and thanked him.

He nodded, and I braced myself for that awkward line of questioning about how I was doing. But he didn't go there, just said again how sorry he was, then changed the subject, for which I was as grateful as for any note of sympathy. We talked the rest of that night, and after last call, he walked me back to my apartment and nonchalantly asked for my number. I told him I had a boyfriend— which was a stretch, I was just hooking up with some baseball player—but wanted to be clear that I didn't like him *like that*. Gabe shrugged and said that was fine, he just wanted to hang out as friends. "I've always thought you were cool."

Because I believed him, and because I was *nothing* if not cool, I gave him my number, and we became instantly tight. Mostly we'd

sit in bars and drink—or sit in one of our apartments and drink. But
we also walked his dog, an ancient black Lab named Woody, and
studied for the anthropology class that neither of us realized the
other was in because we both blew it off so often, and went to see
bands, and smoked an occasional bag of weed.

Our friendship felt unusual because it *was*. Not so much because
of the guy-girl thing, but because we really didn't have all that much
in common, even back when everyone in college had a lot in common. Gabe was outside the mainstream and a little bit of a hipster,
nothing like my girlfriends or the guys I normally gravitated toward.
I found him refreshing, though he had a tendency to playfully put
me down. I quickly lost count of the number of times he looked at
me, incredulous, and said, "How do you not know that?" or "You
really need to read that/see that/listen to that." But I could tell he
appreciated my straightforward simplicity, just as I liked his layers,
and somehow we just clicked.

Over the years, Meredith and my other friends questioned our
platonic deal, accusing us of covertly hooking up. At the very least,
they thought Gabe had a thing for me—or I had a thing for him. I
was always adamant that we did not. Yes, there would probably
always be very fleeting moments of attraction between close friends
of different genders, especially when drinking was involved. But
with Gabe and me, it was never enough to trigger a lapse of judgment, or worse, an ill-fated attempt at an actual relationship. And it
became an unspoken given that neither of us wanted to risk our
cherished friendship in the name of lust, loneliness, or idle curiosity.
In other words, we were living proof that guys and girls could, in
fact, be just friends.

It also helped, of course, that Gabe wasn't my type, nor was I
his. I was curvy and blond and girl-next-door cute, and Gabe liked
petite, rail-thin brunettes, the more exotic the better. His last two

girlfriends had been Asian, and from the neck down, they both looked like teenaged boys. Meanwhile, I preferred broad-shouldered, clean-cut, blue-eyed jocks, a far cry from Gabe's lanky build, dark eyes, and omnipresent five o'clock shadow, which often veered toward an actual beard (which I downright disliked).

"Don't get me wrong," Gabe says now, signaling the bartender for another beer. I can tell by his expression that he's still on the subject of Will. Sure enough, he finishes by saying, "I'm glad you guys broke up."

"Gee, thanks," I say. "You're happy I'm thirty-seven and single and desperate?"

He grins and says, "Kinda."

I smile because I know what he means and feel the same. I'm always a little happier when Gabe is single, and felt total relief when he broke up with his most recent girlfriend, an insufferably snobbish, name-dropping gallery girl. It isn't that we don't wish the best for each other, because we *truly* do. I want Gabe to fall in love and get married and have a family (even though he isn't sure he's cut out for that), and I know he wants the same for me. But it is hard to deny an element of classic misery loves company, not an uncommon dynamic among close, single friends. As an aside—and a backstop— we have always vowed that we will never date someone who isn't cool with our grandfathered-in friendship. In fact, Gabe once called it a screening device, a way to weed out unstable, jealous girls, whom he also calls "the psycho set."

Interestingly, the only person who ever really had a problem with Gabe was Will, who called him "the depressed poser." It was an unfair charge, as Gabe never tries to impress anyone, and really cares little what others think of him, almost to a fault. He isn't exactly depressed either, just a little moody and caustic—which can sometimes wear on people. But he can also be really funny, with a generosity and sense of loyalty that offset his edges. There is no doubt in my mind that Gabe would do anything for me.

"So what's up with Meredith?" he says, changing the subject.

I sigh and tell him the latest—that she and my mother have some big plan they're working up for this December. "You know, it's been fifteen years. . . ."

An intent listener, he looks at me, waiting.

"They want to visit Sophie. In New York," I continue.

"Sophie?" Gabe asks.

"You know, the girl he was dating."

"Oh, right . . ." Gabe shakes his head and whistles.

"Exactly," I say. "So unhealthy, isn't it?"

"It's a little strange . . . I'll give you that." I can tell he is treading carefully, the way he always does around any mention of Daniel.

"It's very strange. Bizarre. They all need to move on with their lives, already."

He raises his eyebrows and looks at me, and I can tell that he is thinking about Will again. I can almost read the bubble over his head: *Isn't that the pot calling the kettle black?*

"What?" I say, feeling defensive.

"Nothing," he says with such purposeful wide-eyed innocence that I'm forced to take drastic measures. I pick up my phone and bang out an email, both my thumbs flying.

From: Josie
Sent: August 18
To: Andrea Carlisle
Subject: Re: Room Mom

Dear Andrea,

Thank you so much for your kind note. Edie is a pleasure, and I can't wait to get to know her better this year. I hope

the Tooth Fairy is good to her tonight! Thank you for volun-
teering to be our room mother—I would love to accept your
kind offer. Look forward to meeting you at Open House.
And yes, it is a small world!

Best,

Josie

I scan it quickly for errors, then send it, listening to the sickening
swooshing sound of an irreversible decision.

"There," I say, showing him the sent message.

He quickly skims it, then hands me back my phone and smirks.
"Whoa. Look at you, Little Miss Well Adjusted."

"I *am* well adjusted," I say, and for one second, I actually believe it.

THAT NIGHT, I wake up around two and can't fall back asleep. I tell
myself that it's just first-week-of-school jitters, or adjusting to an
earlier bedtime, but as morning approaches, I know it runs deeper
than that. I know it has something to do with Daniel and Sophie,
Mom and Meredith, Will and Andrea. And maybe, most of all, it
has something to do with Edie, fast asleep at this very moment. I
imagine her blond curls spilling over her pillow, the shiny coin un-
derneath it, as she dreams her magical dreams. I think of my conversation with Gabe, the person who knows me best and the only one
who knows my secret. My heart aches with regret over so many
things, big and small, including mistakes that have relegated me to
manufacturing boyfriends on faraway continents who are as imaginary as the Tooth Fairy herself.

chapter four

MEREDITH

On Friday night, forty-five minutes before Nolan and I are leaving for dinner with friends, our babysitter cancels via *text. So sorry I'm sick and can't watch Harper tonight. I have food poisoning.* ☹ ☹ ☹

"Liar," I say before slamming my phone onto the bathroom counter, hard enough so that I check to make sure I haven't cracked the screen. Even if I believed she were sick, which I do not, her flippant "so sorry" along with those three emojis would still have pushed me over the edge.

"Who're you calling a liar?" Nolan calls out from our closet, where he is getting dressed.

"The sitter," I answer. "She just canceled."

"Who is she?" Nolan asks, emerging in boxers, socks, and a new light blue linen shirt. One of the many luxuries of being the husband, at least in our household, is that Nolan does not concern himself with domestic logistics like hiring sitters. All he has to do is pick out his own shirt.

"The middle Tropper girl," I say. "I bet she's canceling because of a boy."

"She *could* have food poisoning," Nolan says. "People do get food poisoning, ya know."

"No way. Who gets food poisoning at six-forty-five on a Friday night? And by the way—if you truly *do* have food poisoning, then lie and say it's anything *other* than food poisoning. Because food poisoning *always* sounds like a lie when you're canceling."

"It really does," Nolan says with a laugh. "Why is that, anyway?"

"Because it usually *is*. . . . I should call her out on it. Tell her to go ahead and come anyway, since it's not contagious."

"You can't babysit with food poisoning," Nolan says, missing the point. I watch him unbutton his shirt, then put it back on one of the padded hangers from my end of the closet.

"What are you doing? Put that back on," I say. "I'll see if my mother or Josie can come watch Harper."

"Really?" he says, looking disappointed.

"Don't you *want* to go out?" I say, thinking that I've been looking forward to our plans with the Grahams all week.

"I guess," he says. "But I'm just as happy to stay in. We could order Chinese and watch *Homeland*. We have three episodes left."

I cross my arms and glare at him. "We hardly *ever* go out," I say.

"That's not true," he says. "We just went out to dinner last Saturday."

"Yes, but that was with work people. That doesn't count," I say, knowing that if we stay in, Nolan will watch TV while I put Harper to bed, an arduous, frustrating task that can take hours. I stop short of telling him that I'm desperate to have a few drinks and a grown-up evening without our daughter, in no particular order, and instead say again that I'm going to try my mother and Josie, maybe one of them is free.

"You *know* Josie's going to be busy. When has she ever *not* had plans on a Friday night?" Nolan says, in shirtless limbo. Always in good shape, he's even more fit than usual, gearing up for his next triathlon, his morning training conveniently conflicting with getting Harper ready for school and out the door.

I text them both just in case, but just as Nolan predicted, Josie types back immediately that she is otherwise engaged. My mom writes that she would love to, but already has plans to go to the movies with Kay, her friend from church.

"Dammit," I grumble to myself.

"We could call the Grahams and ask them to come hang out here instead?" Nolan says.

I shake my head, feeling annoyed by the suggestion. "The house is a mess, and we have nothing to eat here."

"So what?" he says. "We can order a pizza."

"I don't want to do that," I say, thinking that I will still be the one stuck putting Harper to bed. "Besides, the Grahams don't want to pay for a sitter for their children only so they can spend the evening with ours."

"All right," he says. "Well, I'm sure we can think of something else fun to do." He gives me his little double-finger gun and wink, and although I know he's trying to be funny, it's also a serious suggestion on his part.

I give him a little noncommittal grunt, wondering where I'd rank sex with my husband these days—before or after putting our daughter to bed.

I KNOW HOW I sound. I sound like a shitty mother and wife. Or at the very least an inadequate wife and ungrateful mother—which is in stark contrast to the image I try to portray on Instagram. *Hashtag happy life. Hashtag beautiful family. Hashtag blessed.* Sometimes, like tonight, I find myself wondering which is more egregious, to pretend to be happy when you're not, or to feel so consistently dissatisfied when you *should* be happy. My therapist, Amy, tells me not to be so hard on myself—which probably has a lot to do with why I keep going back to her. She says that everyone creates a version of her life that she wishes were true and tries to believe. In other words, everyone lies on social media, or at least puts her best foot—and photos—forward. Amy also points out that although I have a lot to be thankful for, I *did* lose my brother in a tragic accident that rocked my family to the core, either directly or indirectly caused my parents to divorce, and left me with a sole sibling who is some combination of selfish and self-destructive. In other words, I'm entitled to my frustration and deep-seated sadness, regardless of how many positive things have happened to me since that horrific day.

As an aside, I also appreciate Amy's forty-something perspective that the thirties are a grind for many, and motherhood isn't the constantly blissful journey everyone thinks it will be when they attend their pink or blue or yellow baby shower. She swears that things get easier as your kids get older and become more self-sufficient, but she also maintains that no matter what their age or yours, motherhood is hard. *Really* hard. Stay-at-home mothers have it rough; working mothers have it rough; and part-time working mothers, like myself, have it rough, even though the first two camps annoyingly insist that we have the best of both worlds when I think we actually have the worst of each. There. I just did it again. Bitch, bitch, bitch. And I mean that as a noun and a verb.

To be clear, I love my daughter more than anything or anyone in the world. She is the best thing I have ever done or will ever do with my life. It's just that taking care of a small child often feels tedious to me, a fact I can admit only to Amy, the person I pay to give me one-hour increments of complete honesty. I can't tell my husband, who labeled me *unmaternal* in a recent argument. I can't tell my friends, because it would undermine my perfect Facebook façade. I can't tell my sister, who desperately wants a child of her own. And I can't tell my mother, because I know she'd do anything to get back a few moments with her firstborn, even the kind of miserable, exhausting moments that I routinely gripe about. Besides, my mother *needs* me to be okay. The child she doesn't have to worry about. The only one who hasn't fucked up or died.

The more pressing issue, and even more closely guarded secret, is the way I feel about Nolan, my husband of nearly seven years. I'm not sure where to begin, other than at the beginning, with the answer to that question *So, how did you two meet?* Every couple has their canned answer, their story that's told again and again. Sometimes the husband will take the lead in the retelling; sometimes the wife will. Sometimes it's a tandem effort, scripted down to the smallest one-liner, suspenseful beat, wistful glance, fond chuckle, serendipitous plot twist. *And then he said this. And then I did that. And now here we are. Happily ever after.*

Sometimes I wonder if part of my problem with Nolan isn't our story itself, the how and why we got together. Because even if I stick to the abridged, upbeat, dinner-party version, and avoid maudlin details such as "Nolan was a pallbearer at my brother's funeral," we always return to Daniel.

Growing up and for as long as I can remember, Nolan was my brother's best friend, although with a four-and-a-half-year age gap, I actually didn't pay much attention to either of them, at least when I was really little. He was just a fixture, like the tweed sectional in our family room or my father's workbench in the garage, part of the backdrop of my childhood, one of the many older boys who came to trade baseball cards or throw a football in the backyard or spend the night, sleeping in the trundle pulled out from under Daniel's twin bed.

By the time I reached middle school, it was harder to ignore Daniel and his friends, if only because Josie was paying such close attention to them. I remember her carrying on about Nolan in particular, and I had to agree that he was easy on the eyes. With wavy blond hair, bright blue eyes, and the kind of skin that easily tanned, he had such obvious Malibu lifeguard good looks that Daniel teasingly called him Baywatch. He also happened to be Daniel's most athletic friend, a natural at every sport he played, though he didn't have Daniel's drive or work ethic, which evened things out for them on the playing fields. But what stood out to me the most was Nolan's sense of humor, the laid-back way he approached everything, in stark contrast to my type A brother. In many ways, they really were opposites, their differences becoming more pronounced over the years, as Daniel graduated as Lovett's valedictorian, then headed north for Harvard, while Nolan focused on girls and parties at Ole Miss, barely eking out a 2.0 GPA (all he needed to return to Atlanta to work at his family's printing business). Yet despite their divergent paths, the two stayed close, always picking up right where they left off. In fact, just a few days before Daniel died, I overheard him telling Sophie that Nolan would one day be his best man.

So it was both fitting and gut-wrenching when we returned home from the hospital the morning after the accident to find Nolan in his black Tahoe parked haphazardly in our driveway, his front door open. As my parents and I got out of our car and neared him, he must have been able to tell that something was wrong—*very* wrong—yet he calmly asked, "Where've y'all been? Where's Danny? We're supposed to shoot hoops at ten." He was eating a glazed donut and licked his thumb, waiting for a reply.

I held my breath, and looked at my father, still wearing the crumpled suit from his business trip, his red tie stuffed into his pocket. He started to answer, but then put his head down and hurried into the house, my mother clutching his arm. Nolan stepped out of his truck, his smile fading.

"Meredith?" he said with a questioning look. "What's going on?"

I was only twenty, not even old enough for a legal drink, yet it was clear that I would be the one to tell Daniel's best friend that he was gone.

"Daniel was in a car accident last night," I said, somehow finding my voice, though my throat was constricting, my heart pounding in my ears.

"Is he okay?" Nolan nodded, as if cuing me for the right answer. "He's going to be okay. Right, Meredith?" He nodded again, his eyes wide.

I took a deep breath, then made myself say it aloud for the first time: *Daniel died.*

Nolan stared back at me, his face blank, as if he hadn't heard what I said or simply couldn't process the meaning of my words.

"A truck hit his car at the corner of Moores Mill and Northside," I numbly reported, still in shock. "He was wearing his seatbelt, but his internal injuries were too great. They said it happened fast. . . . He didn't suffer at all."

I repeated the words exactly as I'd heard my mother tell my grandparents: *He didn't suffer at all.* I wanted so desperately to believe it was true, but would always doubt it, always wonder about Daniel's final thought and whether he knew what was happening to him.

Nolan collapsed sideways onto his front seat, his long legs hanging out the door, his untied high-tops planted in the driveway. I held my breath in horror, as he let out a string of obscenities, his voice a low, guttural moan: *My God, no. Jesus fucking Christ. Oh fffuckkk. Christ, no.*

My instinct was to flee, escape the sound and sight of Nolan. But I couldn't leave him. So I finally walked around the front of his car, opened the passenger door, and climbed in beside him. Only then did I register how cold I was, and that I had left my coat at the hospital.

"Can you turn on the heat?" I asked quietly.

Nolan shifted in his seat, pulled his door shut, and turned the key still dangling in the ignition. The radio came blaring on before he silenced it with his fist, then followed that up with a hard punch to his dash, splitting open his knuckle. I reached into my purse and handed him a tissue, but he didn't take it. Blood trickled down his hand and wrist as he announced that he was going to take off.

"You're leaving?" I said, suddenly panicking, dreading going into my house, literally afraid of seeing Josie, knowing that we no longer had a brother. That it was just the two of us.

"I think I should," he said. "Right?"

I shook my head, staring at the bag of donuts on the seat between us. "No. Please come in."

"Are you sure? Shouldn't it just be . . . family?" Nolan's voice cracked as tears began to stream down his face.

"You *are* family," I said. "Daniel would want you to come in."

ALMOST EVERYONE DESCRIBES the immediate aftermath of death the same way—as a surreal blur, at least for those in the inner circle, in charge of the details. I watched people come and go—close friends, neighbors, and relatives, including some I barely knew. They dropped off food, offered condolences, cried. Mom and Dad picked out a coffin and a cemetery plot with the lady from the funeral home and planned Daniel's service with John Simmons, our longtime pastor. Dad sat in his office and wrote the eulogy, a glass of whiskey on his desk.

Meanwhile, I can't remember Nolan ever leaving, though he must have gone home to sleep and shower. At my parents' request, he sat in the living room with Daniel's computer, going through all of his contacts, emailing and calling his college and medical school friends, one by one. He even phoned Sophie, within hours of her plane landing, and I listened to his conversation, marveling at how he said all the right things, how much Daniel loved her, how special she was to him. He pored through our family photo albums, putting together a collage that would be displayed at the wake. And when there was nothing left to do, he simply sat with me in stunned silence, the forever of it all just starting to sink in.

It was hard to call him a comfort exactly, because nothing could console any of us at that point, but there was something about his presence that was reassuring. He was nothing like my brother, but he was still a strong and powerful connection to him, and I could see so clearly why Daniel had loved him.

ABOUT A WEEK after the funeral, and the day before I returned to Syracuse to finish my junior year of college, Nolan stopped by to say hello and, in his words, "check in on everyone." Standing in our foyer, he glanced up the staircase as I told him my mom was already in bed with a migraine and my dad was at the office, working late.

"And Josie?" he asked. "Is she back at school?"

"Not yet. She leaves next week. . . . I don't know where she is tonight," I said, thinking it was par for the course, before the accident and especially since. I wasn't sure where she'd been going or who she'd been hanging out with, but I had barely seen her for days. We had yet to talk about that night, where she had been or how she'd found out, and I was starting to get the feeling we never would. That Daniel's death was going to push us further apart than we already were.

Nolan shoved his hands in his pockets, looked at me for a few seconds, then asked if I wanted to get a bite to eat. Feeling both surprised and strangely flattered by the invitation, I said yes. For the next hour, we drove around Buckhead, trying to decide where to go, vetoing restaurant after restaurant before we finally settled on the OK Cafe, a brightly lit Southern comfort–food diner. Choosing a booth in the back, we ate barbecue and macaroni and cheese, drank sweet tea, and talked about everything but Daniel. Instead Nolan asked me questions—basic ones—as if he hadn't known me my whole life, which in some ways I guess he hadn't.

"Why'd you pick Syracuse?" he asked. "I've never known a single person from Atlanta to go to Syracuse. Except you."

"Isn't that a good enough reason?" I deadpanned.

"Seriously?" he said with a smile, both dimples firing.

"Yeah, actually. Kind of," I said, smiling a little myself. "Plus they have a really good drama school."

"Oh, that's right," he said. "You're a theater girl. You were in a lot of plays at Pace, weren't you?"

I nodded and said that was my thing—one of the reasons I had chosen to go to a different high school from my brother and sister.

"Daniel was proud of you."

I stared down at my plate, trying not to cry, as Nolan distracted me with more rapid-fire questions. "So you want to be an actress?"

I nodded again.

"But you're so shy," he said, something people often said to me when I told them what I was studying.

"I'm not really *shy*. I'm an introvert." I went on to explain the difference—the fact that being around people didn't make me uneasy, I just preferred to be alone most of the time. "Daniel was an introvert, too. He was selective about who he spent time with. . . . He loved hanging out with you."

Nolan smiled, as it occurred to me that maybe he wasn't just being nice by inviting me to dinner. Maybe I was a comfort to him, too, his closest connection to Daniel.

"How else are you alike?" he asked.

I hesitated, unsure of what tense to use, the present for me, or the past for him. "I have his OCD. And his GPA." I smiled. "Though you can't really compare neurosurgery and Shakespearean theater . . . I'm smart, but he was way smarter."

"What you study has nothing to do with your IQ."

"True," I said, though I was still sure Daniel's had been higher than mine—higher than anyone's in our family.

"You two are more alike than you and Josie, aren't you?" he asked.

I nodded. "Yeah, she's a straight extrovert. Party girl. But it's weird. . . . I'm more like Daniel, but he was closer to her." I felt a stab of jealousy, then guilt for feeling jealous. "Daniel was drawn to people like you . . . and her."

"Fuckups?" He smiled.

"Happy people," I said, wrapping my hands around my warm mug, having switched to coffee. "Fun people. You could always make him laugh."

Nolan's lower lip quivered.

"I heard him tell Sophie that you were going to be his best man. One day."

"He said that?"

"Yeah," I said. "But you already knew that, didn't you?"

"Yeah. I guess I did," he said. "But *he* was the best man. The best friend you could have. God. All the times he had my back . . . the messes he got me out of . . ."

I mustered a smile, recalling some of the funny stories in Nolan's eulogy, how he had so perfectly captured Daniel's loyal, solid essence while painting himself as the foolhardy sidekick.

"I still can't believe it was him—and not me," Nolan said. "God, I wish it had been me."

I shook my head, although I'd had the same wish about myself. *If only it had been me,* I'd thought more than once, *then my parents would still have a daughter to spare.*

. . .

LATER THAT NIGHT, when Nolan dropped me back at the house, he asked if he could see Daniel's room. I hesitated, feeling uneasy. I had yet to set foot in his room and knew that my parents had only been in there once, and that was only out of necessity, to get Daniel's burial clothes. But I said yes and the two of us walked silently into the house, then upstairs and down the hall to my brother's closed bedroom door. My heart raced as I turned the knob and peered inside. The room was dark, the shades drawn, and for a second, I actually found myself praying that we would find a miracle: Daniel asleep in his bed, the whole thing a bad dream. But the sight of his creaseless comforter and tight hospital corners confirmed our nightmare.

"Jesus," Nolan whispered, as we took a few tentative steps into the room, our eyes adjusting to the dark. I tried to speak but couldn't begin to think of what to say. There was nothing to say.

But Nolan found something. "I don't think I've been up here since high school. It looks exactly the same."

I nodded, grateful that my parents hadn't redecorated our rooms the way a lot of parents did when their kids left for school—and wondered if they ever would now. Nolan and I looked around, taking visual inventory of Daniel's bookshelf lined with paperback novels and tennis trophies and signed baseballs and his snow globe collection. We studied the framed baseball jerseys hanging on his walls and the collage of photos tacked to the bulletin board and the stack of medical books on his desk. His suitcase was open and neatly arranged on an ottoman in the corner, and I could see the pajamas Josie had given him for Christmas, the tags still on them. I stared at the jar of Carmex on his nightstand, sitting on top of Malcolm Gladwell's *The Tipping Point,* an index card slipped inside, somewhere around the midway point. I had a sudden urge to read the page he had last read, but didn't dare touch anything. I could tell Nolan felt the same, as if we were standing before a roped-off room in a museum, staring back into history, the end of a young man's life, a moment frozen in time. We looked and looked until there was nothing left to observe, and then Nolan took my hand in his, pulled me to his chest, and wrapped his arms around me. "I love you, Meredith," he whispered in my ear.

Of course I knew what he meant—and in what way he loved me: a fond, surrogate-big-brother way. But the words still caught me off guard, along with the goosebumps that rose on my arms as I whispered it back. *I love you, too, Nolan.*

In that second, I could no longer deny what I had been trying to deny for weeks, maybe even years: I had a crush on Nolan. It was absurd on so many fronts. Even the *word* was flimsy, silly, and stupid amid our monumental loss. Beyond the fact that Nolan was too old and *way* too good-looking for me, he was my brother's best friend, off-limits *before,* and certainly now. Besides, how could I be attracted to *anyone* so soon after my brother's death? It was the kind of inappropriate thing that would happen to Josie, not me. And yet, there it was—as unmistakable as my clammy hands and racing, guilty heart.

I looked away, telling myself that the whole thing was probably in my head, some sort of delusional reaction to grief. Post-traumatic stress. It would pass. And even if it didn't, nobody would ever know. I would never tell him. I would never tell *anyone.*

"We better go," I said, backing away from him.

"Yeah," he said, running his hand through his hair, looking rattled. "I better head out."

A few seconds later, we were back downstairs in the foyer, saying an awkward good night.

"So you're leaving for school tomorrow?" he asked.

"Yeah," I said. "Tomorrow morning."

"Okay," Nolan said, giving me a quick hug followed by a peck on the cheek. "Take care of yourself, Mere."

"You, too, Nolan," I said.

"I'll keep in touch, I *promise,*" he said as sincerely as you can say anything.

I nodded, believing that was his intention, but also doubting it would actually happen. Eventually we would lose touch, my family's connection to Nolan becoming a secondary casualty of our tragedy.

"SO I HAVE a proposal for you," I say to Harper when I find her in her bedroom (my childhood bedroom) after officially canceling our dinner plans and changing into my most comfortable pajamas.

She looks up from her collection of stuffed mice, which live in the bottom drawer of her nightstand, and says, "What is it?"

"Do you know what that means?" I ask, sitting on the edge of her bed. "It's a deal. Do you want to make a deal?"

She gives me a suspicious look but nods, willing to at least hear me out.

"If you brush your teeth and get right in bed, I'll read you *two* bedtime stories *and* . . ." I pause to build suspense. "I won't go out."

With a glimmer in her eye, she says, "No babysitter?"

"No babysitter," I say.

She grins at me. Other than my mom, Nolan's parents, and Josie, Harper *hates* having a sitter, especially at night, and even the fun, young ones send her into a tailspin of separation anxiety and grief.

"But you have to go *straight* to bed after that. Lights out. And you have to *stay* in bed. No shenanigans."

She stares at me, and I can see the wheels turning in her head.

"Do we have a deal?" I say, knowing that I'm up against the single best negotiator in Atlanta.

Sure enough, she has a counteroffer. "*Four* books," she says.

I try not to smile as I say, "Three."

"No, *five*," she says, holding up one fist, then opening it, flashing her fingers.

I shake my head, calmly explaining that it doesn't work that way. Once she says four, she can't go back up to five. But because I admire her moxie, I give in a little bit. "Let's start with three and see how that goes. If it's not too late, we'll do a fourth. Now go on," I say, gesturing toward her bookcase. "You choose, honey."

Jubilant, she skips to her bookcase, strategically selecting three of her picture books with the most words per page. The girl is no dummy. Her first two selections are solid, but then she reaches for *Horton Hears a Who!* and I let out a little groan. Although I love the book's strong moral message of tolerance and equality, I'm not in the mood for Dr. Seuss.

"Can I get one veto?" I say, thinking there are so many great books we've neglected for a while.

"No, Mommy," she says, putting her hand on her hip. "You said I could choose. And I choose *Horton Hears a Who!*"

"Fair enough," I say. "Now, c'mon. Go brush your teeth."

She nods, then heads straight for the bathroom that my sister and I used to share, while I straighten up her toys, tuck in her mice, and settle into her twin bed to wait for her.

A few seconds later, she is back. I resist the urge to tell her she couldn't possibly have brushed her teeth thoroughly in that amount of time, and instead just slide over, making room for her. She climbs into bed, smelling of bubble-gum toothpaste, and hands me *Sylvester and the Magic Pebble*. It is one of my favorites—and one I can remember my mother reading to Josie and me when we were kids. I tell Harper this because she loves hearing about "Mommy and Josie" when we were little. She smiles, her face lit with anticipation as she nestles into the crook of my arm. I open the book and start to read in my most animated voice, savoring the sweetness of the moment. Reminding myself to never take anything for granted.

chapter five

JOSIE

On Friday night, just as I'm about to head out the door on a Match.com date with a physical therapist named Pete, Meredith texts with a last-minute plea to babysit and a rant about a lying teenager. I hesitate before I write her back, actually considering the request because, frankly, I'd *rather* spend the evening with Harper than make small talk with a random guy, even if his profile picture is pretty cute. But I decide to soldier through with my plans because you just never know when you could be canceling on your future husband.

I do, however, decide that this will be it. My final, last-ditch, Hail Mary date. If things don't pan out with Pete the PT, I'm officially done. Admitting defeat. Throwing in the towel on a traditional family and life. I'm not sure what that means, exactly—whether I'll up and move to Africa to do my own goodwill work, like my faux beau Jack, or whether I'll go the sperm bank, single mother route. But I won't continue on this futile path. I've made such claims before, but this time is different. This time I really *mean* it.

I repeat all of this to myself as I drive up Peachtree on the way to meet Pete, realizing that I feel no pressure whatsoever. In fact, part of me actually *wants* the date to outright suck because a bad date is better than a date rating in that murky six-out-of-ten gray area—just enough to get your hopes up, hopes that are inevitably

"His name is *Fudge*?"

"*Her*. And yes. Her name is Fudge. Because she's black. Get it?"

"Wow," I say, shaking my head, smirking.

"What?" Pete asks.

"Fudge?" I say. "That's a *really* weak name."

"My niece named her Fudge," he says. "And now she's dead."

For a second I think he means his niece is dead—and I'm beyond horrified by my ultimate foot in the mouth. Then I realize that he probably means that the *cat* is dead. "Fudge died?" I say.

"Yes. My niece was devastated. It was really her cat, but she lived with me because my brother's wife is allergic. . . . It was hard on all of us, though. Fudge really was a good cat."

"I'm sorry," I murmur, duly noting both his kindness to animals and his closeness to family. "Still. You really should have vetoed the name Fudge."

He stares at me a beat and then says, "Oh, yeah? Well, you should have vetoed Brio. So there."

I burst out laughing. "And why's that?"

"Because . . . it's *Brio*," Pete says with a trace of Gabe-like food snobbishness. "Most girls in your zip code cancel altogether when I pick a chain."

"You *wanted* me to cancel?" I say, noticing the bartender hovering near us. We don't give him an opening, and he moves on to another couple.

"I like to weed out the snobs," he says. "I'm from Wisconsin. Snobs and I don't mix."

"There are no snobs in Wisconsin?"

"Maybe two or three."

"Well, I'm not one," I say with conviction. "But my best friend is—and he accordingly advised that I cancel on you based on your restaurant choice."

"Gay foodie?" Pete says.

"Don't stereotype," I say, smiling.

"Okay. But am I right?"

I shake my head. "No, actually. He's a *straight* foodie."

Pete raises one eyebrow and gives me a circumspect look. "Straight male best friend?"

"And housemate," I say.

"Hmm . . . Interesting."

"You're threatened *already*?" I say, feeling bolder by the second. "Red flag."

"Trying to make me jealous *already*?" he retorts. "Red flag."

A coy staring contest ensues until the bartender reappears. This time we look up and order. I go with a vodka martini, straight up, Tito's if they have it, Belvedere if they don't.

The bartender nods, his gaze shifting to Pete. "And for you, sir?"

"I'll have a Miller Lite. . . . And we'll order a flatbread, too," Pete says, scanning the menu. He asks if I have a preference, and I tell him to pick something with meat.

"Sausage?" Pete asks.

I nod, and as the bartender steps away to put in our order, Pete says, "Good. You're not a vegetarian."

"Or gluten-free," I say, thinking of my sister's latest obsession. "I'm not even sure what gluten is, actually. Is it wheat? Or something else?"

"No idea," he says. "But you know how you can tell that someone's gluten-free?"

I shake my head and say no.

"Because they'll fuckin' tell you," he says, with a very cute smile.

I laugh, as he looks pleased with his joke. "So you're a teacher?" he asks.

"Yes," I say. "First grade . . . I love it. I love the kids."

He nods, his eyes slightly glazed. I try to think of something more interesting to say and then remember that I'm not trying to be interesting—or at least not more interesting than I really am. Instead I ask a question that I'd never *dream* of under normal first-date trying-to-make-a-good-impression circumstances. "How do you feel about kids?"

He hesitates, knowing a desperate, late-thirty-something question when he hears one, but keeps a poker face, as he says, "Kids are great."

"So we have a lot in common," I say as our drinks arrive. "We both like meat, gluten, and kids."

Pete laughs a genuine laugh and raises his glass. "To meat, gluten, and kids."

Our glasses touch, then our knees, before we both take a sip. I swallow, wait a beat, then really go out on a limb. "So," I say. "This is my final date."

He looks at me, appearing both amused and confused, and says, "Are you saying you won't go out with me again?"

"Pretty much. No offense—I decided this before I even got here."

"And why'd you decide that?" Pete asks.

I clear my throat, then say, "Well. As you know from my Match profile, I'm thirty-seven. Almost thirty-eight. So I think it's time to throw in the towel on the whole dating and trying to find a husband routine. On top of that," I say, now on a roll, "my ex-boyfriend's *six-year-old* daughter is in my class. A painful daily reminder that I am way behind and seriously running out of time. So unless you end up being 'The One' and then the father of my children, this is my final date before I go secure the sperm of a stranger. Or, alternatively, move to Africa and devote my life to the poor." I smile. "No pressure or anything."

. . .

Two and a half hours later, our date is over and we are both standing by the valet, waiting for our cars. Although the evening was
more fun than I expected—a solid seven—neither of us mentions
Barnes & Noble.

"So?" Pete says. "Was this your last date, after all?"

I smile, then say, "Yeah. I think so."

"So I shouldn't call you?"

"Did you want to call me?"

"Only if you want me to?"

I carefully consider his question, then tell the truth. "I don't
know . . . Maybe . . ."

He laughs. "Can you give me a little more guidance?"

"Well," I say. "I enjoyed the evening, and I like you, but I don't
think we have that . . . *spark*. . . ."

Pete nods and says, "So . . . does this mean you're headed to
Africa?"

"Or a sperm bank," I say, as I catch the valet giving me a double
take before getting out of my car, the engine running.

"Well, good luck with that," Pete says.

"Thanks," I say, handing the valet four singles, then getting in
my car. I can feel Pete looking at me, so I open my window and say,
"By the way, the cleft in your chin is cute."

Pete smiles. "Is it enough to get me a second date, even without
a spark?"

"You can try," I say, hedging my bets, though I'm really not
going to hold my breath. I wave goodbye, then drive back down
Peachtree, not even waiting to get home before giving Gabe the update.

He answers on the first ring. "How did it go?"

"The seed of solo motherhood has *officially* been planted," I
say. "Pun intended."

chapter six

MEREDITH

After Daniel's funeral, I was secretly relieved to go back to college and escape the unbearable suffering in Atlanta. I called my parents as often as I could make myself, as I knew how much they worried about me, more vulnerable to parental fears than ever. Yet I also tried to push Daniel from my mind, throwing myself into my classes and auditions, anything to stay busy and distracted. Fortunately, my crush on Nolan quickly faded, replaced by a bigger crush on a guy named Lewis Fisher.

Lewis and I met in our stage diction class that semester, and were then cast as Mitch and Blanche in *A Streetcar Named Desire*. A brilliant actor from Brooklyn, he captivated me with his talent, though I also loved his quirkiness and urban sophistication. One night after rehearsal, we lingered backstage long after the rest of the cast and crew had departed, discovering that we had something much bigger in common than acting: we had both lost siblings. I told him about Daniel's accident, and he shared that his only sister, Ruthie, had jumped onto the subway tracks in the path of an oncoming N train a week shy of her sixteenth birthday.

We stayed up half the night talking, analyzing the two tragedies with a brutal frankness. We concluded that although Ruthie's death was more emotionally complicated and troubling, in some ways it felt more unfair to lose Daniel—someone who had been so happy and productive. Lewis had a larger burden of guilt for not saving his sister—whereas my guilt came in the form of being the one who had lived. It was not only cathartic to talk about our losses but also deeply intimate. Our bond felt intense, and our chemistry unmistakable. After crying together, we hugged, then kissed.

By opening night, we were a couple. Even the theater critic at *The Daily Orange,* known for being stingy with his compliments, praised our "palpable heat" as one of the best parts of the production, lamenting that Stella and Stanley didn't share a similar fire. To celebrate the review, we made love. It was my first time, and he said he wished it had been his, too.

Lewis and I became inseparable. We eschewed parties and bar scenes, spending most of our time alone or with a small group of fellow actor friends. We took the same classes, auditioned for the same plays, and spent every night in his bed or mine. We were too young to think about marriage, neither of us particularly aspiring to a traditional life anyway, but we talked about the future, what would happen after graduation—whether we would work in television or theater or film, whether we should move to New York City or Los Angeles. Maybe one of us would make it big and become a splashy commercial success—but that wasn't really our goal. The only thing that mattered was that we were doing what we loved and that we were together.

I was almost happy, as close as I could come given what I'd lost, and for months, everything seemed easy, the effect of true love. Until everything felt complicated—the effect of falling out of love. The unraveling began in the fall of our senior year, when we both auditioned for *As You Like It.* Lewis landed the part of Jaques. A gorgeous blonde named Poppy scored the lead of Rosalind. And I got the insulting role of Audrey, a country bumpkinette goatherder. Lewis and I had never had a competitive dynamic in our relationship, but I found myself feeling insecure, resentful, and jealous, especially of Poppy, whom he seemed to worship.

I developed a mild eating disorder and began to self-loathe and second-guess. I questioned my future as an actor. I wasn't pretty enough, I wasn't talented enough, and I clearly didn't have a thick enough skin. When I confided my reservations to my parents, they both seemed relieved. They said acting had been a good experience but encouraged me to find a more practical profession. My mom said I could always do community theater on the side, and my dad mentioned law school. A trial attorney himself, he pointed out that lawyering was just a different kind of performing. I didn't buy it, but I enrolled in an LSAT prep class and began to research law schools, telling myself it was good to have a backup plan.

Always a bit sanctimonious, Lewis was appalled, accusing me of selling out. I retorted that that was easy for him to say; his parents were bohemian Brooklynites. In other words, he could follow his heart without killing his parents' dreams. Things became more and more strained between us, and our sex, once passionate, turned mechanical.

That Christmas break, just after the one-year anniversary of Daniel's death, my parents sat Josie and me down in our kitchen and announced that they were splitting up—their euphemism for divorce. I knew things had been rocky, and that my dad was drinking again, but I still felt blindsided, devastated by this second huge blow to our family. Without my big brother and the mooring of my parents' marriage, it was as if I no longer had a family at all.

I had even less than that, in fact, because as soon as I returned to school, Lewis officially dumped me for Poppy. He confessed that they had been together since Thanksgiving break, but that he couldn't bear to break my heart before December 22.

"I know how hard that first anniversary is," he said.

"Gee, thanks," I said, doing everything I could not to cry. "That was very big of you."

MY FINAL SEMESTER of college was brutal. I quit acting altogether and fell into a paralyzing depression, the loss of Lewis and my brother hitting me at once. It was as if our obsessive relationship the year prior had simply delayed my true grieving process, and I was back to square one, my mother just waking me up from a sound sleep to tell me Daniel was dead. A professor who noticed my alarming loss of weight and slipping grades insisted that I see a university shrink. Therapy and drugs barely kept me afloat.

The only bright spot came that spring when my acceptance letters rolled in from law schools, including one from Columbia. It wasn't Harvard or Yale, and law school was a far cry from neurosurgery, but it was still the Ivy League, and I knew my news made my parents proud. This, in turn, filled *me* with pride, which was better than being completely empty.

A few months later, I got the hell out of Syracuse, moved to New York City, and threw myself into my first year of law school, doing my best to avoid the theater, plays, or any other cultural offerings. *Maybe Lewis was right,* I thought, when I learned that he and Poppy were living in the Village and had joined the same theater company. Maybe I was a spineless sellout. Then again, maybe I was doing something noble and selfless, putting my parents first. I convinced myself that this was the case, and became determined to be their stable, successful child, the salve on their still-open wounds.

Of course, I think they hoped I would one day have a family, too, preferably in Atlanta. But if that didn't pan out for me, Josie would have that covered. At the time she was dating a generically handsome boy named Will, who hailed from a "good family" (my mother's phrase) in Macon, had impeccable manners, and wore seersucker and white bucks on special occasions. The two quickly became serious, giddy in love, the kind of couple who laid claim to baby names before they're even engaged. She was doing her part to make my parents happy, and we forged a tacit agreement, an unspoken pact: I would accomplish and achieve from afar, and she would marry, become a mother, and provide the beautiful, local grandchildren. Maybe it would make Dad stop drinking. Maybe it would bring our parents back together. At the very least, we would both help them move on in our so-called *new normal,* a term I despised.

At my law school graduation, my parents presented me with my brother's briefcase, the same one they had given him on his twenty-fifth birthday. It was a moment that was more bitter than sweet, and I remember feeling intensely jealous of my sister's end of the bargain. I had a law degree and a briefcase. She had real happiness. Her life as a teacher seemed easy, punctuated by one happy hour and road trip after another. Most important, she had someone to love.

Lest I become bitter, I reassured myself that her choices might actually free me in the long run. *Maybe someday,* I kept telling myself as I passed the bar and went to practice litigation at a top Manhattan firm and billed seventy or eighty hours every week. *Maybe someday* after Josie married Will and popped out a baby, I would follow my heart, too. *Maybe someday* I would be happy.

BUT THEN, BEFORE I could cast off my legal bowlines, Josie fucked everything up in grand Josie style. She called me in the middle of the night (though I was still at work, finishing a brief), bawling, telling me she had screwed up and that Will had dumped her. I asked her what happened, trying to sort out the facts so that I could offer her appropriate counsel.

"It's a long story," she said, her line whenever something was her fault or she didn't want to get into it. "Just trust me. It's over."

"Well, then. You'll get over him—and find someone else," I said. "You're not even thirty. You have plenty of time."

"Do you promise?" she asked so quickly that I couldn't help questioning whether she truly loved Will or she just wanted to get married. Maybe *any* cute boy in seersucker would do.

I obviously couldn't assure her fate, any more than I had Daniel's, but I still told her yes, it's all going to be okay. After all, I thought, the universe owed us both a little mercy.

A week later, I flew back to Atlanta at Josie's pleading, filled with the usual angst of going home. Being back always unearthed grief that I was able to mostly bury in the bustle of my everyday life in New York, where there was no association to my brother. I took a deep breath and braced myself as I rode the escalator up to Delta baggage. To my surprise, there stood Nolan. He still emailed me every six months or so, just to check in and say hello, but incredibly, this was the first time I had laid eyes on him since that night we stood in Daniel's bedroom together.

"Hey," he mouthed, waving at me. I had heard from Josie, who occasionally saw him out at the bars, that he was better-looking than ever, but I still wasn't prepared for how gorgeous he was, standing there in jeans, a T-shirt, and an Ole Miss baseball cap.

"What are you doing here?" I could feel myself beaming. "My dad was supposed to pick me up."

"Yeah, I know. I played golf with him today. I told him I'd get you." He mussed my hair as if I were twelve—although he hadn't actually mussed my hair at any age. "You look great, Mere. Wow."

"So do you. . . . I've *missed* you," I said.

"I've missed you, too," he said, grinning and carrying my bag to his car.

As he drove me home, we quickly caught up. He told me he was still working in his family business, his father grooming him to eventually take over. I told him about my law firm, and some of its juicier politics. We talked about our parents, how sad it was that mine had divorced, but that his really needed to do the same. We gossiped about people we knew in common. Many had left Atlanta for college, but most had returned to settle down and start families.

"Why aren't you married yet?" I asked playfully. "Commitment-phobe?"

"Nah. Just haven't found the right girl," he said. "What about you? Are you seeing anyone?"

"Not at the moment," I said. "I work too much."

Our only moment of silence came as we passed Grady Hospital. Neither of us said Daniel's name out loud, though it hung in the air anyway.

When we got to the intersection at West Paces Ferry, he pointed to the OK Cafe. "Remember the night we went there?" he asked, as if we had shared countless dinners alone together.

"Of course," I said.

"Can you believe it's been almost seven years?" he asked, lowering his voice, staring intently at the road.

"No. I really can't," I said, feeling a stab of pain in my chest. "He's missed *so* many things."

"I know. A lot has changed. *You've* changed. . . . I can't believe I haven't seen you on any of your trips home," he said, as he slowed for a yellow light he could have easily made. I had the feeling he was stalling, prolonging our time together.

"I don't come home that often," I said, thinking of all the times I'd found an excuse to stay at school or work.

He looked at me sideways, his expression suddenly changing from mournful to playful. "Little drama student turned big city hotshot lawyer."

"Nothing hotshot about my job," I said, which was the truth.

"Those heels you're wearing would say otherwise," Nolan said, glancing down at my shoes. "They're nice. . . . Nice legs, too."

"Thanks," I said, smiling out my window.

"You know . . . I'd heard that you'd . . . blossomed."

"Who told you that?" I said, basking in the compliment.

"Just the word around town," he said, shaking his head. "Smart, successful, *and* beautiful."

I nearly pointed out that he was confusing vigilant grooming, compulsive exercising, and general Manhattan polish with true beauty, but decided not to correct him.

A few minutes later, he was pulling up to my childhood home, where my mother still lived. Josie's car was in the driveway, and I anticipated a long night of counseling her through the Will crisis.

"Hey, Meredith?" he said as I was getting out of the car.

I looked back at him, feeling an ancient twinge of attraction and residual adolescent hero worship. "Yeah, Nolan?"

"I know you're here to visit your family . . . but do you think I could take you out while you're home?"

"You mean, like to the OK Cafe?" I asked with a trace of coyness.

"No. Like on a real date." He cracked his knuckles and shifted in his seat to get a better look at me. "Assuming you think Daniel would be all right with it? He had a pretty strict don't-date-my-sister rule back in the day."

I stared into his eyes, my stomach fluttering a little. "Yeah. I know he did . . . but that was really more about Josie," I said with a smile, thinking that she was the one Daniel's friends wanted to ask out. "And besides . . . I think he'd make an exception for us." I was sealing our fate, although I didn't yet know it.

WHEN WE TELL "our story," we always start there, on that night, with the surprise of seeing him at the airport and that innocent lift home. Nolan always brings up my heels—and I laugh and say it was a good thing I'd forgotten to put a pair of flats in my carry-on. We talk about how nice it was to see each other, how we picked up exactly where we'd left off years before.

At this point, we fast-forward past our first date. How we went to dinner at the Lobster Bar, caught a buzz, then returned to his condo, where we drank more wine, then got into his unmade bed, and had sex. If we were to share that part of the story, I'm sure we'd say that it had been a long time coming, that it felt preordained. But in reality, it just sort of shockingly and quickly *happened*. It wasn't like me to have a one-night stand, and in the intimate aftermath, my head on Nolan's chest, I told him as much.

"Well," he said, stroking my hair, "you can't really have a one-night stand with someone you've known your whole life. . . . And besides, who said it was only going to be *one* time?"

I laughed, then confessed my ancient crush, the way I'd felt that night in my brother's room. He pretended to be surprised, then told me he'd felt something, too.

I rolled over, pushed up on my elbows, and looked into his eyes. "Did you *really*?" I wasn't sure why it mattered to me at this point, but for some reason, it did.

He nodded. "Yeah. I felt really close to you that whole night."

"Because of Daniel? Or something else?"

He looked thoughtful and then said, "Yes. Because of Daniel. But not *only* that. After all, I'm not in bed with Josie, now, am I?"

"No," I said, smiling at him. "You're most certainly not."

I resisted asking him if he had ever been attracted to her because I guessed that the answer was probably yes.

"Are you going to tell her about this?" he asked, sounding tentative.

I told him no, that I wanted it to be our secret.

"Okay," he said earnestly. "Whatever you want."

· · ·

ON SUNDAY NIGHT, I returned to New York, wondering when I'd see Nolan again, guessing it would be another half dozen years. But he had other plans for us, showing up at my Upper East Side doorstep only five days later, holding a dozen red roses. Any points that I would have docked for the cliché he more than made up with his usual style and panache.

"Told ya it wouldn't be a one-night stand," he announced.

I laughed and said, "How'd you know I'd be free?"

"I took a chance," he said. "Are you?"

I shook my head and told him I had a blind date.

"He's *blind*?" Nolan said.

I laughed again, and he told me to "blow the guy off." And so I did, then played tour guide to Nolan that whole weekend. I couldn't believe it was happening. But I kept telling myself that it wasn't, not *really*. We weren't embarking on a relationship. We were just having a fling, living in the moment, motivated by sentimentality.

Yet we *kept* living in the moment, visiting each other every couple of weeks while keeping our secret from my family. I didn't want to get my mother's hopes up the way Josie had with Will. Deep down, I think I didn't want to get *my* hopes up, either, and somehow delude myself into thinking that we could ever be a real couple. I wasn't even sure that was what I wanted.

Even after Nolan told me he loved me that Christmas, and I said it back, and we went public with our long-distance relationship, I kept my expectations in check, silently reminding myself that we loved each other but weren't *in* love—nor were we long-term compatible. On paper, I was probably too cerebral for him—and he was too good-looking for me. I was an introvert; he was an extrovert. I loved the arts; he loved sports. I wanted to stay in New York; he couldn't leave his family's business in Atlanta. Our breakup was inevitable, a question of *when*, not *if*.

Then, one muggy Saturday in July, about nine months after our first date, Nolan and I went for a long walk through Chastain Park, ending up on Wilkins Field, where he and my brother had played baseball for so many years. We strolled along the bases and then sat in the empty dugout, looking through the chain-link fence, out over the beautifully groomed diamond. It was just before dusk, the sun casting a golden light over the mound where Nolan had pitched and Daniel had occasionally relieved.

"This was Danny's favorite place in the world," Nolan said, seeming to be talking to himself more than to me.

"Yeah. I know," I said, wishing I had spent less time playing with Josie in the bleachers or making trips to the concession stand, and more time watching my brother play.

In our reflective silence, Nolan took my hand and gave me a soulful glance. I suddenly had the feeling he was going to end our relationship, something that I'd been contemplating lately—or at least anticipating. It had been a good run, and a lot of fun, but something just felt missing. I was still sad, though, hating endings of any kind.

Bracing myself, I mumbled, "Go on. Just get it over with." At least that is Nolan's recollection and where we pick up with our official tale.

He looked at me, confused.

"Aren't you about to break up with me?" I said.

Nolan laughed and shook his head and said, "No, Meredith. I'm not going to break *up* with you." Then he got down on one knee in that dusty dugout and asked the question I had never imagined hearing from him, or anyone for that matter. *Will you marry me?*

For a second I thought he was kidding. Until he produced a beautiful, sparkling princess-cut diamond ring. I stared at it, then at him, feeling stunned and a little scared. In my heart, the answer was no. Or at the very most maybe. But I said nothing, just shook my head, bit my lip, and blinked back tears.

"Say something," Nolan said with a nervous laugh.

"I . . . can't."

I think I meant to say that I couldn't marry him, but it sounded like I was telling him that I couldn't speak. So he just kept talking, giving me a rambling, heartfelt speech. First he told me how much he loved me, that he'd never known a girl like me. Then he went on to tell me how he'd asked my parents for permission and both of them had wept, my mother calling him her surrogate son. He talked about all the memories we had shared over so many years. He said that he and I—*we*—were the only possible silver lining to Daniel's otherwise useless death. He said he could picture my brother up there, rooting for him, just as he had so many times from this field, this very bench.

And with that final comment about my brother, my *no* or *maybe* turned to *yes,* and for better or worse, my uncertain future became something I'd always imagined for my sister.

OUR ENGAGEMENT WAS short, both because I didn't want a big wedding and because I worried that if it were long, one of us might call the other's bluff, point out that for as long as we had known each other, we didn't know each other well enough to get married. After all, we'd been together less than a year, all of it long distance, our time together feeling more like a vacation than normal, every- day life. Despite the horrible thing we had been through so long ago, our relationship itself had never been tested. We'd never even had a major argument. Yet not once did I express any of these res- ervations to Nolan, which I think said a lot, in and of itself.

The only time I discussed my fears at all was with Josie, the weekend she and my mom flew to New York to help me find a wed- ding dress.

"I really don't know if I should have said yes," I blurted out, standing in my underwear, staring at my ring in a posh dressing room at Mika Inatome as the salesgirl left to retrieve another dress. It was the one appointment my mom missed, as she was back at my apartment with another migraine.

"To Nolan?" my sister said, looking appalled.

I nodded.

"You're kidding, right?"

"No," I said softly. "I think I'm having second thoughts."

She furrowed her brow, then reassured me that it was just a little case of cold feet.

"I think it might be more than that," I told her.

"C'mon, Mere," she said, launching into a pep talk that I could tell she believed completely. "You're marrying Nolan Brady. He's gorgeous. He's loaded. He's funny. And he's a really nice guy."

"I know," I said, feeling guilty and ungrateful.

"I mean . . . look at that rock." She took my left hand in her right and shook it.

"I know," I said, gazing back down at my ring. "But it's not really me. Neither are these gowns."

"So what? Those things don't matter. . . . You're marrying a great guy. Are you seriously finding something to be unhappy about here?" she said in the tone of voice I often took with her.

I sighed and tried to explain. "It's just . . . sometimes I feel like we rushed into this . . . that the ring was a bit of an impulse purchase. That *I* might be an impulse purchase."

"C'mon, Mere. You act like you just met at a bar. . . . You've known each other *forever*," Josie said. "For your *whole* life."

"I know, but we haven't been *together* for very long at all. And I don't want him to regret it," I said.

"That's ridiculous," Josie said. "He adores you. He *worships* you."

"Maybe," I said, because I did get the feeling that Nolan admired a lot of things about me. He was proud of my career and how smart I was. *Special* was the word he always used. He made me *feel* special.

I took a deep breath and said, "But is he in love with me? Or the *idea* of me?"

"The *idea* of you?" Josie said. "You're not Julia Roberts. What do you mean, the *idea* of you?"

"I don't know," I said, frustrated that I couldn't describe the way I was feeling to my own sister, though I knew it had something to do with Daniel, and the reasons I had said yes.

"Do you love him?" she asked.

I told her yes, because I did, wishing I could put my finger on the thing that felt missing. I thought of Lewis, not for the first time in recent months. I was way over him, but longed for the intense way I'd once felt. But then I asked myself whether that kind of passion was necessarily a *good* thing—or a feeling that would always, inevitably fade. I was so confused.

"Look, Meredith," Josie said gently. "You're looking for something that doesn't exist. And if you break up with Nolan, you'll regret it forever. Like I'm regretting Will . . ." Her voice shook a little, then trailed off. She still hadn't told me all the details of their breakup, and clearly was never going to, but I knew that Will had already moved on with another serious relationship.

I nodded, having always been motivated by fear of regret, and agreed that she was probably right. "Thanks, Josie," I whispered.

"Of course." She smiled, putting her arm around me, then pulling me into a full-on hug. "Now, come on. Let's do this."

I hugged her back, feeling a tiny bit better, just as our salesgirl bustled in with a new gown—this one more embellished than the others, lacy with extensive beadwork along the bodice.

"Oh, I *love* it," Josie said, turning to me. "What do you think, Mere?"

"Too fancy," I said, shaking my head.

"Just *try* it," she insisted.

I sighed, letting the two of them help me into it, then zip me up and arrange the train at my feet.

"Wow," Josie said as she spun me toward the mirror.

I looked at my reflection and couldn't resist a small smile.

"See?" she said. "I *told* you."

"It *is* pretty good, isn't it?" I asked my sister.

"It's *perfect*. And so is the ring. And so is Nolan. And so is your life, you bitch."

"You're the bitch," I said, smiling back and deciding, once and for all, that I was going to go through with it.

And that was that. In the next few months, everything happened quickly. I resigned from my job, landed a new law firm job in Atlanta, and bought my childhood home on Dellwood from my mother. It was the perfect solution, as she felt that the house was too big for her to live in alone but desperately wanted to keep it in our family.

Then, one beautiful, bright autumn afternoon, I stood in the front of the church where Daniel's coffin had rested and exchanged vows with his best friend.

chapter seven

JOSIE

The morning after my last date ever, Pete calls while I'm still asleep, leaving me a rambling voicemail.

"So I've given it a lot of thought," he launches in without saying hello. "Well, as much thought as you can give something in less than twelve hours, of which seven were spent sleeping. . . . So anyway, contrary to your opinion, I think chemistry can develop over time. In fact, I can think of several significant examples in film and literature in which one or both parties had absolutely no romantic interest in the other at the outset of their interaction—only to find that it blossomed—intensely—later."

I smile as I listen, suddenly genuinely interested—not necessarily in Pete himself, but in where he's going with this.

"So I say we give it another try, just to be sure. . . . In fact, if you're free tonight, I'm going to a rooftop party. I'd love for you to join me . . . and you're welcome to bring a friend—so she can judge me, perhaps offer a second opinion. Soooo . . . give me a buzz and let me know what you think."

I listen to the message one more time, then delete it, shaking my head at the predictability of it all. It is a page right out of one of those dating handbooks—my sudden indifference and independence, neither of which can really be faked, had made me more attractive to the opposite sex.

I call Pete back immediately, something the old strategic me *never* would have done, and say, "So what are your examples from film and literature?"

"Who's this?" he deadpans over loud music.

"It's Josie," I say, mimicking his dry tone. "Your blind date from last night."

"Oh! Yes, hi there, Josie," he says, turning off his music.

"So what are your examples?" I say again. "And do you have any real-life examples or just fictional ones?"

"I'll tell you in person. Tonight."

"So you really are asking me out two nights in a row?"

"Yes," he says. "I really am."

"You know that's, like, 101 of what not to do if you like someone?"

"Who said I liked you?"

"Touché," I say, grinning into the phone.

"So what do you think? About the party? It should be fun. I hear this chick throws Gatsbyesque parties. Over the top."

The description tempts me for a second, but I reply with a quip. "How did Brio boy score an invite to a party like that?"

"She tore her ACL ballroom dancing. I worked on her knee," he confesses. "She told me I was welcome to bring friends."

"She probably meant guy friends," I say. "I bet she likes you."

"Nah. It's not like that," he says. "So are you in?"

I hesitate, but am determined not to succumb to the slippery slope. "I don't think so," I say, holding firm.

"That's it? You 'don't think so'? You're not even going to make something up? Like, tell me you already have plans or something?"

I laugh and say I actually *do* already have plans.

"To do what?" he says, breaking another cardinal rule—don't ask nosy questions during your first phone conversation.

"I'm staying in tonight. I'm going to research sperm banks," I say.

He laughs, but when I don't respond, he says, "You're not kidding about that, are you?"

"Nope," I say, trying not to think about the potential good genes that could be awaiting me on that roof tonight. It's the false promise that has always motivated me, kept me going out weekend after weekend. There is *always* an agenda; the point is *always* to meet someone. Even if disguised in the form of a girls' night out. Even if you're one of those people who pretends to actually enjoy going to the movies or eating at a bar alone. Even if you try to convince yourself that you just want to enjoy a nice end-of-the-summer rooftop party.

"Well, at least that's a lofty pursuit," he says. "Will you let me know how it goes?"

"Are you really interested?"

"Yes," Pete says. "Moderately."

I hang up, wondering if he's talking about me or my project. I have a hunch that it is both, and have to admit that the feeling is mutual. But I remind myself that moderate interest is no longer my thing.

AS PROMISED, I dedicate the rest of the day to donor research, taking detailed notes about fertility doctors and sperm banks in Atlanta on a lined yellow tablet I previously used to jot down interesting profiles (including Pete's) from Match.com. As I surf and read and pop into various chat rooms, I feel increasingly excited and empowered, liberated to let the whole marriage dream die. All I need is some good sperm and a doctor to put it in me. It isn't going to be easy—or inexpensive—but it is much more straightforward than finding "The One," and more important, blissfully within my control.

Every few hours, I go find Gabe somewhere in the house or yard and share nuggets of my newly acquired expertise. He listens intently, the way he always does, but I have the feeling he's mostly humoring me. His interest is finally piqued when I stumble upon a website dedicated to sharing the testimonies, both positive and negative, of parties involved in third-party reproduction, from the egg and sperm donors, to the donor-conceived children, to the surrogate mothers, to the actual parents.

"If you were the product of a sperm or egg donor, do you think that something would feel missing in your life?" I ask him after reading aloud a particularly troubling account of a donor-conceived teenaged girl who knew virtually nothing about her biological father and is now grappling with her identity, concluding with *I will never forgive my mother for her selfish decision, one that has left a permanent hole in my heart and soul.*

"Sounds like a typical melodramatic teenager to me," Gabe says, glancing over his shoulder. A homebody, he has stayed in tonight to watch *Broadcast News,* one of his favorite movies, and hits pause as he finishes his reply. "If she knew her old man, she'd just find something else to hate her mom for."

"Maybe," I say. "So you don't think you'd feel bitter?"

"If I didn't know my biological father?" Gabe asks with a wry look because he actually *doesn't* know his biological father, who died of prostate cancer just after Gabe's birth. The only father he's ever known is his stepdad, the soft-spoken, kindly professor his mother married when Gabe was seven. For a couple of years, Gabe called him Stan, but at some point started to call him Dad.

"But even though you didn't know your real father," I say, trying to differentiate the scenarios, "you at least knew who he *was.* He was never a complete mystery."

"But a sperm donor doesn't have to be a complete mystery, either," he says. "You said yourself, earlier today, that there are all sorts of different arrangements."

"True," I say, thinking of the story I read about the girl who connected with her donor dad and biological half siblings via Facebook. "But that presents another whole set of issues."

Gabe shrugs, still staring at the frozen screen, right in the middle of the scene where Albert Brooks sweats profusely. "Everyone has issues. And at the end of the day . . . you are who you are."

I blink and say, "What does that mean? 'You are who you are'?"

He sighs. "Let's say I found out that I actually came from donated sperm, rather than the man I know from old photos and a few memories. . . . Or let's say that my mom had an affair with the milkman and I just found out. . . . Then I'd *still* be exactly who I am today."

I stare at him blankly.

"I mean, it's just a donated cell," he says. "At the end of the day, it's no different than a donated heart or cornea or kidney."

"It's *totally* different," I say, even though I want to believe in what he's saying. "A cornea is not the same as half your DNA."

"Granted," he says. "But it also doesn't change who you *really* are. Whether I came from my biological father or donated sperm, I was still raised by my mom and Stan. My *dad*."

I take a deep breath and say, "But what if I had a baby with donated sperm and *didn't* ever get married? What if I never gave my child a father of *any* kind?"

"Well, that's a different issue altogether. . . . That's about the people in your life, rather than your identity. And that scenario could happen anyway. People die. They leave. Lots of people grow up without a mother or father. So if you didn't ever marry, then your child would just have you." He shrugs. "So what?"

"So *what*?" I say. "Isn't that sad?"

"Sadder than never being born at all?"

I nod as he offers his final summation. "People just need to be who they are."

I stare at him, digesting his Gabe-like quote, as he hits play on his movie and I move on to an uplifting testimony from a grandmother of a donor-conceived baby being raised by her lesbian daughter and partner. I reassure myself that the positive, inspiring stories with hunky-dory endings seem to far outweigh the tales of woe, especially when everyone involved is honest from the beginning. At the end of the day, it isn't so unlike traditional families, really, all of us vulnerable to tragedy and estrangement, lies and secrets.

"Gabe?" I say.

"Uh-huh?" he asks, this time not pausing the movie.

"Do you think I'm crazy for considering this?"

"Are you *really* considering it? Or is this just like your Buddhist meditation kick?" he asks, still staring at the screen.

"I'm *more* than considering this," I say, feeling my first wave of genuine fear, which in a sense confirms my answer. "Do you think I'm crazy?"

"Yep," Gabe says with a smirk. "But no crazier than usual. And like I said—people just need to be who they are."

THAT NIGHT BEFORE I go to bed, I call Meredith, really wanting to talk to my sister about everything. I can tell right away she's in a bad mood, which is pretty consistent these days.

"What's wrong?" I ask her.

"Nothing."

"You sound pissed off."

"I'm not."

"All right," I say. "So what'd you do today?"

"Three loads of laundry. Grocery shopping . . . oh, and I picked up Nolan's shirts at the dry cleaner's," she says, perfecting her martyr routine.

"That's it?"

"Hmm. Let's see . . . I also took Harper to Buckles."

"Did she get some cute shoes?" I ask.

"No. She pitched an epic fit over a pair of purple glitter sandals . . . and we had to leave."

I laugh, and she adds gratuitous commentary. "Mom says there's no justice in the world since I never pulled stunts like that. That was your department."

Weary of the good girl–bad girl shtick, I sigh, but decide to use it as an opening. "So I guess that means I'll have the perfect child!" I chirp.

She doesn't react to this, nor does she even bother to ask what *I* did today, which is just common fucking courtesy. Instead she informs me that she ran into our old friend Shawna at the shoe store. She was buying her son his first pair of sneakers—little blue Keds.

"How'd she look?" I ask.

"Very good," she says.

"Did she lose her baby weight?"

"Yes. She looked thinner than I've ever seen her."

"Too thin?"

"No. Not too thin."

"Did she seem happy?" I ask.

"As happy as you can be with a toddler," Meredith replies.

"Did she ask about me?" I say against my better judgment. Meredith always accuses me of making things all about myself.

"No . . . but she did tell me y'all haven't talked in months?" I detect a note of satisfaction in her voice, and feel another wave of irritation along with a stab of sibling rivalry at the mention of Shawna, our only shared friend growing up.

"I wouldn't say *months* . . . but it's been a while."

"She wants to get drinks. . . ."

"The three of us?" I ask.

"She mentioned me and Nolan. A double-date thing," Meredith says. "But I'm sure she'd love to hear from you, too."

"Right," I say, thinking this is what I get for wanting to confide in my sister. "Okay, Mere. I'll let you go."

"If you want to go, say you want to go. Don't tell me you'll *let* me go," she says, now just being a straight-up bitch.

"Okay, then," I say, careful to keep my voice light. "*I* want to go."

I HANG UP, pissed off at Meredith and pissed off at Shawna for giving Meredith that kind of ammunition, even unwittingly. She, of all people, knows our complicated history, the three of us going back to 1989, when the Ebersoles moved in across the street from us. Shawna was between us in age, but was precocious and had skipped a grade. Her mother, a Coke executive, had transferred the family from Hong Kong, enrolling Shawna at the Atlanta International School so that she could continue to use her Chinese. It was one of the many things that fascinated Meredith and me, along with her wealth of stories and breadth of travel (in stark contrast to the mainstay destinations of most Buckhead families, which included, give or take, Lake Burton, Sea Island, and Kiawah). The three of us went on long bike rides, built forts along the creek behind Shawna's house, and played Capture the Flag with the other neighborhood kids. One summer, we planted a vegetable garden, then went door-to-door peddling basil and tomatoes from Daniel's old red wagon. I remember Shawna coming up with most of the ideas, doing most of the talking, and generally entertaining Meredith and me. Looking back, I think Mere would agree that it was the only truly harmonious era of our sisterhood.

In middle school, Shawna morphed from our playmate into our fearless, experimental pioneer. The first adult penis Meredith and I ever saw was compliments of Shawna, straight from her parents' very own porn-magazine collection, which they casually stowed in their nightstand along with a tube of K-Y jelly (the purpose of which

Shawna clinically described). I still remember how my sister and I vacillated between horror and fascination at the sight of that large slab of bratwurst-like flesh, slung over the muscular thigh of a burly Nordic man named Big John. We gagged and covered our eyes, then peeked, then gawked, then analyzed, parsing out the anatomy, where his hairless scrotum attached to the long shaft ending with that one-eyed pink head. Shortly after that, Shawna taught us about masturbation, the myriad ways she pleasured herself, even demonstrating the swirling of her two fingers through the silk fabric of her pajama bottoms. There was no such thing as a taboo topic with Shawna—and she was just as likely to research a provocative issue on her own as to ask her parents directly. What was the difference between gay and transgender? How could someone be against abortion except in cases of incest or rape—if killing a baby was wrong, wasn't it wrong no matter what the circumstances? And on and on.

In those years forming the bridge from childhood to adolescence, Shawna was not only our friend and confidante but also the source of many a secret that Meredith and I guarded together. Our parents, both conservative Presbyterian Republicans, liked the Ebersoles well enough, but they called Shawna "out there" and referred to her parents as "permissive" and "liberal." I can vividly remember Dad's face turning bright red when she told us at dinner one night that creationism was an "ignorant myth perpetuated in red states" and how he had stammered a retort that the Bible was most certainly *not* a myth. Only Daniel could calm him down, shifting the conversation to "intelligent design," how it was possible to reconcile Christianity with Darwinism and evolution. It also helped that Daniel enjoyed Shawna in much the same way he loved Nolan. Neither was ever dull.

In any event, we remained a threesome until the summer before Shawna and I entered the ninth grade, when she convinced her parents to let her transfer to Lovett, where Daniel and I went to school. The writing was on the wall, but Meredith fiercely resisted the inevitable shift in our dynamic. Her feelings were perpetually hurt, which only annoyed Shawna and me, as did her tattling to Mom and Dad that we were "blowing her off" and "leaving her out." I insisted that it wasn't like that at all, Shawna and I simply had more in common. We were in the same grade, the same *school*, for heaven's sakes. Beyond that, we had different interests. Meredith listened to downer folk music; Shawna and I danced to R & B and pop. Meredith didn't speak to boys; Shawna and I had begun to date. Meredith was a Goody Two-shoes; Shawna and I sneaked cigarettes and beer.

"What's the big deal?" I'd say to Mom when she pulled me aside and talked to me about my "sister's feelings." She pointed out that Meredith was a bit of a loner, and had come to rely on Shawna and me. I retorted that the age gap had become more significant over time, and that high-schoolers didn't hang out with middle-schoolers. Mom argued that Shawna had always been a neighborhood friend. Not anymore, I said.

Over time, Meredith moved past the big betrayal and made her own theater friends at Pace, but I think it always stung. Shawna remained a longtime sore spot between us. Deep down, I knew I was being insensitive and maybe even a little mean, and looking back, I can see there was definitely a competitive component, too. My sister, like my brother, was a parent pleaser. She wasn't as crazy smart as Daniel, but she got really good grades in honors classes, never got in trouble, and most important, had a genuine passion and talent for acting. Mom and Dad raved about her plays and performances, just like they raved about Daniel's baseball, while I was the classic middle child with no sport or hobby to make me special. It was lame to consider Shawna a feather in my cap, but

I took secret satisfaction in beating my sister in this particular tug-of-war.

After graduation, Shawna and I both decided on the University of Georgia. Our freshman year, we were closer than ever, rooming together, then pledging the same sorority. We even started to look alike, wearing the same clothes and sporting the same superlong, overbleached, flat-ironed hair. Some people confused us, or asked if we were twins, which I found flattering.

Then, sophomore year, Shawna started dating Jacob Marsh, asshole extraordinaire. I couldn't stand him, and made the mistake of telling her as much—which almost always backfires. It certainly did in our case, the two of us drifting apart until Shawna finally came to her senses and dumped Jacob: his cue to leak a video of Shawna masturbating to Madonna's "Justify My Love." It spread within days, not only all over UGA but across the SEC, to Auburn, Alabama, and Ole Miss. Beyond the fact that she was thoroughly humiliated, she was also kicked out of ADPi under the promiscuity clause. A group of us appealed the decision, arguing it wasn't her fault the video got out; it was supposed to be private. But the ladies at the national office weren't budging and Shawna had to move out of our house. She ended up transferring to Georgia State, and we drifted apart even more—much to what I perceived as Meredith's odd vindication. I remember when she heard the news, her first reaction wasn't sympathy—but an off-the-cuff announcement that she "always knew Shawna was trouble."

The next time I saw Shawna was over the following Christmas break, when we ran into each other at a bar in Atlanta. I gave her a hug and told her how much I missed her. She said she missed me, too, but things felt strained. It made me sad, the emotion heightened by the encroaching holidays, but a little bit angry, too. After all, it wasn't my fault that she had trusted such a jerk. As I watched her hanging out with her new friends, I made the conscious decision to have more fun than they were having. I downed my vodka drink, then ordered another, on my way to a blackout drunken night—the kind with big gaping holes, followed by nothingness. In fact, I'm sure the entire night would have eventually been forgotten altogether, except that it happened to be the very night I lost my brother in a car accident.

chapter eight

MEREDITH

About a week later, Josie sends a cryptic group email requesting that my parents, Nolan, Harper, and I join her for dinner the following evening. She tells us "not to worry" but goes on to say that she has "something important to discuss" with us. She acknowledges how busy we all are, and that my parents might not be keen on the idea of seeing each other, but then essentially insists that we join her the night she is proposing. The whole thing is *classic* Josie. Calling shots, making demands, creating drama.

Mom calls me within five minutes of the email appearing in our inboxes.

"Do you think this is health-related?" she asks, panic rising in her voice. "Has she had a recent mammogram? Or any doctors' appointments that you know about? She never tells me anything. . . ."

"Mom, calm down," I say, putting her on speaker so I can continue to work on the answers to a set of interrogatories due by the end of the day. "She wouldn't include Harper if it were to tell us about a lump in her breast or anything dire like that. Frankly, I don't see her including Dad in that conversation, either. At least not initially."

I quickly change the subject, as the only person I want to analyze less than Josie is my father. I'm certainly not going to tell my mother that he has a new girlfriend, although I'm sure Josie will bring that up tomorrow night, too. Hell, she probably invited her in a separate email.

"When did you talk to her last?" she asks.

"Umm . . . last Saturday night," I say. "She called me at some ungodly hour. . . . I was half asleep."

"Did she sound upset?"

"No, Mom. She just wanted to chat. . . . Apparently she can't keep track of my please-don't-call-after-ten rule any more than she can remember not to wear her shoes in my house."

"So . . . do you think Josie might actually have *good* news?" Mom asks with pathetic hope. "Maybe a raise?"

"I doubt it," I say, thinking that it is more likely to be a financial issue than a raise. It certainly wouldn't be the first time that Josie asked to borrow money from one of us.

Mom throws out another theory. "Maybe she met someone?"

"Wouldn't she just tell us that?" I say. "Besides, that doesn't seem possible given her current Will obsession."

"I know," Mom says. "I asked her about the first week of school, and all she really talked about was that little girl. . . . It's sad. . . ."

"Sad meaning pathetic?"

"Be *nice*," she says.

I sigh, taking her off speaker. "I'm trying, Mom. But it's hard. . . . She's so *selfish*. Everything is about her. This email is a case in point."

"Meredith. Please give your sister a chance," she says. "You always assume the worst about her. Maybe she wants to talk about Daniel and our trip to see Sophie. Or—"

I cut her off, confident that this meeting has nothing *whatsoever* to do with Daniel. "I'll tell you what," I say. "Let's see what she wants to discuss. If it's not something completely self-serving, I'll start giving her a chance."

. . .

THE FOLLOWING NIGHT, when Nolan, Harper, and I arrive at my
sister's house, she is nowhere to be seen. Instead, my parents and
Gabe are sitting awkwardly in the living room, a hodgepodge of
Josie's Anthropologie taste and Gabe's more contemporary lean-
ings. Mom and Dad are both perched on hideous matching zebra-
print side chairs that Josie bought at a flea market, while Gabe is
kicked back on his leather sofa with a bored look on his face. Obviously I know he and Josie are housemates, but for some reason, I
didn't expect to see him tonight, and his sullen presence irritates me
more than usual. Or perhaps I'm just a little *more* irritated with
Josie for pulling this stunt, including a non–family member, and not
even bothering to show up on time. It suddenly crosses my mind
that her announcement might actually involve Gabe—that maybe
they've begun to date or are starting some crazy business venture.
But I really think he has more sense than to try either, even though
they clearly have some dysfunctional connection.

I say a terse hello, not even trying to hide my annoyance, while
Nolan overcompensates with a more boisterous than usual greeting,
hugging my mother, then my father, and saying all the right son-in-
law things. They both adore him, although it's hard to say how
much of that is *him* and how much is his connection to Daniel. In
Dad's case, I really think it's the latter, which makes Nolan a constant source of both comfort and sadness to him. Inevitably, when
they get together, the conversation will turn to the past, and they
will rehash the same old stories, Little League games, and inside
jokes. And even if they start out with laughter, Dad always ends up
crying while Nolan does the consoling, proving it's way easier for a
friend to move on than a parent.

"C'mere, Harper sweetie!" Dad says, still standing. His arms are
outstretched.

I glance over my shoulder at Harper, who doesn't move, just continues to pet Revis, Josie's poorly trained rescue dog.

"Harper," I say. "Grandpa's talking to you."

She looks up, with a blank expression, as Nolan propels her forward with an under-the-breath "go hug Grandpa." She begrudgingly obeys, backing into my dad's arms. It is visible evidence that the two aren't at all close—which Nolan blames on me rather than the alcoholic who checked out of our family. Harper makes a quick escape, then heads directly for my mom's lap.

"Where's Josie, anyway?" I say, pacing in front of the fireplace as I inspect her lineup of photographs—various snapshots of her with Gabe and other friends, along with one of Harper. There are none of me, Daniel, or our parents.

"She's just getting out of the shower," Gabe says, his expression inscrutable.

"Harper, honey, go get Aunt Josie," I say, still pacing.

As Harper hops off of Mom's lap and scampers down the hall, I make a snide comment about Josie's time being more valuable than anyone else's. Nobody bothers to defend her because they can't. Instead, I sit next to Gabe and ask him point-blank if he knows what's up.

He gives me a noncommittal shrug. I can never tell whether he dislikes me or just has a prickly personality, but I can count on my hand the number of times he has seemed to be in a genuinely good mood in my presence.

"She hasn't told you *anything*?" I ask him. "I find that hard to believe."

Before he can respond, Harper bursts back into the room, leading Josie by the hand. Her hair is wrapped up in a towel, and she's wearing sweats that could pass for pajamas. "Hey!" she says, all easy-breezy. "How is everyone?"

"Just *fabulous*!" I say as sarcastically as possible as Nolan sits on the other side of me and squeezes my knee, in an attempt to either reprimand or calm me.

Josie stares me down, crosses her arms, and says, "Okay. That was *so* fake."

"Listen, Josie," I say. "We're all a little worried about why you called this meeting tonight."

"It's not a *meeting*. It's dinner," she says, tucking a strand of wet hair into her towel as she plops down onto the floor, center stage.

"But you said in your formal *group* email that you had something to tell us. Didn't you?" I say.

Josie nods.

"Well?" I say. "What is it, then?"

"Jeez. Settle down, Mere," Josie says, which pretty much always has the opposite effect on anyone who is even the tiniest bit agitated.

"Josie," I say, my voice just short of shouting. "Nolan and I are worried. Mom's worried. Dad's worried."

"I'm not really worried, actually," Dad says. "Should I be?"

"Yes," I snap. "You *should* be, Dad." I want to add—*and if you ever thought about anyone other than Daniel, you* would *be*. But I don't want to confuse the main issue.

"No, he *shouldn't* be," Josie says. "There's absolutely nothing to worry about here. It's all good."

I tense up, thinking that it's never *all* good.

"Just tell us you're healthy," Mom says before kissing the top of Harper's head.

"Perfectly healthy," Josie says. "I just wanted to have my family over . . . and talk to you about something. . . ." Her voice trails off.

"Josie," Gabe finally says; he's the only one who can ever really reason with her. "Why don't you just tell them so we can have dinner?"

She takes a deep breath, seeming to relish the moment.

"Wait," I say, as it occurs to me that her news might not be rated PG. "Are you sure this is okay for Harper to hear?"

Josie glares at me. "Omi*god*. Could you have *any* less confidence in me?"

"I'm sorry," I say. "But I have to put my daughter first."

"Look, Meredith," she snaps back. "I really don't appreciate the implication that I'd do anything—"

"Girls!" Mom pleads. "Please, *please* don't fight! This is hard enough—"

"Actually, Mom, there's nothing hard about tonight whatsoever," Josie says. "This is a celebration. I have wonderful news."

I shake my head, feeling certain that I won't agree, as she stands, looks purposefully around the room, and says in a loud, clear voice, "What I brought you here to tell you is that I'm going to have a baby." She takes a deep breath, then smiles, looking triumphant.

At least five seconds of stunned silence pass before Harper begins to clap and cheer, mimicking the reaction to our good friends' pregnancy news last month, clearly unable to distinguish the vast difference between the two scenarios.

"A *girl* baby?" she asks, her eyes bright.

"Oh. That I don't know yet, sweetie," Josie says, beaming as I grind my teeth into my tongue, determined not to be the first adult to speak, especially since the only words coming to mind are *what the fuck*.

"Hey, Jo," Gabe says under his breath. "You might want to clarify here."

She gives him a blank look as it occurs to me, once again, that he might have a role in all of this.

"Your announcement . . . It's a bit . . . misleading," he says.

When she continues to look befuddled, he gives her his best don't-be-such-a-dipshit look, then clues the rest of us in. "She's not *currently* pregnant," he says. "It's just her . . . *plan* to *become* pregnant."

I watch Mom exhale with visible relief.

"Oh. Yeah. Right," Josie says with a dismissive wave of her hand. "When I say I'm *going* to have a baby, I don't mean that I'm pregnant *now*. I mean that I *plan* to get pregnant. As soon as possible."

"And how do you plan on accomplishing that, exactly?" I ask her.

"I'm going to a sperm bank," she says. "That's how."

I glance at Nolan and take twisted pleasure in the fact that he finally looks annoyed. "Josie," he says, gesturing toward Harper.

"Oh, c'mon. She doesn't know what a sperm bank is," Josie says under her breath, which, of course, is Harper's cue to ask what a sperm bank is.

"Harper, honey, why don't you get Revis a bone?" Mom says.

Harper happily takes this suggestion, but before she's even out of the room, Josie says, "I don't think there's anything to be so secretive about. . . . I'm going to want Harper to know where her cousin comes from."

"Fine," Nolan says calmly but firmly. "When she's old enough to understand it . . . But we'd really like to avoid a discussion about the birds and the bees at age four. . . ."

"That was not my intent," Josie says, then launches into one of her know-it-all explanations about child development.

I cut her off. "Well, when you have your test-tube baby, you can make those decisions. But Harper is *our* daughter," I say. "And we would appreciate it if you kept her out of these discussions."

Josie stares at me with pursed lips, then says, "First, I don't think a child should be defined by the circumstances of his or her conception. Second, it wouldn't be a *test-tube* baby."

Before I can respond, Mom says, "What about marriage?"

"What about it?" Josie says, looking defiant.

"Well . . . are you just . . . *giving up* on that idea?"

"Well, Mom. Maybe that will happen later. . . . I hope it does. . . . But I'm almost thirty-eight—"

"Women have babies into their forties now," Dad says, his first contribution to the conversation.

I glare at him, wondering if he has plans to impregnate his court reporter, as Josie says, "Yes. True. Some do. But it's risky to wait."

"You could always freeze your eggs," Mom says.

"I could," Josie replies. "But I'm ready for a baby *now*."

"Well, it's all about what *you* want, isn't it?" I say.

"What's *that* supposed to mean?" Josie asks me. "I'm not allowed to be a mother just because I'm not married? There are plenty of wonderful single parents out there . . . and conversely, plenty of married people with children who are unhappy, terrible parents." She gives me a purposeful look, clearly talking about my marriage, if not my mothering, and I feel my anger burning deeper, hotter.

"Do you *really* think you're in a position to judge *anyone*?" I ask my sister.

"I'm not *judging*. Nor am I asking for advice or permission. I am simply sharing my plan with the people who matter most to me. And I was sort of hoping for a more supportive reaction. Gabe thinks it's a great idea."

I look at him, wondering how soon after the birth he will be seeking a new housemate. "Right. Well. With all due respect to Gabe," I say, "he has no clue what's involved here. He's not a parent, now is he? Shit . . . you told me he forgets to take the dog out when you're not home."

Gabe looks at Josie and says, "That happened *once*."

"Okay. Well, Dad, what do you think?" Josie says, turning to the third-least-qualified person in the room to weigh in on parent-hood.

"I think . . . I think you have to do what makes you happy," he stammers as I predict the number of diapers he will help her change could be counted on one hand.

Mom scowls at her ex-husband, then turns back to Josie. "Honey, you know we want to support you. . . . We're just asking . . . have you really thought this thing through?"

"Yes," she says. "I've given it a lot of thought. And to be honest, since having Will's daughter in my class—"

"I knew it!" I shout, cutting her off. "I *knew* this was about Will."

"It's not *about* Will!" she yells back. "It's about Edie and my realization—"

I interrupt her again. "If you loved him so damn much, why did you screw up that whole relationship?"

Josie looks as if she's just been slapped. "Did you really just ask me that?" she says, her voice quivering.

"Yeah. C'mon, Meredith," Gabe says. "That's not cool."

"Well," I say, crossing my arms and glaring back at him. "She's the one using Will as an excuse to bring a child into the world."

"An *excuse*?" Josie says. "The last time I checked, bringing a child into the world isn't a *bad* thing."

"It is if you can't properly care for it."

"Who says I can't properly care for it? I might not have as much money as you two," she says, "but I have a job—a great job. . . . And I have friends and family who I thought might want to be involved in this child's life . . . but I guess that was too much to ask for."

"That's not fair," Mom says. "Of course we'd want to be involved."

"Of course we would," Dad echoes.

Josie looks at me, waiting.

"Sure." I shrug. "I'll breeze in for a quick game of Twister . . . then be on my merry way. . . . Isn't that what aunts do?"

"*Wow*. That is so unfair," Josie says. "I'm totally involved in Harper's life."

Gabe chimes in, agreeing with her. "She is, Mere. And you know it."

"Okay. Fine. But do you have any *clue* how much easier it is to be an aunt than a mother?"

"Do you have any clue how big of a bitch you are?" Josie says.

"Josie. *Language*," Nolan says, as I announce that we're leaving. I stand up and walk over to Harper, trying to pull her away from the dog as she whimpers that she doesn't want to go, that she wants to stay at Aunt Josie's.

"Fine. Stay with Aunt Josie," I say, fuming. "In fact, why don't you move in with *Aunt* Josie and *Uncle* Gabe? Since they want to play house and have it all figured out."

"Meredith," Nolan hisses, appropriately horrified that I'm taking my anger out on our daughter. My face burns with shame as I catch my breath, then tell Nolan I'll be waiting in the car.

"Can't you just sit down?" he says, looking up at me. "So we can all discuss this calmly?"

"No. I can't," I say, shaking my head. Then, talking about my sister in the third person, I add, "Would someone please tell her that bringing a child into the world is the hardest thing you can do?"

When nobody answers, I finally turn to walk out of the house, catching the look of anguish on Mom's face and knowing, in an instant, she's thinking how wrong I am about this. That watching your child *leave* the world is actually much harder.

chapter nine

JOSIE

"Well, that went swimmingly," Gabe deadpans the second the door closes behind Mom and Dad, the two of them giving new meaning to the expression *eat and run*.

"It's all Meredith's fault," I say. There was no way the rest of us could recover from her outburst and exit, the conversation vacillating between awkward, tense, and downright contentious.

"Yeah," Gabe says as we make our way back to the table and begin to clear the dishes. "But no surprise there. We both knew that was going to happen."

"I guess so," I say. "But I always think she'll be different."

"You know that's the definition of insanity according to Einstein?" Gabe says, raising one eyebrow. "Doing the same thing over and over and expecting different results?"

I sigh and say, "Yeah. Well, I knew she wouldn't embrace the idea, but I thought she'd at least stay for dinner."

"I didn't," Gabe says. "Although it is pretty hard to resist my cooking."

"True," I say, cursorily acknowledging his culinary prowess. "But she wouldn't even listen. . . . Her mind is so made up about *everything*."

"She really *is* closed-minded," he says. "I'll give you that."

"Mom is, too," I say, thinking about some of her remarks during dinner—how many different ways she suggested that I just go on a few more dates.

"Yeah, but it's kind of different. Your mom's just . . . traditional. Conservative. She wants you to follow that set boy-meets-girl path because she thinks that's the only path to happiness. . . . Meredith's not really traditional—she's just judgmental toward *you*. If another friend came to her with this same half-baked idea, she'd be all over it. Praising her independence."

"Exactly!" I say, so excited by how well Gabe always captures and articulates what I'm feeling that I choose to overlook his slightly offensive choice of adjectives. After all, he is correct—the idea hasn't *fully* baked yet. But it *has* been slid into the preheated oven.

"Meredith has no faith in me whatsoever," I continue. "Did you see how she acted about Harper? It was as if she thought I was going to start discussing orgies or heroin in front of a four-year-old."

"You do like a good heroin orgy," Gabe says with a little grin.

I don't crack a smile; I'm too worked up now. "And can you believe she brought up Will like that? As if that is at all relevant at this point . . ."

I return to the table for another armful of dishes as Gabe trails behind me. "Were you at all tempted to set the record straight?" he asks. "She really thinks you cheated on him—"

"No. Not one bit," I say, cutting him off. Because I know what he's thinking, and he knows what I'm thinking, and I see no reason to rehash all of it.

"Okay, okay. Just asking," he says, palms up, facing out. His gesture would suggest that he's offended, but I know it takes a lot more than a few terse words to offend Gabe.

For the next several minutes, neither of us speaks as I rinse our dishes, glasses, and utensils, handing them to Gabe to load in the dishwasher.

"There's no point in discussing ancient history," I finally say, trying to soften my retort. "Especially with Meredith."

"I hear you," Gabe mutters, glancing at me.

"I mean . . . what's done is done," I say, handing him the final few steak knives.

"Right," Gabe says. "What's done is most definitely done."

We are speaking in code, of course, the way best friends do, talking about several layers of things at once. The night Daniel died. And also the night, years later, on which we discovered that there was more to the story than we once thought.

IT HAPPENED ABOUT halfway between then and now, seven years after Daniel died. Gabe picked me up for dinner, no destination in mind, and we landed at Tin Lizzy's, a Mexican dive. It was just the two of us, which had become something of a rarity, as Will and I were approaching engagement, and one of his terms of marriage seemed to be curtailing my time with Gabe. He insisted that he wasn't jealous; he just thought my friendship with Gabe was "odd" (which of course meant that he was jealous). Trying to accommodate him, I mostly obliged his request.

But on that particular Friday night, Gabe and I had Will's blessing, likely because he was going to a bachelor party and figured this was a way to keep me from whining about the strip club antics that were sure to come.

"So ol' Willy gave you a hall pass tonight?" Gabe asked over fish tacos, guacamole, and a couple of ice-cold Coronas.

"Ha-ha. Very funny," I said, feeling defensive. "I don't need his permission to hang with you."

"Oh, yeah, ya do," Gabe said, raising his eyebrows. At that point, he had never directly told me what he thought of Will, nor would he ever tell me he missed me, but I knew the truth, on both fronts. "So what's he got tonight? A bachelor party or something?"

I reluctantly nodded, marveling at his uncanny ability to read a situation.

"Where is it?" he asked, nonchalantly making conversation, though he'd unwittingly stumbled onto very sensitive terrain.

"They started out at Five Paces," I said, feeling myself tense as I looked away. Then I blurted out that I hadn't been back there since the night Daniel died.

"Yeah," Gabe mumbled. "Me neither, come to think of it."

"What?" I asked, looking up at him with a jolt, thinking I must have heard him wrong—or simply misunderstood what he was saying.

But then he clarified. "I haven't been back there since the night your brother died, either," he said, taking a sip of his beer.

"Wait. You were *there* that night?"

"Yeah," Gabe said. "You don't remember?" He let out a nervous laugh, which I would overanalyze later, and added, "Thanks a lot."

As I stared back at him, my heart began to race, and the haziest recollection of Gabe sitting at the bar, wearing a gray hoodie and nursing a pint of beer, returned to me. I wondered if it was a real memory—or just the power of suggestion. "Were you wearing a hoodie?" I asked, squinting into space.

"Hell if I know—" he started to say, then stopped. "Well, actually, I think I was. Maybe . . ."

"Why haven't you mentioned this before?" I asked him, incredulous.

"Because you were *there,* that's why," Gabe said, softening the sarcastic edge I'd usually get with such an answer, given the emotional territory we were in.

"Did we speak?" I asked.

"No. Not really," Gabe said with a little shrug. "We just said hello . . . in passing. That was pretty much it. But I was kind of sitting near you—at the end of the bar. Right at the corner. For some reason I do remember that." He points at the corner of the napkin and says, "You were like this, facing the street . . . and I was right here, facing the back of the bar."

Suddenly I had no appetite. I pushed my plate away and asked who he was with. I wanted, *needed,* to know every detail.

"Nobody, really," he said, which was par for the course. "I knew a lot of people there. But I didn't *go* there with anyone."

My hands turned clammy, the way they always did when I thought about the nauseating minute-to-minute time line of that night. "What time did you get there? What time did you leave?"

Gabe used a chip to scrape the last bit of guacamole from the little bowl between us. "I don't know, exactly," he said, the chip halfway to his mouth before he changed his mind and dropped it onto his plate.

"Well, then, approximately?" I pressed.

He insisted that he truly didn't know—that he couldn't even ballpark it. "My guess would be as good as yours."

"No," I said with a sad little laugh. "Actually that's not true. Your guess would *still* be better than mine."

"Why does it matter?"

"Because it does," I said.

This answer must have been good enough for him, because he said, "Okay . . . well, if I had to guess . . . I'd say I got there around ten . . . and then left around . . . midnight. Maybe twelve-thirty."

I closed my eyes, wondering if we could have been saying hello at the precise minute that Daniel was killed. What was I doing at exactly ten-fifty-four that evening? I had asked myself that question many times, though never with Gabe in the frame. And of course, that was before your cellphone could pretty much give you an answer, providing a near-perfect time-stamped record.

"What else do you remember?" I said. "About me on that night?"

Gabe bit his lip, then said, "Well . . . you were pretty lit. I remember that."

I nodded, feeling a rush of thick shame, not for the first or last time. Shame that I was at a bar at the moment my brother was killed. Having fun. Laughing. Flirting with boys—probably lots of them. Getting blackout, stupid drunk.

"What else?"

"To be honest, Jo . . . that's it. I don't remember anything else."

I could tell he was lying or at least covering something up because Gabe almost *always* told the truth, hence eliminating the need to add the "to be honest" qualifier.

"Yes, you *do*," I said. "Tell me. What was I doing? Who was I talking to?"

"I don't remember. A lot of people."

" 'A lot of people' or you 'don't remember'? Which is it?"

He took a deep breath, then an even longer exhale. "I *honestly* don't remember . . . exactly. A ton of people were there that night. . . . It was near the holidays so everyone was home. . . ."

"I know *that*," I said, frustrated. Of *course* I knew it was near the holidays. It was December freaking twenty-second. I told him to please tell me something I *didn't* know.

"As we've established," Gabe said, sounding weary but patient, "I don't know what you remember, and what you don't remember. So please don't get mad at me here. I'm trying the best I can to answer your questions."

"I'm not getting mad at you," I said, still sounding mad, but feeling something closer to desperation. "Just *please* tell me everything!"

"Okay, okay," he said, holding up his hand. "Shawna was there.

You were talking to Shawna for a while . . . and a lot of the other usual Lovett girls from your class. . . ."

He looked into my eyes as I waited, then waited some more. "I think you were also talking to Nolan Brady at one point," he finally said.

"You *think*?" I quickly replied. Nolan's was the name I'd been waiting for.

"You were . . . but I honestly wasn't paying that close attention. I just knew you were really, really drunk . . . and Nolan looked . . . concerned. That's it. I swear."

I felt as if I might pass out and realized that I'd been holding my breath. I sucked in a few gulps of air as Gabe asked a logical follow-up. "What does *Nolan* say about it? Surely he remembers what you talked about. . . ."

I shook my head, unable to speak.

"He doesn't remember, either?" Gabe asked.

"I never asked him," I finally said.

"Oh." Gabe nodded.

"I've never talked about it with anyone," I said. "Not him or Shawna or Meredith or Mom. Not even that annoying therapist that my parents made me see. No one until now."

"But *we've* talked about the accident before. . . ." Gabe said.

I shook my head. "I don't mean the accident. Or Daniel's death. Or any of that. I mean what *I* did that night. . . ."

Gabe held my gaze and said, "And? What did you do that night, Josie? What do *you* remember?" His expression was so classically Gabe-like, focused and intelligent and compassionate (though he never wanted you to know just how much he cared), that I started to talk. I told him how I had my first drink in my bedroom as I dressed, sipping from my sorority flask. I told him I was in a fight with Meredith because she wouldn't let me wear her pendant that went with my outfit, and Mom had taken her side, and I left the house pissed off.

"How'd you get there?" he asked.

"Kendra picked me up," I said. "But she had a date . . . and left early, so I was hanging with other people. Shawna kind of blew me off, so I was upset. And I just kept drinking. A lot. Mixing stuff. Vodka and beer . . . Things got fuzzy, then fuzzier, then black."

Gabe nodded.

"I don't remember leaving the bar. And I don't know how I got home. . . . Somebody must have brought me back. Or maybe they called me a cab. I don't know. . . . I just remember waking up in my bed. The room was spinning and there was a trashcan next to the bed. Someone put it there. . . . Or maybe I did. I really don't remember. . . ."

I blinked back tears for as long as I could, but at some point, I just couldn't stop myself from crying. I wasn't sure why, exactly, and I could tell Gabe wasn't, either. But he sprung into action, quickly paying the bill, then whisking me to the crowded parking lot. It was still daylight, and I hid my face in the crook of my arm as he opened my door, something he never did—chivalry wasn't really his style.

To my relief, he didn't ask more questions on that ride home. In fact, we didn't talk at all, in that way you can be silent only with a close friend. When we got back to my apartment, he came inside with me. I headed straight to my room to get ready for bed, changing into a long Georgia T-shirt I wore as a nightgown, brushing my teeth, washing my face. At some point, when I didn't come out, he knocked on my bedroom door and asked if I was okay.

"Yes," I lied, quickly turning off my lights so he couldn't see my face.

"Can I come in?"

"Yes," I said again, as I dove under the covers.

He sat on the edge of the bed, stared at me, and said, "What's going on, Josie? Why are you so upset?"

"I don't know," I said. Because I really didn't. It was more of a feeling than anything I could put into words. A feeling that I somehow had something to do with Daniel's accident.

"Yes, you do," he gently pressed. "Talk to me."

"I just feel like . . . it might be my fault. . . ." I finally said.

"How would it be your fault?" he asked. "That's crazy."

"It's not crazy," I said. "Maybe Daniel was coming to get me."

Gabe shook his head, adamant. "I don't think so, Josie. You're being paranoid. He was going to get a burger. Isn't that what he told your mother?"

"Yes," I said. "But . . ."

"But nothing, Josie. You're just experiencing . . . survivor's guilt or something. Your brother had an accident. It had nothing to do with you."

I took a deep breath, my whole body shuddering. Then I told him I didn't want to talk about it anymore. Ever again, in fact.

"Okay," he said, staring at me, his face a mask of concern. "Do you want me to go?"

"No," I said, peering up at him. "Please stay with me."

He nodded, then kicked off his shoes, walked around the bed, and sat beside me, on top of the covers. He leaned against my headboard, his legs straight out in front of him, then reached over to awkwardly pat my back. Once, then twice.

"Thank you," I said, my eyelids feeling heavy.

At some point after I had drifted off, I heard him get up to go. I rolled over and asked him please not to leave.

"Shhhh," he said, rubbing my back through my duvet, blanket, and sheet. "Go back to sleep."

"Don't leave," I said again.

"I won't. I'll stay," he said, and at that point, he took off his jeans and shirt and got under the covers beside me. It would be the only time we ever shared a bed, but nothing about it felt awkward, not even when he rolled over in the middle of the night and put his arm around me. It only felt warm, comforting, safe.

Until just before dawn, when my bedroom door opened and Will walked in. He took one look at us and announced, in no uncertain terms, that he and I were done.

chapter ten

MEREDITH

For days following Josie's announcement, I find myself trying to pinpoint exactly why I'm so angry with her. Yes, I think her plan is ill-advised, half-assed, and selfish. And yes, I think that her child will, at some point and in some manner, become my burden and responsibility. But deep down, I also believe that Josie is right—that *is* what family is for, to help and support one another. And I truly *do* want my sister to experience the awe of motherhood. So why can't I just get on board, wish her good luck, and be happy for her?

One night, as Nolan and I are getting ready for bed, I pose the question to him, bracing myself for an answer I might not like. He's been surprisingly quiet on the topic, perhaps because he doesn't want to tell me that he's actually on her side. "Why do you think I'm so pissed off at her?" I ask.

"I don't know," he says, rinsing his toothbrush, then tapping it on the edge of the sink. "You know I don't understand your relationship with your sister. . . ."

I put on my oldest, most comfortable, and perhaps least attractive nightgown. "Do you think I was too harsh?" I ask.

Nolan gives me a sheepish look, shrugs, and says, "Yeah. Maybe a little . . . You went into attack mode pretty quickly."

I know he's probably right, but still resent his answer.

"Can't you see that she just wants what *you* have?" he continues.

I sigh, thinking that this is how my mother always paints things. How they both insist that Josie's jealous of me.

"I'm sorry, but I just don't buy that," I say.

"Well, regardless. Can't you *roll* with it?" he says, undressing down to his boxers.

"Roll with her having a *baby*?" I pick up his clothes from the closet floor, where he always leaves them, then drop them into the hamper.

"No, roll with her announcement. Humor her. . . . For one thing, the chances are only about fifty-fifty that she actually goes through with it. At *best*."

"You really think so?" I ask, feeling mostly hopeful that he's right, but also an unexpected dash of disappointment, perhaps because I *do* realize that being an aunt is more fun than being a mother.

"Well, let's think about this," Nolan says. "Did she get the PhD or master's she's always talking about?"

I shake my head.

"And remember her big plan to move to California?" he asks, walking into the bedroom.

"Yeah," I say, following him.

"Never happened . . . And what about the fact that she pays rent every month when she's talked for years about buying a place? . . . Enough examples?"

I smile and tell him I'd like one more, please.

"Okay. How about Will Carlisle? She certainly didn't close the deal there, did she?" he asks, as we stand on our sides of the bed and pull down the covers.

"No," I say. "She certainly did not."

"I'm glad *I* closed the deal with you," he says with a wink before climbing into bed.

I smile, then get in next to him, both of us reaching up to turn off our bedside lamps. He gives me a quick kiss on the lips, then rolls over, dropping his head to his feather pillow, while I do the same on my hypoallergenic one.

"Good night, Mere," he says, his back to me.

"Good night, Nolan," I say, relieved he doesn't want to have sex tonight. I wonder if he's tired of being turned down or simply too tired, and hope it's the latter. I try to recall the last time I initiated but can't. It's been that long. I feel a pang of guilt, commingled with worry, but tell myself this is all very normal, happening all over town. "I love you," I add.

"Love you, too," he says, his voice muffled.

A few minutes later, he is breathing deeply, and I can tell he's asleep. I wonder exactly when the snoring will begin, and if it will get loud enough for me to move to the guest room, as my mind returns to Josie, and Nolan's statement that she wants what I have. For a few seconds, I feel sorry for her, but then I remind myself that Josie made her own bed, blazed her own self-destructive path. She could be listening to Will snore right now, or plenty of guys for that matter, but instead she chose to put fun and games with Gabe over a real commitment.

And then it hits me with a jolt: the sudden realization of why I got so upset the other night when Josie told us her news. I suddenly see that it actually has far less to do with the decision, or any of the pitfalls of single motherhood, and more to do with Josie *herself*. The fact that she has always done exactly what she wants, when she wants, how she wants. My sister puts herself first, period. And maybe, for this reason alone, I'm actually the one who is a little bit jealous of *her*.

THE NEXT DAY, Nolan and I take Harper to Isla Graham's fourth birthday party. Isla is Harper's best friend, which is really to say that her mother, Ellen, is my best friend (though Nolan and Isla's father, Andy, are close, too; hence Nolan's attendance at a Pinkalicious tea, wearing a pink checked shirt, no less). We arrive at the party early, as suggested by Ellen, and walk up the long, winding driveway of the Grahams' Brookhaven home. Nolan rings the bell, which Ellen had rewired to, in her words, sound less foreboding, as I simply open the door and head straight through the house to the backyard.

"Wow," I say under my breath, taking in the pink wonderland. Clusters of hot and light pink balloons bob in the breeze. A long child-size table is elaborately set with crystal and silver, pink polkadot linens, and pink hydrangeas. All of the food is in various shades of pink—mini bagels covered with strawberry cream cheese, jelly sandwiches cut into hearts, strawberry yogurt in pink porcelain bowls, cubed watermelon tossed with raspberries, even peeled hardboiled eggs dyed pink. Ellen is a far cry from Martha Stewart, so I know her mother-in-law is behind it even before I see her emerge onto the porch, carrying a pitcher of pink lemonade, Ellen trailing behind her.

"This place looks amazing!" I say, giving them both a hug.

"It's all Stella," Ellen says, gesturing toward her mother-in-law as I notice the goody bags in a basket by the back door, tied with pink tulle and filled with pink candies and pink Play-Doh.

"It was fun," Stella says modestly as I feel a little sheepish about Harper's lackluster farm-themed party in our backyard, complete with a mangy pony, two ornery goats, and a rather pointless flock of dingy brown hens.

Meanwhile, Harper runs to embrace Isla, both girls in pink tutus. Andy hands Nolan a Pabst Blue Ribbon, and the two head inside to watch the second half of the Georgia–Tennessee game.

"Did she buy your dress, too?" I say, once Stella is out of earshot.

Ellen laughs. "Close. I borrowed it from Margot," she says, referring to her sister-in-law.

"I don't think I've ever seen you in anything pink," I say, fondly remembering the day I met Ellen, shortly after I moved back to Atlanta from New York. I was behind her in a long line at the post office, sizing up her outfit the way women do with one another, noticing the details of her faded blue jeans, ripped at the left knee and rolled at the ankles, her bold gladiator sandals, olive-green linen tunic, and layers of funky bead-and-leather necklaces. She looked cool in an effortless way, and although she wouldn't have stood out in New York, she made an impression in the Buckhead sea of brightly colored Tory Burch, Lilly Pulitzer, and Lululemon. Then I glanced down at her package and saw the familiar address of my old New York apartment building in black Sharpie: 22C, exactly three floors down from my 25C. It wasn't like me to chat up strangers, but this coincidence was too great. I tapped her shoulder and said, "I don't mean to be nosy, but your package . . . That's my old building! I lived in 25C."

Her face lit up, instantly elevating her from plain to pretty. "You're kidding! My good friends Hillary and Julian live there. Did you know them?"

"No," I said, smiling back at her. "But small world, huh?"

She nodded and said, "So you're a New Yorker?"

I told her no, I was actually a native Atlantan, but that I'd lived in the city for years. "I miss it," I added.

She nodded and said, "I do, too. I lived there for years myself. Why'd you come back? For a job?"

"My husband's job," I said. We had only just married, and saying the words *my husband* still felt so foreign to me.

"Same here," she said, then introduced herself as Ellen Graham. I told her my name, and we continued to talk in line. I learned that she was a professional portrait photographer, originally from Pittsburgh, married to a lawyer, and I told her my bare-bones biography. She waited as I completed my transaction. Then, on our way out to the parking lot, she reached into her tote bag, handed me a little square business card, and suggested that we go for coffee sometime, maybe grab dinner with our husbands.

"I'd love that," I said, feeling that rush of new-friend excitement that becomes rarer the older you get.

A few weeks later, I called Ellen, and the four of us went to Leon's Full Service, a restaurant in Decatur. It was a very fun night—easy and relaxed—the double-date chemistry perfect. Nolan and Andy were both Lovett grads (though Andy was several years older); both now worked with their fathers; and, perhaps the biggest thing they had in common, both had married women so different than they—women they had met through their siblings. (Andy's sister, Margot, had been Ellen's best friend first.)

As Nolan told our story, he mentioned Daniel, and I watched Andy piece it all together, connecting the dots from my maiden name to the Lovett alum turned Yale med student who had died in the Christmastime car accident.

He turned to me, his face somber. "Was Daniel Garland your brother?" he asked softly.

"Yes," I said, then briefed Ellen so that Andy didn't have to. "My brother died. In a car accident."

Andy mumbled that he was sorry, looking down, exactly the way most people do. But Ellen looked directly into my eyes, took my hand, and said the same words but in such a different way.

"Thank you," I said, feeling a deep connection to her even before she told me that she had experienced a big loss at a young age, too, her mother dying of cancer. "Not that it's the same thing," she quickly added. "Brothers and sisters are supposed to be from the cradle to the grave. . . ."

"Yes, but still . . . I'm really sorry, too," I said. Although the

death of a parent is a more comprehensible void than losing a sibling, because it follows the natural order we expect, I couldn't imagine life without my mother. I especially couldn't fathom losing her
when I was still a teenager. *No matter how you slice it,* I remember
thinking, *life is tragic.*

"Has your family . . . healed?" Ellen asked. "Did it bring you
closer?"

It was such a compassionate question, and I found myself con-
fiding in her, as the guys branched off in a separate conversation
about golf and travel and their work. I talked a lot about Josie, how
walled off she had become, how she refused to discuss Daniel and
seemed to view my desire to do so as unhealthy. I asked Ellen if she
had siblings. She said yes, an older sister named Suzanne. She told
me how different they were, yet still so close. "She really is my best
friend."

It was something I never said about Josie, and I felt a pang of
wistfulness and regret. I wanted to be close like that, but couldn't
imagine it ever happening. "Did losing your mom make you two
closer?" I asked.

"It did," she said, nodding. "But we were always close. . . . My
dad sounds more like your sister. He seldom talks about my mom.
It's funny how grief is different for everyone. . . ."

I nodded, thinking how true that statement was, remembering a
quote from a support group I had briefly attended with my mother.
Grief is a mystery to be lived through, not a problem to be solved,
our counselor—who had lost her nine-year-old daughter—had written on the chalkboard. Maybe she was right. Yet it seemed to me
that talking about it, trying to solve it, was the only way to truly
accept it. The only hope for healing. I said as much to Ellen that
night, and she quickly agreed.

"Absolutely. But I guess my father and your sister just don't see
it that way. And it's hard—really hard—when those we love most

don't handle things in the same way we do. I bet that's why so many marriages break up after the death of a child. I bet couples are more likely to stay together if they handle grief the same way. . . ."

I nodded, then divulged details of my parents' divorce. I told her how certain I was that Daniel's death had caused their split. My mom blamed my dad's drinking—but the drinking was a reaction to his grief. In other words, it all came back to Daniel.

On our way home that night, I told Nolan that I was certain Ellen would become a close friend. Sure enough, we bonded more and more over the next few months, hanging out frequently, emailing constantly, and talking on the phone almost daily, which was something I had never really done with other friends. Josie referred to Ellen as my "girl crush," which annoyed me for several reasons, but mostly because it trivialized our connection. I didn't bother to tell Josie all the things I liked and admired about Ellen. She was passionate about her work—and brilliant at it, too. I could spend hours looking at her photographs of people, marveling at how she made ordinary people look famous and famous people seem ordinary. She was original, yet didn't go out of her way to be different, either— which resulted in unusual combinations that seemed like contradictions only if you didn't know her. Like owning a rescue dog as well as the most beautiful, regal purebred golden retriever I'd ever seen. Like being a hippie at heart, yet marrying a fourth-generation Atlantan blue-blooder. Like driving a beat-up Toyota covered with artsy bumper stickers, yet filling her house with exquisite art and antiques. I loved her raw honesty—that she was quick to acknowledge flaws in herself and her marriage when so many others couldn't even admit they were having a bad day.

As it turned out, Ellen and I got pregnant at virtually the same time, and Isla and Harper were born only five weeks apart. The intense early motherhood experience brought us even closer, both individually and as couples, so much so that we chose each other to be godparents to our firstborns. Josie, of course, was angered by our decision.

"So if you and Nolan die, you're giving Harper to *them*?" she said, cradling our two-month-old daughter with a slightly crazed look. "Someone you've only known a few years? Instead of your own flesh and blood?"

"Oh, for heaven's sakes, Josie, everyone knows that godparents don't necessarily mean guardianship," I said, doing my best not to think about the grisly circumstances that could claim both my life *and* Nolan's. "It's just . . . an *honorary* position."

"So you don't want to *honor* your own sister?"

"You're already Harper's *aunt*. The aunt role trumps that of godmother. Ellen picked me instead of her sister. Or Andy's sister. And they aren't *mad* about it," I said, although this wasn't entirely true. Ellen's sister was fine with her decision, but *Andy's* sister was a little miffed and territorial, too.

"So I *do* get Harper if you die?" Josie morbidly pressed on.

"Josie," I said, aghast, discreetly gesturing toward Mom.

"What? It's important to cover this stuff *now*," Josie said, willing to talk about life and death when it suited her purposes.

"Nolan and I haven't done our will yet," I said, thinking that although we would have much to decide, one thing was for sure: Josie would *not* be Harper's guardian.

"Well, I *want* her," Josie said, as if the decision were just that simple. Sort of like her mindset now. *You want a baby, you get a baby.*

AFTER THE TEA party is under way, I fill Ellen in on Josie's latest antics.

"Interesting," she says, looking intrigued. Although she is always diplomatic and fair-minded when it comes to my sister, this response still surprises me.

"*Interesting?* You don't think it's a horrible idea?"

"It's not the *worst* idea I've ever heard."

"Josie as a *single* mother?"

"She's good with Harper."

"Yeah. For five-hour stints," I say. "We both know that's not how motherhood works."

"Right. But she wouldn't be completely solo. She'd have you and Nolan to help," Ellen says. "And grandparents. And Gabe."

"Friends don't really help when it comes to children," I say. "Not more than a token playdate here and there."

"Maybe not," she says. "But family certainly does."

I look at Ellen, once again reminded of the key difference between the two of us and our respective sister relationships, namely that she both loves *and* likes her sister, Suzanne.

"The baby would have you," Ellen finishes, in case I missed her point.

"But I don't want another baby," I say, just as Nolan passes by us on his way to the cooler. He shoots me a wounded look, grabs another beer, then heads back in the house.

"Shit," I say under my breath. "Nolan heard that."

"He doesn't *know* that?" Ellen says, looking surprised. She and I have discussed it several times before.

"Not *that* directly," I say, thinking it is another difference in our worlds. Ellen and Andy communicate exhaustively, and even do ongoing couples therapy—not because they have any big problems (although they had gone through a rough period before having Isla), but to *prevent* problems. Their marriage isn't perfect, but it is strong, as enviable as her sister relationship, maybe more so.

"You're really sure you don't want a second? Teddy's been such a breeze," Ellen says, referring to her two-year-old son, whom Stella has just taken inside for his nap.

"I'm sure," I say, eyeing Nolan through the glass door. "Besides, what if I had another girl?"

Ellen knows what I'm getting at. "Most sisters get along."

I shake my head and say, "No. Most do not. At least not like you and yours."

"You could have a boy," she says, wrapping her dark hair in a bun on top of her head. "Boys love their mothers. And what if you and Josie *both* had boys? They'd be like cousins *and* brothers. And the brother relationship seems *completely* uncomplicated."

"But I *really* don't want another baby," I say, careful to keep my voice down. "And besides. *Nothing* is uncomplicated when it comes to Josie and me."

"SHE'S OUT COLD," Nolan says to me that night in the family room while I'm straightening up the inevitable end-of-the-day disaster area. He's just returned from carrying Harper up to her bed after she fell asleep on her beanbag watching *Frozen*.

"All that playing in the sun wore her out," I say, tossing her toys into their proper wire baskets. Legos in one, stuffed animals in another, books in the third, dolls and their accessories in the fourth, miscellaneous bits in the fifth.

"All that drinking beer in the sun wore *me* out," Nolan says, yawning as he picks up a pink elephant puppet and jams his hand inside, both of them staring at me. Ever since he took a workshop with Harper at the Center for Puppetry Arts, he's turned into a regular Jim Henson.

"You missed your calling," I say with a halfhearted laugh.

Nolan's face remains blank, his lips motionless, as he somehow manages to make a felt puppet look alert. "It's never too late," the elephant tells me.

"You're a very wise elephant," I say, thinking of all the ways his statement could apply to my life. I sink into the sofa, putting my bare feet up on the coffee table.

Nolan looks at me for a beat, then pulls the puppet off his arm and tosses it into the book basket. I resist the urge to correct him, but he catches me frowning and says, "I know, I know. Wrong basket. I'll get it in a sec."

"It's fine," I say, thinking that the Zoloft might actually be working. Six months ago I would have been unable to resist the urge to move the puppet—and I would probably be sitting over there cross-legged, meticulously organizing the miscellaneous items by size and color. Maybe even ordering more bins from the Container Store.

Nolan sits beside me, his hands on his lap. Remembering his recent offhanded comment that I "never initiate physical contact," I reach for his hand, lacing my fingers with his. His knuckles are a bit gnarled and his middle finger is crooked from various sports injuries, but I've always liked his hands. They are large and strong, and remind me how competent he can be. Handy in a manly way. I put it on a mental list that I'm constantly keeping—*Things I love about my husband.*

"So?" he says, shifting to look at me. "Did you mean what you said today?"

I give him a quizzical look even though I know exactly what he's asking me. "About not wanting another baby?" he says. "I heard you talking to Ellen."

"Oh, I don't know," I say. I feel myself tense, but keep my voice light, a tried-and-true strategy to avoid a serious conversation about family planning or our marriage or sex life—questions that often come after Nolan's had a few beers. I'm not sure whether they make him more philosophical or simply more talkative, but heart-to-hearts are almost inevitable on the heels of his drinking.

"You sounded very . . . definitive," he says, frowning before offering me an out. "Was it just the mood you were in?"

"Yeah. Just the mood I was in," I echo with a little shrug.

"Well, can we talk about it? Another baby?" he asks, his voice tentative.

"Sure," I say, glancing over at him. "You start."

"Okay," Nolan says. He takes a deep breath, stretching his neck to the left, then the right, making a crackling sound.

I wince. "Don't do that. It can't be good for you," I say, although my main reason is simply that the sound grosses me out.

Nolan sighs loudly, then says, "So. I've been thinking . . . about where we are. . . . I mean, we have Harper, and she's awesome. . . . And if that's all we could have, I would accept it. . . . But I just don't feel like our family is complete. I want another baby. I'd actually love two or three more—"

"*Three* more?" I say, cutting him off. "You'd be happy with *four* kids?"

"Yeah. I would," he says, kicking off his leather flip-flops. His big toe angles toward mine, and I meet him halfway, our feet now touching.

"I think big families are awesome," he says. "I always hated being an only child. Still do. It's a lot of responsibility to shoulder—you know, with the family business . . . and now my parents getting older. . . . Besides, it's just kind of lonely. Sad."

"Harper doesn't seem to mind," I say. "She's never asked for a baby brother or sister. I think she likes getting all the attention."

"Yeah, but that's a problem, too," he says. "You say yourself we spoil her too much. Another baby would fix that. . . . Only children have issues."

"You don't," I retort. "You're very *normal*."

I catch my tone of voice just as he does. "Why do you say that like it's a bad thing?" he asks.

"I didn't," I say, even though I know I did—and that sometimes I equate normal with boring. Why do I consider my husband boring when he is frequently the life of the party? Other people always laugh at his jokes, especially women.

"Well, putting aside the pros and cons . . . I just *want* another one. I mean . . . God forbid . . . what if . . ." His voice trails off and I give him a horrified look.

"*Don't* say it."

"Okay," he says, confirming that he was actually going to suggest a second child as an insurance policy against losing Harper. "But you know what I mean. . . ."

"No," I say, appalled. "I don't. That's not a reason to have another baby."

"All right, what *is* a reason, then?" he asks, taking a tactful turn.

"Because you actually *want* one," I say.

"Right," he says. "And as I said . . . I *do*."

I nod as he has made this quite clear for two years now, maybe closer to three. I know the first time he made the suggestion I was still nursing Harper, and had to resist the strong urge to throw a bottle of freshly pumped breast milk at his head. "Got it," I say.

"So, tell me. Where do you stand, exactly? Did you mean what you said to Ellen today? Or not?"

I swallow, tip my head back to look at the ceiling, then close my eyes. "I don't know, Nolan. . . . Right now, I guess I don't want another. . . ."

"But Harper's four—"

"I know how old she is," I snap. "But I'm just not ready."

"Okay. But do you think you'll *ever* be ready?"

"I don't know. Maybe not." I open my eyes, look at him, and make myself tell him the truth. "Probably not. No."

He looks stricken, maybe even devastated, and I suddenly hate myself, not for what I've just admitted to my loving husband and the amazing father to our child, but for what I'm *not* telling him. My full answer.

"Well," Nolan says, releasing my hand and slapping his thighs before he abruptly stands. "Thank you."

"For what?" I say softly, looking up at him.

"For letting me be the *second* person to know. Just after Ellen," he says, then walks over to my neatly organized baskets, picks up the pink elephant, and drops it into its proper container.

chapter eleven

JOSIE

The following Tuesday night, I drive back over to school for our annual Open House, the night when parents meet their child's teacher, visit the classroom, and hear an overview of the curriculum. Afterward, everyone convenes in the auditorium, where the headmaster and a few other administrators give a spiel about how amazing our school is in order to inspire parents, already paying thousands in tuition, to open their checkbooks and donate a few dollars more.

I always dread the parental interaction the night entails—without a doubt, it is my least favorite part of teaching. This year is worse than usual, for obvious reasons, and as I pull into the faculty parking lot, I have the distinct feeling that I might actually pass out from nervousness over seeing Will again. It doesn't help that it's god-awful hot and humid out—or that I've been juicing for forty-eight hours straight in an attempt to fit into an ambitious size-six dress purchased specifically with this evening in mind.

I park my car, unfasten my seatbelt, and blast myself with AC before calling Gabe for a final dose of moral support. When he doesn't answer, I fight the temptation to call Meredith. We haven't communicated at all since she left my house in a huff, and for once I'm determined not to cave first.

Glancing up into the rearview mirror, I carefully apply a fresh layer of lip gloss and mascara as Sydney Swanson, my fellow first-grade teacher and closest colleague, pulls into the spot beside me, making a fish face through her window. Sydney is one of the sunniest, most upbeat women I know, which is especially impressive given that she's thirty-nine and in my dismal relationship boat. She also happens to be six feet in flats, further narrowing her dating pool thanks to her nonnegotiable he-must-be-taller-than-I-am-even-in-heels criterion.

We both step out of our matching Jettas (purchased at the same dealership on the same day for a better deal) as she surveys my outfit, then whistles.

"Whoa! Eat your heart out, Will!" she says a little too loudly, exaggerating her Texas twang for effect. Everything about Sydney is big—her eyes and lips, her hot-rolled hair, her saline-filled breasts, her brash personality—and although I normally embrace her larger-than-life attributes, there are times, like now, that I wish she could be a little more discreet.

I shush her, nervously glancing around the parking lot.

"Re-*lax*, sister," she says. "You got this."

I tell her I think I might faint.

"You do look a little . . . ill."

"*Ill?*" I say, feeling queasier by the second. "Oh, *great*."

Sydney grabs my hand, stops in her tracks, and forces me to look at her as the new choral director, whom we haven't quite determined whether we like, passes us with a terse hello.

"Okay. Listen to me," she says, her voice finally lowered. "You look absolutely fantastic. And skinny."

I thank her, even though I know she doesn't mean skinny—just skinny for *me*. I'll still take it.

She continues, "How many pounds have you dropped since Friday?"

"Six. But they'll all be back tomorrow," I say, putting on my Ray-Bans even though we're steps away from the entrance and already in the shade of the building. "Plus one or two, knowing me."

"Well, we'll worry about tomorrow tomorrow," she says, summing up her philosophy of life as we enter the building and wave hello to a half dozen colleagues. "And seriously, Josie, that dress is *killer*."

Promptly worrying that "killer" isn't really the look you want on Open House Night, I furtively ask if it's too short.

"Maybe too short to play hopscotch in," Sydney says with a laugh. "But it will certainly make Will's wife jealous."

"Um. That's actually *not* my goal here, Sydney," I say, knowing that such a thing is impossible anyway. Not only does Andrea have Will *and* his *two* children, but she also happens to be prettier, younger, and thinner. The damn trifecta. I tell myself there's a decent chance that I'm funnier or smarter or nicer.

"And remind me?" Sydney says. "What *is* your goal, again?"

"I don't know. . . . I guess I'd like to make him a little . . . *wistful*. Maybe give him a small, nostalgic pang," I whisper as we round the corner, then glance down the corridor at a sea of smartly dressed parents, some making effusive small talk while others diligently fill out their name tags at the check-in table.

"Do you see him?" she asks, scanning the crowd along with me. I shake my head.

"Maybe he got fat and bald," Sydney says. "Look for a fat, bald version of him."

"No. I've seen a recent photo in *The Atlantan*. He's definitely not fat or bald."

"Damn. Too bad."

"God, Sydney. I really don't know if I can do this," I say, my voice as weak as my knees.

She looks at me with genuine worry, which only heightens my fear. "C'mon, honey," she says, grabbing my hand. "Follow me and try not to make eye contact with anyone."

I nod, letting her whisk me past the parents, then down a flight of stairs to the first-grade wing. When we reach the safety of my classroom, which is diagonally across the hall from hers, she closes the door, then bolts it shut for added protection. "Sit down," she says, striding over to me. "Right there. On the floor."

I follow her orders, plopping down onto the braided rug, then lowering my forehead to touch my knees.

"I see London, I see France," she's unable to resist.

I reply with a faint groan.

"What have you eaten today?" she asks, sitting beside me and reaching over to rub my back in small, soothing circles.

"Just kale juice and a little black coffee," I confess.

"That's *it*?" Sydney says, aghast. She pulls a PowerBar out of her bottomless bag. "Here. Eat this. At least take a few bites."

"I can't," I say, refusing it. "I'd rather pass out than puke."

"Good point. Puking would be mortifying." She lets out a laugh. "Can you imagine?"

"Sydney! That's not helping," I say, feeling kale rise in my throat.

"Sorry, sorry. You're right. . . ." she says. "Just breathe, honey. . . . In through your nose . . . Out through your mouth."

She demonstrates, and I follow her lead, the oxygen expanding my lungs and lowering my heart rate. "What time is it?" I ask, after a few minutes of silence.

"Almost six-thirty. They'll be coming down soon." She's referring to all the parents, but I only picture Will and Andrea—who right now might as well be the royal Will and *Kate*. "You gonna be okay?"

I peer up at her and nod. "I think so."

"Just remember," Sydney says, "she doesn't know you're single. And neither does he."

I nod again, thinking of how often I'm told that men *can,* in fact, sense when you're desperate. But maybe that doesn't apply to the married ones who have already dumped you. Besides, I'm no longer desperate, I remind myself. I have a game plan, finally, which I've already confided in Sydney, too.

"And remember—you only have to get through the next hour or so," she says, grabbing my hands and pulling me to my feet.

"No," I say, shaking my head. "I have to get through the next *nine* months."

Sydney's eyes widen, her thick fake lashes at attention. "What? Wait! Are you already *pregnant?* Is that why you're sick?"

"No, dummy. I meant I have to get through the school year," I say.

"Oh. You will. No problem," she says. "Just stand up straight and smile. And wipe the lipstick off your front tooth."

I rub my teeth with my finger and thank her, wishing she were my sister. Hell, if that were the case, I'd actually be the responsible one in the family.

On her way to the door, she glances over her shoulder, gives me a thumbs-up, and says, "No matter what happens, that dress was a great fucking call."

OVER THE NEXT ten minutes, my classroom quickly fills with parents, filing in two by two. Meanwhile, I focus on breathing and smiling, scanning name tags and shaking hands. Once I have that down, I graduate to autopilot small talk, working the room like it's a cocktail party minus the flattering lighting, music, and cocktails. *Hello! Welcome! It's so nice to meet you! You're Lucy's mother? My goodness, I see the resemblance! The summer sure did fly by! I'm so excited for the school year!*

As the last few stragglers enter, and the slightly slow wall clock over the dry-erase board clicks to six-forty-five, Will and Andrea have yet to arrive, and I start to become hopeful that they won't be coming at all. It *could* happen. Maybe they had a previous engagement. Maybe one or both had a non-life-threatening but contagious and unsightly illness like, say, hand, foot, and mouth disease or pinkeye. Maybe, just *maybe,* they got into a huge fight over *me.* One could hope, I thought, as I tried to imagine the accusatory eruption on their way out the door. *You still have feelings for her, don't you?! . . . No, I swear I don't! . . . Then why are you wearing cologne?*

Whatever the explanation, though, it is time to get started. Tugging nervously at the hem of my dress, I clear my throat and say hello, my smile feeling frozen. The room instantly quiets, everyone on their best behavior, the Pavlovian response to being back in a classroom, no matter what your age.

"Welcome! Welcome, everyone!" My voice sounds unnaturally high, like that of a sorority rush chair who has just downed a Red Bull. I swallow, making a concerted effort to lower my voice an octave, along with my eyebrows, which feel maniacally raised.

"Thank you so much for being here tonight," I continue, sounding a bit more normal. I glance at the door, praying that it doesn't open, and move on with my script. *It's only been a couple of weeks, and already I can tell what a wonderful group this is. It's been such a pleasure getting to know your children—and I'm thrilled to meet you all. This evening, I'm going to briefly go through the curriculum for the school year—some of the fun things we're going to cover in reading and math, as well as our specials, which include science and social studies. Please take this opportunity to explore the classroom, visit your child's cubby, perhaps leave him or her a little note for tomorrow. And of course, feel free to ask any questions you may have. Remember, as I tell your children, there are no stupid questions—and my door is always, always open!*

Then, as my Charlie Brown teacher voice drones on, it happens. The door swings open, and in walk Andrea and Will. As everyone turns to look at the latecomers, I make the shocking observation that the perfect couple is not only late but also flustered and slightly out of breath. At least she is—I won't let myself look directly at him. Andrea still qualifies as beautiful, but to my relief, she isn't quite as perfect as I remember from my Whole Foods sighting. She has gained a few pounds and her hair is overdue for color, a dull brown stripe streaked with gray at the crown of her otherwise golden head. More satisfying are the sweat-soaked armholes of her marigold-yellow silk blouse. *Rookie move wearing silk on a day as hot as this one,* I think, as she makes furtive eye contact with me and whispers, "Sorry we're late."

I wave off her apology with the same magnanimous smile I'd give to a child who has just wet his pants (which still occasionally happens in the first grade). "You're totally fine," I say, my heart fluttering in my chest, my role as scorned ex-girlfriend suddenly supplanted by my position as poised, punctual, and most forgiving educator.

AN HOUR LATER, the exhausting dog-and-pony show is finally over, and I make an announcement that everyone can head toward the auditorium unless they have any remaining questions. After a mass exodus, only two pairs of parents remain: (1) the Eddelmans, who have asked roughly sixty percent of all questions tonight, most of which are completely specific to their child, Jared, who, we have all learned, has a nut allergy, a latex allergy, a phobia of birds, and a propensity for nosebleeds; and (2) Will and Andrea.

I take a deep breath and address the Eddelmans, who give me a three-minute monologue about Jared's EpiPen, while, from the corner of my eye, I watch Andrea and Will inspect Edie's cubby. I nod earnestly, reassuring the Eddelmans that I am very well versed in life-threatening allergies but also fully confident that parents will respect the strict no-nut policy.

"We are very, very careful," I say, acknowledging their concern. "Please rest assured that Jared will be safe at school."

Finally appeased, the Eddelmans thank me and move along, leaving only Will and Andrea. My heart is in my throat as I turn to them.

"Hello," I say, my fake smile back in full force. I focus solely on Andrea, glancing at her gray roots, feeling grateful that I've yet to find one on my own head. A small victory.

"Hi, Josie. I just wanted to introduce myself. I'm Andrea," she says. She gives me a genuine smile as she starts to shake my hand, then stops, perhaps because her hands are as clammy as mine.

I take a deep breath and tell Andrea that it's very nice to meet her, too. At this point, I decide that I can no longer delay making eye contact with Will, so I force myself to meet his gaze. I feel a stab of pain in my chest. He is as perfect as I remember. Even more so. "Hi, Will," I say. "It's nice to see you."

"Hi, Josie," he says.

I drop my gaze to the two open buttons of his teal checked Vineyard Vines shirt, and remember how soft his chest hair used to feel against me when we were making love.

"It's been a while," I say, my eyes shifting to the whale logo on the breast pocket.

"Yeah," he says, nodding. "How's your family?"

"They're well. My parents . . . are . . . still divorced," I stammer, "but both are pretty happy. Meredith married Nolan and they have a daughter."

Will nods and says, yes, he heard that—and I give him credit for not pretending that I hadn't crossed his mind once in all these years and that he knew nothing about my life. He glances at Andrea and quickly explains, "Nolan was Josie's brother's best friend."

She nods, clearly aware of exactly who all the players are, and oddly, I'm both touched and annoyed by this. On the one hand, how dare he talk about my brother to her, especially when he never even met him. And yet, deep down, I know I'd feel worse if Andrea had no clue who Daniel was.

"That's really cool that they got married," Will says, shifting his weight from one foot to the other, perhaps second-guessing his use of the word *cool*. Is it really cool when two people connected to a terrible tragedy wind up together? I mean—it'd be cool if Daniel were still alive. But he's not.

I let Will off the hook and quickly agree, though, because I don't want to talk more about my sister's marriage or my brother's death. In case this isn't clear, I make my face as blank as possible, a tough thing to do when you're churning with emotion, but something I've become good at over the years. *Impassive,* I remember Will calling me during our final fight—a charge that led to me shutting down completely.

"So anyway, we just wanted to say hello," Andrea says. "Because otherwise it might be sort of awkward . . . given your history with Will." She chooses her words carefully. "I mean, I guess we just wanted to acknowledge the elephant in the room."

"Yes. Thank you," I murmur, surprised by what appears to be her complete lack of an agenda aside from pleasantness, courtesy, perhaps even kindness.

Andrea smiles. "We were so happy when we got the teacher assignments. We heard that you're the best teacher in the grade."

"All the first-grade teachers are fantastic," I say. "But I was happy to see Edie on my list, too." The statement suddenly doesn't seem like a lie, if only because she really has been the catalyst for my life-changing plan.

"She really likes you," Andrea says. "She talks about you all the time."

I'm not sure I believe this until Will nods in vague agreement. "Yeah. We heard about your doctor boyfriend. In Africa." He flashes me a fleeting look of skepticism that I can only interpret because I once knew him so well. He clearly doubts my story.

Deciding I no longer need a Jack in my life, I give a little dismissive wave of my hand and say, "Oh, yes. Jack. We actually broke up. Last night . . . well, it was morning for him."

"Oh," Andrea says with genuine concern. "I'm sorry to hear that."

"Long distance . . . It was inevitable. . . . But I think we'll stay friends," I babble, trying to make my story more believable.

Andrea nods. "Yes. It's always nice if you can stay friends," she says, then glances at Will uneasily.

"Or not," I say cheerfully, throwing her a lifeline.

"Or not," Will echoes with a nervous chuckle.

AFTER SEEING WILL, I experience a brief setback, granting myself a few days of self-pity and regret. But I remind myself that motherhood is what matters most to me, and that once I have a baby, I won't want to change a single thing about my past, including the fact that I lost Will, because all those steps will have been what led me to my child. I just have to get on with things.

So that Friday night, I throw myself back into my research, surfing a reputable sperm-donor site. I've yet to submit my credit-card information and pay for full access to the database; I just want to get my feet wet. As I read, I start thinking about other women in my shoes, as well as married couples who are here because the husband's sperm isn't good. Somehow, it helps to remember that I'm not the only one in this boat—and I tell myself to just take it one step at a time.

"Do I care about eye color?" I blurt out to Gabe at one point as I go through the menu of genetic options, making selections just for the hell of it.

"I don't know. *Do* you?" he asks with a yawn. He is reclined on the sofa, his feet propped up on two pillows.

"Well, I prefer brown-eyed guys," I say. "But I'm not *dating* the guy. And I think I'd rather my child have my eye color."

"Narcissist," he says.

"I'm not a *narcissist,*" I say. "It's just—all things being equal—it might be nice if she looked like me."

"She?"

"Or he. For some reason, I picture a girl," I say, standing to refill my mug of coffee from the stale pot left over from this morning, then making a mental note to cut back on caffeine, starting tomorrow. I sit back down at the kitchen table, click the blue-eye box, summarizing aloud for Gabe. "Okay. So this is what I have so far. . . . Caucasian, brown hair, blue eyes, medium or medium-dark skin tone—"

"Why not fair-skinned?" he asks.

"Because she'll be less likely to burn—and therefore less likely to get skin cancer."

"All right," Gabe says, sitting up and stretching. "I buy that."

"Okay. Next: ethnic background," I continue, scanning the continents and choices, as I check all the Eastern and Western European boxes, from Austrian and Belgian, to Finnish and French, to Scottish and Slovak, with a running commentary to Gabe as I move my mouse and click.

"What about that Brazilian guy you dated for a while? You contemplated getting accidentally knocked up by him, didn't you?"

"That was a joke. But he was pretty hot," I say as I click the

Brazilian box. "And . . . let's see . . . I'm also going to throw in Native American, Lebanese, and Israeli."

"Why's that?" Gabe asks, appearing amused.

"Because you've got some Lebanese blood," I say. "And I've always liked your face."

"Gee, thanks." He stands, stretches, then makes his way to the kitchen table, looking over my shoulder.

"And Israelis are badass," I continue.

"I think that comes from living in a war zone rather than genes. . . . Buckhead might not have that same effect," Gabe says, sitting across from me.

"Maybe," I say. "But I'm still keeping that box checked. . . . And I think it would be cool to have Native American blood. . . . Don't you?"

"I guess," he says, now scrolling through his texts. "But FYI, there aren't a lot of blue-eyed Native Americans out there."

"True," I say. "But it could happen. Recessive genes and all that . . . Now. What about astrological sign? You think that's important?"

"To idiots it might be," Gabe says, knowing I read my horoscope on a regular basis.

"C'mon, Gabe," I say. "You promised you'd be my adviser here."

"What do you think I'm doing?" He leans toward me, his elbows on the table. "I'm advising you *not* to be an idiot."

I shake my head and say, "Well, I'm sorry . . . but I just can't do an Aquarius. They're notoriously cold. Detached," I say, thinking of Will.

"You'd rather have an *attached* sperm donor? Isn't that sort of the point of using an anonymous donor instead of someone you know?"

"Yes, but I don't want an emotionally detached *child*," I say.

"Okay. But zodiac signs aren't genetic," he says. "Assuming you believe in that crap, the sign of your child is determined by when your child is born, right?"

I laugh and say, "Oh, *yeah*! Good point! See? This is why I need you! . . . Religion . . . ? Hmm . . . I guess Christian, right?"

Gabe raises his eyebrows and says, "What about your Israeli tough guys?"

"Good point," I say, clicking the Jewish box, then deciding religion doesn't really matter to me at all and clicking the "all" box. "How about this one? Favorite pet."

"Favorite *pet*? Is that really on there?"

"Yes," I say, reading off the choices: dog, cat, bird, fish, reptile.

"That's ridiculous," he says. "Who cares? . . . But if you're picking one, you gotta go dog."

I nod, then think of Pete the PT and his cat, Fudge, and check the cat box, too.

Gabe says, "What if he's allergic to dogs and cats? And can only have a fish?"

"All the more reason not to pick him," I say. "I don't want my kids to have allergies."

Gabe nods, then says, "Okay . . . but have you ever noticed that smart people seem to have more allergies?"

I laugh and say, "You only say that because *you* have allergies. . . . Although Adam Epstein had bad hay fever, and he was probably the smartest guy I dated."

"Well, there you go," Gabe says.

"Okay," I say, looking back at the computer. "Next up is education. . . . I want a college graduate, right?"

"As opposed to a dropout?"

"Yes."

"But Bill Gates and Ted Turner both dropped out of college," Gabe says. "Can you get their sperm? Ted's right here in town. . . ."

"C'mon, Gabe. Focus," I say, trying not to smile. "This is serious. . . . How about grad school?"

"If you can exclude lawyers."

"Right," I say, thinking of Meredith and pretty much any colleague of hers I've ever met. "What about hobbies?" I read off the categories: musical, athletic, culinary, craftsman, creative/artistic, technology, and outdoor recreation.

"Go craftsman," he says.

I can't tell whether he's kidding. "Why?"

"Why not?"

I smile, skipping this section for now, suddenly thinking that this entire exercise feels bizarre, borderline preposterous.

"Let's see," I say, scrolling down to the final question. "This one's called 'personal goals.' . . . They ask the donors what matters most to them. . . . We have 'fame'—"

"Hell, no," Gabe says, cutting me off.

I nod in agreement. "Financial security?"

"Nah. Too risk averse . . . You don't want dweeby sperm."

"Religious slash spiritual?"

"Maybe. But is that one box?"

I nod.

"Well, I like spiritual, but not religious. You don't want to get a rigid, judgmental extremist."

I give him a look and say, "Not all religious people are rigid, judgmental, or extreme."

"True. But you avoid those types if you don't click that box."

I nod, grateful that he's finally being serious. "Okay. How about 'community service'? Or 'improve environment'? Or just a nice general 'help others'?"

"Yeah. I like all those. Check them, for sure."

"How about 'travel'?"

"I like that, too," Gabe says. "Adventurous spirit."

"Marriage and family?"

"Hmm. Nah."

"Why not?"

"Because if marriage is his goal—and he's donating sperm? Doesn't that seem to indicate that he's not very successful in achieving his goals?"

I laugh. This is Gabe at his absolute best—funny and insightful. "How about this one—'to be happy'?"

Gabe pauses, deep in thought. "Hmm. It's a little simplistic . . . verges on hedonistic."

"It says *happy*," I say. "Not *pleasure seeking*."

"Yeah, I know. But is the point of life to be happy—or to make other people happy?"

"Well, doesn't making other people happy make *you* happy?"

"I wouldn't know," Gabe says with a smirk.

I laugh.

"But I like it," he continues. "If I were you, I'd check that one, the travel box, and all the ones about helping others."

"Okay," I say, nodding in agreement.

"But, Josie?" he says, putting his hand lightly on my arm. It's not unheard of for him to touch me, but it is unusual, always catching me slightly off guard.

I look up from my computer. "Yeah?"

"All of this is sort of bullshit, isn't it?"

"Why do you say that?" I ask. Although I have the same general feeling, I want him to put it in words for me.

"I don't know. It's just—whatever the donor dad is doesn't necessarily mean the kid will turn out that way, especially when you remove nurture from the equation."

I nod and murmur my agreement.

He continues, "And you're going to love your kid whether it's a boy or a girl. Or a fair-skinned, reptile-loving woodworker—or a brown-eyed, sporty . . . aloof Aquarius."

I smile and say, "I know. . . . It feels a little ridiculous, checking the boxes for a baby. Maybe I should pay up and just get to the essays and photos." I scroll down the site, clicking on the price menu.

"Definitely. Let's do that," Gabe says, as I pull my credit card from my wallet and begin typing in the numbers. It feels a bit hasty, especially when I'm not even sure this is the sperm bank I will ultimately use, but I'm afraid of losing momentum, as well as Gabe's attention. Before I click the final button making payment, I say, "You really think I should pull the trigger here? This isn't cheap."

"Yeah. I do," Gabe says, nodding. "I think this will give us a good gut feeling."

I look up at him and say, "But you're always saying I have bad instincts when it comes to guys. . . ."

"You *do*," Gabe says, smiling. "That's why I said give *us* a gut feeling. Now. Move over, and let's read these essays."

chapter twelve

MEREDITH

If you don't want to have sex with me, maybe I should find some-one who will.

Those are Nolan's exact words when I rebuff his Monday morning advances, and the first thing I share with Amy once I'm settled on the white slipcovered sofa in her Midtown office for my monthly appointment. The comment has been echoing in my head all day as I draft a response to an emergency motion to compel, prepare for a hearing on a motion to dismiss, and attempt to negotiate a global settlement on behalf of one of my top (but least likable) clients.

"He *said* that?" Amy asks, leaning forward in her usual straight-back chair across from me, looking the slightest trace appalled. She doesn't often overtly disapprove of Nolan, but I relish it when she does. It is my validation, an excuse to feel the way I do.

"Yes . . . He said it jokingly," I reluctantly confess. "But he still said it."

Amy nods, her calm, inscrutable mask returning. "And how did you respond?"

"I told him to go for it," I say, reclining into the sofa cushions. "If he can find someone who wants to have sex at six-thirty A.M. on a rainy Monday, all power to him."

"Did you really say that?"

"More or less, yes," I say, as I admire Amy's polished ensemble—

wide-legged, cuffed navy trousers, a bright white button-down blouse, and black pumps that look fresh-out-of-the-box new. Everything about Amy is crisp, uncluttered, smart—her clothing, mannerisms, and advice.

"Hmm. Well, try to avoid responses like that in the future," Amy says. "Joking or otherwise."

"He started it," I say.

"Yes. But you don't have to play along. . . . He just might take you up on your suggestion."

I shake my head and say, "He would never do that."

"Never?"

"Never."

"Don't be naïve, Meredith," Amy says. "Pretty much all men— and all *people*—are capable of cheating under the right circumstances."

It is the sort of concrete insight that sets her apart from so many other therapists, and the main reason I keep coming back to her. She actually adds to the conversation, rather than just listening to me talking away self-indulgently.

She adds, "Do you know how easy it is for a nice-looking, successful man like Nolan to find someone who will have sex with him?" She taps her mechanical pencil on her tablet, the rhythm of a rhetorical question.

I give her a little shrug.

"Well. It's easy to be cavalier when you're confident nothing is going on," Amy says. "But what if he actually had an affair?" She crosses her legs. "How would you feel?"

I sigh and tell her that I can't fathom Nolan ever cheating on me. "He's far from perfect, but he's not a liar," I say, thinking that his flaws fall more under the heading of *not* doing things. Not listening. Not helping with Harper. Not putting his clothes in the hamper.

"Well, I'd like you to try to imagine it anyway," she presses. "Picture Nolan . . . spending time with one of his more attractive female friends. Innocent at first . . . They simply enjoy a strong rapport—a genuine, platonic affection."

"He doesn't have female friends," I say.

She gives me a skeptical look.

"What?" I say. "He really doesn't."

"Okay. Then perhaps a colleague. Someone he likes and respects at work."

"Honestly, I can't picture anyone that fits that bill," I say, just as Diane West, our new neighbor and a recently divorced mother of one teenaged son, pops into my head. Diane is a decade older than I am, somewhere in her mid-forties, but has a fantastic figure, an elegant sense of style, and an impressive career as an equine veterinarian.

"Okay. I just thought of someone," I say, deciding to play along with Amy's game. "Our neighbor Diane."

"Okay." Amy nods. "Tell me about her."

"She's a horse vet. She also rides. Pretty, very confident."

"Comfortable in her own skin?" Amy says, an expression she often uses, and one of her litmus tests for happiness.

"Yeah. That's a fair description," I say, thinking that Diane also looks quite comfortable in tight riding pants.

"Okay," Amy says, nodding as if we're finally getting somewhere. Her sleek black bob swings forward, then settles right back in place. "So one night, Diana—"

"Diane," I correct her. Somehow this seems like a relevant detail.

"Right. *Diane* stops over to borrow a cup of sugar—"

I laugh. "Does anyone do that anymore? That's so . . . fifties."

"Please forgive my gender stereotyping . . . especially given Diane's remarkable career. . . . Do you know it's harder to become a vet than it is an MD?"

I roll my eyes at her transparent attempt to make me jealous. "Hmm, yes, I've heard that. Go on."

"Right. So Diane drops by to borrow a . . . Phillips screwdriver. Her washing machine is on the fritz. . . ."

"Pity," I say.

"Yes. So Nolan finds one in the garage, then offers to take a look. While you stay home with Harper—in mid–temper tantrum—Nolan and Dr. West depart together."

"And then what?" I ask, smirking. "Wait! Lemme guess. . . . Do they have sex atop her broken washing machine?"

Amy doesn't react. "No. Not as far as you know, anyway. He simply returns over an hour later, mission accomplished. The machine is all fixed. . . ."

"Nolan's good deed of the day," I say, rearranging the loose pillows behind me and shoving one against my stiff lower back. "Good for him. Good for her. All's well that ends well."

"Yes . . . Yet you also notice that his teeth are a bit red . . . stained from a glass of pinot noir. She happened to have a bottle open. . . ."

"Nolan doesn't drink red wine."

"Fine. Then you note a trace of bourbon on his breath. She poured him a glass while he worked. One for herself, too. She loves whiskey. They toasted the fixed machine and finished their lively discussion about thoroughbreds."

"*How* lively?" I ask, still more amused than jealous.

"*Very* lively. He finds her work—and her rapport with such large animals—fascinating."

"Actually, I think he does," I grant her. "He's mentioned it more than once."

"Right," she says, nodding. "So then it doesn't altogether surprise you when Diane begins to drop by on a fairly regular basis. Just to say hello. Always when Nolan's home. Often when you're not. One evening, she drops by with a book. The one she told him about. The one she promises he will *love* . . . She casually touches his arm, but looks a little too comfortable in doing so. . . ." Amy cocks her head and bites her lower lip suggestively.

"Okay, *okay*," I say. "I get your point."

Amy nods vigorously, smugly, as if we've just had a major breakthrough when what I'm really feeling is standard-fare competition with another woman. "So I don't want my husband to cheat on me," I say. "So what? Who would want *that*?"

"Some women do," Amy says.

"Why's that?" I ask, although I'm pretty sure I know the answer.

"So they have an out," she says. "So they can do the same thing, guilt-free. So their situation becomes black and white, and they can get out of their marriage."

"Well," I say. "I *don't* want that."

"You don't want Nolan to fall in love with Diane West?" she says. "Or you don't want to get a divorce?"

"Neither," I say firmly.

She nods, then writes one word on her tablet. I strain to see it, but can only make out a capital *D*.

"What did you just write?" I ask. "*Divorce?*"

"No," she says. "*Diane.*"

"Oh, for heaven's sakes. Nothing is going on with Diane! Or anyone else, for that matter," I say, now full-fledged perturbed, which happens about once a session, to Amy's clear satisfaction. "Why are you trying to scare me?"

"*Are* you scared?"

"No," I say. "I'm not. I mean, nobody *wants* to be the fool. Nobody wants to be deceived. And I like to think that the father of my child has more integrity than to cheat on me. Or have some meaningless affair—"

Amy cuts me off, which she seldom does. "Okay. Well, let's make it a deep emotional connection. . . . But they never cross that physical line, both of them too principled to cheat."

"I'd still be hurt," I admit. "Is that what you want me to say?"

"I don't *want* you to say anything," Amy says, which for the most part, I believe. "I simply want you to understand your feelings on this subject."

"Okay. Well, I would be very upset if Nolan cheated on me, whether physically or emotionally," I admit, just before I let the word *but* slip out of my mouth.

"But what?" Amy's expression is misleadingly placid.

"But if he simply wanted a divorce . . . without an affair . . . or another woman involved . . . I could probably live with that," I say, wondering why I feel so tricked into this admission. I remind myself that Amy is on my side, or at least neutral. Besides, she's a professional secret keeper—and certainly not in the business of judging.

"So you could live with it," Amy says. "But it isn't what you *want*?"

I say an emphatic no, it isn't what I want.

"Do you ever think about divorce? What it would be like?"

I say no, not really. I tell her my thoughts mostly consist of how to get through the day.

She stares at me, perfectly still, a wax therapist statue.

"But if we got a divorce, I think it would be fairly amicable. I don't see us fighting over money or *things*. Over really anything," I say, talking quickly now, words spewing out of me. "Except maybe time with Harper . . . though I would be willing to share custody fifty-fifty. I think that's only fair, really. To him and to Harper. He's such a good father—and she loves him so much. . . . I think she'd be resilient. . . . It would kill my parents, though. And his. Especially mine. Our friends would be shocked, too. . . . Everyone thinks we have the perfect life. Once we have that second child, that is." I stop suddenly, Amy familiar with the controversy over a second child.

"Have you made any progress with that?" she asks.

"No. I'm still not ready," I say, the statement suddenly ringing hollow, the word *ready* a farce. You get *ready* for a vacation, or a job interview, or a move. You even get ready to actually give *birth* to a baby. But do you really get ready for pregnancy? Especially a second pregnancy? Or do you just take the leap and *do* it?

As if reading my mind, Amy asks the exact question Nolan posed to me. "Do you think you'll *ever* be ready?"

"I don't know," I say. "I think so. At some point. Maybe."

"Is that why you didn't want to have sex this morning?"

I shake my head. "No. I'm on the pill. . . . I didn't want to have sex with him this morning because I didn't want to have sex with him this morning."

"Fair enough."

"But regardless . . . I don't think there's anything wrong with having just one child."

"Of course not."

"There are actually advantages to being an only child," I say.

"Certainly," Amy says, knowing a smoke screen when she sees one. I wait for her to call me on it, get back to the real subject at hand, and when she doesn't, I'm almost disappointed.

"Tell me what you're thinking," I say, knowing that it has nothing to do with the pros and cons of being an only child.

"Okay," Amy says, nodding, her hair swinging again. "I was wondering whether you love Nolan. . . ."

The question, veiled as a statement, is so simple that it catches me off guard. Yet my answer is easy, automatic. "Of course I do. He's a good man. A great father," I say, thinking that we've covered these points exhaustively—along with our history, the fact that

Nolan was Daniel's loyal and kind best friend. That he was there for me and my family. That now he *is* my family.

"Yes," Amy says. "I know that you love Nolan and care for him as a person and a partner and the father of your child. But are you *in* love with him?"

I stare at Amy, feeling rankled over what, for years, I've told myself is an adolescent distinction. The fact that my heart doesn't race over Nolan, and I never feel overwhelmed by lust, and I don't melt when our eyes meet across a crowded room (hell, I seldom even *look* for him in a crowded room), doesn't mean I don't love him or that I'm not committed to our marriage.

Yet deep down, I know what she's asking me, just as I know the answer, and have since that day in the dugout. It is an immutable fact, the same as Daniel being dead, impossible to change simply by wishing things were different. So I finally make myself confess the truth. I am telling my therapist, but as these things go, I'm really telling myself.

"No," I say aloud. My voice is soft and low but clear and very, *very* certain. "No, I am *not* in love with my husband."

chapter thirteen

JOSIE

I've never understood precisely what Murphy's law is, but I'm pretty sure it applies when I finally break down and go out with Pete the PT for the second time, this time to Bistro Niko, an upscale French restaurant, wearing the same dress and shoes I had on at Open House, and spot none other than Will and Andrea Carlisle, enjoying a cozy steak dinner. It doesn't help matters that Pete just got a self-proclaimed bad haircut that approaches a buzz, and is wearing a short-sleeved button-down shirt, the combination evoking a door-to-door missionary. Nor does it help that Will is sporting my favorite look—jacket and no tie with jeans—along with a sexy five o'clock shadow.

As the hostess leads us right past their table, I avert my eyes, praying that we'll go undetected, but then hear Andrea calling my name over the dull din of diners. With Pete trailing behind, I stop abruptly, feign surprise, and say, "Oh, *hey* there!"

"Hey!" Andrea says as I notice that she got her hair colored, the grays eradicated, her rich golden highlights fully restored. "Nice to see you again!"

"You, too. Recognize the dress?" I let out a nervous laugh, regretting the comment immediately.

Andrea blinks, playing dumb, which I find mostly kind, but also annoying since I'm then forced to say, "I had it on the other night."

"Oh, *yes*! I *do* remember it now," she says, nodding effusively. "It's such a pretty dress."

"Thank you," I say, allowing myself a quick glance at Will, who peers up at me, his dark eyes shining in the candlelight. I can't read his expression, but his half smile makes my chest ache.

"Hi, Josie," he says, then shifts his gaze to Pete, now directly beside me. When Andrea does the same, I feel forced to make an introduction.

"Pete, this is Andrea and Will. I teach their daughter," I say as succinctly as possible.

Pete nods, smiles, and says, "Ah. Nice."

"So?" Andrea asks with a girlfriendy lilt. "Are y'all on a date?"

I say no just as Pete replies yes.

Andrea manages to wince and smile at once. "Oops. Sorry. None of my business!"

"No. It really isn't," Will mumbles into his wineglass. His tone to his wife isn't exactly rude, but it is slightly reprimanding, evoking his subtle but pervasive sense of superiority, something I had forgotten or, more likely, buried. I think of how he'd nudge me under the table when I said something he perceived as inappropriate. Sometimes he was right; usually it felt like needless nit-picking. The memory is a slight comfort, offsetting those damn brown eyes.

"No worries," I say, entirely for Andrea's benefit. "It's sort of a date—but we're really just friends."

"Yeah, technically this is our second date. But because we had no chemistry on our first date, Josie's already given up," Pete says, trying to be funny, but making everything exponentially more awkward. "I still have hope, however."

Andrea nods earnestly and says, "Yes, these things sometimes take time."

"Was that how it was for you two?" Pete asks, as I stand there in disbelief that this conversation is *actually* happening.

"Um. Not exactly," she mumbles, as Will calmly cuts his next bite of steak, raising his fork to his lips.

The opposite of love is indifference, I remind myself, but feel an intense wave of bitterness.

"Not *exactly*?" I say with an acerbic laugh. "Not at *all*. Andrea and Will got engaged *very* quickly. Immediately after he and I broke up, in fact." I snap my fingers for dramatic effect.

Pete laughs, then realizes I'm not kidding, his expression mirroring Andrea's—something between pity and discomfort. Meanwhile, Will begins to cough. The three of us glance at him with mild concern, as the coughing quickly escalates to a disturbing choking sound.

"Honey? Are you okay?" Andrea asks.

Will answers with a loud gasp, then goes silent, his eyes wide, watery, and panicked.

"Will!" Andrea shouts, rising from her seat as the hostess steps toward our table and the couple next to us begin to stare. "Will? Can you breathe?"

He doesn't reply—because clearly he can*not* breathe—as Andrea yells, to no one in particular, "He's choking!" She looks around the restaurant and shouts, "Is there a doctor? Does anyone know the Heimlich maneuver?"

"No. That's not recommended yet," Pete says, holding his hand up to calm Andrea while stepping toward Will, intently watching him.

"He's in the medical field," I tell Andrea, hoping that physical therapists are trained in choking first aid.

"Try to cough," Pete calmly instructs Will. "Can you cough at all?"

Will shakes his head, making a faint wheezing sound. Andrea continues to yell for help. I watch in horror, picturing a gruesome image: Edie standing beside her daddy's casket.

"Okay. Stand up, man," Pete says, helping Will out of his seat, bracing him with his arm around his waist as he strikes Will's back with the heel of his hand three times in a row. Thwack, thwack, *thwack*. Nothing happens, except I notice Will's lips start to turn a tinge blue. Then, with the fourth hard, loud blow between his shoulder blades, Will heaves the stringy bit of red meat out of his mouth. It lands on the white linen tablecloth, just past his plate. I stare at it, marveling that it could have been as lethal as a bullet to the head, while diners around us begin to clap and cheer. Will gasps for breath.

I watch Andrea put both hands over her heart and rush to her husband's side, throwing her arms around his neck. He allows a brief embrace, then says something to her under his breath, before pulling away and sitting back down.

"Oh my God, thank you *so* much," Andrea says, turning to Pete, tears in her eyes.

Pete modestly shakes off her gratitude and asks Will if he's all right.

"Yeah, yeah, I'm fine. . . . It just went down the wrong pipe," Will sputters, before taking a long drink of water. As he puts his glass back on the table, I watch his expression of relief morph into one of mortification.

"You can sit down now," he mumbles to his wife, as I think how much he's always hated a scene. Andrea takes her seat, still profusely thanking Pete.

I watch as Will tries to discreetly scoop the glob of meat into his napkin. It takes two tries and to my secret satisfaction, leaves a telltale stain on the tablecloth, almost as red as the hue of Will's neck and ears. Only then does Will reach up to shake Pete's hand and thank him for the first time.

"No problem, buddy," Pete says. "Happy to help."

· · ·

LATER THAT EVENING, after Will and Andrea send a bottle of wine over to our table, Pete begins to laugh.

"What?" I say.

"That guy really dumped you and married her?"

"Yes," I say. "What, exactly, is so funny about that?"

"Well, talk about revenge. You almost made him choke to death."

I smile, shrug, and say, "No. *Happiness* is the best revenge."

"Trite but true," Pete says, nodding. "So are you? Happy?"

"I'm working on that," I say. Then, lest he get the wrong idea, I give him the update on my single motherhood research, telling him all about my checklists on issues like finances, childcare options, health insurance coverage, and maternity leave. I then go on to tell him about the essays by sperm donors that Gabe and I spent hours reading together. "Of course, we narrowed it on the basis of health first . . . only considering donors with a stellar medical history."

Pete listens intently, then says, "Do you have a front-runner?"

"Maybe," I say, then reach into my purse and hand him the essay by a donor named Glenn S that I printed last night.

I watch as he unfolds it, raises his brow, and begins to read:

I am a 27-year-old straight male, documentary filmmaker. I attended Cal Berkeley for my undergraduate degree where I majored in communications and ran track—mostly middle distances. I am fit, slim, healthy, and eat a completely plant-based diet. My eating habits are a result of three factors: first and foremost, a compassion for animals and a desire to avoid contributing to their suffering; secondly, a lifelong interest in health and nutrition; and finally, for environmental reasons, as meat and animal products are the number one cause of destruction of our planet. My recipient need not share my beliefs, but should be happy to know that her donor is both compassionate and healthy. Currently I am working on a documentary film about the visceral reaction most humans feel when they see animal suffering, and the disconnect and rationalization they engage in when continuing to eat and wear those same animals. I decided to be a donor because I do not believe in the societal norms that mandate that I raise a family, nor do I want to contribute to the further destruction of the resources of our planet by having my own child. However, I do have a great deal of compassion in my heart for women who want to be a mother and cannot, for whatever reason. If someone is determined to bring a new life onto our planet, I would rather that life come from intelligent, compassionate genes.

Pete finishes reading, his brows raised. "That's from a sperm donor?"

"Yes," I say, taking the paper from him and putting it back into my purse. "My friend Gabe helped me select him."

Pete nods, then asks if I know what he looks like.

"His baby picture was cute. That's the only photo you get," I say. "But his description sounded good. . . . Blue eyes, light hair, athletic, six feet tall."

Pete smiles and says, "Sounds great." Something about his voice sounds fake, though—or at least hesitant.

"You think it's weird, don't you?" I say, wondering why I want his approval.

"No," he says, shaking his head. "Not at all."

"Do you like the sound of his essay?" I ask a bit eagerly.

"Well, sure. He sounds nice . . . very compassionate and princi-pled. . . ." He takes a sip of his wine, then adds, "Maybe a little extreme, though?"

"Yeah. I know what you mean," I admit, because Gabe and I thought so, too. "But he was the best of the bunch. . . . And I like that he's not donating for money. Many seem to be, though they try so hard to disguise it. . . ."

"Money? Or an egotistical need to spread their seed across the planet?" Pete asks, smiling.

"Gabe said the same thing. Is that the way you guys really feel?"

"I guess. Kind of," Pete admits. "Not enough to donate my sperm, though."

We stare at each other an awkward beat before he cracks up.

"What?" I say.

"Nothing . . . I was just thinking that your ex choking on red meat might be a sign to go with the raging vegetarian."

"Maybe so," I say with a smile.

LATER THAT NIGHT, Pete and I leave the restaurant in a shared Uber car. When we pull into my driveway first, he leans over to kiss me on the cheek.

"That was fun. Thanks."

"It was," I say, smiling at him. "I'm glad you were persistent."

"Me, too," he says, grinning back at me.

I turn to open the car door, and he stops me with his hand on my arm. "Wait."

I laugh and remind him that he's paying by the minute here.

He nods, then clears his throat. "Any chance of you inviting me in for a nightcap?"

"A *night*cap?" I say, laughing. "You sound like my dad."

"Your dad sounds like a cool guy."

"He's sixty-four. You sound sixty-four."

"C'mon. Invite me in. I just want to talk some more. That's it."

I hesitate and smile, wondering what our driver is thinking. Surely he's heard this conversation before, though he's politely pretending not to listen.

"Okay," I say, noticing that Gabe's car is gone. "Would you like to come in for a nightcap?"

"Well, how nice of you to ask!" Pete says. "But I'd really rather have a cup of herbal tea."

I smile and roll my eyes, then say, "And now you sound like my grandmother."

About ten minutes later, after I've apologized for how messy the house is and I've made us tea, we head into the backyard with Revis. The night is pleasantly cool, and we both murmur how nice it is.

"The mosquitoes are gone, too," he says.

I glance at him, smile, then say, "Are we really talking about weather and bugs?"

"We are," he says.

"We can do better that that," I say. "C'mon. What do you got?"

Pete gives me a serious look, then says, "Okay. I was actually just thinking of that donor guy's mission statement."

"Oh, yeah? And?"

He nods and says, "Yeah. I have to say . . . it is pretty noble."

"I know," I say. "I don't think I could donate one of my eggs like that. . . . Could you? Donate sperm?"

"Maybe," he says. "For a friend. If I believed she would be a good mother. For you I probably would." He raises his eyebrows and shoots me an earnest sideways look.

I laugh, but he doesn't.

"Are you serious?" I ask, feeling the tiniest flutter in my stomach. "Or is this some kind of a ploy to sleep with me?"

Pete gives me the Boy Scout's three-finger honor sign and says, "I swear it's not a ploy. Besides, I totally had a turkey baster scenario in mind. Isn't that how they do it?"

I nod. "Something like that . . . I think it's a little more sophisticated, though."

We both take sips of our tea as I wonder if he's starting to feel at all uncomfortable. Shockingly, I am not. "Would you make me pay for your sperm?" I ask jokingly. "Or give it to me for free?"

"I'd give you my friends and family rate," he deadpans.

I smile, looking into his eyes. It's too dark to really see them, and I suddenly can't recall their exact shade. "What color are your eyes, exactly?"

"Hazel," he says.

"I never know what that means. . . . What is hazel? Besides a trendy girls' name."

"A nicer way of saying brown . . ." Seeing right through my line of questioning, he adds, "Anything else you'd like to know that you didn't glean from Match and our two dates?"

"This isn't a date, remember?" I say. "And I think I have all relevant data. I have your height, eye color, profession. You seem like a nice guy—"

"I *am* a nice guy."

"And," I say, "you just saved a man's life. So you're sort of a hero."

"True," Pete says with an adorable full-on grin.

"How's your health?"

"Good," Pete says. "I just had a physical. . . . My resting heart rate is fifty-eight. Blood pressure one ten over seventy."

I nod, even though I don't know what these numbers mean. "How about your family's medical history?"

"My grandfather died of a heart attack at fifty-nine, but he smoked a pack a day. . . . My other three grandparents are still alive, along with one great-grandparent. Healthy midwestern stock."

"Do you have OCD? ADD? Depression?"

He shakes his head.

"A mean streak?"

He smiles and says, "Nope. I'm pretty simple."

"*How* simple?"

"Not *too* simple."

"What's your IQ?"

"No clue," he says. "But I took all the AP courses in high school."

"And where did you go to college again?"

"University of Wisconsin. I had a three point six in a hard major. Biology."

"Are you athletic?"

"Decently coordinated . . . I have a good golf swing. I shoot in the low eighties. I played baseball and tennis in high school."

"Varsity?"

"You really think I would mention JV?"

I smile. "Are you artistic or musical?"

"Not really. Is that important to you?"

"Nonessential," I say, deep in thought, studying his face, my eyes finally adjusting to the dark. He really does have a good bone structure and even, symmetrical features, almost pulling off the buzz cut. I like his complexion, as well as the color and texture of his hair. And then there's that cleft.

"Let me see your hands," I ask, putting down my mug and reaching for them.

He puts his mug down next to mine and shows them to me, palms up, then down. They're on the large side, but not so big that my daughter might end up with man hands. I nod and murmur, "Nice."

"Thanks," he says.

I clear my throat and say, "So . . . if you were ever to really do something like this . . . would you want to be *involved*?"

The question feels monumental, though I'm not sure what I want his answer to be. I remind myself that this is all completely theoretical. He's not really offering his sperm up on the spot.

"You mean with the baby?"

I nod.

"You mean . . . like . . . paying child support?" he asks.

"No," I say as adamantly as I can, thinking that with money comes strings, complications. "There would be no child support. You'd be the donor, not the father. You'd have no parental rights whatsoever. I'm talking emotionally."

"I don't know. . . . It might be cool if I could take him—or her—to an occasional baseball game. Would you allow that?"

"Maybe," I say. "That might be nice. . . . But if I ever married, which I hope to one day, I'd want my husband to adopt my child. And then—"

"You might not want me coming around?"

"Maybe not," I say. "Would that make you feel bad?"

"Maybe," Pete says. "But it would be your child—and your decision. I would respect your wishes." He starts to say something else, then stops.

"What?" I say. "Tell me."

"Well . . . what if you *wanted* me to take your kid to a baseball game . . . and I didn't want to. Would your feelings be hurt?"

"Maybe," I say, as I marvel at how honest and candid we're both being. So much more so than if we were actually interested in each other romantically. "But I really don't think so. I think that would be the deal going in. You'd be the donor. Period."

"Period," he echoes.

We stare at each other, both of us on the verge of smiling. Yet we don't.

"Would you really consider this?" I ask, part of me starting to believe he might be serious—or at the very least not just humoring me as a way of getting in my bed. "I mean . . . you barely know me."

"I know you better than the vegan track star does," Pete says.

"True," I say.

Pete stares into my eyes. "I know. It's crazy. But I think I might be a bit serious here."

"Why?" I say, my heart pumping a little more quickly, essentially asking him to answer the essay question. "Why would you want to do this?"

He shakes his head and says, "I don't know. . . . To help you . . . to do something worthwhile with my life . . . in addition to saving lives at Buckhead restaurants, that is."

I love this answer, and can't help smiling.

He smiles back at me. "Any other questions?"

I think for a second, then say, "There are twelve hundred elephants in a herd. Some have pink and green stripes, some are all pink, and some are all blue. One third are pure pink. Is it true that four hundred elephants are definitely blue?"

"Wait," Pete says. "Say that again?"

I repeat the question, but no more slowly.

"Well, no, it's not *definitely* true," Pete says. "But it could be true."

"Correct," I say, grinning.

"C'mon, that's a layup. I'm a math-science guy, remember?"

"Yeah," I say, thinking that I'm more verbal—a nice balance.

"So? What do you think?" he asks, leaning forward and staring into my eyes.

I gaze back at him, smile, and say, "I think . . . you have definite potential."

chapter fourteen

MEREDITH

One steamy evening in late September, Ellen and I meet for a walk in Chastain Park. A few minutes in, she tells me that she heard from Andy, who heard from his sister, Margot, who heard from a girl on Margot's tennis team, who heard from Will's wife, Andrea, that some guy Josie is dating saved Will's life last Saturday night at Bistro Niko.

I give her an incredulous look, stopping on the paved path so suddenly that a runner nearly collides with us. "*What* . . . in the *world*?" I say.

As the runner swerves past us and we begin to walk again, Ellen explains that, according to the report, Josie just happened to be randomly passing by Will and Andrea's table at the very moment that Will began to choke on his steak. Josie's date, who does something in the medical field, administered the Heimlich maneuver or some such procedure, dislodging the meat and saving Will from his untimely demise.

"Unbelievable," I say. "And yet somehow . . . *not*."

Ellen laughs and says, "Yeah. You'd practically think Josie planned it, but how could she?"

"If anyone could, *she* could," I say. "And I bet it wasn't a coincidence they were at the same restaurant. . . . At the very least, she'll use this as an excuse to talk to Will. Call to follow up on his airway." I roll my eyes, disgusted. "Andrea better watch her back."

"You don't think she'd really do that, do you?" Ellen asks.

I shrug. "Probably not, no. Although my therapist says that most *everyone* is capable of an affair under the right circumstances."

Ellen murmurs her pensive agreement as I find myself thinking about her marital problems from several years before. I don't know the details, or if anyone else was involved, but somehow I got the impression that the rockiness was more her fault than Andy's.

"Have you ever been tempted?" I ask.

When she doesn't immediately respond, I mumble, "Sorry. That's none of my business."

"It's okay," Ellen says, pausing to stoop down to retie a shoelace. "You can ask me anything. You know that."

I pause and wait for her to secure the knot, then tighten the other. She doesn't speak until we're walking again. "Remember Leo?" she asks as her pace quickens.

"Of course," I say, recalling one of several long conversations we had about our two most significant exes, Lewis and Leo, and specifically how similar they were. Both were artist types (Leo was a journalist, Lewis was still acting, mostly on Broadway but occasionally appearing in small indie films). Both were native New Yorkers. Like Lewis, Leo had been very intense and had broken her heart.

"Well, a few years back," she continues, "I started to have . . . contact with him again."

"What sort of contact?" I say, struggling to keep up with Ellen's stride, her legs so much longer than mine.

"Mostly just emailing and texting . . . but I also saw him a couple of times. Once on a shoot in L.A. Once in New York . . ."

"Did you . . . ?" My voice trails off.

"No," she says firmly. "We didn't have sex or anything close to that. It was really more of an emotional thing. But it was still pretty bad. . . ."

"I'm sorry," I say, feeling vague disappointment that my suspicion has been confirmed, but no judgment whatsoever. If anything, I feel reassured by the evidence that people can recover from major marital setbacks. "Does Andy know?"

"Yeah. He knows," she says, her voice thick with regret. She then confesses that although it was mostly an emotional affair, she did kiss Leo once.

"One kiss isn't so bad," I say, although I'm not sure I entirely believe that.

"Yes. Maybe not. But I contemplated much more than that . . . including leaving Andy altogether." Ellen finishes abruptly, and it takes me a few seconds to respond.

"What made you stay?" I ask.

She looks back at me with wide, earnest eyes. "Love," she says.

"Aww, *Ell*," I say, moved by the sincerity and purity of her reply, especially when I was anticipating a more cynical answer: fear or guilt or a sense of duty or that she was already pregnant with Isla. "I'm so glad you worked it out. You're really perfect together."

"Well, nothing's perfect," she says. "But I do think Andy and I truly belong together. And things are really good now."

"Did you love Leo?" I say, lowering my voice, as if his name might still hold some power over her.

"Maybe. But it wasn't a true, deep, real love, like the kind I have for Andy. . . . It was always more of an obsession . . . an unhealthy addiction. . . . And to a certain extent, maybe I was just feeling that sense of *what if*? . . . What if I had married Leo? What would my life be like?"

I nod, thinking the whole concept of the path not taken is partly what has always troubled me. Not so much in terms of Lewis, though I do think about him once in a while. But in terms of a different life altogether, the one I might be living if Daniel hadn't died and I hadn't married Nolan, the two events always seeming so intertwined.

"So Andy just . . . forgave you?" I ask.

"Well, not right away . . . We definitely had a rough couple of months. Really a pretty shitty year . . . By the time I met you, though, things were a lot better. And when Isla came—*wow*." Ellen's voice becomes light, yet also awe-filled. "She really took us to a higher place. Fixed things . . ."

"She did?" I say, finding it a little hard to believe that a baby could have that effect when Harper definitely caused a strain for Nolan and me. Then again, Isla has always been easier than Harper in pretty much all respects.

"Well, I guess I shouldn't say she *fixed* things. We did that on our own with a lot of hard work. But she definitely renewed our commitment. It was almost as if her birth gave us something of a clean slate. Put everything in perspective."

I nod, thinking that this part I understand. Motherhood really does give you a broader perspective about so much.

Ellen continues, "I think the whole ordeal, as horrible as it was, made us stronger in some respects. Maybe that's just me trying to justify things, but I really think it's true."

"So you never hear from him anymore?" I ask. "Leo?"

"No," she says. "Not in a very long time . . . About a year after everything happened, he called. But I never called him back. I did send him a short letter, telling him an official goodbye and asking that he please not contact me again. . . . Honestly, he could have *died* for all I know."

"Yeah. He could have choked to death," I say, forcing a smile.

She smiles back just as halfheartedly, then suddenly shifts gears. "Are you and Nolan doing okay?"

"I guess so," I say, wiping my sweaty forehead with the back of my forearm. "I don't know. He's pretty frustrated with me."

"Because of the second baby thing?"

"Yeah. That . . . and you know, the usual complaints—not enough sex . . ." I stop, never having been comfortable discussing my sex life with even my closest friends. "That's how the subject of infidelity came up with Amy at my last session. She said, more or less, that if someone isn't being satisfied on that front, they may start to look elsewhere. . . . I guess it's not really a revolutionary concept. . . ."

Ellen nods and says, "Yeah. I guess not. Pretty cynical, though."

"Yeah. Amy's a cynic," I say. "Or at the very least a realist . . . but I really can't imagine Nolan cheating on me."

"Yeah. I can't, either," she says. "He's such a good guy."

"So's Andy," I say. "We're both really lucky."

"Yeah. Hashtag blessed."

I smile.

Ellen laughs, as we've both made fun of those nauseating Facebook posts that use a religious concept to justify their thinly veiled bragging. We walk in silence for a minute or more, both of us becoming a bit breathless, before she asks her next question. "So what about you? What if Lewis came back the way Leo did? Would you be at all . . . tempted?"

"I really don't think so," I say, almost wishing my dilemma were that straightforward. If I were contemplating an affair, or following a lustful impulse, then I could just stop, confess, and recommit, like Ellen did. Or, alternatively, I could make the other choice and go ahead and have the affair—which might be a catalyst for a different change altogether. "Not that I judge you," I quickly add.

"Oh, I know you don't," she says.

"It's just that I think I finally got over Lewis when I was practicing law in New York—and sneaked in to see him in a two-man off-Broadway show." I smile. I've never admitted this to anyone.

She laughs. "He was that bad?"

"No. He was fucking *brilliant*," I say. "But he seemed a little . . . I don't know . . ."

"Self-important? Pompous?" she guesses.

"No. Just over the top . . . a little *flamboyant*," I say.

We both laugh, and she says, "Could he be gay?"

"Nah," I say, thinking of how incredible the sex with him was. "I doubt it. But I did try to convince myself that he *might* be. And that helped."

She laughs again as I continue, "The thing that I miss the most about Lewis isn't Lewis . . . but the way I felt when I was with him."

"Do you think part of what you miss is just being young? In your twenties?" she asks.

I shrug. "Maybe a little. But I don't think that's it, exactly. Especially because my twenties were pretty rough."

She nods, knowing that I'm talking about my brother.

"It's more the way being in love made me feel about life. . . . Our love even eased my grief over Daniel—at least for a while—and it just felt like we could do *anything*. . . . Go anywhere, do anything, be anyone. . . . The possibilities felt *endless*," I say, holding my breath for a few seconds, remembering the crazy, intoxicating highs that came before the fall. "And then he broke my heart. Which felt a little bit like death."

"Yeah. Broken hearts really do feel like death," she says as we near the top of the hill, overlooking the baseball fields. "But it all worked out. Because you got Nolan."

She says Nolan's name the way people say *The End*. In other words: *All's well that ends well.*

"Right," I say, biting my lip.

In the distance, I can see Wilkins Field—and the exact spot in the dugout where Nolan proposed—and am saddened to realize that it's more of a queasy memory than a magical one.

"And Harper," she says.

"And of course Harper," I say, thinking that sometimes my daughter is the only thing that keeps me from wanting a do-over.

As we continue to walk in silence, my mind drifts from Harper, to the second baby I don't want to have, to Amy's final question in my therapy session, to Ellen's explanation of what kept her with Andy—*a true, deep, real love*—and I'm suddenly overcome with an intense wave of guilt and grief. For what I don't have. For what I can't give my husband.

"Meredith?" I hear Ellen say as I realize that I've stopped walking. "What's wrong?"

"I just need a second," I say, drifting over to sit on the stone wall that separates the sidewalk from the steep slope below. She sits beside me, our backs to the ball fields, our shoulders touching.

"Are you okay?"

"I don't know. I'm just not happy. With Nolan and our marriage. Sometimes I think the whole thing was a mistake. . . ." My voice breaks, my vision blurs, and I have to stop talking to keep from bursting into tears.

Ellen takes my hand and does her best to soothe me, telling me that all marriages are complicated and messy and mysterious and flawed. That maybe I'm just confusing the burdens of unglamorous everyday life with something missing in my relationship. That it might sound simplistic but sometimes you just have to love the one you're with. I know her advice is mostly sound, but deep down, I also know how very different our situations are. She hit a bump in the road, whereas I'm on a road I never should have been on in the first place. She lied to Andy in her marriage, whereas my *whole* marriage sometimes feels like a lie.

. . .

LATER THAT NIGHT, after being held hostage in Harper's darkened room for over two hours, I fall asleep in the glider next to her bed, awakening to the sound of my phone vibrating. I find it in the cushions and see Ellen's name.

"Hi, there," I whisper, tiptoeing out of Harper's room.

"Are you alone?" she asks.

"Yeah. I was just putting Harper to bed," I say, walking downstairs, where I start cleaning the kitchen.

"Where's Nolan?" she asks.

"At a work dinner."

"So I've been thinking about earlier," she says.

"Me, too. Listen—I'm sorry—I don't know what came over me. I think I'm just hormonal . . . about to get my period—" I'm lying to my friend, but only because I don't want to burden her.

"No, *I'm* sorry," Ellen interjects. "I shouldn't have tried to tell you how you should feel. And I hope I didn't imply that my marriage is perfect now. Because it's not. Far from it."

"I know," I say. "I didn't think you were doing that."

"Okay, good. Because sometimes I have the feeling that everyone thinks that everyone *else* is living a fairy tale. Especially in the South. People fake things so much. Put on a happy face and show off your perfect life."

I murmur my agreement as she continues, "And I just wanted to say . . . that I hope you stay with Nolan, but no matter what happens, I'll always be here for you."

"That's really nice," I say. "Thank you."

"Of course," she says, then hesitantly asks if I've considered marriage counseling. "I mean, I know you go to Amy . . . but what about *couples* therapy?"

"Yeah. Maybe we'll try that," I say, although I'm pretty skeptical about it as a solution for us. It seems to me that counseling might help with a lot of relationship issues, but that it can't make you love someone you just don't. I'm also beginning to realize, sickeningly, that the only real solution is to tell Nolan the truth.

"It's going to be okay," Ellen says. "You just need a little time."

"Right," I say, thinking that the notion of time healing all might be an even bigger lie than the foundation my marriage is built upon. Daniel's death taught me that much; some things will *never* be okay.

chapter fifteen

JOSIE

The week after the choking incident, I'm at school, enjoying a blissful free period while my kids are in music, when an email from "William Carlisle" appears in my inbox, the subject line ominously blank. Shamefully, my heart races as I click it open, then feel a rush of disappointment when I see only a few words appear on my screen. *Josie, Could you please give me a call at your convenience?* He then leaves his mobile number (which I still know by heart but no longer have programmed into my phone for fear of an unfortunate pocket call, or worse, a pocket FaceTime), along with a formal *Thank you* and his initials: *W.C.*

I reread it a few times, debating whether to consult Gabe or Sydney first. Instead, I simply call him, convincing myself that I'm not being too eager—that I just want to "get it over with"—and further, that he doesn't warrant a lot of time and analysis.

"This is Will," he says, answering on the second ring.

"Hi, Will," I say, my stomach churning. "It's Josie. I got your email."

"Hi, Josie," he says. His voice is distinctly uneasy, which somehow makes me a little less so. "Thanks for calling."

"Sure. What's up?" I say, trying to sound light and casual.

I hear him take a deep breath. "First, I just wanted to . . . thank you again for the other night. I mean, thank your friend for . . . you know . . . intervening. . . ."

"Sure. I'll tell him again . . . but it's really no big deal. I'm sure you would have been fine either way," I say, although I can still envision another scenario, and feel a little chagrined that I used to wish disaster upon him—never death, but occasionally financial ruin, partial paralysis, or mild disfigurement.

"Yeah. Well . . . that was really embarrassing."

I already knew he was embarrassed, but am surprised and disarmed that he is admitting it to me so candidly, days later. "No, it's not," I say with an odd feeling of déjà vu that must be stemming from a similar, distant memory, a time when I felt protective of his pride or feelings. "It happens a lot. Do you remember when George Bush choked on a pretzel?"

"George W?"

"Yeah," I say. "Remember he was watching football at the White House and choked, then passed out."

"Yeah, vaguely," he says, his voice lighter.

"Can you imagine? All that Secret Service surrounding and protecting him, and he nearly died alone, watching football?"

Will laughs, and I get a sharp pang of nostalgia. I always loved his laugh—a low, breathy chortle—and I especially loved when I was the source of it. He didn't laugh easily, sometimes only smiling during *really* funny movies, so it always felt like an accomplishment when I could make him laugh.

"So what else?" I ask. "Is everything okay with Edie?"

"Oh, yeah. She's doing great," he says, sounding a little stiff again, but no longer overtly uncomfortable. "At least she is at home. How's she doing in school?"

"Great," I say. "They're in music now. It's my free period. That's why I could call you in the middle of the day."

"Oh, yeah," he says. "That makes sense."

"Uh-huh," I say just to fill the silence, wondering if that's all he has to say. "So? Was there . . . something else?" I ask casually, determined not to let my voice betray the hopeful, needy way I feel—although I have no idea what I want him to say. For years, my fantasy was for him to call me, tell me that he was getting a divorce, that he'd made a big mistake, that he wanted to be with me and only me. But now I wouldn't want that to happen to Edie.

"Um, yeah. Kind of," he says. "I just . . . I wanted to . . . I don't know . . . clear the air. About us . . ."

"Us?" I say, my pulse quickening again.

"Well, not *us*. But you know, the past—what *happened* with us. I just feel badly about how things ended. . . ."

"*Bad*," I say, making a conscious decision to correct his grammar.

"What?"

"*Bad*. Not *badly*," I say, smiling a little, remembering how many times I tried to explain to him that the adverb *badly*, when modifying the verb *feel*, means you have poor tactile sensation, perhaps from a severe burn on your fingertips. *Feeling badly* would make it difficult to, say, read braille. *Feeling bad*, on the other hand, means you have negative feelings on a subject. "You know, the adjective versus the adverb."

"Oh, yeah, right, grammar girl. *Bad*. I feel *bad* about how we ended things."

I resist the urge to point out that *we* didn't end things; *he* did that. All on his own. "It's okay," I say instead, feeling healed by his pseudo-apology all these years later. "But, Will . . . I *didn't* cheat on you. . . ." My voice trails off.

"Yeah. Well, whether you did or didn't, I was a little harsh. . . . Everyone makes mistakes. . . ."

"Yes, but I really and truly didn't," I say, remembering that terrible night. Maybe the second worst of my life.

"Okay," he says.

"Do you believe me?" I ask him.

He hesitates, then says, "Josie—you were in bed with him. . . . I caught you in bed with him."

"But it wasn't like that," I say. "I swear . . . I've never told you the whole truth about that night. But only because I couldn't. . . ."

"You couldn't?" he asks.

"I thought I couldn't," I say. "It was just . . . so complicated and had nothing to do with us. It had to do with Daniel . . . but I regret it. At least I regretted it for years. I wish I'd been straight with you. . . . I'm sorry."

"Don't be sorry. It all worked out," he says. "Right?"

I swallow, then bite my lip. "Right. You have a beautiful family," I say, feeling proud for taking the high ground.

"Thank you," he says.

"I really like Andrea," I add.

"Yeah. She likes you, too," he says, as it occurs to me that she may have put him up to this call. There is suddenly no doubt in my mind that, at the very least, she has made him a kinder, more compassionate version of who he once was.

"So. Yeah. Things worked out," I say, perhaps a little too cheerfully to be convincing.

Sure enough, he hesitates, then says, with distinct concern in his voice, "So what about you?"

"What about me?"

"Are you happy now? Things are good with you, too?"

"Oh, yeah. Things are great," I say, my cheeks beginning to warm. I then overcompensate and blurt out my birth plan. "I'm actually planning to have a baby . . . with a sperm donor. . . ."

"Really?" he asks, sounding more than a little surprised.

"Yeah," I say, feeling a rush of internal peace and confidence, confirming that I'm making the right decision. "It's something I've

wanted for a long time. . . . Motherhood, that is . . . I'm really excited."

"That's great, Josie. I think you'll be a terrific mother," he says,
his tone sincere, but also filled with unmistakable guilt and pity—
and maybe a trace of condescension. "I'm so glad to hear that things
are working out for you . . . after all."

"Thanks, Will," I say, wondering how I can feel touched and
offended at once. In an odd sense, I preferred his self-righteous silence to his sympathy, and I try to think of something else to say,
something along the lines of *I know that I'm going to have the baby
I'm meant to have, the child I wouldn't have had if you and I had
stayed together.* But then I hear the sound of clamor in the hallway
and know that I'm out of time. One beat later, the door swings
open, Edie's sweet face the first to appear.

"Okay! Gotta go. My kids are back," I say. "Well, *your* kid . . .
my class . . ."

"Right . . . okay," he says. "Thanks for the call, Josie. I appreciate it."

"Thank *you*, Will," I say. "And remember—there's no reason
for you to feel bad . . . or badly, for that matter."

AFTER WORK, I come in the house and spot Gabe on the back deck
with a girl. She is his usual petite-verging-on-emaciated type, but
blond instead of brunette. They are playing Uno, drinking beer in
frosted mugs, and laughing. I watch them for a second, trying to
place her, but can't.

"Hi, there!" I call out, through the screen door.

"Oh, hey," Gabe says, glancing at me over his shoulder, his voice
unusually chipper. "Come on out and join us."

I slide open the door and step onto the porch as he says, "Meet
Leslie."

"Hi, Leslie," I say, smiling. Getting a closer look, I decide that she is very pretty—and very young.

"Hi. You must be Josie," she says, pushing aviator sunglasses up on her head and giving me a broad smile. Her teeth are disproportionately large for her face, but in a striking, not horsey, way. "I've heard a lot about you."

"You, too," I lie as I admire her outfit—a feminine white eyelet peplum top, paired with faded boyfriend jeans.

She laughs a high Tinker Bell laugh, and Gabe gives her a smitten glance before looking back at me.

"What's so funny?" I ask.

"We just met last night," Gabe says.

"Oh," I say with a shrug. "Well, then. Busted."

"Yeah," she says, laughing again. "But you're a good roommate to cover for him like that."

"Yeah," I say, raising my eyebrows at Gabe, the noun *roommate* instead of *friend* not lost on me. "I try to be."

At this point, she throws down a wild card and shouts, "Uno! Green!"

"Son of a bitch," he says, throwing down his cards. "I give up."

"That's five in a row," she says, looking jubilant.

"Yeah. Well, don't play him in backgammon," I say. "I don't think I've beaten him in nearly twenty years."

"You've known each other twenty years?" she says.

"Longer than that," I say. "I've known him since we were kids. But we didn't become close until college."

"Ah, I see," she says, nodding, then reaching out to put her hand playfully on his. I expect him to leave it there a beat, at most, before pulling away. Instead, he flips his hand over, rearranging their fingers in an intimate clasp. For Gabe, this qualifies as PDA.

"So where did you meet?" I say, trying to recall where Gabe went last night, but drawing a blank.

"The Iberian Pig," he says. "Remember? I was there for Dale's birthday."

"That's right." I nod, wondering how she and Gabe got from Dale's birthday to a game of Uno on our back deck in less than twenty-four hours. As Gabe continues to hold her hand with a goofy grin, I have a pretty good guess what's happened in between.

"So, Leslie?" I say, feigning oblivion to the strong third-wheel vibe I'm getting as I walk around their chairs and plop down on the top step. "What do you do?"

"I'm in grad school," she says. "At SCAD."

"Fashion design?" I guess, eyeing her funky metallic espadrille wedges. They are open-toe, her nails painted a deep navy.

She shakes her head and says, "No. Sequential art. But I do love fashion."

"Oh," I say, nodding and smiling.

"Do you even know what that is?" Gabe says, calling me out for the second time.

I glare at him as she laughs and says, "Don't worry, he didn't, either."

"I'm sorry," I say. "I don't, actually. What is sequential art?"

"Broadly speaking, it's an art form that uses images for graphic storytelling."

"Like comic books?" I ask.

"Yeah," she says. "Although that's not really my thing. I do animation."

"Oh," I say, nodding.

"Leslie just got a job with Pixar."

"Wow," I say. "That's exciting."

"Yeah. I guess we both have a passion for children," she says. "Gabe tells me you're a teacher?"

"Yes. I teach the first grade," I say, wondering why I suddenly feel that my work is so pedestrian. I remind myself that there is nothing more important than good teachers—except maybe doctors. But even doctors needed good teachers along the way.

"That's awesome," she says a little too exuberantly, which only heightens my insecurity.

"Thanks," I say. "I love my job. . . . So where's Pixar based?"

"Emeryville, California," she says. "Between Oakland and Berkeley."

"So you're moving there soon?" I ask, wondering why I want her gone already.

"Not until next summer," she says. "After I graduate."

I smile and nod, quickly running out of things to ask her. "Okay. Well. I'll leave you two to game six," I say, pointing to the deck of cards as I stand and walk toward the door. "Good luck, Leslie. I'm rooting for you."

I DON'T SEE Gabe again until two days later, when we run into each other in the driveway. I'm on my way to the gym, and he's all gussied up, at least for him.

"Where've you been the last few days?"

"At Leslie's," he says, putting on his sunglasses.

"What's the deal there? Are you, like, in love already?"

"Please. I've known her less than a week."

"Okay. But have you not just spent three nights in a row with her?" I ask, puzzled as to why this is so annoying to me when Gabe has had plenty of girlfriends and flings over the years.

He grins and shrugs.

"*God,*" I say, rolling my eyes. "So you've already had sex with her?"

"That's none of your business," he says, an unprecedented reply that means not only yes but that he really likes her. Usually he tells me these things.

"How old is she?" I ask. "Or is that top secret information, too?"

"Twenty-six."

"Twenty-*six*?" I say, although I'm pretty sure his last girlfriend was younger than that. "Lemme guess—she's very mature for her age?"

"Well, she is," he says. "She's smart and talented and driven, too. Do you know how hard it is to land a job at Pixar?"

"How hard?" I say.

"Very," he says.

I cross my arms and say, "Well, anyway . . . Do you realize you've ignored my last three texts?"

"Did not," he says. "I wrote you back."

"Hardly," I say, thinking that writing only three words—*He's a loser*—in response to my text *I talked to Will on the phone* was not only unsatisfying but downright neglectful.

"Don't you want to know what Will had to say?" I ask.

"What did he have to say?" Gabe asks, now looking down at his phone and texting someone. By the expression on his face, I'm guessing it's Leslie.

"Never mind," I say with a loud sigh.

Gabe looks up. "Why are you being this way?"

"I just feel like you don't care lately," I say, my voice sounding whiny. "About what I'm going through."

"Did I miss something?" he asks. "What, exactly, are you going through, again?"

"Oh, nothing major," I say. "Just teaching my ex-boyfriend's child, not speaking to my family, and gearing up to have a baby alone. No biggie."

"Josie," he says, sliding down his sunglasses to look me directly in the eyes. "You're a real pain in the ass, you know that?"

"Yes," I say, staring back at him. "But I'm *your* pain in the ass. And don't forget it."

chapter sixteen

MEREDITH

It takes an emergency session with Amy, in which she tells me, more or less, that this has been a long time coming, and another few heart-to-hearts with Ellen, before I build up enough courage to even make a *plan* to talk to Nolan. I'm not sure exactly what I'm going to say, or where I'm going to say it, only that I have to say *something*. I give myself a deadline, vowing that the conversation must take place on or before our swiftly approaching seven-year wedding anniversary.

Naturally, after several years of pretty much ignoring our anniversary or, at most, only going to dinner and exchanging cards, *this* is the year that Nolan decides we need a romantic getaway.

"We haven't gone away, just the two of us, in *years,*" he says one night as he comes in from a long run, removing his earbuds and toweling off his sweat in the kitchen. On my list of pet peeves, it is minor, but I have told him before that I wish he'd cool down out-side—or at least in a room other than the kitchen.

"What about Napa?" I say, trying to resist the macaroni and cheese that Harper didn't finish, reminding myself that her leftovers aren't free calories.

"Yeah. That was *three* years ago," he says, gripping the counter as he stretches his hamstrings. "And that doesn't count—we were there for a wedding."

"It still *counts*. Harper wasn't with us. And we stayed a few extra days," I say, recalling the trip and how pleasant it was to be away with him. For a few seconds, I'm filled with self-doubt. Maybe Ellen's theory is correct—we are just going through a rough patch and need a little time and effort to work on our marriage. I ask him what he has in mind, trying to keep mine open.

"Oh, I don't know. Something beachy . . . but it's probably too late to get flights." He frowns. "I'm sorry I didn't think of it sooner."

"It's okay," I say, quickly absolving him. I fleetingly wonder if he feels as conflicted as I do about our anniversary, but I want to let him off the hook either way. "I know you're busy at work, too."

Nolan nods and says he's going to grab a quick shower—then we can talk about it.

Thinking that he has never taken a quick shower in his life, I say, "Okay. I'll see you in an hour or so."

As PREDICTED, ABOUT an hour later, Nolan finds me in the laundry room, folding towels. "What about Blackberry Farm?" he says, referring to the astronomically expensive resort in the foothills of the Tennessee Smoky Mountains.

"Way too pricey," I say.

"Oh, c'mon. Don't be such a frugal Frieda," Nolan says. "You can't take it with you."

"I know you can't take it with you. But wouldn't it be nice to leave some for Harper?" I say, remembering that our first and only trip to Blackberry, also for a friend's wedding, happened to be the weekend Harper was conceived. I had just gone off the pill the month before, so we weren't really trying yet—a fact that Josie sometimes brings up when she's listing all the ways I'm "the lucky one."

"Two nights at Blackberry isn't going to break the bank," Nolan says. "And we still have fourteen years to save for Harper's college."

Fourteen *long* years, I think, but only say, "Okay. Sure. Give them a call. But I bet they're booked."

Nolan shakes his head, and as he leaves the laundry room, I hear him say, "Frugal Frieda. Negative Nellie."

As IT TURNS out, Blackberry has just one room available and it's "all ours for just nine hundred a night."

"Nine hundred dollars?" I say. "Or yen?"

"Ha," Nolan says. "The cottages are nearly double that."

"Oh. So this is actually a *bargain*," I say.

"Exactly," he says. "So can I book it?"

"I don't know," I waffle, worried that he will feel even more betrayed by what I think I'm going to tell him if the conversation takes place in a nine-hundred-dollar-a-night room at Blackberry Farm. Then again, maybe it will soften the blow, remind us both that no matter what happens in our relationship, we will continue to cultivate beauty in our lives—and always share a special history.

"I need a yes or a no," he says. "The guy is only holding the room for ten minutes."

I sigh and say yes because, as I have learned, yes is usually the easier answer.

A WEEK LATER, I drop Harper off at Mom's, with one duffel bag of necessities and two additional bags of toys that Harper insists are necessities. "You're visiting for the weekend or the month?" Mom asks, bending down to kiss Harper.

Harper looks at me for the answer and I say, "Just two nights. We'll be back on Sunday afternoon."

"Well, no rush," Mom tells me, smiling. "I'm so glad you and Nolan are doing something nice for your anniversary. It's a special spot for you two." She gives me a knowing wink.

"Ugh. Mom, c'mon," I say, rolling my eyes. I can't remember ever sharing the where and when of Harper's conception, but obviously I did at some point.

"What?" she says, playing dumb. "I just meant . . . I know you like it there. I'm glad you're getting away."

"Uh-huh," I say, then launch into weekend instructions, even though Harper enjoys fairly regular sleepovers with her grandmother.

"Is she still allergic to cinnamon?" Mom asks.

"It's not really an allergy," I say. "Just a slight intolerance."

"I get a bad rash here," Harper says, pointing to her upper lip.

"Nolan's turning her into a hypochondriac," I say under my breath.

"Okay, sweetie. We'll just avoid cinnamon," Mom says. "Anything else?"

"I don't think so," I say. "Do *you* have anything else?"

"Have you heard from Josie?" she asks, completely off point.

"Nope," I say, determined not to be sucked into a conversation about my sister. "Well, I better go. Nolan wanted to get on the road before rush hour."

"Sure. Sure. Go," she says, straightening a stack of MLS listings on the kitchen table, a three-and-a-half-million-dollar house on top.

"Is that your listing?"

She shakes her head. "No. I'm just showing it. New client."

"Are you sure this weekend is okay?" I say, knowing that weekends are her busiest times. "Because Ellen said she could take her. . . ."

"It's *totally* okay," Mom says. "Now. Go have fun with your husband."

"Okay," I say, kissing my daughter goodbye, fighting a wave of distinct sadness and separation anxiety, and trying not to imagine a life of every-other-weekend goodbyes.

. . .

ONCE NOLAN AND I get out of Atlanta traffic, the drive to Tennessee becomes pleasant and easy. Few cars on the highway, bright blue skies. It doesn't yet feel like fall, the trees still green and lush, but the high heat has finally passed and I'm wearing a light sweater for the first time this season. Nolan's mood is always pretty good—but it's downright chipper today, as he whistles, chats, and cranks the volume on his quirky, high-energy "road trip" playlist. As he belts out the lyrics to Katrina and the Waves' "Walking on Sunshine" and then Wham!'s "Wake Me Up Before You Go-Go," it's hard not to feel happy.

Our plan is to drive the whole way and arrive hungry, the Blackberry cuisine rivaling the mountain vistas, but two hours into the trip, we break down and stop at Cracker Barrel—which Nolan unabashedly loves as much for the food as for the peg game and gift shop.

I start to order a salad with grilled chicken but at the last second copy Nolan's order of dumplings—essentially a big bowl of starch and empty calories. We play the peg game, taking turns until Nolan steals a second board from a nearby table and we begin frantic parallel play. My best is a pathetic four pegs remaining—while he reaches three, then two, looking jubilant.

"We should do this more often," he says after our food arrives.

I butter an already buttery biscuit and murmur my agreement.

"You need to get away from that firm," he says.

"You mean quit?" I ask, feeling a hopeful surge.

He laughs and says, "No, I meant more vacations . . . weekend getaways . . . but you *could* quit. If you want."

I shake my head. "No. We need the money," I say, taking a small bite of my biscuit.

"No, we really don't," Nolan says. "What part of 'successful family business' don't you get?"

"The part that feels dirty," I say with a smile although I'm only slightly kidding.

He smiles back but looks a little offended. "*Dirty?* What the heck does that mean? You act like it's mafia money or something."

"Okay. Strike 'dirty,' " I say. "It's just that sometimes . . . I wish we had made our own way, Nolan. Your money comes with strings."

"*Our* money," he says. He stirs sugar into his tea, as I wonder what I always do—why doesn't he just order it sweetened? "And there really are no strings. I like working with my dad."

I think of the occasional skirmishes he gets into with his father, and start to contradict him, but then decide, for the most part, I'm being unfair. I've been very lucky in the in-law department.

"I mean, look at Ellen and Andy," Nolan says. "You think they could afford that house of theirs, plus their New York City apartment, on his salary and her part-time photography work?"

"Probably not," I say, knowing from my mother what they paid for their house. Plus another half million, at least, for their renovation. And Nolan is right—Ellen seems to have no problem with it. Her mother-in-law sometimes annoys her, but she mostly just adores the Grahams, thrilled to be part of their clan. Maybe that's the difference, I think, the dumplings suddenly looking like they've been marinated in Elmer's glue.

"And we live in *your* old house that we paid for ourselves," Nolan continues, "which is perfectly nice, but far from . . . *lavish.*"

I nod, thinking that he is the one who always insists that we can never move, never break that tie to Daniel. After several years of following my mother's lead and treating his room like a museum, we finally packed away most of his personal stuff and got a new queen-size bed to replace Daniel's twin. Ostensibly, it is now set up for guests, but we seldom use it that way and often still refer to it as "Daniel's room."

"So anyway . . . the point is . . . you don't *have* to practice law."

"I know," I say, conceding this much.

"You just seem so miserable there. . . . What's the point in that?"

I nod, thinking this is the perfect opening to begin a serious discussion, but also wondering if maybe what I'm *doing* isn't a bigger problem than who I'm *with*. After all, if you're not happy with your own life, can you really be happy sharing it with another? It sounds like something Amy would say. In fact, I think she *has* said it. "You're right," I say. "I'm *not* happy."

It feels like a huge first step, a breakthrough of sorts.

"So quit," Nolan says. "Quit Monday, first thing. I triple-dog dare you."

The thought is so liberating that I can't help smiling. "Maybe I will," I say, feeling a weight lifted from my shoulders. I tell myself that there isn't a more supportive man in the world. Was I crazy to think that he was the problem, when it had to be that vile job and all the pressure to bill, bill, bill, *bill*? I think about acting and how much I miss it—and consider all the other creative possibilities, ways I could be spending my time and life.

Then, like a record screeching to a halt, the next words out of Nolan's mouth are, "Just think. You could be a stay-at-home mother with complete freedom."

I give him a blank stare, thinking that there is pretty much *nothing* liberating about staying home with Harper all day, every day. And that, as much as I hate to admit it, even to myself, I would probably rather bill hours than be trapped at home twenty-four-seven.

"And then . . ." he says with a slow smile. I hear a dramatic drumroll in my head before he finishes his sentence exactly as I predicted, "we can have another baby."

My heart sinks, confirmation that something is very wrong in our marriage, and that I must tell Nolan how I feel. I almost pull the trigger right there at Cracker Barrel, but tell myself we need to get back on the road. Then I tell myself that Nolan needs to concentrate on driving. Then we arrive at Blackberry, and we're too busy unpacking. Then Nolan wants to go for a quick run and we both have to shower and get ready for the evening. Then we're on the back patio, sitting on oversize wooden rocking chairs, sipping organic martinis as we watch the sun set behind inky blue mountains—too serene a moment to taint. Ditto to our exquisite five-course dinner at The Barn, the award-winning, romantic restaurant on the property. Then, once back in our room, we both crash, too full of fine foothills cuisine and wine pairings to even stay awake, let alone have a big talk.

BUT THE FOLLOWING morning, after I wake up in the high four-poster antique bed and take a few seconds to process where I am and what day it is, I know it's finally time, that I am out of excuses. I roll over and look at Nolan as his eyes flutter halfway open.

"Good morning," he says, his voice scratchy with sleep.

"Good morning. Happy anniversary," I say, even though I have the sinking feeling that neither will be good or happy.

"Happy anniversary," he says through a big yawn and stretch. "What time is it?"

"I don't know," I say, squinting at the window. Sunlight is working its way through the closed blinds, but it's not very bright yet.

Nolan rolls over and reaches for his phone on the nightstand. "Wow. It's almost eight-thirty," he says. "I slept like a rock."

"Me, too," I say. "Did we fall asleep with the lights on?"

"Yeah. I woke up around two and turned them off." He smiles, then says, "Wow. No alarm. No Harper. Nowhere to be."

"Yeah," I murmur, feeling myself tense as he shifts a few inches toward me, one leg slung over the covers, the other still tangled up in the sheets. I glance down and see his standard morning erection making an appearance in the opening of his green gingham boxers. Although it crosses my mind to *just do it,* so to speak, I clear my throat and issue a preemptive, foreboding statement. "We need to talk."

Nolan nods, pulling me toward him, looking into my eyes. If we were any closer, we'd see each other in double. "What do you want to talk about?" he asks.

I take a deep breath and say, "Remember yesterday at Cracker Barrel? When you were talking about me quitting and us having another baby?"

"Yes?" he says, looking so hopeful that I fleetingly consider changing course. Saying *anything* to avoid hurting his feelings. "You think it's a good idea?"

I slowly shake my head, the high-thread-count pillowcase smooth under my cheek. "No," I say. "I don't."

"Oh," he says. Then, after a long pause, "And it's not the job, is it?"

"No," I say again, this time in a whisper.

"It's us, isn't it?" he says.

"I don't know," I say, my heart starting to race.

"Yes, you do," he says softly. "You *always* know."

He's right, at least this time, so I take a deep breath and make my confession. "Yes," I tell him. "I think it's us."

When he doesn't reply, I continue, starting at the beginning. "Do you remember when you asked me to marry you? In the dug-out?"

"Of course," he says, his brow furrowed.

I brace myself but keep going. "I had no idea you were going to propose," I tell him. I've said this before, many times, but have always couched it in terms of a wonderful surprise instead of shock bordering on dismay. "I really wasn't ready for that. . . . I almost said no. . . ."

He frowns, then says, "So why didn't you?"

I take another deep breath, then push up onto my elbow, still meeting his gaze. "Because of Daniel," I finally say.

"*What?*" he says, abruptly sitting up and leaning against the headboard. "What does *that* mean?"

I sit up and face him, searching for the right words, wanting them to be honest but gentle. "I just mean . . . we were there on that field, the two of us, alone. . . . But it was like Daniel was there with us . . . and I just felt . . ." I shake my head, my voice trailing off because there is simply no gentle way to put it.

"You felt *what?*" he asks.

"I just felt that I *should* say yes. Because of Daniel," I say again, knowing we are going in circles. "Sort of in his memory."

"Whoa, whoa, whoa," Nolan says, putting both hands to his temples like his mind is being blown. "You're telling *me* that you *married* me because your *brother died* in a car accident?"

"That's not what I said," I stammer, but then realize that he has accurately paraphrased my answer, boiled things down to their essence. If Nolan had popped the question while my brother was still alive, off doing his residency somewhere, then he probably wouldn't have entered my head at all. Nor would I have considered my parents, who had also factored heavily into my answer.

"Well, then. Please explain," he says, shaking his head in disbelief.

"C'mon, Nolan," I say, going on the offensive. "Are you honestly going to sit there and tell me that you would have dated me if Daniel hadn't died?"

He gives me an incredulous look. "What the hell is that supposed to mean? You think I dated you out of *pity?*"

"Not pity," I say. "But . . ." I look up at the ceiling, trying to articulate what I've always felt to be true.

"But *what*, Meredith?"

"I just think we got together because of Daniel."

"What does that *mean*? 'Because of Daniel, because of Daniel,' " he says, imitating me, his voice growing louder. "You keep saying that, but I have no idea what that means!"

"Yes, you *do*!" I say, raising my voice back at him.

"No! I *really* don't, actually."

I swallow, breathe, and try to calm down before I explain. "Well. For starters, you wouldn't have played golf with my dad that day you picked me up from the airport . . . or asked me out . . . or slept with me that next night . . . or flown up to see me a week later. . . . None of that would have happened if Daniel had been alive."

"But, Meredith, that's just . . . *circumstances*," he says. "That's like saying that a married couple who met in a bar wouldn't be together if one of them hadn't gone to the bar."

I shake my head. "No. It's not the same thing at all." I bury my face in my hands and catch my breath, before looking back up at him. "I think we were both searching for meaning."

"Oh, Christ, Meredith. Is this Amy talking? Or you?"

"It's both," I say. "I said it first, but she agrees with me. . . . You asked me to marry you, and I said yes, because we both wanted the silver lining to a terrible tragedy. Daniel's best friend marries Daniel's sister. Happily-ever-after can't ever happen—not with him gone . . . but this is the closest we can come—"

"That's *horseshit*," he says, cutting me off, roughly throwing aside the covers, then getting out of bed and heading for the bathroom.

He slams the door, but I can still hear him urinating, then flushing, then running water. A long minute later, he emerges, wearing workout clothes. The neck of his T-shirt is wet, along with his hair-line, and I can tell that he's just splashed water on his reddened face.

He looks at me for several long seconds, holding on to the bed-post, then says, "I asked you to marry me because I loved you." His voice is low and calm, but unsteady. "Not because Daniel died."

"Okay," I say, nodding. "I'm sorry. I didn't want to upset you."

"Well, that strategy isn't working," he says, dropping his hand to his side. At first I think he's referring to how upset he is currently, but then he clarifies. "You don't say yes to a marriage proposal because you think saying no will upset someone."

I try to interrupt him, but he continues. "And you don't say yes because you happen to share a tragic story with someone, either. In fact, most people who share a tragic story end up splitting. Look at your parents."

"I know, Nolan. I'm really sorry. I just thought I should tell you . . . I thought you should know. . . ."

"Okay, Meredith. Well, now I know," he says. "So what am I supposed to do with this information? More than seven years later? What do *you* want?"

"I want . . . Daniel back," I finish, suddenly hating myself more than Nolan ever could.

He throws up his hands in utter disgust. "Well, we can't have that, Meredith. So short of a resurrection—or . . . or going back to 2001 in a time machine, what do you want?"

"I want to figure this out," I say as meekly as I've ever said any-thing.

"How?" he shouts.

"I don't know," I say, wincing. "Please stop yelling at me."

He blows into his hands, as if he's warming them on a cold day, before turning, walking over to an ottoman, and sitting down to put on his socks and running shoes.

"Where are you going?" I ask.

"For a run."

"May I come?"

He looks up at me. "Because you *want* to come? Or because you think you *should* come?" he says, his eyes narrowing and flashing. "Or because you think I *want* you to come?"

"Because I *want* to," I say, but I hear my voice rising in an unconvincing question.

Nolan hears it, too, because he stands, shakes his head, and says, "Actually, Meredith, I think *I* want to be alone for a while."

chapter seventeen

JOSIE

After our second date/nondate, Pete and I text and talk daily, sometimes more than once. During one flirtatious late-night exchange (in which he jokingly offers his services to impregnate me "the old-fashioned way"), it flits through my mind that there might be romantic potential between us. But for the most part, our interaction remains platonic—and I stay focused on my goal, determined not to lose more precious time, waffling and stalling, looking for excuses not to go through with my plan, whether using Pete's sperm or an anonymous donor.

At certain moments, the whole process reminds me of adopting Revis. First, I had to decide that I truly wanted a dog—*any* dog—and that the pros outweighed the many cons. Then I had to choose my *actual* dog. For months, I tirelessly researched breeds and breeders, while also pulling up images of homeless pups on various pet finder websites. I drove all over Georgia, visiting shelters, and I frequented the Humane Society on Howell Mill Road to such an extent that I became a de facto volunteer. Eventually I ruled out a purebred, feeling compelled to rescue, and then eliminated all puppies after discovering that they have a much easier time finding homes than adult dogs. But I still remained paralyzed by indecision, reluctance, and endless second-guessing, always focusing on the particular drawbacks of individual dogs. Some barked too much;

others shed excessively; many simply had a notoriously aggressive breed in their mix—like pit bull or Rottweiler. (I hated to be prejudiced against a breed, but my sister was adamant that I not take the chance with Harper, and ultimately I agreed with her.)

Then, one day after work, I decided it was time to pull the trigger. So I drove over to the Humane Society, walked into the adult big-dog room (always less crowded than the puppy and small-dog rooms), and spotted Revis, a new resident, staring adorably up at me from the corner of his cinder-block kennel. A three-year-old black Lab–collie mix, he was larger than what I ideally wanted, with loads of fluffy black hair that I knew would end up on everything, particularly in my all-white bedroom. Two strikes. Then I read his story, typed up and posted on his kennel, about how his former owner had dropped him off, unable to deal with Revis's "separation anxiety"—which I knew was a nice way of saying he destroys shit when left alone. Three strikes.

I almost kept walking, headed for a gnarly-looking but very sweet beagle-retriever mix named Betty, also a new resident. But something made me stop and kneel down before Revis.

"C'mere, boy," I called out softly. "C'mere, Revis."

Revis gave me a skeptical stare before standing, wagging his fluffy tail, and trotting over to me. He pressed his pink and black mottled nose against the Plexiglas partition, staring into my eyes.

A moment later, I had retrieved the key to his padlock and was letting him lead me around the courtyard outside the shelter. He was attentive, alert, and good on a leash, and as we sat in the shade, quietly bonding, I whispered into one cocked ear, "Hey, buddy. Are you my dog?" Revis looked up at me, right into my eyes, and I swear he smiled and nodded. I was smitten.

Of course even then, when I was utterly convinced he was the dog for me, it still took me another ten days, two additional visits, and an introduction between Revis and Gabe (after which Gabe voted an unequivocal no, wary over the "separation anxiety" description) before I finally paid my fee, signed the papers, overrode Gabe's veto, and made it official. That was three years ago, and despite what a giant pain in the ass Revis can be, I have never once, even fleetingly, questioned my decision to adopt him, rescue him, make him mine.

When I draw this comparison to Gabe one evening, he looks up at me from his book. "You're comparing having a baby to getting a dog?"

"No, I'm comparing Pete to Revis," I say, sitting on the chair across from him.

Gabe closes the book, marking his spot with his thumb. "Look, Josie. Don't make me go all Meredith on your ass."

I shift in my chair, and give him a sheepish smile. "I just mean . . . I *have* to make a choice. I have to just *do* this. And the more I shop around, the more confusing it gets. And maybe I should just go with Pete—"

"*Shop* around?" he interjects, tossing his book onto the coffee table. "Do you know how that sounds?"

"Shop. Look. Research. It's all the same thing," I say. "It's just like Petfinder or Match—no matter how you try to sugarcoat it, I'm *shopping* for sperm. Just like people shop for pets or spouses."

Gabe nods, surrendering the point in a way that makes me feel jubilant. But then he says, "Okay. Maybe so . . . but I still think this Pete thing is a terrible idea at best."

"And at worst?"

"A really, *really* terrible idea."

"See that?" I say with a smirk. "You thought Revis was a really, *really* terrible idea, too."

Lying on the floor between us, Revis hears his name and glances over at me without lifting his head.

"He *was* a terrible idea," Gabe says, pointing at the leg of the coffee table that Revis recently gnawed during a thunderstorm. Gabe tried to sand it down and camouflage it with a brown Sharpie, but the shades of brown don't match.

"But you love him," I say.

Gabe raises his brows at Revis, then shakes his head, having learned not to be sidetracked by my meandering debating style. "Okay. But are you really comparing the father of your child to a mutt you rescued from the Humane Society?"

I stare back at him, a stubborn standoff ensuing. Several seconds later, after Gabe blinks first, I say, "Would you at least meet him? Tomorrow night? I invited him over for dinner."

"Are you just trying to get me to cook?" he says, narrowing his eyes.

"Maybe," I say. "But we could also order a pizza."

"I have plans with Leslie," he says.

"She can meet him, too."

"So now you're taking a poll?"

"No, I'm not taking a *poll*. I don't care what Leslie thinks," I say, already tired of hearing her name, at least the way he says it, so reverently. "I want *your* opinion as my best friend."

He folds his arms across his chest and takes a deep breath, but I can tell I've reeled him in with this last line. "Is Pete aware that he's being interviewed?"

"Interviewed? No. Because he's not. Is he aware that I want him to meet my best friend? Yes. He is, and he wants to meet you, too."

"Why? Because he likes you? Or because he's seriously considering donating his sperm to you?"

"Are they mutually exclusive?"

"They should be."

"Okay. The latter, then," I say. "In fact, this whole thing was actually his idea."

"It's called wanting to sleep with you, ding-a-ling."

"No," I say. "It's not like that. We wouldn't have sex. . . . We'd go through the proper channels. . . ."

We have another staring contest, and this time Gabe wins. "So if he randomly donated to a sperm bank . . . you're telling me that his jizz would be your first choice?"

"Please don't call it 'jizz,'" I say, cringing.

"Okay. His *seed*. His *sacred* seed."

"Yes. It might be, actually. Hence, the reason I want you to meet him. . . . You read the essays—so what's the difference?"

"There's a big difference," Gabe says. "But okay. I'll screen this dude for you."

THE FOLLOWING NIGHT, Leslie and Pete arrive at the same time, and are introducing themselves as I open the door. They are both dressed casually in jeans and T-shirts, though Leslie has on crazy high sandals and her hair looks suspiciously blown-out.

"Hey! Come in," I say, feeling genuinely happy to see Pete and only a little annoyed to see Leslie.

Pete gives me a slight grin, followed by a friendly, one-armed hug. "Thanks for the invite."

"Yes, thank you," Leslie says, handing me a bottle of red wine with a funky Andy Warholesque label. "This'll go with pizza, right? Gabe says we're having pizza?"

"Yes, we are," I say. "And yes, anything goes with pizza."

I smile, and she smiles back at me, but there is something about her expression that seems insincere. It's almost as if she thinks she's doing me a favor by hanging out tonight—which I guess, in a sense, she *is*. But I don't think she's earned the right to feel that way, still in a trial period herself.

"Your hair looks great, Leslie," I say, as Gabe walks into the foyer behind me.

"Thanks," she replies so flatly that I decide to call her out in front of her new beau.

"Did you get a blowout?" I ask casually.

The question catches her off guard, and she hesitates before mumbling yes, she just didn't feel like doing it herself so stopped in at Drybar.

Feeling a tad guilty for breaking at least a footnote of the girl-loyalty code, I smile and say, "Oh, yeah. It's such a pain to do it in this humidity."

She murmurs her agreement, then looks past me, her face lighting up as Gabe steps forward to kiss her on the lips, making that gross *hmmm* food sound, like the one Aidan used to make on *Sex and the City* every time he kissed Carrie. As their faces separate and he slips his arm around her waist, I make a mental note to tell him never to make that noise again unless he's eating insanely good chocolate cake, and maybe not even then.

"Pete. This is Gabe. My best friend in the *world*," I say as much for Leslie's benefit as Pete's. They shake hands as I continue my introduction. "And, Gabe, this is Pete." I pause, then add, "My newest friend—and potential sperm donor."

Everyone stares at me with identical expressions of surprise, which I take secret delight in.

"She's all about shock value," Gabe says to Pete.

"I can see that," Pete says with a laugh as Gabe turns, now taking Leslie's hand, and leads us into the kitchen, where he's prepared a simple spread of blue tortilla chips and homemade guacamole.

"Margaritas, anyone?" he asks.

We all say yes.

"Salt?"

Pete and I say yes, and Leslie says no, which I find a bit predictable and irritating. We watch as Gabe artfully runs a lime wedge over the rims of three glasses. He then presses them into a coaster of coarse sea salt and pours four glasses from a pitcher with bartender precision.

"Help yourselves," he says with a flourish.

We each take a glass, murmuring our thanks, as I warn Pete and Leslie of the potency of Gabe's recipe.

"They're pretty much straight tequila," I say. "With a little lime juice."

Gabe winks (which I've only seen him do about twice before), then lifts his own glass eye-level, his face somber as he delivers an unexpected toast (Gabe gives toasts about as often as he winks).

"To new relationships," he says. "And all that they may hold in store."

We clink our glasses together as I roll my eyes. Gabe gives me a sheepish shrug.

"So," he says, turning to Pete. "Josie says you're from Wisconsin?"

Pete nods, easy small talk ensuing about the Midwest, specifically camping and skiing, two passions they share. This, in turn, leads to a conversation about college, work, even politics (Gabe and Pete are both self-proclaimed libertarians). Leslie and I interject along the way, while I make a point to ask her polite sidebar questions, but I try to let Pete and Gabe bond as much as possible. By the time we finish our margaritas, I can tell they genuinely like each other. At least I can tell Gabe likes Pete, which is what really matters here.

"You two are a lot alike," I remark not so subtly during one lull. "I knew you'd hit it off."

They both nod and smile, and Gabe says, "Awkward."

"It's not awkward," I say. "I'm just happy you like each other. That's all."

"If you're happy, *we're* happy, right, Pete?" Gabe says.

"Oh, she's one of those?" Pete asks, his brows raised. "If she ain't happy, nobody's happy?"

"Oh, yeah," Gabe says, nodding. "She's *totally* one of those."

"No, I'm not," I protest, even though I know I kind of am.

At this point, I catch Leslie giving me a critical once-over. Maybe it's in my head, but I have the feeling that it's hard for her when I'm the center of attention—at least Gabe's attention—and I suddenly feel just a tad self-conscious. So I change the subject, open our junk drawer, pull out a deck of cards, and give it a shuffle. "Y'all wanna play Hearts?" I ask, looking up at Pete first.

"Sure," he says. "But I should warn you—I'm *really* good."

"Counting-cards, shoot-the-moon good?" I ask him.

"Yes," he says, holding my gaze. "That good." He then turns to Gabe and says, "She just wants to test my intelligence. The other night she actually quizzed me at the dinner table. With *brain teasers.*"

"Well?" I say. "I want a smart kid."

"Yeah," Gabe says. "She wants to raise the gene pool."

"I resemble that," I say, an old joke between us.

Gabe chuckles and says, "Yeah, I know. That's the problem. You *do* resemble that."

I punch him, then turn to ask Leslie if she plays cards. "Other than Uno?"

She hesitates, folding her arms across her flat chest, then says, "A little. But I've never played Hearts."

"We can teach you," I say.

"If you want . . ." Leslie says, glancing at Gabe, as if transmitting a private message.

"Nah. I'm not in the mood for cards. Let's just talk," he says, deftly interpreting her look to mean that *she's* not in the mood for cards.

"Okay," I say with a shrug. "It was just a suggestion."

Gabe clears his throat and says, "Maybe we should order the pizza now?"

"Sure," I say, grabbing my phone. "I'll call Blue Moon. What does everyone like? Sausage and mushroom?" I look at Pete, fondly remembering the flatbread from our first date.

"Sounds good to me," he says.

"Leslie's a vegetarian," Gabe says.

"You are, huh?" I say, giving her a closed-lipped smile.

"Yes," she says, raising her chin a few centimeters.

Here we go, I think, then toss her a softball she can hit from her soapbox. "Because of health or animal rights?"

"Both," she says.

"Hmm. Then do I have the sperm donor for you," I say, thinking of Glenn S, the animal rights activist. "If you ever end up needing one."

She smiles her smug twenty-something smile, then says, "Thanks. But hopefully that won't be necessary."

LATER THAT NIGHT, after our two pizzas arrive (one sausage and mushroom, the other gluten-free veggie) and Gabe, Pete, and I all eat three slices, and Leslie eats one, minus the crust, I find myself wondering what my beef with her is (vegetarian pun intended). Am I just jealous of her fresh, unlined face and raging fertility? Or feeling territorial over Gabe, selfishly clinging to our status quo, wanting to keep my best friend all to myself, especially as I embark on an overwhelming, downright scary endeavor?

As the evening wears on, I have the feeling it has more to do with Leslie herself—something I can't quite pinpoint, but that I just don't like about her. It's nothing she says or does; it's more what she *doesn't* say or do. She answers all my questions to her, whether how many siblings she has (one sister) or where she studied undergrad

(Tufts) or where she grew up (Alexandria, Virginia), but never asks a single question of her own. Instead she just sits there, emitting her smug, artsy vibe. To be fair, maybe Gabe's already told her all about me. But I don't think that lets her entirely off the hook.

"So," Gabe says at one point after I make another reference to sperm donors. "Are you two really serious about this thing?"

I look at Pete, and he looks at me, then smiles. I smile back at him and say, "I am."

"I am, too," Pete says. "But it's up to Josie. I'm sure she can find better."

My smile grows wider, thinking that his response is generous but humble.

"So how would this work?" Gabe asks. "I mean—not mechanically speaking . . . but, you know, how would the whole *thing* work?"

"We haven't really gotten that far," Pete replies. "But that would be up to Josie, too."

"So *everything's* up to Josie?" Gabe asks with a measure of skepticism, suddenly sounding like a father interviewing a new boy-friend.

I hold my breath, awaiting Pete's reply, realizing how much I want him to pass the test.

"I'm not going to say *everything's* up to her," he says.

Gabe raises an eyebrow, and I half expect him to exclaim *aha!* But instead he waits as Pete crosses his legs, looking contemplative, then continues, "I guess what I'm saying is . . . I'm not offering her *everything*. Just . . . my sperm." He lets out a nervous laugh.

Gabe doesn't smile back, but I can't tell if he's disapproving or just worried. "So not . . . financial support, for example?"

"Correct," Pete says. "Though I might help out here and there. I really don't know. . . . We haven't figured the whole thing out . . . but it wouldn't be traditional. I wouldn't be the baby's *father*. . . ."

"You wouldn't?" Gabe says.

"I mean, I *would* be the biological father . . . but not the *father* father."

"So what if she got pregnant—then never wanted to see you again?"

"We talked about that. . . ."

"And?"

"And I'd understand."

Gabe stares at him for a few seconds, then says, "So what's in it for you?"

"Does something have to be in it for me?"

"I guess not." Gabe shrugs. "But people usually act in their self-interest."

"Yes. But not always . . . Don't you give blood?"

"Blood and sperm are kind of different, don't you think?" Gabe asks.

I interject, feeling defensive of Pete. "Gabe. You argued the opposite just a few weeks ago. You compared this to organ donation. Remember?"

"Yeah," Gabe fires back. "And *you* said it wasn't the same at all. Remember?"

I start to answer, and he keeps going. "Besides. This isn't about what I think. It's about what Pete thinks. I'm trying to understand how *he* feels." Gabe swallows, still looking tense as he turns back to Pete. "So. Describe your ideal scenario."

"My ideal scenario . . ." Pete starts, then stops. "Let's see . . . my ideal scenario—"

"You're putting him on the spot," I say, half expecting Pete to get up and walk out. Why should he put up with an interrogation?

Pete shakes his head and says, "No, he's fine. I'm just thinking." He tries again. "My ideal scenario is that I donate my sperm . . . and

Josie gets pregnant . . . and then gives birth to a beautiful, healthy baby. . . . *Her* child . . . but . . ."

"But what?" Gabe says, pouncing.

"But maybe she'd allow me to be involved in some limited way."

"Define *limited*," Gabe says.

"I don't know. A once-a-year outing. Maybe an annual Braves game—"

"You're a Braves fan?" Gabe asks, as if this is pertinent.

"No. Brewers. But since I'm assuming road trips are out of the question, I'd settle for the Braves." Pete smiles.

"And what if you took your kid to that Braves game . . . and got attached?" Gabe fires back.

"I'm sure I probably would," Pete says.

"And? You don't see that as a problem?"

"Gabe," I say, finally getting a little angry. "Why are you trying to talk him out of helping me?"

"I'm not," he snaps back.

"It's fine," Pete says calmly. "It's actually helpful. Go on."

"Okay," Gabe says, nodding, then taking a deep breath. "Well, I did a little research."

I shoot him a pointed look, wondering why he didn't tell me about his research first.

"And even if you have a legal document in place, courts can sometimes overturn them. Which means"—he pauses dramatically—"there's a possibility that Josie could sue you for child support." Gabe points to me but continues to stare at Pete. "And there's a chance you could sue *her* for paternity. Even joint custody." He gives me a hard look now.

"I wouldn't do that," I say, borderline pissed now.

"Neither would I," Pete says.

"But you both *could*," Gabe says. "It happens. It's a risk."

"Not if we used a licensed doctor," Pete retorts. "In those cases, agreements are almost always upheld."

I look at him, surprised, and he gives me a slight but adorable smile. "I did some research, too."

I smile back at him, touched. "You *did*?"

"I did," he says, nodding.

For a few seconds, I forget that Gabe and Leslie are in the room until Gabe clears his throat and begins his closing argument. "Look, guys," he says. "I have to be honest here—I just don't think this is a good idea. At all."

"Well, I do," Leslie suddenly chimes in, completely unexpectedly.

Everyone stares at her as she continues, "Josie wants a baby. And Pete wants to help her. So why not?"

Her words are nice enough, but her body language, tone, and entire demeanor are loaded. She shifts on the sofa, drops her head to Gabe's shoulder, then yawns wearily, clearly ready for this portion of the evening to end.

Pete ignores her, directing his reply to Gabe. "We obviously have to give it some more thought. There's a lot to discuss. And we'd have to talk to professionals in this field. A doctor *and* probably a lawyer." His voice is steady, strong, reasonable. "Most likely, I think I would donate, then disappear. That would probably be best for everyone involved."

I feel a wave of disappointment before he adds a *but*. I wait, feeling hopeful, though not sure what *for*.

"But Josie and I can make our own rules," he says, meeting my eyes with a tenderness that makes me catch my breath. "Right, Josie?"

"Right, Pete," I say with a big smile, feeling almost as lucky as a girl in love.

· · ·

THE FOLLOWING MORNING, while I'm still in bed scrolling through my Instagram, Gabe returns home from Leslie's and knocks on my door.

"Come in," I say, putting my phone down and sitting up.

He opens the door, looking disheveled and tired, but extremely animated.

"It's a terrible, horrible, no good, very bad idea," he says, referencing my favorite children's book, which I keep on my nightstand, along with *Harold and the Purple Crayon* and *The Five Chinese Brothers*.

I play dumb and calmly reply, "What is?"

"This thing with Pete. It's a complete and utter disaster waiting to happen." He glances around my room, looking suspicious, then says, "Did he spend the night?"

"No!" I say, sounding aghast. "Of course not."

"Uh-*huh*," he says, crossing his arms.

"He *didn't*!" I say. "God. What's your deal?"

"It's a disaster," he says again.

"You don't like him?" I say.

"I *like* him just fine," he says, sitting on the foot of my bed. "But this is truly one of your all-time worst ideas."

"Why do you say that?" I ask.

"Because it is," he says, then starts to enumerate all the things that could go wrong, several rehashed from last night. He could get too attached and sue for partial custody. My husband could resent him. His wife could despise me. I could end up with my kid's half siblings living in town. I finally interrupt him, during a completely far-fetched hypothetical about my daughter being torn over who should give her away at her wedding. "She can't decide between her sperm donor father and the man you married. . . ."

"But *I'm* not even married—and you're already marrying *my daughter* off?" I say. And then, before he can get started again, I add, "There are always risks in relationships. Look at you and Leslie. You could have knocked her up last night. Then what?"

"First of all, I actually *couldn't* have knocked her up last night. Because we didn't have sex."

"Yeah, right," I say, thinking of that gross *hmmm* sound he made when he kissed her. "You guys never stopped touching each other all evening."

"Well. If you must know, we got in our first fight last night."

"I'm sorry to hear that," I say, resisting the urge to ask him about it. Then I say, "But at some point, you *could* end up getting her pregnant—or just marrying her—and then realizing that she completely *sucks*." I say the last word with as much fire as I can muster.

"That's totally different," he says as I notice dark circles under his eyes and a massive underground zit emerging on his forehead. "And you know it."

"Well, *every* situation is different," I say.

"Yes," he says. "And this one is way, *waaay* too messy and complicated and fraught with dangers and pitfalls. If I got just one veto in your life, this would be it."

I picture Leslie's uppity little nose, then ask if I get a veto in his life, too.

"And you know what the biggest problem here is?" he asks, ignoring my question. "In a sea of really big problems?"

"What?" I ask at my own peril.

"Dude *likes* you."

I stare at him, confused, and he clarifies. *"Pete."*

"I know who 'dude' is," I say. "But I don't get your point. Of course he likes me. He wouldn't do this for me if he didn't like me."

Gabe shakes his head. "No. He *likes* you. As more than a friend. As more than a 'hey, let me loan you some sperm.' He wants to sleep with you. Date you. Maybe marry you."

"You're nuts!" I say, laughing and throwing a pillow at his face. "No, he does *not*."

He lofts the pillow into the air, and we both watch as it falls neatly in place. "I'm a guy," he says with calm certainty. "I can tell. I know. And I promise you—this would be an absolute *fucking* disaster. As in . . . the biggest disaster you've ever put in motion. And that's saying a lot."

His face falls as soon as the words are out. "You know what I mean," he says, looking guilty.

"Yeah," I say, feeling crushed, knowing that we both know that there will always be a far worse and much darker disaster in my past.

chapter eighteen

MEREDITH

In true Nolan ignore-the-issue style, he returns from his run several hours later (after I've cried and showered and dressed and cried some more) and tells me he thinks we should just enjoy the weekend. The coward in me is relieved, but at the same time, I am incredulous, frustrated, and worried that nothing is going to change—in my heart, our marriage, my life.

And that feeling grows larger when, that evening, we exchange anniversary cards, have another long, romantic dinner, and then return to our room, where I reluctantly initiate guilt-driven but resentment-filled sex.

While it's actually happening, I make my mind as blank as possible, which in turn makes me realize just how much of sex is mental. In other words, it's virtually impossible to make it a purely physical act. It is always more than that.

Afterward, Nolan curls his body around mine and says, "Did you . . . ?"

"You couldn't tell?" I murmur.

"Just confirming," he whispers.

"Yeah," I say. "I did."

"Good," he says, tightening his embrace. His arms are strong, warm, comforting—and the feeling that washes over me is a complete contradiction to everything I told him this morning.

I kiss the side of his elbow, the only thing I can reach, and say, "I'm sorry, Nolan. For earlier."

Then, as I get ready to backpedal, he shushes me and says, "Let's just go to sleep, Mere."

I close my eyes, deciding that for now, I'd rather doubt myself than doubt my marriage.

THE FOLLOWING MORNING, right after breakfast, we drive back to Atlanta, heading straight to my mother's house to collect Harper. It's been less than forty-eight hours since we dropped her off, but it feels like much longer, and I can tell Nolan misses her as much as I do, both of us practically running into the house. He gets to her first, picking her up out of her chair to give her a big hug. I hover beside them, waiting for my turn as I inhale her strawberry Lip Smacker scent. But before I can hug her, she scrambles back down to the table, returning to her elaborate art project incorporating crayons; rubber cement, tape, *and* paste (because you can never have too many adhesives); and copious amounts of purple glitter.

"I want a hug and kiss, too," I say, stooping down to her eye level.

She turns her head a few degrees and gives me a perfunctory kiss on the cheek.

"How about a hug?"

She shakes her head and says, "Later, Mommy. I'm very busy now."

They are clearly words she's heard many times before, and I feel a stab of guilt knowing she is quoting me.

"What are you making?" I ask, sitting at the table beside her, and wondering why my mother didn't put down a drop cloth or newspaper, glitter already working its way into the crevices of her rustic wooden table. I resist the urge to clean, waiting for her answer.

"A castle. And that's you," she says, pointing to an oval-faced brunette peering out of a half-moon third-floor window. I'm not quite frowning, but certainly not smiling, my mouth a straight, smudged line of red crayon.

"What's Mommy doing up there?" Nolan asks, sitting on the other side of Harper.

"Just looking out," Harper says. "At this tree. And this blue bird." She points to each as I notice that her fingers are beginning to lose their chubbiness, becoming little-girl slender.

Nolan and I exchange a glance, as I wonder if he's trying to psychoanalyze her art project as much as I am.

"And where are you?" I ask, even though it is clearly her standing in the front yard, wearing a pink A-line frock. Beside her is a strapping, smiling man that has to be Nolan.

"Right here," she says, pointing to herself. "With Daddy."

"That's a mighty happy pair," I say under my breath, but Harper hears me and quotes me back.

"A happy pair," she says, smiling, nodding.

"So did you and Nana have fun?" I ask, changing the subject.

"Yeah," she says.

"You mean 'yes'?" I say, gently correcting her.

"Yes," she says, shaking more purple glitter into the flower bed in front of the castle.

"We had a marvelous time," Mom says, gazing at Harper adoringly. "And how was your anniversary weekend?"

"It was great," I say, forcing a cheerful tone. "Very relaxing . . . It's such a beautiful place."

Nolan quickly echoes my comments.

Mom looks pleased. "I'm so glad you had a good time," she says.

"So what else did you two do?" I ask, glancing from Mom to Harper.

"Let's see. We watched movies. . . . Right, Harper?"

Harper nods and says, "*Lady and the Tramp* . . . and *101 Dalmatians.* And *Lassie Come Home.*"

"Oh, a little dog theme, I see," Nolan says pointedly, glancing my way.

In addition to a second child, he has been trying to get Harper a puppy for months now, but I have held out, knowing that I will be the one taking it out every morning, feeding it, and scooping up its poop from the yard.

"And speaking of dogs," Mom says. "Aunt Josie came over with Revis for a late breakfast. You actually just missed her."

"Drats," I say, my voice completely flat.

Mom says my name as a warning.

"What?" I ask, feigning innocence.

"Be nice," she says. And then—"Have you still not talked to her?"

"No," I say, positive that this fact was discussed, and knowing how adept Josie is at making me out to be the bad guy.

"You really need to talk to her."

"And why's that?"

I know her answer before she says it: *Because she's your sister.* She clears her throat, then adds, "*And* because she's going to have this baby, and we need to support her decision."

"Do you think she'll really go through with it?" Nolan asks.

Mom nods and says, "Yes. In fact, she picked her donor."

I flinch, but remain silent, determined not to ask any questions and indirectly validate what Josie's doing. Of course Nolan doesn't get this nuance and eagerly asks for the scoop.

Mom takes a deep breath, then starts rattling off the detailed bio of a complete stranger. "His name is Peter. He's from the Midwest—Wisconsin, I think she said . . . but he currently lives in Atlanta.

He's forty-one. I think she said he's five-ten or five-eleven. . . . He has brown hair and hazel eyes."

She takes a deep breath, Nolan looking rapt while I pretend to be completely disinterested. "And let's see. . . . He's Irish and German by descent. . . . He was raised Catholic, but isn't very religious. He is spiritual, though. He believes in God. He likes outdoorsy things—camping and biking and skiing. He's very fit. Very healthy. He went to college, then got a graduate degree in physical therapy, which he practices now. He's very smart, especially in math and science. . . ."

"If he does say so himself?" I say.

Mom ignores my snide comment and says, "Oh—and she says he has a cleft in his chin. Which Josie has always liked."

"Well, *super,*" I say.

"Meredith," she says sternly. "You really need to change your attitude."

"Why? She never changes *her* attitude," I say, knowing how immature I sound. "She never resists a single impulse."

"Actually," Mom says, her voice gentle. "That's not true. She's really trying lately."

I cross my arms and raise my eyebrows. "Oh? How so?"

"Well, for one—she has agreed to go to New York with us. In December."

"We'll see about that. I bet you a hundred bucks she backs out," I say, thinking that's one of Josie's signature tactics—bow to pressure, then come up with an excuse later.

Mom shakes her head. "No. She's really come around on the idea," she says so earnestly that it breaks my heart. "And I think it will be good for her. For all of us, but maybe especially for her."

"Why's that?"

"She needs to face her grief," Mom says. "She never really has. I think seeing Sophie might help with that. . . . So anyway, we should all probably book our tickets and hotel soon. . . . New York is so busy around the holidays. . . ." Her voice trails off and her eyes grow glassy, as she is obviously thinking about Daniel, that time of the year, trees and decorations and Christmas carols, all completely synonymous with death in our family.

I look away, watching Harper add another large tree to the castle grounds, this one an evergreen. Nobody speaks for a long stretch, the only sounds those of Harper's crayon pressing against the paper and Nolan tapping the table with his thumbs. Annoyed by the monotonous rhythm, I reach over and put my hand on his, silencing him.

He glares at me, then clears his throat. "Speaking of New York," he says. "Meredith might go up there sooner than December. . . ."

I look at him, confused. Ellen and I have recently discussed going to the city for a girls' weekend, but I don't recall mentioning this to him, probably because I knew it was a long shot given my workload at the firm.

"Oh?" Mom says, glancing at me. "For work?"

"No," Nolan quickly replies. "She just needs a break. A little getaway."

"Wasn't that the point of this weekend?" Mom asks, clearly as confused as I am.

"Oh, she needs a longer break than *that*," he says. "A *real* break. From her job. And Harper. And me." He flashes a fake smile, then forces a chuckle. "Don't you think that would be good for her?"

Mom nods, but remains pensive. "Well, I guess time away can be good for all of us. . . . How long of a break do you need, sweetie?"

"I don't *need* a break," I say, feeling both agitated and defensive.

Nolan musses my hair, feigning lightheartedness, and says, "Oh, yeah you do. A couple weeks will do you good."

"A couple of *weeks*?" Mom and I reply in unison.

"What about Harper?" she asks as I glare at my husband.

"Oh, I have that covered. Hell. Josie's going to be a single parent. Surely I can handle a couple of weeks on my own," he says, as I stare at him, wondering when all of this came to him. On his run yesterday? Last night after we had sex? On the virtually silent drive back this morning?

He whistles a few bars of an unrecognizable song, then says, "Maybe I'll take some time off, too. Do a little father-daughter bonding. Wouldn't that be fun, Harper?"

"Uh-huh," she says, without looking up.

"And I'm sure Nana can help a little . . . and Gran and Pop," he says, referring to his parents. "And Josie, of course. Good ol' Aunt Josie."

Mom frowns, looking confused by the contradiction between his maniacal mood and the undertones of his message. Deep lines appear on her forehead as she asks her standard question. "Should I be worried here?"

"No," I say.

"Oh, *no*," Nolan says. "Not one bit. Meredith just needs to do some thinking. Right, Mere?"

I bite my lip and mumble a noncommittal *yeah,* as Mom asks what sort of thinking.

"Deep thinking," he chirps. "*Soullll* searching."

"About?" Mom asks.

At this point, I'm in damage control mode, so I simply say, "About my job."

"So you're seriously thinking about leaving?" she asks, her frown lines easing a bit.

I start to reply with a watered-down statement about feeling burned out, but Nolan once again answers for me. "Yes," he says decisively, a word he almost never uses, which is why Harper continues to say *yeah* and *uh-huh*. Then he turns and looks into my eyes. "She's *seriously* thinking about leaving."

"WHAT THE *HELL* was that about?" I ask Nolan as soon as we're back at the house and alone—as alone as you can be with Harper in the next room. My voice is measured and low, but inside I'm enraged.

"What?" he says with a passive-aggressive shrug. "I think it's a great idea. You need some time to think."

"Any reason you didn't mention this idea to me *first*?" I ask, using my fingernail to scrape a piece of hardened shredded wheat from a cereal bowl Nolan left in the sink two mornings ago. It's now as hard as superglue. I finally give up and put it in the dishwasher.

"Any reason you didn't mention that you think our marriage is a joke?" he asks.

"I never said that. Nor do I think that."

"Okay. Any reason you didn't mention that you think our marriage was a big mistake?"

"I didn't say that, either, Nolan," I say, spinning around and staring at him.

He stares back at me with defiance and disdain. "What *did* you say, then?"

"I don't know, Nolan. . . . I'm just . . . confused."

"Well, as I said, I think you need to go away and figure it out."

"I can't just *go away,* Nolan," I say, my hands on my hips. "What about Harper?"

"I told you. I can handle things here."

I look at him, thinking that he doesn't have the first clue about how to run the washing machine, let alone handle the myriad details of Harper's daily routine. I think about the last time I went on a work trip and how he didn't even get the mail for three days. "What about my job? Can you handle my job, too?" I say.

He shrugs. "Take a leave of absence. People do it all the time. Or just quit. You hate it. What's the point of doing something you hate?"

"I don't *hate* it," I say, thinking that his oversimplification of everything is part of the problem.

"Yes, you do," he says. "You *despise* it. You wish you had stayed in New York and become a famous actress."

I open my mouth to correct him, as I never desired fame. I just wanted to be a working stage actress. At most I dreamed about a Tony—and how many Tony Award–winning actresses are household names? But this seems rather beside the point.

"Instead you're an attorney in Atlanta. Married to me. Huge, *huge* mistake," he says.

"Nolan," I say, my voice beginning to rise. "Would you please stop with this crap? I *didn't* say that."

"Oh, but you *think* it," he says. "Don't you?"

My mind races for a response, as I realize that he is partially right. And maybe, but for Harper, *completely* right.

"And you know what?" he continues. "There's nothing stopping you from getting a do-over."

I pretend we're both talking about my job, and not a divorce, wondering how long it will be before one of us utters the word aloud. "I'm too old to change careers," I say.

"No, you're not," he says. "Isn't acting like riding a bike? Surely it's all still there. . . . Just . . . go to some auditions. . . ."

I swallow, a huge lump in my throat. "It's not that easy," I say. "And besides. We can't leave Atlanta."

"Yes, *you* can," he says. "You can do anything you want to do, Meredith."

I turn away from him, looking out the window over the kitchen sink, just like in Harper's drawing, and I feel myself tremble with the tantalizing, terrifying thought that he might be right.

chapter nineteen

JOSIE

On Monday morning, I take a giant leap forward and call the office of Dr. Susan Lazarus. According to my research, Dr. Lazarus is the leading fertility specialist in Atlanta, known for both in vitro fertilization and intrauterine insemination. My heart sinks when her receptionist briskly informs me that her first available appointment is nearly two months away. I tell her that I'll take it, then ask if she can please put me on a waiting list.

"If there's any cancellation . . . I'll drop everything and come in at a moment's notice. I'm pushing forty and a little bit panicked here. . . ."

"I feel you," she says with a little chuckle, dropping her professional persona. "I turn forty next week. Ugh."

"Do you have kids?" I ask.

"Yes. Ten-month twins, thanks to Dr. Lazarus."

"Wow. Congrats," I say, feeling bolstered by the anecdote, though the mere thought that I could somehow end up with twins fills me with pure terror. "Boys or girls?"

"One of each," she says.

I congratulate her again as she suddenly informs me that I'm in luck, she just noticed a cancellation on the calendar for this coming Friday at eleven, confirming my belief that sometimes small talk can really pay off.

"I'll take it," I say.

. . .

I GIVE SYDNEY my entire update at recess that day, the two of us
taking our usual supervisory spots on a bench overlooking the playground. As I watch Edie hanging upside down on the monkey bars,
her arms dangling, her tiny torso swinging, and her face turning red,
I fill Sydney in on Pete, as well as my upcoming appointment with
Dr. Lazarus.

"I'm so proud of you, Josie," she says, turning to give me a sideways hug. "And a little jealous."

"Hey, why don't you do it with me?" I say excitedly.

She laughs. "Matching cars and kids?"

"I'm serious! Would you ever consider it?" I ask, as I hear Meredith scoffing in my head, proffering my suggestion as further proof
that I'm not taking motherhood seriously.

Sydney shakes her head and gives me an adamant, animated *hell
no.* "I'm seriously impressed that you're doing this . . . but person-
ally? If I had to choose just one, I'd rather have a husband than a
baby. But definitely in that order."

I nod, thinking that although I want both, too, the baby part of
the equation has always been more important to me—at least since
Will and I broke up. And if I'm honest, I think I might have even felt
that way then. I loved him, yes, but he also felt like a prerequisite
for motherhood. The means to an end.

She gives me a thoughtful look, then says, "Are you scared?"

"A little," I say. "Mostly just about logistics."

She murmurs her agreement, then asks if I will still live with
Gabe or move into my own place.

I frown and tell her I haven't figured that out yet, as I hear Meredith's voice again, mumbling that this is par for the course.

"Gabe knows your overall plan, though? That you want to have
a baby?"

I nod and say of course, Gabe knows everything.

"And?" she asks. "What does he think?"

"He's supportive. . . . Unlike my sister, who is her usual judgmental self." I pause, then say, "But he's not really down with the idea of Pete as my donor."

Sydney raises her eyebrows. "That's 'cause he's jealous."

"Stop it right there," I say, knowing exactly what she's getting at. "How many times do I have to tell you men and women can be friends?"

She smirks. "Yeah. That's what Harry and Sally said."

"I'm *not* Sally," I say.

"Maybe not. But he's definitely Harry," she says.

"No, he's *not,* Syd. . . . Didn't I tell you about his new girlfriend?"

"Yeah, yeah. Whatever," she says, rolling her eyes.

"I'm serious. . . . He really likes her."

"Yeah. But only because he can't have you."

I shake my head. "No. His objection to Pete is purely a practical one. He thinks I should use an anonymous donor rather than someone I know. He's worried that it would get too . . . weird. Messy."

"And you say . . . ?"

"I say I'll take that chance. Pete's smart, attractive, and really sweet. It just feels . . . right."

"Oh, *reeally,* now?" she says, her voice dripping with innuendo of the sexual kind.

"The right *donor,*" I say. "I have no interest in dating him, either."

"Well, then," she says, sitting up straighter. "Introduce us."

I laugh and say not a chance.

"Why not? He could be my soul mate. You'd deprive me of that?"

"Yes. Because *that would* be too weird," I say, feeling oddly possessive, if not of Pete, then at least of his sperm.

. . .

THAT EVENING, I find Gabe out back, grilling three hot dogs while listening to Bob Marley.

"Hey," I say, leaning against the deck.

"What's up?" he says, without looking my way.

"Is Leslie coming for dinner?"

He shakes his head. "Nope. And she's a vegetarian. Remember?"

"Oh, right. How could I forget?" I say, only a little snidely.

He either misses or ignores my tone, and asks if I'm hungry. "I threw an extra dog on just in case."

"Sure. Thanks," I say, then ask about his day. Gabe's worked for the same company for nearly a decade, but I'm still not exactly sure what he does for a living—other than that it involves graphic design, computers, and a lot of high-maintenance clients.

"Everyone and everything annoyed me."

I laugh and say, "So, the usual?"

"Pretty much. How about yours?"

"It was okay," I say. "I told Sydney about my baby plan. And my appointment with Dr. Lazarus on Friday."

He nods without looking at me. "So what exactly is going to happen on Friday?"

I shrug and say I'm not sure. "It'll probably just be an introduction and a discussion of my options."

"Is Pete going with you?" Gabe asks as he turns down the flame on the grill.

"No," I say, though the thought did cross my mind earlier today.

"Why not?" he asks. "Have you changed your mind about . . . using him?"

"No," I say. "He's still kind of at the top of my list. But there's no need for him to go with me . . . not at this point. . . . I was thinking of asking my mom. It'd be nice to have someone there. You know—for moral support." I give him a needy look, then add, "Hint, hint."

Gabe rolls his eyes and says, "You want me to go?"

I put my hands together in prayer. "Would you? Please?"

"I guess," he says with a big sigh.

"You think Leslie'll be okay with it?"

"Why wouldn't she?" he asks.

Because she's controlling and clearly doesn't like me, I almost say, but decide to treat it as a rhetorical question. "That'd be really awesome, Gabe," I say. "Thank you."

"No problem," he says with a nonchalant shrug. "Besides. I want to be there to hear this doctor tell you that acquaintance sperm is a really shitty idea."

"Acquaintance sperm?" I laugh. "Is that a scientific term?"

"Yes . . . I mean . . . this Pete guy seems nice and all . . . but he could be a serial killer with . . . a recessive cystic fibrosis gene, for all you know."

I laugh.

"Well, he *could* be," Gabe says, transferring the hot dogs to a plate, then turning to walk inside.

"I'm sure Dr. Lazarus will do thorough testing," I say, following him into the house.

"The ol' serial killer test?" he says, glancing over his shoulder.

"Well, any sperm donor could be a serial killer," I say. "So could any boyfriend, for that matter. Hell, for all you know, Leslie could be one. . . ."

"I've never heard of a female serial killer," he says.

"Well, even if she's not a full-fledged murderer, she could be shady. . . . She could have all kinds of skeletons you know nothing about."

"I guess," he says. "But the difference is . . . I'm not planning on impregnating Leslie anytime soon."

"Not anytime *soon,* huh?" I say, my hands on my hips.

"Stop changing the subject," Gabe says. "We're not talking about me. We're talking about you and your . . . capricious choice."

"It's not a capricious choice," I say, although I can't remember exactly what the word means.

"Okay," he says, pulling a bag of hot dog buns out of the bread drawer. "Tell me again, then. One more time. What's so special about Pete? Why him?"

"Why not?" I say, unable—or maybe just unwilling—to articulate my gut feeling about using Pete.

"That's your answer?" He gives me an incredulous stare as he tosses a bun to me. I miss it, and watch it land on the kitchen floor.

"Yep," I say. I pick it up and put it on my plate, deciding to go with the five-second rule. "That's my answer."

ON FRIDAY MORNING, after Gabe and I both call in sick to work, we walk into a nondescript Midtown office building for my appointment with Susan Lazarus. As we sit in the waiting room, I fill out endless forms, answering exhaustive questions about my medical history, while Gabe plays solitaire on his phone. At one point, I glance over his shoulder and read a text from Leslie that says: *Where are you?*

With Josie, he writes back, which both surprises me and piques my curiosity enough to covertly read the rest of the conversation, in real time:

Oh. At lunch?

No. Just out and about.

Can you call me?

Can't at the moment—but will in about 30?

Sure . . . Imy.

Out of the corner of my eye, I see him smile, then type: *Imy2.*

At this point, he catches me reading over his shoulder.

"Nosy," he says, tilting his phone away from me, just as my name is called by a young woman in lavender scrubs.

I stand and look at Gabe. "You coming?"

"You want me to?"

"I want you to," I say.

A moment later, we are ushered into a small office. A diminutive woman with a pixie cut sits behind a large, antique desk that seems too heavy and ornate for her. She stands and says, "Josephine?"

"Josie," I say, nodding.

"Josie," she repeats, giving me a warm smile. "Please come in. I'm Susan Lazarus."

I like her immediately—perhaps because she uses her first name—and I smile back at her as we shake hands. "This is Gabe," I say.

She nods, shakes his hand, then tells us to please take a seat, gesturing to the chairs across from her desk.

"So," she says brightly, "what brings you here today?"

"Well, um, I want a baby," I say, overcome by a sudden rush of excitement.

She gives me an even wider smile, then says, "Well, you've come to the right place. . . . So tell me, Josie, have you been trying to conceive?"

I shake my head and say, "No. Not at all. I'm not married. . . . I'm single. . . . I want to use a sperm donor."

She nods, completely unfazed. "Perfect," she says, then turns to Gabe. "And will you be donating your sperm?"

"Nope," he says. "I'm just here for moral support."

"That's *wonderful,*" she says. "And so very important given Josie's journey ahead." She turns back to me and says, "Have you thought about your donor?"

"Yes," I say. "I've been reading and researching quite a bit."

"Good," she murmurs, nodding. "And tell me about that."

"Well. I've read a lot about sperm banks . . . women who have gone that route. Children who were conceived that way . . . and I don't have a problem with it. . . . I get that it's more straightforward, with fewer strings attached . . . but I just think that I'd like to use . . . acquaintance sperm," I say, exchanging a look with Gabe.

"You mean the sperm of an acquaintance?" she asks with a calm poker face.

"Yes. A guy I've recently met. I guess you could call him a friend," I say. "Do you think that's a bad idea?"

"I think this is entirely a personal decision. A *very* personal decision."

Gabe makes an exasperated sound and says, "But aren't there a lot of *risks* to doing this with some guy she barely knows?"

"There are pros and cons to every reproductive scenario," Dr. Lazarus replies. "We believe in helping women make a choice that is right for them . . . and supporting that choice, both medically and legally. We have a family law practice we work closely with. . . . They can help you draw up a contract that works for you. And of course we would handle the insemination in the office."

"See?" I say, looking at Gabe, jubilant. "I told you, if I do it at the doctor's office, it's foolproof."

"I wouldn't say *foolproof*," she interjects. "Nothing ever is foolproof when it comes to the ever-shifting body of reproductive law . . . but the way we handle it is as close to ironclad as you can get. And we've done it that way for many women."

I glance at Gabe, who crosses his arms in not-so-subtle protest.

"Of course there are emotional issues that can't be provided for in a contract. And it sounds as if that might be your concern?" she continues, now looking at Gabe.

"Yes. As a matter of fact, it *is* my concern," he says, nodding. "What if this guy she barely knows turns out to be crazy? And he won't leave her or her kid alone? What then?"

"Well, that could happen with any guy," I say, turning to him. "And I'd handle it the same way I would if I were *dating* the guy and he turned crazy. With a restraining order."

"You'd be okay getting a restraining order against the father of your kid?" Gabe's voice is slightly raised and agitated.

"He wouldn't be the *father*," I say.

"Right. He'd just be the creepy sperm donor you got a restraining order against," Gabe says with a shrug. "No biggie."

Before I can reply, Dr. Lazarus clears her throat and tentatively interrupts our sidebar. "Might I make a suggestion?"

"You may," I say, feeling fairly confident that she will be on my side.

"Let's focus on *you*, Josie," she says, pointing at me. "Because we know that part of the equation. We know you want to use one of *your* eggs and carry *your* child, correct?"

"Yes," I say, nodding emphatically. "We do know that."

"So. Let's focus on *your* preconception care and check for any potential risks to you during your pregnancy."

I tell Dr. Lazarus that I think that's a fabulous idea.

She continues earnestly. "No matter which donor sperm you decide to use, we want you to be your healthiest self, both physically and emotionally."

I nod, feeling another burst of excitement, as Gabe manages to look slightly less glum. We both watch and listen as Dr. Lazarus puts on her reading glasses, glances through my forms, and begins to ask detailed follow-up questions about my health history. She then asks me if it's okay if Gabe stays while we discuss my reproductive history. I tell her yes, he can hear anything. "We're best friends."

She smiles, nods, then asks if I've ever been pregnant before.

"A few scares," I say with a laugh. "But no."

"So no miscarriages?"

I shake my head. "I don't think so. I mean . . . occasionally I'm a little late and have a really heavy period . . . and sometimes I wonder if that could be a miscarriage. . . . But no, I don't think so."

I glance at Gabe, who grimaces, then crosses his arms, as Dr. Lazarus continues to ask questions about my cycle, menstrual history, vaccinations, and contraceptive use. I tell her I have a very regular twenty-eight-day cycle, that I'm all up-to-date on my vaccinations, that historically I've been on the pill *and* use condoms, though I went off the pill a few weeks ago, and have not been sexually active in several months.

"Any abnormal Pap smears?"

"Umm . . . just one," I say. "It turned out to be nothing, though. Just a yeast infection."

"All righty, then," Gabe says under his breath. "Can I please wait out there?"

"No," I hiss, glaring at him. "You can't."

Gabe sighs and stares at the ceiling as Dr. Lazarus segues into a conversation about nutrition and exercise, alcohol and nicotine. I tell her I don't smoke, but I do drink socially.

She nods. "Okay. A glass of wine here and there is fine before conception, but try to limit it to that."

"What about coffee?" I ask.

"I recommend limiting your caffeine to three hundred milligrams per day. . . . So about two eight-ounce cups."

I get out my pad and start to take a few notes, but she reassures me that all the advice will be on my printed materials. "I'll also give you a prescription for a prenatal vitamin, as you will need plenty of folic acid. Additionally, you should make sure you're eating a variety of foods rich in fiber, calcium, and other nutrients. Avoid sugar and processed foods. . . . You just want to be as healthy as you possibly can to get your body ready for pregnancy."

"Okay," I say, feeling determined. "Gabe's a great cook. And we live together."

"Well, that's a big help," she says, smiling at him, then me.

I smile back at her. "So is that it?"

"Almost," she says. "I'd like to do a quick physical exam and then we're going to take some labs."

Gabe looks horrified.

"You may skip the exam," Dr. Lazarus tells him with a smile. She stands, walks around the desk, and shakes his hand. "It was very nice to meet you, Gabe. Josie's lucky to have you in her life."

The comment seems to catch him off guard, but he mumbles a polite thank you.

"I trust you'll help her make a sound decision about her next steps?" she says.

I hold my breath, awaiting his response, half expecting something snarky to come out of his mouth. Instead, he simply nods and says, "Yes. I will. We just want a healthy baby. Right, Josie?" He turns to look at me.

I swallow, feeling a little teary, then tell him yes, that's all we want.

chapter twenty

MEREDITH

Nolan and I barely talk the week following our anniversary, and when we do, our exchanges are strained and formal. I'm not sure whether I'd call it a stalemate or a standoff or simply the calm before the storm, but I find myself seriously contemplating his "suggestion" that I go to New York. I can't imagine leaving Harper for more than a few days, but the prospect of spending some time alone becomes something of an obsession. It doesn't help my mental state that I've just been staffed on a mammoth product liability case with Larry Goldman, the biggest asshole partner in the firm, who gave me a scathing review last year because I dared to miss a deposition when I came down with a 103-degree fever.

When I give Ellen the update over the phone one morning, she tells me I'm welcome to stay at her apartment in the city.

"Are you sure?" I ask.

"Of *course*," she says. "Absolutely."

"Oh, *thank* you . . . It would only be for a few days. . . ."

"Stay as long as you want. Stay a week."

"I don't know . . . I think I'd feel too guilty leaving Harper for longer than a couple of nights."

"You shouldn't feel guilty," Ellen says. "I'm often gone from Isla a week at a time, and she's totally fine with Andy and his parents."

"That's different—you're actually *working*," I say.

"Yes. But we all need time to ourselves sometimes," Ellen says. "It doesn't make you a bad mother."

"Maybe not," I say, thinking that it might not make me a bad mother, but I'm pretty sure the way I'm feeling does make me a lousy wife.

THE FOLLOWING MONDAY, I call in the big guns and meet with Amy, telling her everything I told Ellen, only more candidly. She listens intently, then says, "Why New York?"

I frown, thinking for a few seconds before I say, "I don't know why Nolan suggested New York. Maybe because that's where I lived when we started to date . . . maybe because he knows I'd have a free place to stay there—my friend Ellen has an apartment. . . . Honestly, though, it doesn't have to be New York. I just want to get away. From him. From work. Even from Harper."

I wait for a lofty psychological explanation—something about how common my feeling is among mothers with young children.

Instead, she simply says, "You should do it, Meredith. You should go *now*." She looks into my eyes with her trademark confident, clear-eyed stare.

My heart skips a beat. "Really?"

"Yes. Really." She nods again, her bob in full motion.

"And do what, exactly?" I say, wanting to be clear about the permission slip she's signing for me.

"Take a vacation. Maybe even a short leave of absence, as Nolan suggested. Go to New York. Alone."

I shake my head. "They'll never let me take a leave, especially now that I'm on this big case. . . ."

"Yes, they will," she says. "Especially if you tell them you need the time for your health."

"You mean imply I have cancer or something?" I look at her, appalled.

"No, I'm talking about your *mental* health. Which can be just as critical."

I sigh, considering the implications. "If I admit to some mental problem, then I'll *never* make partner. Even if I go back to full-time."

"First of all, they legally can't hold that against you. Second of all, I didn't realize that making partner was your dream?" she says, calling my bluff because she knows that making partner has never been something I cared much about. I mean, it would be a satisfying accomplishment; it would translate to more money; and it would make my parents very, *very* proud. But basically, I'm perfectly fine as a senior associate.

"It's not my *dream*," I say. "You know that."

"Well, then? What's your next excuse?"

I stare at her, my heart now racing. It was one thing when Nolan told me to go to New York. And even Ellen. It's another thing altogether hearing it from Amy. "I guess I don't have one," I say.

"Okay, then. Tell your firm you need some time off. They'll put someone else on this case. You're replaceable."

"What if I'm so replaceable that they fire me?"

She shakes her head, adamant. "They wouldn't do that . . . especially not if you cite your health. . . . But who knows? Maybe you'll quit when you get home."

"Maybe," I say, wondering why I haven't already. Was it nerve that I lacked? Or simply a viable alternative?

"There's really no downside here," Amy says. "So go home and book your flight, pack your bags, and head to New York City for a week or three. . . ."

"*Three* weeks?" I say, her advice suddenly sounding so rash and extreme that I fleetingly question *everything* she's telling me. "That's out of the question. I could never be gone from Harper for longer than a week. . . . Besides, wouldn't that constitute *abandonment*?"

Amy shakes her head. "Absolutely not. A few weeks away does not an abandonment make . . . and after all—it was *Nolan's* idea. Your *husband* made you the very kind offer to take some time to think—"

I interrupt her, shaking my head. "I wouldn't call it 'kind.' I'd call it passive-aggressive. I actually don't think that he thinks I'll do it."

"All the more reason," she says.

"How do you figure?"

"Because this is just another sign that you aren't on the same page. He's challenging you, your love for your family, maybe even your mothering."

"Okay . . . so doesn't going to New York simply prove to him that I'm somehow inadequate?"

"Do you *feel* inadequate?" Amy asks.

I consider the question carefully, then say, "Sometimes. Yes."

"Because you need some time to yourself?"

"Well, yeah," I say, biting my lip. "Because I want to be alone. Among other reasons."

Amy pushes her hair behind one ear, then the other, and says my name calmly, reassuringly. "Meredith, all mothers occasionally fantasize about an escape. Taking some time off. You, however, are in the unique position to actually *take* that time. You have financial security . . . and a husband who has given you his permission, albeit passive-aggressive permission. So go. Think. Decide what it is *you* want and need. Maybe it's a divorce. Maybe it's a new career. Maybe it's nothing more than a little time to yourself and a fresh perspective on things. Regardless, I do believe that you'll be an even better mother on the other end of some reflection."

I smile, grateful for the inclusion of the word *even*. I tell myself that I *am* a pretty good mother, otherwise I might have been long gone by now.

"If you end up happier . . . this could really be a gift to Harper in the long run."

"Maybe," I say, frowning as I picture my daughter's face peering at me in her darkened bedroom, telling me that she needs another story, a drink of water, or simply a "mommy cuddle." She can't even fall *asleep* in her own bed if I'm not sitting in the rocking chair beside her. How will she ever be okay for a week or more without me? I suddenly shift gears, fast-forwarding years from now, picturing Harper as a young woman sitting in an office like this one while she discusses her deep-seated issues. How they all stem from the time her mother left her when she was only four.

I hear Amy say my name.

I look at her. "Hmm?"

"What are you thinking?" she asks.

"I don't know," I say, shaking my head. "I just don't know if I can do this. . . ."

"Yes, you can," she says.

I take a deep breath, then exhale as Amy reassures me that Harper will be fine. "She'll be with her father and grandparents and aunt, in competent, loving hands."

"I wouldn't call my sister particularly competent," I say, but feel my first real urge to talk to her since our fight, if only for Harper's sake.

"Harper will be fine," Amy says again. "And *you*, Meredith, need to find a way to be fine, too."

THE NEXT MORNING, I wake up and decide to go for it. Take Nolan's dare, Ellen's offer, Amy's advice, and most important, follow my own gut. I take a shower, put on my best black suit and heels, and get to the firm early, even before the most dogged associates with no children or personal lives. I head straight for my office and promptly begin to take inventory of my cases, realizing, with some mixed feelings, that Amy is right—I am indispensable on absolutely nothing. A very small, insignificant, albeit overworked cog.

About an hour later, I work up the nerve to send an email to our managing partner, Mike Molo, requesting a short meeting with him. I am pretty sure Molo has no clue who I am, our only real interaction occurring on the elevator when he asks me to push the button for floor sixteen, one above mine. So I'm flabbergasted when I spot him in the hallway outside my office, reading my name plate, an expandable Redweld file in one hand, a Starbucks Venti in the other. After confirming that he has the correct utterly replaceable associate, he takes a sideways step, now filling my doorway, and says, "Good morning, Meredith."

"Good morning, Mike," I say, my heart pounding as I stand to meet his gaze.

"You wanted to talk about something?" he asks, his voice as imposing as his frame.

"Yes. . . . Yes, I do . . . but I would have . . . come to you," I stammer.

"It's okay. I was in the neighborhood. Why don't we have a seat?" he says, pointing to my desk chair.

I sit back down as he walks the rest of the way into my office, glances around the crammed quarters, then eases himself into the chair across from my desk.

"So what's up?" he asks, taking a long sip of coffee, as if we're old pals, or at least equals.

I take a deep breath, then give him my rehearsed opener. "Well, first of all, I'd like to say that I've been working at this firm for more than seven years . . . and that I've had mostly excellent reviews. . . . And I have met or exceeded my billable requirements every year, both as a full-time associate, and after my daughter was born, as a part-time associate."

"Yes. You have an excellent reputation. Thank you for your fine work and commitment." He nods, looking serious, but I detect a sparkle of something in his eyes, like he knows what's coming and is somehow amused by it. "So what are you working on these days?" he asks.

"The Lambert case," I say, trying, likely unsuccessfully, to hide my distaste. "Pretty much exclusively."

He whistles, then winces. "Ohh. Sorry to hear that. Goldman's a real charmer, isn't he?"

"Yes," I say, giving him a genuine smile. "He is, indeed."

Molo grins, then says, "So is that what you wanted to talk to me about? Goldman?"

"Oh, no. Not exactly. Actually, not at all . . ." I babble. "I just wanted to talk about work in *general. . . .*"

"Okay. Let's cut to the chase. Are you resigning? Or just requesting a leave of absence?" He takes his last sip of coffee, then aims the cup toward my wastebasket, a full four or five feet away. He makes the shot, then says, "Because I would really recommend the latter."

Stunned, I say, "Yes, sir. The latter. I would love the latter."

"How long do you want?" he asks.

"Two weeks? Maybe three?"

He raises his brows and says, "You sure that's all?"

"Three would be amazing."

Molo nods, then says, "How about a month?"

My smile turns into a grin. "Thank you so much. A month would be amazing."

"Fabulous. Enjoy," he says, glancing at his watch, then abruptly standing. "Just tell Goldman and HR I signed off on this. See you in a month. I hope you come back. But Godspeed either way."

Then, before I can thank him, let alone process the magnitude of the gift he's just bestowed upon me, my boss's boss winks and walks out the door.

chapter twenty-one

JOSIE

The Wednesday morning following my first appointment with Susan Lazarus, and three days before I turn thirty-eight, Gabe walks into the kitchen with an extreme case of bed head.

"Nice hair," I say.

He runs his hand through it and thanks me.

"Why are you up?" I ask, glancing at the clock on the microwave. It's only six-forty, about five minutes before I have to walk out the door, but a good hour before Gabe normally hits his snooze button for the *first* time.

"I wanted to catch you before you left," he says, yawning as he opens the refrigerator. He pulls out a jug of grapefruit juice, gives it a shake, then pours some into a glass. "Your birthday's coming up."

"I thought you forgot," I say.

"I did until this morning," he confesses without a trace of remorse. "Why didn't you remind me like you usually do?"

I put my peanut-butter toast down on a paper towel, wipe my fingers on the edge of it, and say, "I'm trying to be less self-involved as I approach motherhood."

"And how's that going for you?" he asks, rubbing his eyes.

"It's not easy," I say. "I was starting to feel like Samantha Baker."

"Who?" he asks, which surprises me; normally he nails movie trivia.

"C'mon. Molly Ringwald? *Sixteen Candles*? Remember how everyone forgot her birthday?"

"Facebook wouldn't let that happen to you."

"You're not on Facebook."

"But I'm sure Pete is." He gives me a coy look, clearly testing me.

"Good point," I say.

"So do you have plans with him?"

"No. I don't have any plans," I say, making a big show of taking my folic-acid-filled vitamin with a long swallow of now-room-temperature green tea.

"Well, what do you wanna do?" he asks.

I think for a second and say, "I want to go out and get really drunk."

"Spoken like a mother."

"It'll be my last hurrah. Hopefully my last birthday without a child . . . Will you make a reservation somewhere fun?"

"Can't Sydney handle that?"

"Gabe," I whine. "She's not my best friend. *You* are."

"Fine," he says with a sigh. "But can I get some guidance? Where do you want to go and who do you want to invite?"

"I'm sure you'll make the right decisions," I say. Then, in case that's not enough pressure, I add, "You're the one person who *never* lets me down."

"Okay," he says. "Just send me Donor Boy's number. I assume you want him there?"

"Sure," I say. "That'd be great."

"How's his sperm count doing, anyway?"

"Well, let's see. He switched from briefs to boxers. He gave up cycling. And he's avoiding the sauna and hot tub. The boys function best at ninety-four to ninety-six degrees," I say, gathering up my things.

"Tell me you're kidding."

I *am* kidding, but I give him a shrug, enjoying the rare role reversal. Usually I'm the gullible, confused one. Gabe mumbles something under his breath about me being insane as I head out the door, feeling inexplicably triumphant.

ODDLY ENOUGH, DR. Lazarus leaves me a message later that morning, saying that she got my test results and would like for me to call her back at my convenience. I listen to it twice, and although her voice is perfectly neutral, my heart fills with dread and despair. I feel certain that she's going to give me disastrous news, and can barely keep it together during my ensuing science lesson on the differences between solids, liquids, and gases. The second the school day ends, I call her back, launching right in with "Just give it to me straight. I can't have a baby, can I? I need to start looking into adoption?"

She pauses for a few horrifying seconds, then laughs and says, "Not at all, Josie. It's not that dire. . . ."

"Not *that* dire?" I say.

"It's not dire at *all*."

I blink back tears of relief as she calmly continues. "You're fine. Just *fine*. And very healthy."

"So I *can* have a baby?"

"Yes. You should be able to have a baby . . . but your ovarian reserve result, which measures the quantity and quality of your eggs and is a major indicator of fertility, *is* a bit on the low side for your age."

"So . . . I'm more like forty than thirty-eight?"

"Something like that," she says, with what I can tell is a smile. "It's nothing to panic about . . . but at the same time, if this is something you're really certain about, I don't think you should wait for very long."

"Like, how long do I have?" I say.

"It's not that scientific," she says. "But if I were you? . . ."

"Yes?" I say, putting all my faith in her reply. "If you were in my shoes . . . what would you do?"

"I would start trying immediately," she says. "As soon as you make your donor decision."

"Okay," I tell her, instantly picturing Pete. "I will."

THAT NIGHT, JUST after I've given Gabe the update on my ovarian reserve, Pete calls to chat. Although we've been talking on the phone fairly regularly, there's still a little nervous energy when we do. Both of us are working to be witty, as is often the case with new friends, regardless of gender and whether one is considering donating his sperm to the other. About ten minutes into our conversation, he mentions that Gabe called him about going out on Saturday night.

"Oh, yeah . . . I know it's last minute. But thirty-eight isn't a birthday to get too excited about. . . ." I say, thinking that that's especially true when your eggs are more like forty. "No worries if you have plans . . ." I try to sound more nonchalant than I feel.

"I'm in," he quickly says.

I smile and tell him good, I'm glad to hear it.

"I've been thinking about what to get you," he says.

"Oh, you don't have to get me anything. Your presence is present enough," I joke. Incidentally, Meredith actually included that line on Harper's last birthday invitation—which I thought was a little bit pretentious. I mean, *puh-lease,* just let people get your kid a twenty-dollar gift, already.

"Oh, is it?" Pete asks.

"That . . . and your sperm," I add with a laugh.

"Just tell me when and where to make the deposit," he says.

I know it's only banter, but I seize the opportunity to tell him about my doctor's appointment last week. "They call it prenatal consultation," I say. "It was interesting. I really, really liked the doctor—Susan Lazarus. She was very nice, very smart. Gabe liked her, too, and he's harder to please. . . ." I bite my lip to halt the babbling, deciding not to tell him about my test results.

"Cool. So are you thinking of using Gabe now?" Pete asks. "For your donor?"

"Oh, *God*, no. Not at all. Never. He just went for moral support." I take a deep breath, then add, "I told Dr. Lazarus about *you,* actually."

"Oh, you did, did you?" he says, sounding flattered.

"Yeah. I told her that I had an excellent prospect. . . ." My voice trails off, as I wonder how I'm ever going to take this conversation to the next level.

"And?" he asks.

"And . . . she . . . listened," I say with a nervous laugh. "So would you want to meet her?"

"Sure," he says, without a second of hesitation. "When?"

"At my next appointment?" I say, now sweating. I pick up the brochure that Dr. Lazarus gave me and start fanning myself with it.

"Sure," he says again. "So would it be like a preliminary interview? Or more like a look-at-porn-and-ejaculate-into-a-vial kind of deal?"

"C'mon!" I say, pretending to be offended. "That's disgusting."

"Sorry. But isn't that how it works?"

"I guess," I say. "But can I make one request?"

"Go ahead. Though something tells me that it won't be your last."

"I really don't want to know if porn is part of my journey to motherhood," I say, laughing.

"Fair enough," he says. "I'll light some candles and bring some roses and think romantic thoughts instead."

I smile and tell him that's a much better visual. "Thank you."

"No problem," he says. "Oh, and Josie?"

"Yeah?"

"You're welcome to join me. . . ." he says jokingly.

"Ha-ha," I say, pretending that my heart didn't just skip a beat.

ON SATURDAY MORNING, my actual birthday, I wake up in a good mood and feel even happier when Gabe comes into my room and informs me that we have a reservation at The Optimist at eight.

"Perfect!" I say, as I start to make my bed. "Who all's coming?"

Gabe gives me a cagey look and says, "I thought you wanted to be surprised?"

"I never said that. I said I wanted you to *handle* the details," I say.

"Well, I *did* handle them."

"And?"

He sits backward on my desk chair, Fonzie-style, and says, "It's me, you, Leslie, Sydney, Meredith, Shawna, and Donor Boy."

"Interesting," I say, freezing in mid–pillow fluff.

"Okay," Gabe says with a sigh. "What's your beef?"

I have several beefs, Leslie among them, but simply say, "*Meredith's* coming?"

"Yeah. She texted me yesterday and asked," he says. "I had to include her."

"What about Nolan?"

Gabe shakes his head and says he can't make it.

"Why not?" I ask, feeling disappointed that he can't be their family representative and also a little worried that he might be mad at me, too—that my sister managed to rile him up and somehow turn him against me. I remind myself that this hasn't happened to date, so I'm probably okay now.

"Meredith didn't say," Gabe replies.

"What about Stacey, Kendra, and Leigh?" I ask, referring to my three closest college friends, none of whom Gabe particularly likes. "Did you invite them?"

He pauses, then confesses. "You left it up to me, so I *might* have exercised a little bit of discretion. . . ."

I cross my arms and whine his name.

Gabe isn't having it. "Look. Do you have any idea how hard it is to get a table for seven people at The Optimist on three days' notice? Can you just focus on the positive here?"

"It's not so hard when you've had relations with the head bartender," I say.

Gabe gives me a sheepish look. "That was a long time ago."

"That you had sex with her or that she sent you a naked selfie?" I ask, remembering how I accidentally glimpsed a rather spectacular full-frontal nude of her on his phone.

"Both," he says, cracking his knuckles.

"But that *is* how you scored a last-minute reservation," I say. "Isn't it?"

He smirks. "Maybe."

I roll my eyes and ask if Leslie knows about her.

"Yes, Leslie knows I'm friends with a bartender at The Optimist."

"No, Gabe. *We* are friends. *That* was something else altogether. But whatever," I say, then switch gears. "So Shawna's coming?"

"Yup. Meredith's idea. She gave me her number."

"Huh," I say, a little surprised. Even though Shawna and I both made an effort to repair our friendship after Daniel died, it has been several years since she joined one of my birthday outings.

"When's the last time you talked to her?" he asks.

"It's been a few months . . . and I don't think I've seen her since Oliver was born."

"I figured it had been a while. . . . She asked if you were seeing anyone."

"What did you tell her?"

"I told her no. . . ."

"Did you tell her anything about Pete?"

"No," he says. "How do you plan on introducing everyone to him, anyway?"

"Like this," I say, pausing for dramatic effect. "Pete, meet Meredith, Sydney, and Shawna. Ladies, meet my sperm donor."

Gabe shakes his head, muttering that I have serious issues, as he stands and walks toward the doorway.

I clear my throat and say, "Um? Did you forget something?"

"Oh, yeah," he says, glancing over his shoulder. "Happy birthday, *Samantha*."

"Thanks, Duckie," I say with a grin.

"Duckie's in *Pretty in Pink*," he says, stepping into the hallway, then turning toward the stairs. "Get your Brat Pack flicks straight."

"Well, then, thanks, *Long* Duk *Dong*!" I shout after him.

THAT EVENING, GABE and I take an Uber to The Optimist well ahead of our reservation. We sit at the bar, eating oysters and drinking champagne, as we wait for the others to arrive, getting progressively more buzzed. Leslie shows up first, upstaging me in a clingy black dress with a plunging neckline, which with her flat chest creates a kind of Kate Moss effect. I chalk the wardrobe choice up to jealousy over the bartender, and tell myself to give her a chance, as Gabe stands, kisses her cheek, and offers his stool. She refuses it, saying she's fine standing, then turns to wish me a happy birthday. "Have you had a good day?" she asks, giving me a hesitant hug.

I nod and say I have, that I went shopping, then got a manicure. I hold up my fire-engine-red nails, which she promptly compliments, although she doesn't seem like the red-nail type. She puts her clutch on the bar, covertly but furtively glancing behind it.

"Don't worry," I say with a smile. "The ho's off tonight."

To Leslie's credit, she doesn't play dumb, but laughs and says, "Oh, good!"

"Besides, you're way prettier," I say—which is actually true.

"You totally are," Gabe says, nodding earnestly.

Leslie laughs again and says, "You have to say that."

"No," I say, shaking my head. "Gabe's painfully honest."

"And that's a *bad* thing?" he asks.

I ignore his question and look at Leslie. "Just don't ever ask him if something makes you look fat. Not that you could ever look fat. But still."

"Hold the phone, birthday girl. I have *never* told you you look fat. Not one time," Gabe says, then shifts his gaze to Leslie. "She's always asking whether I can tell she's gained weight. . . . Sometimes I can't. Sometimes I can. But I've never called her fat."

"All right. Fair enough," I acquiesce, as Leslie gushes about how refreshing it is to be with an honest man. I nod in agreement, deciding that they really are a pretty cute couple, though they could almost pass for brother and sister.

"You two look sort of related," I blurt out.

Gabe shrugs, throws his arm around Leslie, and says, "Yeah. Well, what's sexier than dating yourself?"

The bartender comes by and I order an Old Salty Dog, a vodka and grapefruit cocktail. I warn Leslie that they go down like water, as she orders one, too.

By the time Sydney, Shawna, and Pete walk in, pretty much all at the same time, I can hear myself starting to slur my words a tiny bit as I make the requisite introductions. A moment later, just after Gabe hands me his glass of water and discreetly suggests that I "slow down," the hostess finds us at the bar and leads us to our table. I slide into the middle of the banquette. Sydney and Pete end up on either side of me; Gabe, Leslie, and Shawna across from us—

which leaves the awkward seventh chair on the end for Meredith, should she ever decide to show.

"So happy you all came tonight!" I announce, overcome with a warm feeling of affection for everyone at the table. I tack on a special postscript for Shawna. "Thanks for making the effort . . . I know it's hard when you have a baby . . . and I *really* appreciate it. Please thank Lars for me, too," I say, knowing that her husband is home with their son.

"It's our pleasure," she says, reaching across the table for my hand. She gives it a little squeeze, followed by a smile that reminds me of the way things used to be between us—like she's about to share a very juicy tidbit of gossip. Instead, she turns her gaze to Pete, staring at him through funky dark-rimmed glasses.

"So, how did you and Josie meet?" she asks. "Are you a teacher, too?"

Pete shoots me a fleeting glance, clearly looking for guidance, but when I provide him none, he simply says, "Um, no. I'm a physical therapist, actually."

"Oh," she says, nodding enthusiastically. "Do you have a specialty?"

"Sports and orthopedics," he says.

"He works with a few Braves players," I brag.

She looks impressed as he modestly adds, "*Ex*-Braves."

As we all begin to peruse our menus, I decide to blurt out my news. "So Pete's also going to be my sperm donor," I announce.

Sydney claps and lets out a jubilant yelp. Gabe rolls his eyes and shakes his head. And Shawna, after a glance at Pete confirming that I'm not joking, begins to fire questions at me. Pete and I answer together, as he repeats what he's said more than once. That he wants to help me—and do something good with his life. That he thinks he has pretty good genes. That he would love to have a relationship of some kind with my kid—but that he will respect my decision regarding his involvement. Shawna listens intently, without a visible trace of judgment or condescension, although at one point, as she murmurs how "absolutely fantastic" it all is, I wonder if she might be overcompensating a little. At the very least, I bet she's relieved that she's not in my shoes. Regardless, I appreciate her supportive reaction, and tell her as much, openly contrasting it to Meredith's. As Gabe chimes in, Sydney jabs me with her elbow and announces, "Shh. She's coming."

Sure enough, I look up and see my sister marching toward the table, wearing a big scowl and the most boring outfit imaginable—dark jeans, a plain black tank, and her standard Manolo pumps, which would be okay except she gets them in a too-short-heel height (the only thing worse, the dreaded kitten heel). Her only accessories are stud earrings, her wedding ring, and a watch. *Yawn.*

"Sorry I'm late," she says when she gets to the table. She hands me a gift bag stuffed with tissue paper and says happy birthday. She then crouches slightly to give me a stiff, awkward hug, patting my shoulders twice.

"Thanks," I say, taking the bag, then pointing to her chair. "You're over there."

She takes a step in that direction, then stops, looks at Pete, and introduces herself. "I'm Meredith. Josie's sister," she says, formally extending her hand.

"Hi, I'm Pete," he says, shaking it.

"Hi, Pete. I think I heard about your heroic efforts at Bistro Niko." She takes her seat, looking pleased with herself for having this nugget of information, probably because she knows I'm wondering how she heard it.

Pete laughs modestly and says he'd hardly call a "slap on the back *heroic.*"

"Certainly not like donating sperm." Sydney tees me up with a big grin, practically rubbing her hands together.

"Oh, yes . . . I was just telling Shawna that Pete plans to donate his sperm to me," I say, looking straight at Meredith.

My sister slides her chair in closer to the table and flashes a prim smile, her hands folded in her lap. "Yes, Mom told me about your donor. I didn't realize you were the same Pete," she says breezily, then looks up at our waiter, who has returned to take our drink orders, and asks for a Coke Zero.

"You don't want a glass of wine?" I ask, not trying to hide my annoyance.

She shakes her head and says, "Unfortunately, no. I'm not drinking tonight. We have early church tomorrow. Harper's singing in the cherub choir."

Of course any announcement containing the words *church* and *cherub* when you're out to dinner has a fun-sponging effect, and I'm forced to go in the opposite direction, instructing our waiter that we'd love to kick things off with a round of tequila shots.

He smiles, nods, and glances around the table. "So, seven shots?"

"No. Six," Meredith quickly corrects him.

"No. *Seven*," I say. "I'll take hers."

DESPITE MEREDITH'S BEST buzz-kill efforts, my birthday dinner is a blast. I can tell Shawna and Sydney both *really* like Pete, and even Gabe seems to put aside our reproductive controversy for the evening. He is loose and happy, cracking jokes and telling stories, which is not his usual style. At one point, Sydney makes this observation, and jokingly asks Gabe if Leslie deserves the credit for his "improved mood."

He nods with a little smile and says, "Yeah. Maybe so."

"*Totally* so," I say, deciding to throw Leslie a bone. I turn to her and add, "You're good for him."

She smiles, reaches for his hand, and says, "You think so?"

"Yes," I say. "But here's the real test. Can you get him to go to Johnny's Hideaway tonight?"

Sydney laughs, knowing of my secret agenda to end up at one of my favorite, and Gabe's *least* favorite, venues in town.

"*Hellll*, no," he says. "No fuckin' way."

"Who's Johnny?" Pete asks.

"You don't know Johnny's Hideaway?" I say. "And you've lived in Atlanta for how long?"

"Four years," he says. "And no. Never heard of it."

"Me neither," Leslie says.

"You're missing absolutely nothing," Gabe informs them.

"Is it a bar?" Pete asks.

"It's a nightclub," I say. "And an Atlanta *institution*."

"Please," Gabe says. "It's a creepy midlife-crisis meat market where you go to listen to ABBA and Neil Diamond."

"I like Neil Diamond," Pete says.

I flash Gabe a jubilant smile as he shakes his head at Pete. "You might like Neil Diamond when you're driving around in your car . . . but a bar full of cougars belting out 'Sweet Caroline' while dirty old men look on with cigars under a disco ball? Not a pretty sight."

Pete laughs and says, "That sounds like fun, actually."

Gabe looks at him for a beat, then turns to me and asks in his dry monotone, "And you still want to use his sperm?"

Everyone laughs, except Meredith, who has already asked our waiter for the bill and is glancing impatiently in his direction.

"It's *very* fun," I say. "In a disco throwback-to-the-seventies kind of way."

"Half the people in there *are* seventy," Gabe says. "And one hundred percent of them are cheesy."

"Not true," I say, insisting that it's become a mixed crowd, trendy and cheesy living in harmony.

Meredith pulls her AmEx out of her wallet as she announces, "I'm with Gabe. Johnny's Hideaway is vile."

Gabe snaps and points at her and says, "Finally. We agree on something."

"Well, you two can just head on home. Syd and I are going to Johnny's," I say, then ask Shawna, Leslie, and Pete if they want to join us.

"Yep. I'm in," Shawna says, without hesitating, reminding me of what I used to love so much about her.

"Me, too," Pete says. "I wanna see this place."

I smile, then turn to Leslie, expecting her to decline. Instead she nods, then bursts into the first lines of "Sweet Caroline." Syd and I continue in unison.

"Oh, good grief," Gabe says.

"C'mon. Please come?" I beg him. "For me?"

"Nope. I don't do Johnny's," Gabe announces in the same tone that someone might say *I don't do drugs*. Then he turns to Pete and says, "My man, you're on your own tonight."

JUST BEFORE MIDNIGHT, Shawna, Sydney, Leslie, Pete, and I join the line outside Johnny's—which is housed in a nondescript building at the end of a retail strip on Roswell Road. In front of us is a loud, cackling pack of fifty-something women all wearing tight animal prints. After Sydney strikes up a conversation with them, we discover that they are attending a cougar-themed bachelorette party. The bride's sash announces that this will be her LAST NIGHT ON THE PROWL.

"When's the big day?" I ask her.

"Next Saturday," she replies, adjusting her headband, which is actually a leopard-print thong. "Here's hoping third time's the charm!"

We all laugh and wish her good luck, then pay the suit-clad

doorman our five-dollar cover, making our way into the dimly lit, black and red lounge, pulsing to the rhythm of "Little Red Corvette." A large disco ball spins, casting glittering light onto the parquet dance floor.

"Wow. This place is awesome," Pete says, glancing at the walls, adorned with photos of celebrities from Frank Sinatra to Arnold Palmer to Britney Spears to George Clooney (who apparently came by the club one night, as he is posing with our same doorman).

"Told you," I proudly reply.

Leslie, his fellow Johnny's virgin, nods in agreement, murmuring that Gabe's really missing out, as I tell her for about the third time how impressed I am that she came without him. "It's just so cool of you," I gush, then admit that I like her more now than I thought I did at first—the sort of confessionary thing you blurt out when you're drinking.

"Well, thanks," she says. "Gabe told me how important you are to him . . . so . . ."

"Ah, so you're just being strategic? Like the way to a man's heart is through his stomach. But for Gabe, it's Josie?" Sydney asks her.

Leslie laughs and says, "Honestly, I just wanted to see this place."

"Is it everything you hoped it would be?" I say.

"And more," she says as we sail through a cloud of cigar smoke and sidle up to the bar lined with red upholstered swivel chairs.

"What do you girls want?" Pete asks, pushing a credit card across the bar. "Should we go with a retro cocktail? Harvey Wallbangers? Manhattans? Tequila sunrises?"

I say, "You know what? I'll take a whiskey sour."

Shawna makes a face and says, "I forgot how we used to drink those! Make it two."

Syd and Leslie say they'll stick with red wine—and Pete orders a

Miller Lite, starting a tab despite Shawna's insistence that he's only getting the first round. Moments later, drinks in hand, we squeeze onto the packed but demographically diverse dance floor—from hot sorority girls to Virginia Slims–smoking divorcées to businessmen in crumpled suits. As the DJ spins hits from the fifties through the nineties, we dance in a sweaty cluster, occasionally merging with gyrating strangers or posing for provocative group selfies. At one point, my left breast even makes an accidental cameo.

A few rounds later, as Pete and I pair off and slow-dance to Poison's "Every Rose Has Its Thorn," I feel a surge of happiness. Although I recognize that it's probably just an alcohol-and-eighties-music-induced euphoria, I wonder if it might be a little more than that. If maybe it might actually have something to do with *Pete*.

"I'm so happy we met," I say, smiling up at him, my arms around his waist.

"Me, too," he says, grinning back at me. "No matter what happens with us."

"Meaning what?" I ask. "Are you backing out . . . ?"

"Nope," he says, expertly dipping me. "I just meant regardless of what happens *tonight*."

I laugh and say, "Wait. Are you hitting on me?"

"Uh-huh. I think I am," Pete says, putting his hand on my ass. "But at Johnny's, it's called making a pass. . . . Can you dig it?"

"Oh, I can dig it," I say, racking my brain for seventies slang. "You're such a Casanova."

He gives me his cheesiest wink, then does a groovy spinning dance move. "Don't you know it, girl."

I beam up at him, then say, "You know what?"

"What's that?"

"I was just thinking that you're hot. Really hot . . . but it's probably just the booze talkin'."

"A drunk mind speaks a sober heart, baby," he says, pulling me closer.

"Actually," I say. "I don't think it's the booze. I think it's that your buzz cut is finally growing out."

"*Jerk,*" he says, pretending to be offended.

"A drunk mind speaks a sober heart," I remind him, staring at the cleft in his chin. "But seriously. You really do look good tonight."

"Good enough to kiss me?" he asks as the DJ starts playing "Jessie's Girl," one of my all-time favorites.

"Maybe," I say, giving him a coy smile.

"Well?" he says. "What's it gonna be?"

As Springfield bursts into his refrain, I decide to go for it. I stand on my tiptoes, lean up, and kiss him for just long enough to know that I like it.

"Wow," he says, as we separate, his eyes still closed. "That was pretty nice."

"*Pretty* nice?" I say.

"*Very* nice," he says, then leans down and kisses me again. Our lips part.

"Get a room!" I hear Shawna shouting behind us, bringing back college memories.

I pull away from Pete, quickly wipe my mouth with the back of my hand, and say to Shawna, "You didn't see that."

"Did, too," she says, then points at Leslie and Syd. "And so did they."

"It was nothing," I announce to the group. "Just a little birthday kiss. Right, Pete?"

Pete nods in earnest agreement. "Yep. That's all it was."

I stare at him, wondering if he's bluffing or telling the truth. I decide it's likely the latter, feeling a dash of disappointment. After all, it's very difficult to let go of the lifelong dream of finding love—and at the very least it would be nice to feel wanted. But then I remind myself of the greater picture, a bigger dream. I tell myself not to let one stupid kiss muddy the waters. That one day, it will just be a cute story to share with my daughter—or son—about my thirty-eighth birthday. How one night, shortly before my insemination, I kissed her biological father on the dance floor of Johnny's Hideaway.

ABOUT AN HOUR later, after we shut the place down (no easy feat), and Sydney drops me off in her Uber car, I walk in the house, ravenously hungry, heading straight for the kitchen. As I open the refrigerator, scouring for leftovers, I hear footsteps behind me and jump, dropping a Chinese take-out box that spills all over the floor.

"Hey," I hear Gabe say.

"Jesus, you scared me," I say, bending down to pick up the container and a big clump of white rice. "What are you doing creeping around like that?"

"Um. I live here?" Gabe says.

"Well, still," I say, kicking off my heels, knowing that my feet aren't going to recover for days. "What are you doing up?"

"I can't sleep."

"Are you hungry?"

"No."

"Well, I'm fuckin' starving," I say, swearing more than usual, as I always do after a few drinks. "Do we have anything other than rice?"

"There should be some beef and broccoli in there, too," he says.

I look again and spot another white container behind Gabe's carton of whole milk. "There it is," I say, grabbing it and putting it on the counter. Then I pull a fork out of the utensil drawer, deciding that it's not worth the effort to get a plate or put anything in the microwave. Instead, I dive straight in.

"Nasty," Gabe says under his breath, both because he never eats cold leftovers and because he thinks all food, even that which is consumed at three in the morning, should be put on a plate and eaten with a little civility. His words.

"Whatever," I say. "*You're* nasty."

"No, *you* are," he says. "And you smell like an ashtray."

He gives me a knowing look, leading his witness, as always. When I don't respond, he adds, "I heard you were smoking cigars tonight."

"Paul Jolly was there. You know—our old neighbor? I took, like, *one* puff of his cigar. Who's your informant?"

"I talked to Leslie."

"She called you *already*?" I say, thinking that she left only about twenty minutes before the rest of us.

"No. I called *her*."

"Failed attempt at a booty call, eh?" I say.

"I *never* fail at my booty calls," Gabe says, which is probably close to the truth.

"Well, then, why isn't she here?" I ask.

"Because I didn't invite her. I was just starting to worry about where *you* were. . . . I called you first. . . . Check your phone."

"It died. . . . I took a lot of videos. I caught Leslie in some hot girl-on-girl action," I say, thinking of the impressive grinding she and Sydney did to "Pour Some Sugar on Me." Granted, it was all initiated by Syd, but still.

"Yeah. Well, I hear you were caught in some girl-on-*boy* action," Gabe says. "Makin' out on the dance floor, huh?"

"Holy *fuck*, she's a snitch," I say, taking another bite of beef.

"Oh, so you wanted to keep it a secret from me?"

"No, it's not a secret," I say, with my mouth still full. "But she's exaggerating."

"Right," he says, folding his arms across his chest. "You know what, Josie? . . . Johnny's Hideaway is bad. But *making out* at Johnny's Hideaway is on a whole other level."

"I did *not* make *out* at Johnny's," I say, scraping up the last bite.

His arms still crossed, he cocks his head to the side. "So you didn't kiss Pete tonight?"

"Yeah, I kissed him," I say, rolling my eyes. "But that's a far cry from making out."

Gabe gives me a disapproving stare.

"What? Don't give me that look," I say, then add, "You know . . . if I didn't know any better, I'd think you were jealous."

It is the sort of thing I would never say sober, which begs the question—is it really what I deep down think?

"Jealous of *what*?" Gabe retorts. "I mean, if you want to choose his mediocre sperm, go right ahead. But I'm ninety-nine percent sure you'll be sorry."

"Mediocre sperm!" I laugh. "Wow. You *are* jealous. That's really cute."

"I'm not *jealous*," he says. "I just think it's a *really* bad idea to be making out with your sperm donor. If you want to date him, date him, but then put this project on hold."

"I don't want to date him. I just want a baby—and some sperm."

"Okay. Well, then, frankly speaking . . . I think you could do better than Pete."

"That's mean," I say. "He's a really nice guy."

"I know. But in the world of sperm? He's your top pick? C'mon, Josie . . ."

"Well, who's better?" I say, grateful that I switched to water when I did, that I can at least hold my own in the debate. "The vegan runner? Gabe, c'mon, read that essay again. He sounds like a freak. Besides . . . I just don't like the idea of using a stranger. I'd rather go with a known quantity."

He stares at me, nodding, then uncrosses his arms and presses both palms onto the counter. "Okay, well, how about a *really* known quantity?"

I deposit the beef container into the trash and start in on the rice. He snatches it away from me and throws it in the trash, too.

"Hey!" I say.

"You told me to never let you eat white food late at night. I'm trying to be your friend here. . . . So. Back to the known quantity . . . What about using a close friend instead of some guy you just met on Match?"

I narrow my eyes, confused. "How close of a friend?" I ask. Surely he can't be suggesting what he seems to be suggesting.

"Like . . . I don't know . . . a best friend?" he says, averting his eyes, looking distinctly nervous.

"You're kidding, right?" I say with a laugh.

He meets my gaze and shakes his head, stone serious.

My heart flutters even more than it did on the dance floor when Pete and I kissed. "I thought you didn't like messy?" I say.

"I don't," he says. "I still think you should go with a complete stranger. But if you won't do that . . . you should go with someone you can trust. Someone who would always have your back. And your kid's back."

"You mean *you*?" I confirm.

"Yes. I mean *me*."

"And what would that make you?" I ask, my mind racing.

"What do you mean?" he asks.

"Would you be just the donor? Or, like . . . the father?"

He swallows, then says, "Well. Both, I guess."

"So more than a donor?"

"Yes," Gabe says. "More than a donor. More than you'd get with Pete. I'd be the dad, too."

"And what about us?" I ask, fleetingly wondering if he isn't about to reveal some sort of crush on me—like Andrew McCarthy in *St. Elmo's Fire.*

"What *about* us?" he asks.

"Well . . . you're not suggesting . . ." My voice trails off as I motion between us, but his face remains blank.

I finish my thought. "You're not suggesting that we have *sex*?" I say. "To get pregnant?"

"Oh. God, no," Gabe says, making a face. "Nothing like *that.* We'd still use this doctor lady. And we'd be totally status quo on the friendship front. . . ."

"Okay," I say, nodding. "But wouldn't that be weird?"

Gabe shrugs. "Maybe . . . but I don't know . . . I think it would be more like having Revis together."

"But Revis is a *dog*," I say.

"I know that."

"And besides, Revis is *mine*."

"C'mon, that's a technicality and you know it. Who walks him more? Who takes him out at night? Who paid that last monster vet bill when he ate that sock?"

"It was *your* sock," I say. "That you left out."

"C'mon, Josie. Whose bed does he sleep in if given the choice?"

"It's fifty-fifty," I insist.

"Bullshit. That dog loves me more, and you know it."

I start to protest, but Gabe is on a roll. "Bottom line, I love Revis as my own. I'd do anything for him. And I'd take him if anything ever happened to you."

"What if we got into a fight?" I say.

"We *do* get into fights."

I shake my head. "No, not like stupid arguments over leaving dirty dishes in the sink," I say. "A *real* fight."

"Don't be dumb," he says. "You know that wouldn't happen."

"It *could*."

"Okay. You're right. It could. And if it did, we'd be like other divorced couples who share custody. Only we were never married in the first place. We'd just be skipping that part."

I nod, though I'm having trouble believing what I'm hearing. "What does Leslie say about this?"

"I haven't discussed this with Leslie."

"You think she'd be okay with it?"

"I do, actually," he says, so quickly that it's clear he's given it thought. "I mean—here's the way I look at it. What if I already had a kid? Would she *not* date me?"

"I have no clue," I say. "I barely know her. Maybe she wouldn't."

"Well, if not, that would make her shallow. And I don't do shallow. So better to find out now."

"I don't necessarily agree with that," I say. "I'm not sure I'd want to be with a guy who is having a baby with another girl."

"Well, then *you're* shallow," he says with a smile. "And anyway, I really like Leslie . . . but she's not the deal breaker here."

"Are you sure?" I say. "I thought you might be falling in love."

"I might be," he says. "But that's irrelevant. If we did this— it would be *our* decision. You and me. Together."

I stare at him for a dizzying few seconds, trying to process everything. "So are you telling me that you actually *want* a baby?"

"No," he says. "I never said that. But I don't *not* want a baby. And I want *you* to have a baby if that's what you want."

"That's not very convincing," I say.

"I'm not trying to convince you," he says. "I'm just making an offer. Take it or leave it. . . ."

I give him a hug, welling up a little, whispering that this might be the nicest thing anyone's ever offered to do for me.

"Yeah, yeah," he says, pulling away with a big yawn. I notice that his eyes stay open, a telltale sign that it's a *fake* yawn, and that he's merely looking for a transition, uncomfortable with my display of emotion. Sure enough, he announces that he's going back to bed, then turns and abruptly walks out of the kitchen.

"Good night, Gabe," I call after him. "I fuckin' *love* you!"

"Love you, too, potty mouth," he mumbles on his way up the stairs.

chapter twenty-two

MEREDITH

The Friday after Josie's birthday, on the afternoon I'm supposed to fly to New York, Harper has a meltdown that has absolutely nothing to do with me leaving—or her earlier realization that I will be missing trick-or-treating on Monday, a source of considerable maternal guilt. Instead, in a case of life imitating art, she has seemingly lost her beloved stuffed animal, just like the little girl in *Knuffle Bunny,* Harper's favorite Mo Willems book.

"Where did you last see it?" Nolan asks her—a question that has always mystified me, and seems especially ridiculous when posed to a hysterical four-year-old.

"I. Want. Raaaaa-bby!" she sobs in response.

"I know, sweetie," I say, looking under the sofa, though I know he's too big to fit under it. "We'll find him. I promise."

Nolan clears his throat and says, "Um. We probably shouldn't make any promises. If you get my drift."

I look up at him, still on my knees, and my heart drops, considering that they just returned home from a father-daughter outing to Legoland.

"Nolan," I say slowly. "Are you trying to tell me something here?"

"Maybe?" he says, his voice rising in a question, looking panic-stricken.

"Please, please, for the love of God, tell me that Harper did not take Rabby to Legoland," I say, standing and looking directly into his eyes.

Nolan stares back at me, but he doesn't reply, as a wave of terror passes through me. I remind myself that I still have Harper, that there hasn't been a kidnapping, that we're talking about a stuffed animal, an inanimate object.

"I'm positive we had him in the car," Nolan says, looking *anything* but positive.

"How positive?" I say.

"One hundred percent positive," he says. "I remember seeing Rabby in the rearview mirror."

For one second I'm relieved. Then I say, "Wait. On the way there? Or on the way home?"

Nolan scratches his head and shrugs. "*That* . . . I'm not sure about," he says.

"Nolan!" I groan, pressing my hands to my forehead. "How many times have I told you not to let her take Rabby out of the house? You *know* it would be a disaster if he gets lost for good!"

"I didn't know she had him when we left," he says.

I take a deep breath, my mind racing. "Did you call Legoland?" I say, as Harper's sobs begin to ramp up.

"Of *course*," he says. "Multiple times. I've left two messages and also talked to some guy at the front desk."

"And?"

"Nobody's turned it in yet."

"So you *did* leave it there?"

"I don't know, Meredith," he says, then blurts out an irrelevant fact. "I took her there so you could pack in peace. . . ."

"So this is my fault?"

"I didn't say that. . . ."

I turn away from him and say, "Harper, honey. C'mere, baby."

"I want Raaaa-bbbyyy!" she wails, rubbing both fists into her eyes, her face coated with a mixture of snot and tears.

"I know, sweetie," I say. "Daddy and I are doing our best to find him."

She repeats that she wants Rabby, then adds that she misses Rabby very, very much.

"I know, baby," I say, my stomach in knots, as I glance at my watch.

"What time's your flight?" Nolan asks for at least the third time today.

"Seven," I say. "But obviously I'm not going now."

"Why not?" Nolan says.

I ask him if he's serious, and he replies that yes, he is serious. "You being here won't change anything," he adds.

I bite my lip, nod, and say, "That's *really* nice, Nolan. Thank you."

"I mean in terms of the *damn* rabbit," he says under his breath.

The phone rings before I can reply, and I make the mistake of glancing at caller ID and seeing Josie's name. Deciding it really can't get any worse, I answer the phone.

"Hi, Josie. We're kind of in the middle of a crisis here," I say before she can speak.

"What's wrong?" she asks.

"We can't find Rabby."

"Oh," she says, clearly thinking that we've simply misplaced Rabby, as opposed to leaving him at *freakin' Legoland.*

I walk out of Harper's earshot, cupping the receiver as I fill Josie in. "On top of that," I add, "I have a flight that leaves in a few hours. . . ."

"Where are you going?" she asks.

"To New York."

"For work?"

"No."

"For what, then?"

I hesitate, wondering why I don't have this answer more prepared, then say, "I just need to get away for a few days."

"A few days? So you'll miss Halloween?"

"Yes. But Harper's butterfly costume is ready to go . . . and besides, Nolan's always the one who takes her trick-or-treating. I just hand out candy. It's no big deal," I say, still trying to convince myself of this fact.

"Huh. Okay. . . . So are you going with Ellen?"

"No," I say. "I'm going alone . . . but I don't know if I can go at all now. . . ."

"Why? Because of Rabby?" she says.

"Correct," I say, glaring at Nolan. "Because of Rabby."

"Do you want me to come over?"

"Why?" I blurt out, instantly regretting it.

"Never mind," she says.

"I'm sorry," I say. "When I said 'why'—I just meant, are you coming to look for Rabby? Because I don't think we're going to find him. . . ."

"I just meant to come be with Harper. So you can go . . . while I distract her."

I hesitate, not because I don't desperately want to take her up on the offer, but because it's difficult to admit that we need her. That I need her. My concern for Harper trumps this, though, and I say, "That would be great, actually. . . ."

"Okay," she says briskly. "I'm almost home. I just need to let Revis out. . . . I can be there in forty-five minutes? Does that work?"

"Yes. Thank you," I say. "I'll let Nolan know."

"All right," she says. Then, after a long pause, she makes an even greater offer. "I can stay over tonight, too . . . if Nolan wants? I can be her Rabby substitute?"

I almost say that there is no substitute for Rabby, but Aunt Josie might be the lone exception to that. "Could you really do that?" I say, swallowing the rest of my pride. "That would be amazing. Thank you, Josie."

MY FLIGHT LANDS at La Guardia just after 10:00 P.M. I power on my phone as soon as we hit the runway, checking my texts, praying for good news on the Rabby front. Nothing, I discover. No word at all from Atlanta, other than a text from Ellen wishing me a good trip and telling me to call her if I have any questions about her apartment. I thank her, then send Josie and Nolan a joint text asking about Rabby. *Still MIA? How's Harper?*

Thirty minutes later, after I've retrieved my suitcase and joined a blessedly short cab line just outside of baggage claim, I have yet to receive a response from either of them. I assume the worst, but tell myself that there is nothing I can do. So I put my phone in my tote bag, close my eyes, and inhale the glorious scent of Queens—a mix of exhaust and garbage and falafels.

Suddenly, I'm overcome with exhaustion, and all I want to do is sleep. I remind myself that I can do just that. I can sleep *all* day tomorrow. I can sleep for the next week. For the first time since Harper's birth, I have absolutely no responsibilities, at least not in an hour-to-hour sense. Yet, as I get into my cab and give my driver Ellen's address on East Tenth Street, I realize it's not as simple as sleep or freedom, and as the billboards and buildings whiz by me, I feel about as lost as poor Rabby, wherever he may be.

chapter twenty-three

JOSIE

Meredith calls my cell the following morning while I'm still curled up with Harper in her twin bed.

"Did you find Rabby?" she demands before even saying hello.

"No," I whisper, rolling over toward the wall and keeping my voice low, though Harper could sleep through an air raid. "Not yet."

"*Shhit,*" Meredith sighs. "How's she doing?"

"She's fine. Still asleep. I'm here with her now. . . ."

"In her bed?"

"Yes."

"Did she kick you all night?"

I laugh and say it wasn't too bad.

"Where's Nolan?"

"I don't know. . . . I haven't gotten up yet."

There is a long pause before she says, "I texted you both last night. Did you not get the message?"

"Harper and I went to bed early," I say. "Nolan went out."

"Oh," she says, sounding surprised. "Where'd he go?"

"I don't know. I didn't ask. . . ." I hesitate, then ask as gently as I can, "Is everything okay with you and Nolan?"

"Yes," she says. "We're fine."

Her terse retort, combined with Nolan's rare moodiness last night, only adds to my suspicion that some sort of trouble is brewing. But I know how private and guarded Meredith is about her marriage—and that it's pointless to press her on something she doesn't want to talk about. So I change the subject. "I bet Rabby'll show up today. But just in case . . . I did go ahead and order another one."

"Another *Rabby*?" she asks.

I tell her yes, that I recalled the Jellycat tag, and after a quick Google image search, located the same beige bunny on Nordstrom's website. "I'm having it overnighted," I say.

"But she'll *totally* know the difference," Meredith says. "Remember how Mom tried to replace Bongo?"

I smile, thinking of the completely random name I gave our blue-and-yellow betta fish. "Yeah. That didn't fly."

"It sure didn't," she says. "And Harper's savvier than we were. . . ."

"I know," I say. "But I figured it was worth a try. I was thinking I could let Revis play with it for a few days . . . roll it in the mud . . . throw it in the dryer on a high setting. . . ."

"She'd still know," Meredith says with a sigh.

"Yeah. I guess you're right," I say, wishing she'd at least give me a little credit for the idea and effort. For the fact that I'm here in bed with her daughter. "So what are you up to today?"

"I'm not sure yet," she says. "What about you?"

I tell her I'm not sure, either, but that I planned to spend it with Harper. "If that's okay with you?"

"Of course it's okay," she says, her voice softening a little. "Thank you."

"You're welcome," I say. "And, Mere?"

"Yeah?"

I hesitate, searching for the right words. "Please let me know if you want to talk . . . about anything."

"Thank you," she says again. "I really appreciate that, Josie."

LATER THAT DAY, after Harper has broken down over Rabby about three times (fortunately never on the phone with Meredith), Nolan walks in the family room, where I'm folding laundry, and asks how I'd feel about visiting Daniel.

"You mean at the cemetery?"

It's a stupid question—where else would we visit Daniel?—but Nolan is gentle with his response. "Yes. . . . I was going to take Harper. . . . I'd love for you to come, too. Will you, please?"

I look at him, so surprised by the directness of his request that I find myself reluctantly nodding. "Okay," I say, my heart filling with dread.

A FEW HOURS later, despite my multiple attempts to divert us, Nolan, Harper, and I slow to a stop along the circular drive of Arlington Memorial Park. Our three car doors open, then close, in rapid succession, echoing in the serenity of the scenic cemetery. My stomach clenches as I steel myself against an onslaught of memories from December 26, 2001, the last time I was here. They come anyway, of course. The biting cold. The sensation of my heels sinking into the wet earth. The gaping red-clay hole in the ground. That solitary bluebird in the barren oak tree overlooking my brother's coffin.

We walk in silent single file toward Daniel's grave, Nolan leading the way, Harper between us. She is holding a bouquet of flowers. I have a lousy sense of direction, but I could find this spot without any assistance, that old oak giving me my bearings. Sure enough, I spot my brother's name, his headstone in the partial shade of the tree. A few leaves have fallen on his plot, and I watch Nolan brush them aside. Meanwhile, I stand awkwardly to one side, clueless about cemetery etiquette, but feeling certain that you're not supposed to stand directly over a grave.

The sun has been in and out all day, but the sky is overcast now, a slight chill in the air. I shiver, then zip my fleece up the whole way, hugging my arms across my chest before I force myself to look down at my brother's headstone. The flat gray granite marker bears his full name, the dates of his birth and his accident. Below that is the engraving of a cross and the words my mother came up with sitting in the kitchen with my dad and our pastor. *Beloved son, brother, friend.*

I remember thinking that the epitaph was too simple. That it left a lot of things out—*grandson, nephew, cousin, boyfriend,* to name a few. I very nearly pointed this out, in a burst of what felt like post-traumatic stress Tourette's, but managed to restrain myself. Instead, I went up to my room, where I pretty much remained until the funeral, out of everyone's way.

Nolan clears his throat now and says in a low, soothing voice, "Harper, honey, do you want to put the flowers down?" He points to the base of the headstone.

Looking over-the-top solemn, like a child actress in a funeral scene, she nods and kneels, slowly lowering the bouquet to the ground. A mix of carnations and roses, the Publix flowers look cheap, borderline garish, the green cellophane wrapper and flimsy rubber band not helping matters. If Meredith were with us, it would be different: the flowers would have been purchased at a fancy florist, and Harper would be wearing a dress, not a stained T-shirt. The biggest difference, though, is that I would not be here—the burden of her expectations too great for me to bear.

"Good job, sweetie," Nolan whispers, kneeling down beside her, then carefully angling the blossoms toward the stone. "Do you want to pray?"

Clearly accustomed to the drill, Harper presses her palms together, scrunches her eyes closed, and says, "God bless Uncle Daniel."

"God bless Uncle Daniel," Nolan echoes.

Although I often think of my brother's unborn children, I have never really considered the loss from my niece's perspective. I put it on my long mental list of things to feel sad about later. But for now, I do my best to stay as numb as possible.

Meanwhile, Nolan says the Lord's Prayer—which I find oddly formal or at least old-fashioned. I know I should say it along with him, but do not. I don't even close my eyes, which remarkably Harper does for the entire prayer, right down to his *Amen*. Then she says it, too, a long drawn out *Ahhh*-men.

Afterward, they both stand, and Harper wanders off, a carefree child again. Nolan's arm wraps me in a quick but tight, sideways embrace.

"Are you okay?"

Realizing that I've been holding my breath, I exhale and tell him yes, I'm fine.

"When's the last time you've been back here?" he asks, as I wonder if he knows the answer.

A breeze blows my hair into my eyes. I corral the strands behind my ear before confessing. "I haven't," I say.

"Not *ever*?"

"No. Not since the day he was buried," I say, feeling ashamed.

"Oh," he says, his lips remaining parted.

"You think that's awful, don't you?"

Finally closing his mouth, he shakes his head. "No," he says, though I'm not sure I believe him.

"I just don't think he's here. In the ground," I stammer. It's the excuse I always give when I'm justifying the decision not to visit my brother—whether to myself or to my mother and sister.

Reliably kind, Nolan nods and says he understands.

I squint up at the sky and say, "I like to think of him up there."

He follows my gaze and nods again. "I know what you mean . . . but I still feel him more strongly when we come here. . . . They say a portion of the soul is always present at the grave site. . . ."

I nod, listening to the sound of silence, then realizing that it's not silent at all. Leaves rustle in the breeze. A dog barks in the distance. A car engine turns over. Meanwhile, I feel Nolan looking at me, and know that he expects a reply.

"To each his own," I finally say, worrying that I might sound flippant. Meredith would definitely hear it that way.

But Nolan isn't Meredith, fortunately, and only murmurs his agreement. "Yes, everyone is different about these things . . . but you definitely do believe he's *somewhere,* right?" His brow furrowed, he looks directly into my eyes.

I hesitate, thinking that sometimes I do, but sometimes I do not. "I don't know," I finally say.

He looks at me, aghast. "But, Josie . . . you *have* to," he says. "Otherwise . . ."

"Otherwise what?" I retort.

"Otherwise, how do you make sense of it?"

"I *don't* make sense of it," I say under my breath, thinking that more than anything, I hate that notion of "God's plan."

Before I can say more, his phone rings, saving me. He pulls it out of his front pocket, glancing at the screen. I think we both expect it to be Meredith—at least I do. But he holds it up, showing me an unprogrammed 404 number. Mumbling that he has no idea who it is, he answers it anyway.

"Hello?" he says, his voice as anxious as I feel.

I hear a woman's high voice droning and assume it's a telemarketer. Until Nolan begins to grin.

Watching him smile is like watching the sun come out, I remember my mother once saying, before Daniel died, back when she used to make such poetic observations. It was and still is true.

"That's awesome! Thank *you*," he says excitedly. "We'll be right there! Thank you so *much*."

He hangs up, slides his phone back into his pocket, and looks up with tears in his eyes. "Harper, sweetheart! Guess what?"

"What?" she yells back, shielding her eyes with her hand.

"They found Rabby! He's safe and sound at Legoland!" Nolan shouts to both of us.

As Harper cheers and sprints toward us, Nolan beams, giving me an I-told-you-so look. "See?" he says.

"See what?" I reply, though I know what he's thinking because I've heard him say it many times before. Something about Daniel being Harper's guardian angel. Something about him looking out for all of us.

As if "God's plan" would ever, in a billion years, include taking a young man but saving a stuffed rabbit.

LATER THAT NIGHT, after I've rather easily put Harper to bed (with Rabby's assistance), I come downstairs to find Nolan eating the remains of Harper's macaroni and cheese directly from the pot with a big wooden spoon. He gives me a sheepish smile, wiping his mouth with his hand.

I smile back at him and say, "Don't worry. I do it, too. Why is food always better when you eat it right off the stove?"

"I don't know, but it really is," he says, taking one last bite. "Are you hungry? We could throw in a pizza or order something?"

"No, not really," I say. "I was actually gonna take off. . . ."

"Right now?" he says, looking disappointed. "Do you have plans?"

"No," I say, though Pete did send me a text about an hour ago asking what I was up to. "But now that we have Rabby back, I figured you didn't need me. . . ."

"I don't *need* you. But why not stay and hang out for a bit?" he says. I remember Meredith once told me that Nolan can't stand to be alone. "One beer?"

"Sure," I say. "Why not?"

Nolan smiles, heading straight to the refrigerator. He opens it, grabs two Budweisers from the door, and hands me one before sitting at the kitchen island. I stand across from him, leaning on the edge of the counter, twisting the top off.

"So? How's life?" he asks, taking the first sip.

"It's fine," I say with a shrug. I fleetingly consider telling him about the latest development with Gabe and his offer, but decide against it, knowing he has enough on his mind. "How's *your* life?" I ask him.

"Oh, it's totally *swell*." He gives me two thumbs up to reinforce the sarcasm, and I take it as an invitation to ask him point-blank what's going on with Meredith.

"Who knows?" he says with a long sigh.

I take a sip of beer, choosing my words carefully. "Why is she in New York, exactly?"

"She's just taking a little break. . . ." he replies, his voice trailing off.

"Is anything . . . wrong? With y'all?" I press, knowing that the situation must be fairly dire if Meredith is missing Halloween—right up there with Christmas when you have a four-year-old.

Nolan looks up and to the left, which, according to body language experts, is strong evidence of an impending lie. "No," he says. "Nothing's wrong."

"Okay. But just so you know," I say. "Liars always look up in that direction."

Nolan gives me a halfhearted smile, then says, "Well. I guess it takes one to know one."

"Seriously," I gently press. "What's going on with you and Mere?"

"I don't know, Josie," he says, shaking his head. "She's just not happy. . . ."

"So what else is new?" I say. "Mere's been in a bad mood since she came out of the womb."

"I know," he says. "But it's worse than usual."

I ask him why, feeling annoyed that my sister can't just snap out of it and be happy, especially given all that she has to be happy about. "Do you think she's depressed? Like clinically?"

"No. I don't think that's it. . . . She definitely had depression after Harper was born. . . ." His voice trails off as I remember Mere's postpartum baby blues. They were mild, but still concerning, especially to my mother.

"But this is different," he continues. "This is almost like a midlife crisis."

I stare at him, thinking that it is such a loaded term, almost always referring to infidelity of some kind. I tell him my sister would never cheat.

"Oh, I know," he says, staring at the label on his beer. "I don't mean that kind of midlife crisis. . . . I just mean . . . maybe she'd rather be alone than married to me."

"She wants a *divorce*?" I say, floored.

"Yeah. I think she might," he says, meeting my gaze.

"No way. That can't be it," I say, shaking my head.

Nolan gives me a look that can only be classified as sad. *Deeply* sad. "I think it is, Josie. . . . She pretty much told me that it was."

"But you're the *perfect* husband," I blurt out, feeling a wave of animosity toward my sister. How dare she do this to him?

He gives me a small smile, but still looks mournful. "Yeah. Well, thanks. But I think we both know it doesn't work like that. . . . Looking back . . . I don't think she ever loved me."

"Of course she did. *Does*," I say, as I'm bombarded with a distant memory of my sister and me sitting in the dressing room of the bridal shop where Meredith purchased her gown. I remember how she talked about having cold feet, being unsure about Nolan. It seemed ridiculous at the time. It *still* seems ridiculous. She could never do better than Nolan. Nobody could.

"What?" Nolan asks. "What're you thinking?"

I glance away and say, "Nothing."

"You just looked up and to the left," he says. "Now *you're* lying."

I swallow, almost telling him about that moment in the dressing room, then quickly deciding it isn't my place. Besides, what good would it do at this point? Instead, I take a deep breath and say, "I just think Meredith is hardwired to be dissatisfied . . . and she always second-guesses herself. Think about her chosen profession. . . . What was that all about, anyway? She *always* wanted to be an actress . . . so why did she go to law school?"

"Exactly," he says. "But Josie—that's my point. . . . I'm the relationship equivalent of law school. She regrets law school. She regrets me. She regrets her whole *life*."

"That's not what I meant," I say, realizing that I've just made him feel worse. "I just meant . . . Meredith is complicated. . . . She's always been that way . . . and she got way worse after Daniel died."

He gives me a surprised look.

"What? That can't be a revolutionary concept, can it?" I ask, thinking that we *all* got worse after Daniel died; Meredith was just a little darker to begin with.

"No . . . it's not that," he says. "I just think this might be the first time you've *ever* brought up Daniel with me. It's always *me* bringing him up with *you*."

I nod, my stomach clenching like it did in the cemetery. "I know," I say.

"Why is that?" he asks. "Why don't you ever want to talk about him?"

I swallow, sweat beginning to pool under my arms. "I don't know. . . . It's like we said in the cemetery today. . . . Everyone is different about this stuff. About death . . . and dealing with it."

"Yes . . . but it's always struck me as odd. . . . I've always thought you would be more like Meredith . . . and she'd be more like you. . . . You know?"

I shake my head, not following. "Why's that?"

"Because generally speaking, you're more of an open book . . . and you're more glass half full. . . ."

"Maybe," I say with a little shrug. Then, hoping to change the subject, I ask how we got from his marriage to me.

"I think it's all related," he says, without missing a beat.

I force a laugh and try to sidetrack him. "What? How do *I* have anything to do with *your* marriage?"

"You don't," he says, my decoy not working. "I'm talking about your family . . . what Daniel's death did to your family. To all of us."

I know what he's getting at, and I desperately don't want him to go there. He does anyway, staring into my eyes in a way that I can't escape. "Can we please talk about that night, Josie?" he asks.

My throat feels too tight to reply, so I just shake my head.

"It's been almost fifteen years . . . and we've never talked about it. . . . Doesn't that seem strange to you?"

"Not really," I manage to say, averting my eyes. "I mean . . . what's the point?" My voice cracks, then trails off.

"Josie," he says. "I think we both know the *point*. And I think it needs to happen. *Now*."

My heart starts to pound in my ears as I try one last time to make it all go away, just as I've been doing since the night I first suspected the truth, the night Will found me in bed with Gabe. "Do we have to?" I whimper.

"*Yes,*" he says. "We *do*. I mean, Josie, *shit*. . . . We were *together* the night Daniel died—and yet we've never talked about—"

"We weren't *together,*" I cut him off, bracing myself, praying that maybe, just maybe, I'm actually wrong about my hunch. "We were just . . . at the same bar. Lots of people were there. . . ."

"I know. Lots of people who had absolutely *nothing* to do with Daniel . . ." he says, holding his bottle cap between his finger and the counter. He flicks it hard, and we both watch it spin, then stop, before making eye contact again.

"Josie," he says, the color draining from his face. "I have to tell you something."

"No," I say, my heart pounding in my chest, my instinct to flee kicking into high gear. I take a few steps backward, actually looking around the room for my best exit, but Nolan darts around the counter, putting his hands on my shoulders, holding me in place.

"I *have* to," he says again, more forcefully.

"I know what you're going to say," I say, my vision blurring.

"I don't think you do," he says, still holding on to me.

"Yes. I do," I say, shaking free, fighting back panicked tears. "He wasn't getting a burger that night, was he?"

Nolan stares at me a beat, then shakes his head slowly. "No," he says. "He wasn't."

"He was coming to get *me* . . . wasn't he?"

The tortured look on Nolan's face confirms my worst fear, even before he nods and says yes.

"Fuck," I say, trembling. "I knew it . . . I knew it was my fault. *Fuck.*"

"No, Josie," Nolan says. "It wasn't *your* fault."

"Of *course* it was my fault," I say, choking back a sob. "He was coming to get *me*."

"But don't you see, Josie?" He stares at me.

"See what?"

"Don't you see that *I* was the one who called him. . . . I was the one who told him to get in his car and come get you. So see? It was *my* fault. Not *yours*."

"But if I hadn't been drunk—"

"But I *wasn't* drunk, Josie. Don't you get that? I wasn't drunk at all. All I had to do was drive you home. . . . I was talking to some girl. Some stupid girl I wanted to sleep with . . . I didn't want my fun interrupted. So I called Daniel to come get you . . . and then I left the bar. . . . I didn't even wait for him to get there. I didn't know he never got there. Not until the next morning when Meredith told me." His face crumples, and he begins to break down and cry in a way that I have never seen a grown man cry. Not even my father when Daniel died.

My flight instinct grows stronger, and this time I manage to break free to the family room. I sink into the sofa, burying my face in my hands. Nolan's footsteps are behind me. I can see him in my peripheral vision and feel his weight on the cushion next to me, his arm enveloping me.

"Josie," he says. There is so much pain in his voice. "Please look at me, Josie."

I do. For his sake.

"I'm sorry," he says, tears streaming down his face. "I'm so *fucking* sorry, Josie."

"I'm sorry, too," I say, refusing to let him shift the blame from me. "He always told me not to drink so much. . . . He always warned me about being like Dad. . . ."

"Yes. But he told me, just the day before, that I should stop chasing stupid girls and try to find someone I really cared about . . . like Sophie. . . ."

"Well, neither one of us listened to him, did we?" I say.

"But if only I had taken you home myself. . . . It was my fault."

We continue like that for some time, making disjointed, parallel confessions. *I was having sex with some girl when he died. . . . I was wasted when he died. . . . I didn't know until the next morning. . . . You knew before I did.*

At some point, when there is nothing left to say, he reaches for my hand. I give it to him. It should be awkward, sitting there holding my sister's husband's hand, but it's not. It's actually the opposite. He feels like my brother. Not Daniel, but another brother. We sit in silence for a long time before I finally ask the question burning a hole in my heart. "Does Meredith know?"

I look at him, holding my breath, waiting for the answer, thinking that a yes would explain so much of her animosity toward me. Yet I can't imagine her holding this back for so many years—not when she throws far smaller things in my face.

Sure enough, Nolan says, "No, she doesn't know any of this. Nobody knows. . . . Everyone thinks he was going to get a burger." His voice shakes, but he continues. "The next day, when your parents asked me to call Daniel's friends, I took his phone. . . . I knew his pass code . . . 4265. . . ."

"Why was that his pass code?" I ask. It is beside the point, but I still want to know.

"It spells *Hank*. For Hank Aaron."

"Oh," I say, thinking of the baseball card that he used to keep in his wallet. How my parents had tucked it into the breast pocket of his jacket right before they closed the coffin. I swallow, willing myself not to throw up.

"So, anyway, I knew his pass code," Nolan continues. "And got on his phone and checked his call log. . . . I prayed that he'd called someone else after we talked . . . maybe Sophie before she got on her flight. . . . But no." He shakes his head, then takes a deep breath, trying to keep it together. "The last two calls were with me."

"*Two* calls?" I say.

"Yes," he says. "The first was fifty-two seconds. When I asked him to come get you."

"And then you called back?" I ask softly.

"No. Then he called me about fifteen minutes later . . . to tell me he was leaving the house. On his way."

"Do you remember that call?"

"Of course I do," he says. "It was the last time I ever heard his voice. It was the last time *anyone* ever heard his voice. . . ."

"How long did you talk that time?" I ask, sure that he knows the answer.

"Fourteen seconds. Fourteen *fucking* seconds. You know why it was only fourteen seconds?"

"Because he was driving?" I ask, thinking of how responsible Daniel always was about driving. About *everything*.

"No." He shakes his head. "Because I was in a hurry to go. . . . That girl I was talking to was on her way outside . . . and I didn't want her to leave without me. . . ."

"Was she gone?" I ask.

"Almost," he says. "But I caught her on the way out the door. . . . I went back to her apartment . . . and I had sex with her. . . . And now?"

I squeeze his hand, giving him the strength to continue. "Now I can't even remember her goddamn name. . . ."

chapter twenty-four

MEREDITH

On Sunday morning, I awaken to the sound of distant church chimes and a sharp chill in Ellen's simple whitewashed bedroom. Shivering, I pull the goose-down comforter up to my chin, rolling over to face the window. The curtains are drawn, but sheer enough for me to make out the silhouette of a ginkgo tree, its twisted, bare branches bending toward the windowpanes.

I wonder what time it is, but can't tell by the flat northern light. It could be as early as seven, as late as nine. I decide it doesn't matter, a realization that is more disorienting than liberating. So I reach for my phone, shocked to see that it is a few minutes past ten, about the latest I have slept since Harper was born, at least when neither of us is ill. The mere thought of her sets off a fresh quake of homesickness. No matter how surly she is in the morning, I am always happy to see her face first thing, her cheeks flushed, her hair a tangled mop. I close my eyes and can almost smell the odd maple-syrupy scent of her skin after a long sleep.

Suddenly desperate to hear her voice, I call Nolan. He doesn't answer, just as he didn't answer last night or yesterday afternoon, my only update coming from Josie when she texted me a photo of Harper embracing Rabby, along with the caption *Reunited and it feels so good!* My heart flooded with relief as I texted her back immediately, virtually begging for the details, adding extra exclamation points and question marks. But three hours passed before she wrote back a glib reply: *Found at Legoland. All's well that ends well. Enjoy your vacation.*

I call Nolan again, listening to the futile sound of ringing, followed by his chipper outgoing message. This time I leave a message. I calmly ask him to please call me back as soon as he can, doing my best to keep agitation out of my voice. I know I have little standing to be angry, yet I am anyway. Yes, I am the one on a boondoggle in Manhattan, but it all unfolded at *his* prodding. His virtual *insistence.* And now he is punishing me. Cutting me off. Making a point. *This is what your life will be like without me, without us.* I tell myself to get up, seize the day, and embrace my soul-searching sabbatical.

So after a quick shower, I change into my city uniform—jeans with a black sweater, a black leather jacket, and black boots. I put on oversize sunglasses, throw my hair into a utilitarian ponytail, and sail down four flights, out the heavy front door of the brownstone, into the crisp fall day. It is windier than I expected, more unpleasant than invigorating, but I tell myself I will warm up. I just need to keep moving.

For the next five hours, I aimlessly wander the city on foot and by subway, from the Village up to Chelsea and the far reaches of the Upper West Side, then across the park, down Fifth Avenue, and the whole way into SoHo. Along the way, I duck into coffee shops and browse boutiques, stopping whenever and wherever my fancy strikes. I sit on random benches, people watching. I speak only when necessary, to order a sandwich, ask a clerk a question, thank the man who slid down to make room for me on the subway. Otherwise, my inner monologue and urban solitude are uninterrupted, my life examined from every angle.

I think a lot about the past, particularly the years I lived here, feeling as disconnected from those memories and friends as I do

from my college years and acting. I have no desire to get in touch
with anyone I used to know, even to meet up for a drink, and I can't
help but wonder what this says about me. I like to think of myself
as merely introverted, but is it something stronger? Am I a patho-
logical loner? An outright loser? If so, no wonder my marriage feels
empty, like something's always missing. No wonder I can't get
along with my sister. Maybe our turbulence is more my fault than
hers. I think of how happy she looked the other night at her birthday dinner, how fun always follows her, how fiercely loyal her
friends are to her, especially Gabe. I tell myself that I have Ellen, but
deep down I know it's not the same, perhaps because Ellen has
Andy, and that *he* is her best friend, the person to whom she is the
most loyal.

By dusk, I am freezing, and my heels are beginning to blister,
and all I want to do is go home and take a bath. But I stop at a
Duane Reade on the outskirts of Chinatown, buy a Diet Snapple
and a box of Band-Aids, then head back outside to hail a cab.

"Where to?" the driver asks as I slide into the taxi, which reeks
of artificial evergreen.

"I don't know yet," I tell him. "Could you just drive, please?"

He nods, indifferent as long as his meter is ticking, while I study
the bridge of his nose, forehead, and eyes in the rearview mirror,
trying to determine his ethnicity based on his features and last
name—Abrama. He could be Mexican, Italian, Portuguese, Span-
ish, Israeli, the possibilities as endless as my potential destinations.

"Where are you from?" I finally ask, caving to the curiosity.

He raises his chin, answering proudly. "I'm Calabrese," he says
in the way people from home tell you they are third- or fourth-
generation Atlantan.

"Oh. Beautiful," I say, though I've never been to that part of
Italy. "That's the toe of the boot, right?" I ask him, reminding myself of my sister and how she always chats with strangers.

Mr. Abrama nods again, unimpressed by my command of world geography.

A few minutes pass before he asks, "Did you decide?"

"Decide what?" I say, thinking of Nolan.

"Where you want to go?"

I clear my throat, then say, "Yes. Could you please take me to Times Square?"

TWENTY MINUTES LATER, I pay my fare and am deposited one block away from the pulsing neon heart of the city. I head directly for the TKTS booth under the red steps, suddenly craving a live performance. I'm in the mood for low-key and talky, not slinky or razzle-dazzle, but it is nearly seven o'clock, so I take what I can get, ending up with a ticket to *Chicago,* a show I've seen twice before and don't particularly love. Still, as I make my way to the Ambassador Theatre and settle into my balcony seat, waiting for the curtains to part, I feel something come alive inside me.

By intermission, I feel like a new person—or maybe just my old self. I check my phone in the theater lobby and see that I finally have a missed call from Nolan. I press myself into a reasonably quiet corner and call him back.

"Hi," he says, his voice barely audible. "Where are you?"

"At a show," I say.

"With who?"

"I'm alone."

"Oh . . . Are you having fun?"

"I wouldn't call it 'fun' . . . but it's nice. . . . How are you? How is Harper?"

"We're fine," he says. "We got Rabby back."

"I heard," I say. "Josie told me."

"Oh. Right," he says.

"Can I talk to Harper?" I ask, though the second warning to return to our seats has just been issued.

"She's asleep," he says. "She has school tomorrow. I'm taking off for her Halloween parade."

"Oh. That's great. . . . So, what else is going on?" I say as the lobby empties.

"Well . . . Josie and I went to the cemetery yesterday. With Harper. We took flowers."

"*Josie* went?" I ask, more than a little shocked.

"Yeah."

"Wow. I take it that was your idea?"

"Yeah," he says. "It was . . . but she went . . . and we had a really good talk."

"About Daniel?"

"Yes," he says.

I shake my head, thinking of how many times I've tried to get my sister to go to the cemetery or have a substantive conversation about our brother. Never to any avail. Resentment builds inside me— toward both my husband and my sister. "Well, thanks for the call. I need to go . . . intermission's over," I say, thinking of how he, annoyingly, always calls it *halftime*.

"No problem," Nolan quickly says. "Enjoy the show."

chapter twenty-five

JOSIE

For several days following my conversation with Nolan, I try to delude myself, a skill I've honed over the years. I keep telling myself that my actions were just *one* piece of a giant, tragic puzzle, and that a hundred little things had to happen for Daniel to die. A *thousand*. If you back up far enough, *tens* of thousands.

Take, for example, Scott Donahue, the driver of the Denali that hit Daniel. I have never laid eyes on the man, but somehow I know his part of the story. I know that on the night of the accident, he was headed to Walgreens to buy cough medicine for his three-year-old son. So right there alone, I can see that Mr. Donahue and his wife had to meet, marry, and conceive that particular child, who would then get sick that very week in December (perhaps picking up a virus at one of those bouncy venues that Meredith despises); that the Donahues had to be out of children's cough medicine (maybe they both forgot to pick it up earlier that day); and that Mr. Donahue had to go out precisely when he did (perhaps he stalled a few minutes to watch news coverage of the shoe bomber, the big story that broke that day). And on and on and on.

Yet no matter how I slice it, or what other factors may have been at play on that fateful night (and in the weeks, months, and years leading up to it), the inescapable, bottom-line, stone-cold truth remains: Daniel would be alive today had I not gotten drunk—no, *wasted*—on the night of December 22, 2001.

Obviously, there is nothing I can do about the past except live with it, but my agonizing dilemma becomes what to do moving forward. Do I make a joint decision with Nolan to tell Meredith what really happened that night? Do I confess to Meredith on my own, regardless of what he decides? Do I tell my family the truth simply because they deserve to know every detail of Daniel's final hours—or will telling them only burden them with more heartache? I think about the repercussions of a confession and worry that my father might blame himself for my excessive drinking. I can certainly see my mother feeling that way. I can also see her lamenting that she hadn't been stricter during my teenaged years. Most of all, I know beyond a doubt that a confession will only further poison my relationship with Meredith, perhaps end it altogether, and that it might also be the death knell for her marriage. I know my sister, and I just can't imagine her forgiving either one of us for keeping such an enormous secret.

After several torturous days and restless nights, I decide to talk to the one person I can always trust. So I knock on Gabe's door late one evening, finally catching him alone, without Leslie.

"Yeah?" he calls out, sounding exhausted.

I open the door a crack and peer into his darkened room. "Sorry. Were you asleep?"

"Nah," he says, rolling from his back onto his side to look at me. "I just got in bed. . . . You okay?"

"Yeah . . . yeah. . . . I just wanted to talk. . . ."

"Well, come on in," he says.

I hesitate one beat, then take a deep breath, climb onto his bed, and talk as quickly as I can, before I can change my mind, spilling my whole disjointed, raw confession.

"Well, you always thought this might be the case. . . ." he says after I'm finished, his tone sympathetic yet matter-of-fact.

"Yeah," I say, nodding as I hug my knees. "But I also always hoped I was wrong."

"I know," he murmurs.

"It sucks," I say.

"Yeah . . . but aren't you just a little relieved to *know*?" he asks. "Now you don't have to wonder anymore?"

I nod, impressed with his usual insightfulness. "Yeah. I guess. Maybe a little . . . I probably should have talked to Nolan a long time ago."

"He should have talked to you, too," Gabe says, loyally shifting the blame. "And I really can't *believe* he never told Meredith. . . . *Wow*."

"Well, I kept a secret from her, too."

"Yeah, but you aren't *married* to her."

I nod.

"Besides," Gabe continues. "Nolan *knew* the truth. You only *suspected* it. . . ."

"I guess," I say, having considered all of these angles as I searched for ways to absolve myself, or at least mitigate my culpability. "But we're still *both* to blame for what happened."

Gabe props himself up, cradling his head in his left hand. "Nobody is to *blame,* Josie. It's not like someone was drunk *driving* here. . . . It was an *accident* . . . an accident *nobody* could have foreseen."

"Still," I say.

"Still *what*?" he says, his brow furrowed.

"I *still* played a role in it . . . and I still have to tell my family. They deserve to know the truth. . . ." I stare into Gabe's eyes, hoping he'll talk me out of it, tell me there's no point—or at least no upside. "Don't you agree?" I ask, holding my breath.

He hesitates, then slowly nods. "Yeah . . . I think you're proba-bly right. . . . But I think you need to tell them for *your* sake more than theirs . . . so that *you* can move on—"

"But I *have* moved on," I say, cutting him off, thinking that is a large part of my guilt—the fact that I moved on with my life so ef-fortlessly, never visiting my brother's grave until last week, barely even mentioning him to friends *or* family.

Gabe shakes his head. "No. You haven't, Josie. You haven't moved on at *all*. You carry this with you everywhere."

I stare at him, knowing that he's right, and wondering how he can tell.

"And look what it's done to you," he finishes softly.

"What's it done to me?" I ask, lowering my eyes, afraid of his reply, his always brutal honesty.

"Well, for one," he says, "you didn't tell your boyfriend why I was in your bed that night."

"So?" I say, bristling at the mention of Will.

"*So?* You would rather have had him think you *cheated* on him than know the truth about the night your brother died. What does that tell you?"

"Are you saying I *should* have told Will? That I could be mar-ried to him if I'd told him the truth about why you were in my bed? About everything?" It is a thought that has occurred to me count-less times over the years, and even more in the last few days.

"No," Gabe replies, adamant. "That's not what I'm saying at all. . . . I think if Will had been right for you, he would have be-lieved you when you told him nothing happened with us. . . ."

"Yes. But it did look pretty bad," I say, wondering why I'm still defending Will after all these years.

Gabe shakes his head, his voice becoming louder, passionate. "So *what*? So it looked bad? Nothing happened."

"Well, jeez, Gabe. I *know* that. . . . I tried to tell him that many,

many times," I say, getting sickening flashbacks to our final few escalating fights and the lonely, empty aftermath, when it slowly began to dawn on me that he wasn't coming back. Ever.

"You could have done a much better job of convincing him, and you *know* it. If he had been your soul mate," Gabe says, using a term I've never heard him use before, "you would have confided in him . . . or he would have taken your word and trusted you. You would have trusted *him* enough to tell him everything. . . . Instead, you let him think the worst about you. . . . So he did."

"Killing my brother is worse than cheating on Will."

Gabe cringes, dropping his head back to his pillow. "You didn't *kill* your brother, Jo. Don't ever say that again."

"Well, it feels like I did. . . . Do you know how many times Daniel gave me lectures about drinking? About how I needed to be more careful because of our dad? Jesus, Gabe, just a couple days before, he talked to me about it . . . and I brushed him off."

"You were a college kid, Josie. Lots of college kids drink too much."

"He never did," I say. "Meredith doesn't, either."

"Well, *you're* not *them*," he says. "And you're not your father. You're *you*. Did you have too much to drink that night? Absolutely. Did you drink too much the other night when you made out with Pete at Johnny's?" He smiles, clearly trying to cheer me up.

"We didn't *make out*," I say, quibbling with his verb, but he raises his hand and continues.

"The point is, I don't think you've ever had a drinking problem. Maybe an attitude and behavior problem," he says, smiling again. "But not a drinking problem."

"Well, my behavior, along with my drinking, resulted in my brother's death," I insist. "Whether directly or indirectly, it did. And . . ."

"And what?"

"And I deserved to lose Will because of it," I finish decisively, truly believing this.

"As your punishment?" Gabe asks.

"Yes," I say. "As my punishment."

Gabe shakes his head. "I disagree. I *strongly* disagree. . . . You and Will broke up because he wasn't right for you, Josie. . . . That was clear. . . . Hell, that was clear to me long *before* you broke up. . . . You were never yourself around him. . . . You were . . . a fake Josie . . . and you haven't loved anyone since Will because you won't let yourself."

"That's not true," I say, thinking of all the guys I've gone out with, and slept with, and tried to love, and tried to make love me.

"It *is* true. And you need to stop punishing yourself." Gabe stares up at me with a mixture of pity and love, before reaching out to gently touch my arm. The gesture, along with the feel of his skin on mine, instantly floods my eyes with tears.

"Aww, Jo. Don't cry," he says. "C'mere."

"Where?" I say, desperately needing a hug, even from one of the world's most awkward huggers.

"Right here," he says, patting his chest twice before pulling me down beside him, wrapping both arms around me.

"I'm so sad," I say, as it occurs to me that we are lying together exactly the way Will found us all those years ago—and that nothing has really changed since that night.

"I know," Gabe says, his breath warm in my hair. "But you need to forgive yourself. It's time, Jo."

"But what if my family doesn't forgive me?"

"They will."

"But what if they don't?" I say, thinking specifically of my sister.

"Well, then . . . *I'll* be your family."

"You mean my baby daddy?" I ask, smiling, only partly kidding.

"Yeah, that, too," he says with a little laugh.

"Are you really serious about that?" I ask. "Would you *really* do that for me?"

"Of course I would, Josie. . . . I'd do *anything* for you," he says.

I try to thank him, and tell him that I feel the same, but can't get out the words, too overwhelmed with gratitude. Besides, I know he doesn't expect a reply, that he's simply stating a fact I already know. Instead, I close my eyes and let myself drift off in his arms, doing my best to memorize the moment I will one day tell my son or daughter about. . . . *That was the moment I made my decision. The moment I picked your father. The moment I knew.*

chapter twenty-six

MEREDITH

Four days, two off-Broadway plays, one musical, and endless hours of wandering the city later, I can't tell if I'm feeling a little better or much worse. I decide it's closer to the latter when I get a call from Josie, gushing about how cute Harper looked in her butterfly costume. "Did you get my photos?"

"Yes. Didn't I thank you?" I say, knowing that I did.

"Yes," she says. "You did."

"I'm really glad you stopped over to see her . . . because of course Nolan only took one shot. And it was dark and blurry."

She laughs and says, "Typical guy."

I murmur my agreement, and a long pause ensues before Josie brings up her visit to the cemetery.

"Yeah. I heard y'all went," I say, tensing. "How was it?"

"It was nice," she says. "Difficult, but nice . . . I feel a little better."

"Well . . . good. Great . . . Does Mom know you went?" I ask, feeling certain that the answer is no.

"I don't think so. . . . Unless Nolan told her . . . I haven't mentioned it to her yet."

"Well, maybe you should tell her? You know—since she's been wanting you to go for *years*," I say.

"Yeah. I know. I will," she says. "I actually need to talk to both of you. . . ."

"Oh?" I say. "About?"

"About . . . some things," she says. "When are you coming home?"

I lean back on Ellen's sofa and stare at a large water mark on the ceiling as I tell her I don't know.

"Soon?" she presses.

"I don't know," I say again, irritation creeping into my voice.

A long silence follows, but I am determined to outlast my sister. "*Are* you coming home?" she finally asks.

"Now, why would you ask that?" I bark, enraged by her insinuation that I would abandon my child.

"God. *Sorry*," she says. "I didn't mean to offend you. . . . I'm just worried . . . about you and Nolan. And Harper."

"Well, don't be," I say. "You have your hands full with your own life."

I know my response is over-the-top bitchy, and I brace myself for a brawl, or at the very least, one of her signature hang-ups, but Josie floors me by taking the high ground.

"You're right, Mere. I do," she says. "But I'm really trying here."

"Trying to do what, exactly?" I snap.

"Trying to get it together . . . and I just really, really want to see you in person. If you're not coming home, do you think I could come up there?"

I shake my head and roll my eyes, getting the sudden feeling that Josie is using my crisis to justify a trip to New York *and* score a free place to stay. "Is it really that urgent?"

"Yes, Mere," she says. "It kind of is, actually."

I sigh, telling myself not to fall into Mom's trap and start worrying that it's something dire or health-related. "Can you at least tell me the topic?" I ask, betting that it involves Will, or her sperm donor guy and their half-assed birth plan, or maybe even some other new guy, Josie never going very long before some new male character emerges in her life.

A long pause follows—so long that I think we've been cut off. "Are you still there?" I say.

"Yes," she says. "I'm here."

"Okay? Well? What's the topic?" I ask again.

"It's about Daniel," she says, her voice cracking. "I need to talk to you about Daniel."

All of my instincts tell me to say no—that Josie is somehow manipulating me and my situation, or otherwise pulling some sort of attention-grabbing stunt. But of all the things my sister's been dramatic about over the years, our brother has never been one of them. I think back to the days immediately following the accident, how she disappeared into her room for hours on end while the rest of us milled about the kitchen. I think about her demeanor at the funeral— how self-contained and withdrawn she was. I can't recall her crying at the service at all, and have a vivid memory of her standing apart from our family at Daniel's graveside until my grandmother pulled her over to the front row of folding chairs, practically forcing her to sit down.

So on the off chance this is all legitimate, I sigh and say yes, she is welcome to come to New York this weekend.

JOSIE'S FLIGHT LANDS around seven on Friday night, and she pulls up in a taxi less than an hour later, just as I'm arriving home from the corner bodega. She sees me first, calling out my name through her open cab window. She is wearing her hair wavy and natural around her unmade-up face, and my first thought is that she looks stunning—*way* prettier than when she spackles on the makeup and irons all the life out of her hair. I try to wave, but my grocery bags are weighing down my arms, so I simply smile and yell hello, waiting for her to get out of the car. It takes her an unusually long time to pay her fare and finish chatting with her driver, and I feel myself growing annoyed. She is the kind of person who will finish her phone call and touch up her lip gloss while someone waits for her spot in a packed parking lot. It makes me crazy.

I tell myself to stop my mental rant, then take a deep breath. I have enough on my plate right now. A few seconds later, her door swings open, and she plants a black suede platform boot onto the street, before heaving a giant roller bag out of the backseat.

"Perfect timing!" she declares as she gets out of the taxi, slams the door, and waves goodbye to her cabbie.

"Yeah, I just ran to the store." I smile brightly while eyeing her suitcase. "That's a lot of luggage for two nights," I can't resist saying.

"I know, I *know*. . . . I'm a terrible packer. I just threw a bunch of stuff in before school this morning." She steps toward me, then throws her arms around me. "It's *so* good to see you, Mere."

I lower my plastic bags to the sidewalk and hug her back, stiffly at first. Then I relax, as I realize that in spite of my cynicism, I'm genuinely happy to see her. We separate, and I watch her glance up, then down the block, as if to get her bearings. She then squints and points up at Ellen's building. "That's it, right?"

"Yes. Fourth floor. It's a walk-up," I say with a grimace. "No elevator."

"That's okay. I need the workout," she says, making a muscle, then motioning toward my grocery bags and asking if we're eating in tonight.

That hadn't been my plan, but I say yes anyway, trying to gauge her reaction. "Would that be okay with you?"

"Sure," she says, passing the test—at least for now. "Whatever you want to do is cool with me. . . ."

I smile, then turn and lead her up the stone steps of Ellen's building. We walk into the bare-bones lobby, past the small grid of mail slots, then enter the musty stairwell. All the while, Josie rambles about how tired she is, what a long week it's been, how exhausting it is to be a teacher, especially with young children who have no self-control or respect for your personal space. After two flights, she's completely winded, and by the third, she has to put her bag down to catch her breath.

"How many pairs of shoes did you bring? Tell the truth. . . ." I say.

"Oh, I don't know . . . four or five." She flashes me a sheepish, yet somehow still proud smile.

"Including the pair you're wearing?"

"Okay. So five or six," she says.

"And yet . . . you'd be okay staying in?" I say as we climb the last flight.

"I said *yes*," she says. "Why do you keep asking me that?"

"I've only asked you twice."

"Right. But I already said yes. . . . Whatever you want is fine, Mere."

"Okay," I say, rounding the corner, then unlocking Ellen's door and pushing it open. Once inside, I put my groceries down and slowly remove my boots, lining them neatly up next to the doormat, her cue to do the same. But of course she does not, sauntering right past the entryway, her filthy airplane-airport-city-sidewalk boots clunking on the hardwood.

"Hey, Josie," I say. "Your shoes?"

She rolls her eyes and says she was just about to take them off; would I *please* give her a chance?

"Okay. *Sorry,*" I say, though I don't actually believe her. "You know it's my thing. . . . You overpack; I obsess about germs."

"I know," she says, retreating a few steps. "But still. Don't you remember how Mom used to tell us to say 'thank you' before we had a chance to spit the words out?"

"Yeah," I say with a laugh. "The cupcake wouldn't yet be transferred to our hands before she was like, 'Gir-*ls*! What do you *saaay?*' "

Josie sits on the floor, pulling off her boots. "Exactly. And don't you remember how much it always annoyed us? Because we were totally *going* to say it? Only *now* . . . we no longer got the credit for having good manners? We just looked like a couple of dolts. . . ." She stands and looks at me, her brows raised.

I smile, thinking, not for the first time, that although some of our worst sibling rivalry involves vying for our mother's favor, some of our best bonding has come at her expense.

I carry the groceries into Ellen's tiny galley kitchen, putting away the few perishable items before washing my hands. Josie does the same, this time without prompting, then turns and eagerly asks for a tour.

"Well, this is pretty much it," I say, gesturing toward the living room. "Plus her bedroom in the back."

"It's nice," she says, walking over to the windows and looking out to the street below. "Very cute . . . and cozy . . . What's the rent run?"

"They bought it. And I have no idea what they paid for it," I say, despising the way Josie talks about money.

"Must be nice," she says under her breath, "having that kind of loot."

"Better than being broke, I guess," I say, refraining from my usual commentary about how money can't buy you happiness.

"Yeah . . . that's an understatement," Josie says with a laugh, picking up a little bronze Buddha from an end table. "This is cute."

I nod, thinking Ellen probably isn't going for *cute*. "Yeah. She has good taste."

"What would you call her style, anyway?" Josie asks, putting down the Buddha and running her hand up and down the base of a lamp made of cork.

"Oh, I don't know . . . eclectic? The opposite of Andy's?"

She nods, then inspects Ellen's coffee table books, now in full-on nosy mode. She opens one on photography, reading the inscription from Andy, then flipping randomly to an edgy black-and-white portrait of Lenny Kravitz. "Cool shot," she murmurs.

I nod.

"Did Ellen take any of these?" she asks, still flipping through the pages.

"I don't think so . . . but maybe," I say, thinking that Josie seems to have such love-hate feelings about Ellen, sort of the way I felt about Shawna in high school, both fascinated by and disdainful of her at once—which often boils down to jealousy. "She's shot a few famous people."

"Oh, I know. She's told me," Josie says, rolling her eyes, implying that Ellen brags—which couldn't be further from the truth. "Does she know I'm here this weekend?"

I nod. "Uh-huh."

"What did you tell her?"

"I don't remember *exactly*. Just that you were coming for the weekend."

"And?"

"And *what*?"

"Did you tell her *why* I was coming?"

I raise my eyebrows and stare at her pointedly. "Um. No . . . How could I do that?"

She gives me a blank look.

"I don't *know* why. Remember?"

She glances away, crossing her arms over her chest as she sits on the far end of Ellen's contemporary sofa. "God. This is *so* uncomfortable," she says. At first I think she's talking about the two of us, until she adds, "Why would she buy a sofa that's this *hard*?"

"Maybe she likes it," I say. "To each her own."

"Not possible. It's *terrible*."

I shrug. "Well, I don't think she sits around here very much. . . . She really just works and sleeps when she's in the city."

"So . . . was she okay with me staying here?" Josie asks expectantly, almost as if she *wants* the answer to be no.

"Yeah. She was totally fine with it. . . ." I say, sitting on the other end of the sofa. It is the truth, but I leave out the part about how Ellen and I analyzed the subject for nearly thirty minutes, unable to come up with any possible Daniel-related topic that would necessitate an urgent, face-to-face dialogue.

"I doubt that," Josie mumbles.

Against my better judgment, I ask her why she always thinks the worst of Ellen.

"I don't think the *worst* of her," Josie says. "I like her *fine*. . . . I just get the feeling she thinks the worst of *me*."

I shake my head. "That's not true," I say, because it actually *isn't*. "She often defends you. . . ." My voice trails off.

She narrows her eyes and says, "Oh? Why would she need to do that?"

My mind races for a clever retort, but I come up empty-handed. "Because you drive me nuts," I say, smirking at her. "That's why."

"Well, you drive me nuts, too," she says, with a little pout that takes a few seconds to dissipate. "But I'm still really glad to see you."

"Me, too," I say, wondering how I can have such mixed

feelings—and how they can shift so quickly and radically, even from one minute to the next. "So how long do you think we can go without arguing?"

"*Jeez,*" she says with a little laugh. "It's like you *want* to fight with me."

I tell her that's silly, that I *hate* fighting with her.

"Me, too," she says. "God. We've had some doozies, haven't we?"

I nod, almost fondly.

"Remember Chick-fil-A?"

"Of course." I laugh, conjuring the details of perhaps our most epic fight, occurring when she was sixteen and I was fourteen. Every morning, she drove me to school in our family's ancient Volvo, dropping me off at Pace before she headed the couple of miles over to Lovett. The problem, of course, was that we could never agree on our departure time, and she was *always* running late. (She must still hold the record at Lovett for the most tardies in a school year.) On that particular morning, though, Josie had promised me, multiple times, that she would do her best to get me to school early, as I had left my math book in my locker and needed to finish my homework.

All was fine, until she pulled into the Chick-fil-A on Northside, announcing that it would only "take a sec" to get a chicken biscuit. Incredulous, particularly after I observed the long drive-thru line, I tried to talk her out of it, even resorting to begging.

"Too late," she said as a car pulled up behind us, trapping us in line. "Sorry, Charlie."

"God. Why do you have to be such a *bitch*," I said.

"Why do you have to be such a nerd," she replied, then went on to mock me for caring so much about my math homework.

Our arguing quickly escalated as we inched along, until I went too far, making a snide comment about how she really didn't "need those extra calories." As soon as the words were out, I regretted that particular brand of meanness, especially knowing how self-conscious she was about her weight, and how hard she'd been trying to drop a few pounds before prom. But before I could apologize, she hauled off and backhanded me as hard as she could in my left breast. It hurt so much that tears immediately filled my eyes, and I remember thinking that a blow to a guy's balls couldn't be any more painful. So of course I slapped her back, and within seconds, a wild hair-pulling, name-calling melee ensued in the middle of the Chick-fil-A drive-thru. Of course, I got to school late that morning, disheveled and miserable, and for days afterward, I worried that her blow to my boob might somehow cause breast cancer. A small part of me even *hoped* for some real damage, if only to reinforce to my parents that I was their nicer, better daughter, and that their middle child might be the most selfish person on the planet.

"God. That was *so* redneck," Josie says now, laughing.

"I know," I say. "Total white trash."

She continues to smile, but informs me that I've just used "a racist expression."

"How do you figure?" I say, weary of her political correctness, which I know she simply parrots from Gabe.

"Well, why specify 'white'? Name another instance when you actually specify the majority. . . . It just seems to imply that all other races are de facto trash," she says.

I roll my eyes and say, "That's a bit of a reach, but whatever. . . ."

We stare at each other an awkward few beats, before she slaps her thighs and says, "You know what? I think we should go out, after all. Is there a low-key spot around here?"

"Of course," I say. "We're in the Village. It's all low-key . . . but did you want to talk about Daniel first?"

"Nah," she says, waving me off. "We have all weekend. . . . That can wait."

At Josie's request for a burger, we decide on the Minetta Tavern for dinner. We have a nice, relaxed time, without so much as a fleeting undercurrent of tension, and an even better time once back at Ellen's. Against all odds, we fall into one of our rare, lighthearted zones with lots of reminiscing, mostly about our childhood, before our adolescent friction set in.

Daniel's name comes up here and there, but only in the context of family lore from before we lost him. As we get in bed and start to fall asleep, it really hits me how much Josie and I have shared over the years. I think of the expression *from the cradle to the grave*—and the fact that she is the only person in the world I can say that about.

The next morning is equally nice. After sleeping in, we get up, shower, and head to my favorite generic neighborhood diner for breakfast, then walk up Fifth Avenue, all the way to Bendel's, where Josie spends a small fortune on makeup.

We leave the store, crossing Fifty-Seventh Street and passing Bergdorf's and the Plaza, before winding our way into the park. The day is cold, but bright and sun-filled, and my heart feels lighter than it has in weeks, maybe months. I almost tell her this as we stop to sit on the bench, but get distracted as we both read the small silver plaque screwed to the back of it: FOR CAROLINE, WHO LOVED THE PARK, AND GEORGE, WHO WAS ALWAYS WITH HER.

Josie runs her hands across the words and says, "Wow. What a sweet dedication."

I murmur my agreement as we sit, our backs to the inscription. "Do you think the kids did it for their parents?" I say, hoping that Josie and I are one day that unified, when Mom and Dad are gone and it truly is just the two of us.

"Probably," she says, with a faint smile. "I picture a little old couple who sat right here, every morning, with their little dog and matching canes . . . until one night, they died in their sleep. Together . . ."

I nod and smile. "That's about as happy an ending as you can get," I say, thinking that even the happiest possible endings still ultimately end in death.

I share the observation aloud, and she looks at me and shakes her head. "God, Mere. What a *downer*."

I shrug and say, "Well? It's the truth."

"I know, but *jeez*."

We both laugh, then sit for a stretch of silence, before she shoots me a serious glance.

"So . . . do you want to talk about what's going on?" she asks, her voice soft. "With Nolan?"

For the first time in a long time, I actually want to confide in my sister. So I go with it. "I don't think I married the right person," I say, squinting up at the cobalt, cloudless sky and wishing I'd worn my sunglasses.

I wait a beat, then meet her gaze. Her expression is more sad than judgmental, the opposite of what I expected.

"I know," she says, nodding. "Nolan sort of told me. . . ."

"He *did*?"

"Yes. Don't be mad at him."

I shake my head. "I'm not. What did he say?"

She swallows, staring down at her pearly pink manicure. "He's scared you want to divorce him."

I freeze. That word.

"Do you?" she asks, glancing up from her hands to look at me.

I slowly nod and say, "I think maybe it's the right decision."

"But . . . why?" she asks, sounding so innocently mournful. "He loves you so much."

"First of all, I don't know that that's true—"

She cuts me off and says, "Oh, Mere, it *is* true. Don't you see the way he looks at you? He *adores* you. He respects you. God . . . you're so *lucky*."

And just like that, I feel my sadness morph into defensiveness and resentment. "I'm *not* lucky," I say. "I married someone I was never really in love with. I cried on my wedding day. That's not lucky. That's just . . . *lame.*" I look at my sister, unsure of whether I want her to argue or relent the point.

"But you have a good marriage," she says. "Don't you?"

"In some ways," I reply. "Okay . . . in a *lot* of ways, maybe. . . . But sometimes I want more . . . for both of us. . . . I want both of us to have the *real* deal . . . what Daniel had with Sophie."

"I know," she says softly. "I use them as a benchmark, too."

"You do?" I say. "I thought you used Will for that?"

She nods. "Yeah. For a while I did. I *wanted* Will to be my Sophie. On paper, he seemed to be. . . . But looking back . . . he wasn't." She gives me a funny look, then says, "Speaking of . . . she actually wants to have dinner with us tonight."

"Sophie?" I say, thinking I must be confused.

"Yeah. I got in touch with her the other day. On Facebook . . . I told her we were going to be in town and gave her my phone number. She texted last night and said she'd love to meet us for dinner. . . ."

"She texted you *last night*?" I say, my voice rising. "And you're just mentioning it to me *now*?"

"Yeah . . . I wasn't sure I wanted to do it."

I close my eyes, shake my head, and say her name under my breath.

"What? I thought you wanted to see her," she says, her voice now raised and whiny. "How could you possibly be upset with me for arranging something that you and Mom wanted in the first place?"

"Well, for one," I say, "Mom's not here."

"I know . . . but we can always see Sophie again in December . . . with Mom."

"So we wait fifteen years and then see her twice in a matter of weeks?"

"Well? Why not?"

"Doesn't that seem a bit . . . excessive?"

"Sorry, I didn't check the etiquette guide on this topic. . . ." She pulls her phone out of her purse and mumbles that she'll just text her back that we can't make it.

I exhale with disgust, then reach out and put my hand on her forearm. "Stop. Don't text her *that*. That's rude. . . . I just need to think for a second. . . ."

"About what?"

"About whether I'm up for seeing Sophie tonight, with absolutely no warning whatsoever."

"Why do you need warning?" she says. "I mean, what's the difference? Now or next month?"

"I just wish we had discussed it together."

"That's what we're doing now," she says. "Isn't it?"

"Yes, but . . ."

"But what? Why does everything have to be exactly on your terms?"

"It doesn't," I say, thinking of how many times she's called me a control freak for simply having an *opinion* that differs from hers. "I just—"

"You just what, Meredith? Why are you always so dissatisfied with me?" She stands and looks down at me, her hands shoved into her pockets.

"I'm *not*," I lie.

"Yes, you are. And so are Mom and Dad. . . . *God*. I'm sorry I'm not perfect like you and Daniel," she says, stalking away from me.

I get up and quickly catch up to her. "Could you *stop* it with the pity party?"

She stops and glowers at me. "It's not a pity party at *all*," she says. "I'm just sick and tired of your constant judgment. I'm here this weekend to talk about Daniel. . . . That's why I reached out to Sophie. I'm trying to do the right thing here. Can't you see that?"

I stare at her, fleetingly seeing things her way. But like Rubin's famous optical illusion, I quickly return to my view, that white vase so much more obvious than the dual black profiles. "Okay," I say, giving in. "Text her back. Tell her we'll meet her for dinner."

"Is that what you really want?" she asks, as it occurs to me that she could be calling my bluff. Hoping that *I'm* the one who will decide against seeing Sophie.

Instead, I give her a breezy shrug. "Sure," I say. "Let's do it."

chapter twenty-seven

JOSIE

I should have known Meredith would find a way to be pissed off at me for contacting Sophie. It had actually crossed my mind to vet it with her first, but then I thought—no, I should just be proactive, handle something on my own for once. Besides, I really didn't expect Sophie to reply so quickly. I thought there was a very good chance she wouldn't respond until next week, which would mean I'd get credit with Mom and Mere for reaching out to her without actually having to endure yet another emotional encounter.

Then, last night, when I got Sophie's response, I didn't want to bring up anything heavy when Meredith and I were having such a good time, joking and laughing and bonding. It felt so nice and natural—the way I see so many other sisters getting along. I just wanted to savor it, especially given the dread I felt over my impending confession and the very real possibility that Meredith will never forgive me for my role in Daniel's accident.

But of course my strategy backfired, and as we walk through the park, I watch her do a complete one-eighty, her mood going from cheerful to dour in record time.

"All right," she briskly announces. "I'm ready to head home."

"Now?" I say, thinking that I wanted to shop a bit more on the way back.

"Yeah. But you don't have to come with me," she says, slipping into full-on passive-aggressiveness. "You know your way."

I shake my head, knowing she will only hold that against me, too, and can practically script her rant. *How can you go shopping at a time like this?*

And really, she'd be right. That magical Manhattan feeling quickly dissipates as I process that I now have not one, but *two* big things to dread. "No, I'll go back with you," I insist.

She nods, quickening her pace as we head west through the park, the opposite direction from which we came.

"Why are we going this way?" I ask, practically jogging to keep up.

"This is the way to the subway."

"Oh. You don't want to walk back?"

"No. I want to take the *subway.*"

"Well, all righty, then," I mumble.

A silent, sullen fifteen-minute journey later, we enter the subway station at Fifty-Seventh and Seventh, dipping underground, then standing in more silence on the dank platform.

"Look," I finally say, mouth-breathing to avoid the stench of urine and garbage. "We really don't have to see Sophie tonight. We can tell her we have plans. We can tell her we'll do it another time. . . ."

"No. It's fine," she says—which, with Meredith, means it's *not* fine, but she's going to play the martyr.

"So you want to go?" I confirm.

"I said yes. It's *fine.*"

I look at her, frustration welling inside me. "I just don't see why you're so mad at me," I say, as a train roars toward us.

"I'm not mad," she shouts back at me over the vibrating clamor of metal on metal.

"Okay. What are you, then?" I ask, as the train screeches to a halt and we board a mostly empty car. She waits for me to sit, then chooses a seat diagonally across from me. "What are you then?" I repeat.

When she still doesn't answer, I offer her a multiple choice. "Upset? Annoyed? Frustrated?"

"All of the above," she says, crossing her arms tightly over her chest.

"Why?" I say, genuinely wanting to know. "I just don't see why."

"Well, for starters, let's back up here. . . . I've been trying to get you to go to the cemetery *forever*—Mom, too—and you finally go when I'm out of town and you don't even tell Mom you're going. . . ."

"It was a last-minute thing," I tell her.

"But that's even *worse*," she says. "You go on a *whim*? Without us?"

I let out a weary sigh, then try to explain. "I was at *your* house, spending time with *your* daughter because *your* husband lost Rabby. . . ."

"So?" she says. "And your point is . . . ?"

"My point is . . . it just came up. . . . Nolan asked me to go with him. . . . I wanted to say no, but I felt sorry for him, you know, with everything going on. . . . So I said yes. . . . How can you be pissed at me for that?"

Meredith doesn't answer the question, just stares at me, then presses on to her next point. "Second of all, I *specifically* told you that Mom and I wanted to plan something for this December . . . for the fifteen-year anniversary."

I once again wince at her use of *anniversary* in this context.

"And then you pull this stunt," she says. "This was supposed to be about you and me and Mom doing something together. In Daniel's memory."

"Well, we're together now," I say.

"I know, but Mom's not here, and, *shit*, Josie," she says, throwing her hands up, then letting them fall back onto her lap. "Don't you get my point? At all? That we always do things *your* way . . . on *your* terms?"

"Yes, I get that it might seem like that. . . . But things change. . . . Neither one of us thought you were going to take a leave from work and flee to New York and plan a divorce—"

"Can we please leave Nolan and my marriage out of this?"

"Fine," I say, catching an older woman staring at us. I slide down a couple feet, so I'm directly across from Meredith, then lean forward, lowering my voice. "But I think it's all related."

She shakes her head and says, "No, it's *not* all related."

"Yes. It *is*," I insist, my heart now racing. "It all goes back to Daniel. Don't you see that? . . . Nolan . . . your marriage . . . Sophie . . ." I nearly blurt out my confession right there on the subway, just to get it over with, and win the debate. Show her just how much it's all so *fucking* interrelated. But she is now glaring at me with such animosity that I back down, afraid. "My issues, too," I simply say. "And I really want to sort those things out before I have a baby . . . before I become a mother."

"*Exactly!*" she says, raising her voice and pointing at me, just like the lawyer that she is. I stare back at her, wondering what point she thinks I've just made for her.

"What?" I say. "Is there something wrong with that? *God,* Mere. Why do you hate me so much?"

"I don't *hate* you," she says, giving me a look like she does. "I'm just sick and tired of everything revolving around you. *Your* timing. *Your* plans. It's always about *you*, Josie."

My cheeks on fire, I say, "That's so unfair. . . . I came here to see you, Meredith—and to make sure you're okay. I was really hoping to work on our relationship—which is why I didn't want to spoil our good mood last night with anything serious."

She starts to speak, but I hold my hand in the air, determined to make my last point. "And I also came here because I *need* to talk to you about Daniel."

"Yeah. You keep saying that," she says, shaking her head. "When's that conversation going to happen, anyway?"

"Tonight," I say, knowing that things are about to get much, *much* worse between my sister and me.

WHEN WE GET back to Ellen's, I text Sophie, telling her that we would love to meet up with her tonight. She quickly writes back, suggesting we come to her place on the Upper West Side for a drink before dinner and she'll make a reservation somewhere casual.

In the hours that follow, Meredith and I both react to the stress of our plan in our typical ways: she changes into workout clothes and announces that she's going for a long run. I change into sweats, crawl back into bed, and fall into a deep sleep.

I awaken sometime later to my vibrating phone, feeling disoriented, and even more so when I see Pete's name. I suddenly remember where I am, as I answer with a groggy hello.

"Hi, you," he says, his voice chipper. "Were you asleep?"

"No," I fib, wondering why I always deny being asleep or drunk.

He asks me what's going on, and I tell him I'm in New York, visiting my sister. I haven't spoken to him in a few days, and have yet to tell him about my decision to use Gabe as my donor. I feel bad, having gone so far down this path with Pete, especially given his generosity throughout. I don't want to hurt his feelings or seem mercurial. But these factors just can't override the bigger picture. Contrary to what Meredith might think, I have no illusions about how serious this undertaking is, that we are talking about a child's life here. Anyway, Pete might even be relieved to be off the hook.

Surely, he's had his share of doubts and second thoughts, too. But at the same time, I'm more than a little worried that it will extinguish any romantic possibility between us, and maybe even end our odd, fledgling friendship. And I have the sad, sinking feeling that I'm really going to miss him.

"Oh. Cool," he says. "I didn't know you were going up there."

"Yeah. It was kind of last minute. . . . My sister and I really need to sort some things out. . . ." I say, as it actually crosses my mind to tell him everything. As in, *everything*. Instead, I stick to the broad strokes about Sophie and our plan to see her this evening.

"It'll be the first time we've seen her since my brother's funeral," I say.

Pete whistles. "Wow. That sounds intense."

"Yeah. It's probably going to be pretty awkward. . . ." My voice trails off.

"Is she married?"

I tell him I don't know, that her Facebook page is vague. She mostly posts articles or random, funny, Seinfeldesque observations. "It looks like she has a son," I add. "There's one little boy on there a lot. But I guess it could be her nephew or a family friend . . . you know, like you and Fudge."

"Right," he says with a laugh. "Good ol' Fudge."

"So anyway . . . what's going on with you?" I ask, mentally refuting Meredith's accusation that I'm self-absorbed.

"Not much," Pete says. "I was just kinda missing you."

I smile, pleasantly surprised by his answer. "Really?"

"Yeah," Pete says. "I mean not a *lot*. But a *little*."

"A little, huh?"

"Yeah. A smidge."

"Well, I miss you a smidge, too," I say, as I get an unexpected tingly feeling.

"Well, good," he says. "So when're you coming home?"

"Tomorrow," I say. "My flight lands around five, I think."

"You need a lift home?" he asks. "I'd be happy to come get you."

"Aw, thanks," I say. "That's really sweet . . . but I drove."

"Well, then . . . how about dinner? Monday night?"

"That'd be great. I actually wanted to talk to you about something. . . ."

"Oh?" he says, his tone turning serious. "About?"

"Just . . . some things," I say.

"You mean baby-daddy stuff? Or our kiss at Johnny's?"

I laugh, remembering the feel of his lips on mine. "Both, actually," I say.

TWO HOURS LATER, Meredith and I are cabbing it to the Upper West Side. I feel queasy for the obvious reasons, but also a little intimidated by the idea of dining with an accomplished, sophisticated British doctor. I can tell Meredith is uneasy, too, as she keeps checking her makeup and fiddling with her hair.

"You look great," I say, glancing at her sideways.

Looking sheepish for being caught primping, she snaps her compact closed and stows it back in her purse, murmuring a dismissive thanks.

"At least there're two of us. There's only one of her. . . . I bet she's more nervous than we are," I muse aloud.

"I'm not nervous," she quickly says.

I shoot her a skeptical look and say, "C'mon, Mere. How could you not be nervous?"

"I'm just not," she insists. "I'm a little apprehensive, maybe. . . . I mean, she's sort of a stranger."

"She's *completely* a stranger. We haven't laid eyes on her since Daniel's funeral. . . . I don't even think I talked to her *that* day."

"You didn't talk to *anyone* that day," Meredith says with an accusatorial edge.

I ignore the dig, and ask her if we should have a signal.

"A signal for what?"

"A signal for 'let's get the hell outta here.'"

Meredith purses her lips and shakes her head, adamant. "No. No signals. We have to be warm and engaging—no matter what. . . . We have to make a good impression . . . for Daniel. . . . You know?"

It occurs to me to accuse her of being too wrapped up in appearances (which she is) or to point out that if Daniel really is up there watching us, our making a good impression on Sophie surely would be among the least of his concerns. But the last thing we need right now is another tiff, so I simply say, "Yeah. I guess so."

A few minutes later, we arrive at Sophie's building on Central Park West. Meredith and I get out of the cab and walk into the marble lobby of a stuffy doorman building.

"Movin' on up!" I start singing the theme song from *The Jeffersons,* mesmerized by a big crystal chandelier.

Meredith hisses at me to *stop it,* as the doorman smiles, then asks if he may help us.

"Yes," she replies, her voice high and prim. "Could you please tell Sophie Mitchell that Meredith and Josie are here to see her?"

He nods briskly, picks up an old-fashioned telephone, and says, "Yes. Hello, Dr. Mitchell. Meredith and Josie are here. . . . Very well. Will do." He hangs up, points to the elevator, and says, "Ninth floor."

Mere thanks him, and we head that way. Once inside the elevator, we wait for both sets of doors to close—the outer, then the inner accordion-like grate—before lurching upward.

After a slow ascent, we grind to a stop, and the doors open in reverse order into a small vestibule flanked by two apartments. Before we can select the correct door, one swings open, and there stands a surprisingly faded version of Daniel's Sophie. I'd still characterize her as attractive, in a Euro sort of way, and she is wearing a very chic jumpsuit and pointed patent flats. But she has a less-than-svelte figure and heavily sun-spotted skin.

"Hello. Come in, come in," she says, her voice exactly as I remembered, her English accent undiluted by so many years in the States. I can tell she's nervous as she steps forward to give us each a stiff, arm's-length hug, in our birth order. "It's so nice to see you both again."

"It's nice to see you, too," Meredith says.

"Yes, thank you for having us over," I add as Sophie leads us into her living room. I note that there are about a dozen places to sit, including an L-shaped sectional, two huge armchairs, and several plush ottomans, yet no television in sight. I have a sudden random recollection of her telling us that she wasn't allowed to watch it growing up.

"You have a beautiful home," Meredith says.

"Thank you," Sophie says. "We just completed a renovation. This used to be the dining room . . . but nobody entertains that way anymore. . . ." She laughs, then adds, "And I still can't cook."

I catch the *we*, and feel sure Meredith does, too, yet still see no signs of a husband, or a child for that matter, though I do see several framed photos of the boy from her Facebook page.

We follow Sophie into her all-white contemporary kitchen, as she asks what we'd like to drink. "A cocktail? Or a glass of wine?"

Meredith and I both say sure, we would love a glass of wine.

"Red or white?" she asks.

"Whatever you have open," Meredith says, until Sophie insists that we choose.

"Red would be great, thanks," I finally decide, when I notice that Sophie is drinking red. Her stemless lipstick-stained glass rests on the counter next to an artfully arranged charcuterie board. She may not be able to cook, but she certainly can entertain.

"And for you, Meredith?" Sophie asks with a charming lilt.

"Red would be *lovely*," my sister says, sounding pretentious.

Sophie reaches up, plucking two glasses from her open shelving, then fills them both a little more than halfway. Meredith and I each take one as Sophie lifts hers, a smile frozen on her face. An awkward beat follows as it becomes clear that she is poised to make a toast. "To old acquaintances," she finally says, looking into my eyes, then Meredith's.

"To old acquaintances," we echo. I force a smile, as I think of how contradictory the two words are, acquaintances always seeming as if they should be brand-new, either progressing to full-on friendship or falling back into obscurity. Then again, I can't think of a more accurate categorization—so I give her a pass as we all sip our wine. An awkward lull follows, Sophie speaking first.

"So you're a lawyer?" She looks at Meredith.

"Yes," Meredith says. "Though I just took a sabbatical."

I cringe at the term, wondering why she didn't call it a "leave of absence" like she has before, as Sophie turns to me. "And you're a teacher?" she asks.

"Yes, I teach the first grade. How did you know that? From Facebook?"

Sophie shakes her head and says, "No. Your mum told me . . . the last time she wrote. . . ."

"And when was that?" I ask, uncertain of the timing or frequency of their communication, and wondering if Mom's been in touch about a December visit.

"Oh, several years back," she says. "Maybe two thousand ten or eleven . . . I can't recall exactly. How is she doing?" Sophie's brow furrows with concern.

"She's fine," I say. "She got her real estate license."

"Mmm," Sophie says, a British response that I've never been able to decipher. Does it mean "Oh, really?" or "Tell me more" or "I already knew that"?

"And I guess you heard our parents got a divorce?" I say.

Sophie drops her eyes, as she says yes, she knew that. "I'm so sorry," she adds.

For some inexplicable reason, I feel the urge to make it worse. "Yeah. Mom couldn't deal with Dad's drinking. He was on the wagon until . . . everything fell apart."

"Okay, then," Meredith says in a brisk, upbeat voice. "Enough of that."

I smile, then say to no one in particular, "Okay. Meredith says enough of that."

"I just think we can find more cheerful things to discuss," Meredith says under her breath.

I raise my brows, thinking, *Oh? Like the last time we all saw each other, at Daniel's funeral, perhaps?*

"Anyway. She sends her best," Meredith says, which I'm pretty sure is a lie, unless she happened to talk to Mom this afternoon while I was napping.

"Tell her I said hello, too." Sophie smiles and nods, but can't mask her pained, pitying look. I know it well—it was the way so many people looked at me for so long after the accident—and feel a rush of annoyance, though I know it's not fair. How else do I expect her to look right now? And would I really want her *not* to feel pity?

Silently granting that she is in a lose-lose situation, I pluck a piece of ropy Serrano ham from her appetizer spread, pop it into my mouth, and change the subject. "So?" I say, still chewing. "Are you married, Sophie?"

Meredith interjects with a high, nervous laugh, then says, "Well. That's a little direct."

"Oh. It's fine," Sophie says, as I recall one of her letters to Mom about a year after Daniel's death. It was several pages long, both front and back, and written in the most beautiful handwriting, covering every subject imaginable—from her family to her residency to her travels. But there was not one single mention of her romantic situation, only an awkward paragraph about how she still thought of Daniel "every single day." I remember folding it back up and thinking this should be a given, hardly worth mentioning—and that this seemed to be a sign that she was seeing someone.

In any event, she seems perfectly comfortable with my question now. "I'm actually divorced. But we had a good run . . . almost ten years."

"I'm sorry," Meredith says, bowing her head.

At least he didn't die, I think.

"Thank you," Sophie says. "It was hard . . . but I'm in a good place now."

I imagine her saying these same words to her ex-husband about Daniel and feel another irrational wave of resentment at just how adept she is at getting over big wounds.

"Do you have kids?" Meredith asks.

"Yes," Sophie says, smiling. "I have a seven-year-old son. Calvin."

"Oh, yes. I think I saw him on your Facebook page."

She smiles, nods, and says, "Yes. That's him."

"That's a cute name," Meredith says, as I think that I can't picture my brother going for a name like Calvin. But frankly, I can't picture Daniel with Sophie at *all* anymore. Even when I try to adjust his age in my mind—a difficult thing to do—I just don't see them together as she is now.

"Thank you. He's a sweet boy," Sophie says, perking up the way parents so often do when the subject turns to their kids. "Do you have children?"

"I have a daughter. Harper. She's four," Meredith replies, a look of pride flickering across her face.

"Oh. That's a *great* age," Sophie says.

Meredith nods her agreement, then says, "Josie's planning on having a baby soon, too. . . ."

I look at her, surprised, as Sophie asks me, "Oh? Are you pregnant?"

"No," I say. "I'm planning to do it via donor insemination . . . soon."

Sophie cocks her head to the side, giving me a look that can only be interpreted as one of respect. "That's marvelous. Good for you," she says.

"Thank you," I say. "I'm really excited."

"You should be," she says, and as we segue into a lively conversation about pregnancy, childbirth, and motherhood, I wonder how long it will be before one of us finally brings up Daniel.

NEARLY AN HOUR later, we are seated in a cozy corner booth at Cafe Luxembourg, a bustling bistro where Sophie seems to be a regular. She orders another bottle of wine, which I hope will facilitate a deeper conversation. But by the time our entrées arrive at the table, Daniel's name still has yet to be uttered. I decide that I can't wait another moment. Searching for my opening, I find it when Meredith compliments Sophie's wine selection.

"I'm glad you like it," she replies. "I actually don't know much about wine, but I've been to this particular vineyard."

"You don't know much about wine? That's surprising. . . . Daniel used to brag about how worldly you were. . . ." I say, thinking that wine selection seems to fall squarely into that purview.

She smiles, then says, "I think he confused my accent with worldliness. I was actually quite green when I met Daniel."

"Yeah, right," I say, feeling oddly jubilant that I finally got her to say his name.

"I *was*," she insists.

I roll my eyes and laugh, but not unkindly. "C'mon, Sophie. You were a *Yale* medical student . . . and didn't you go to Oxford and some fancy boarding school before that?"

"Yes," she says, pushing a carrot with a tine of her fork. "But I was only a day student. . . ."

"Oh, a *day* student." I smile. "Well, that changes *everything*."

Sophie laughs at herself, but then grows earnest. "Truly. I grew up in much the same way that you did. Very comfortably, but not lavishly . . ." She hesitates, then adds, "I loved your family home . . . and Atlanta is such a *beautiful* city. Urban in some ways, yet so green and lush . . . You really had an idyllic life—" She stops abruptly, looking slightly mortified. "I mean, that's what I remember thinking when I was there. . . . You know, with Daniel . . ." Her voice trails off as her face reddens and she looks down at her plate. In other words—when she visited the first time, *not* when she came back for the funeral.

It is so awkward that I can't help feeling sorry for her, and reach out to touch her arm. "We know what you meant," I say, speaking for my sister, too, as I wonder, for really the first time, about how it all unfolded for her.

"Where were you when you found out?" I say, chasing the question with a gulp of wine.

Sophie takes a measured breath, then another. "I was on my way to Royal Albert Hall with my grandmother. We were going to the Carols by Candlelight. Our little tradition . . ." She pauses and bites her lip, a faraway look in her eye. "My mobile rang. I saw Daniel's name—and was so excited to hear from him. . . . I'd been gushing about him to Gran—and had been trying to call him since

I landed that morning. . . . But it wasn't Daniel, of course," she says. "It was his friend . . . Nolan."

My eyes still on Sophie, I nod and point to my sister. "That's Meredith's husband. . . ."

Sophie looks surprised. "Is it?" she asks.

"My mom didn't tell you that?" I ask, knowing that she must've, and wanting to call Sophie out on forgetting.

"Maybe she did, come to think of it," she says, now looking at Meredith. "That's so nice. For your family."

I watch Meredith tense up, her eyes becoming expressionless, almost steely. "Yes. We got married and moved into our family home. . . ." Her voice trails off.

"It *really* is a *beautiful* home," Sophie says. "And I just love Atlanta."

"Do you think you would have lived there?" I ask. "If you had married Daniel?"

Sophie gazes back at me, blinking. She opens her mouth, starts to answer, then stops, as if the thought has never really occurred to her, one way or the other. "I don't know," she says, blinking back at me.

"Well," I press. "Do you think you would have married Daniel?"

A painful silence follows, but I refuse to speak first, unwilling to offer her an out. I am relieved that Meredith doesn't, either.

"Oh, Josie," Sophie finally says, her voice and expression laden with guilt. "I just don't know the answer to that. . . . There are so many variables."

"Such as?" I ask.

"Such as our residencies. Whether we would have matched at the same place . . . then our fellowships . . . We were so young—and those were grueling years."

"But did you love him?" I ask, thinking there's really only *one* variable that should matter.

"Yes, I loved him, but . . . I just don't know. . . ."

Her answer, along with the uneasy look on her face, confirms my hunch. Although I appreciate her honesty, I can't help feeling betrayed on Daniel's behalf, and part of me is tempted to shout, *How dare you not tell us that our brother was the love of your life, the best person you've ever known, and that you've never gotten over the loss?!*

I glance at Meredith, and can tell in an instant that she feels the same, which is somehow reassuring. It occurs to me that as different as we are in our behavior and decisions, our most basic, knee-jerk emotional reactions to really big things are often remarkably similar. And it is in these moments that I am most grateful for my sister.

Meredith clears her throat, then picks up my interrogation where I left off, her feelings of decorum apparently having dissipated. "The night you flew back to London . . . right before the accident . . . Daniel sat in the kitchen and talked to Mom about you. Did she ever tell you about that conversation?"

Sophie shakes her head and gives a terrible answer, once again. "Maybe. I don't recall for certain. . . ."

My sister raises her chin and continues, her voice strong and clear. "Well, I'll tell you what he said. . . . He said you were the most incredible person he'd ever met—and that he wanted to marry you for a lot of reasons, including that he knew you'd be a fabulous mother."

"Goodness. That's so incredibly sweet," Sophie says, finally looking mournful.

"Yes," Meredith says. "And I think that's why you have remained so important to our mother. . . . You're a connection to him. . . ." Her voice cracks, so I finish where she left off.

"I guess we just want to know if you *really* and *truly* loved him?"
I say, giving her one last chance. "That it wasn't just some passing
romance?"

Sophie shivers, pulling her cashmere wrap more tightly around
her shoulders, taking her time answering. "Yes, I did love him. . . .
It's just hard. . . . It's hard for me to really remember that time. . . .
So much life has happened since. . . ."

"Yes. For everyone but Daniel," I say, wanting to shame her.

It seems to work as she nods and adjusts her wrap again. Deep
down, I know I'm not being fair. It's not Sophie's fault that Daniel
died and she lived. I can also tell that she is trying her best. It just so
happens that her best sort of sucks. So I attempt one last angle.
"Was your ex-husband much like Daniel?" I ask.

It feels like a softball, given that the marriage ended. An easy
way for her to tell us how much better Daniel was.

"In some ways," she says. "But not really."

"Is he American? A doctor?" Meredith asks.

"Yes. And yes," Sophie says. "But he's not a surgeon like Daniel
wanted to be."

"What is he?"

"A dermatologist," she says. "And the stereotypes of those spe-
cialties really fit. He's much less intense than Daniel was . . . more
outgoing. . . . Daniel was smarter. . . ."

I nod, thinking, *Damn right he was.*

She shrugs, then finishes. "I don't know. . . . They're very different people."

"Was he jealous of Daniel?" I ask, instantly realizing how ridiculous the question sounds. "I mean, of your *relationship*?"

"No. Todd's not wired like that. He doesn't really get jealous. . . .
He's not the sensitive type. Hence . . . our divorce, perhaps." She
laughs nervously. "My boyfriend before Todd was more jealous, I
think. . . ."

"Of how much you loved Daniel?"

"Yes," she says.

Finally, I think, a satisfying answer.

"Are you dating anyone now?" Meredith asks.

I take a final bite of my filet, only mildly curious about Sophie's answer, and for some reason fully expecting it to be no. But when I look up, I watch her face come to life, even more so than when we asked about Calvin. She tells us yes, there is someone.

"Is he a doctor, too?" Meredith says.

"She," Sophie says. "And no, she's a writer."

She goes on to eagerly explain how they met—at some yoga retreat in Arizona—but I mostly tune her out, exchanging a glance with Meredith. It is a fleeting one, but I am now positive we feel the same. That we're totally over this evening and Sophie, and especially her love for someone who isn't our brother, whether a man or a woman.

Sure enough, during the next pause in the conversation, Meredith cranes her neck to signal the waitress for our bill, then presses her palm to her lips in what I can tell is a completely fake yawn.

"Oh, listen to me," Sophie says, still smiling. "I'm so sorry for prattling on like this."

"It's fine," Meredith says. "We're really happy for you. Right, Josie?"

"Yes. Of course," I say. "Very happy for you."

"But it *is* getting late . . . and Josie has an early flight," Mere lies.

"Yes. A very early flight," I say, locking eyes with my sister, unable to think of a single time I have loved her more.

chapter twenty-eight

MEREDITH

"Well. I didn't see that one coming," I say after a virtually silent cab ride home. I carefully remove my shoes and hang up my coat as I make the decision not to mention Josie's boots. Hell, she can sleep in them tonight, for all I care at the moment.

"Yeah. Me either . . . I mean, I knew she had moved on . . . but *damn*. . . ." Looking glum, Josie strides over to the sofa and collapses onto it. "It was like he meant *nothing* to her."

"That's not necessarily true," I say as I wash my hands at the kitchen sink. "We don't know that she didn't love him deeply. . . . She could have been as committed as he was at the time. . . ."

"Okay . . . but did you get that feeling?" Josie asks. "Because I didn't. I mean—she didn't even mention his name until we got to the restaurant. . . . It just felt like she moved on, like, a couple months later."

"Yeah. But she just gave us the CliffsNotes version of her life. . . . She did say that one ex was jealous of Daniel. . . . I mean, she could have been heartbroken for *years*."

"Well, it would have been nice to hear that," Josie says.

I nod again, silently noting that irony—that it would have been nice to hear a lot of things from my own sister over the years, too. It would have been nice to discuss our feelings. Or visit the cemetery together. Or acknowledge Daniel's birthdays—and all the painful anniversaries of his death.

But I stick to a more constructive point and one I've come to learn well in my own life. "It's impossible to understand someone else's relationship. They seemed very happy together . . . and maybe we need to focus on that . . . the fact that Daniel was happy when he died."

"She would have broken his heart," Josie says.

"Probably so," I agree.

Josie sighs, a deep frown on her face. "So? Did you really tell Mom we were having dinner with her?"

I shake my head.

"I knew it," she says. "Should we tell her?"

I shrug, having already asked myself this question several times since we left the restaurant. "We should probably tell her we saw her. But skip the details."

Josie nods in agreement. "It would upset her more than us."

"For sure . . . Sophie's been a symbol to her. Or at least a comfort . . . Think about the stories she always tells about that visit . . . and her last talk with Daniel at the kitchen table. She loves knowing that Daniel was truly happy and deeply in love . . . that he experienced the sweetness of that. . . ."

"Even if he loved her way more than she loved him?" Josie says.

"Even if," I say, my mind drifting to Nolan again, wondering if that isn't the happier place to be—the one loving *more*. "Do you want a cup of tea? Or a decaf?"

She shakes her head. "No. But I'll take some bourbon or something. . . . Is there any hard stuff here?"

"Yep. You're in luck," I say, standing on an acrylic stepladder to reach the cabinet where Ellen keeps her liquor. I pull down a bottle of Widow Jane whiskey, along with a rocks glass. Then, on second thought, I grab another glass for me, pour about two shots in each, then toss in some cubes of ice from the freezer.

"God, this is depressing," I say, walking over to the sofa and handing her one of the glasses before I sit down beside her. "I mean—what are we doing here, anyway?"

"Well. *You're* here on a *sabbatical,*" she says. "Remember?"

"Yeah, yeah," I say. "You know what I mean. . . . Look at us. . . . Here we are . . . fifteen years later . . . all screwed up . . . and begrudging someone else her happiness. Maybe we just need to move on?"

Josie kicks her boots off, leaving them sprawled under the coffee table, then takes a long drink. She makes a face, puts down her glass, and nods. "Yeah. I know. We really do. . . . That's what I was sort of trying to say earlier, when I said that all of our problems seem related to Daniel. . . . It just feels like we've never really gotten over the loss . . . the way Sophie did."

I nod. "Yeah. But you can't compare a short romance—even an intense one—to a relationship with a sibling."

"True," she says, her face twisting into an expression of deep, profound sadness. "You really can't."

A long moment of silence passes before she says my name, then turns to face me, leaning on one arm of the sofa.

"Yeah?" I say, looking at her.

"I need to tell you something. . . ." She frowns, staring down at her hands clasped in her lap.

"Okay," I say, turning to sit sideways, facing her.

"It's the thing I came here to tell you . . . about Daniel," she says, glancing up at me with a worried expression.

Feeling suddenly cold, I pull Ellen's nubby throw blanket from the back of the sofa and drape it over our legs. "What is it?" I say.

Josie's big blue eyes grow glassy, her lower lip quivering. It conjures a memory of how she used to cry on demand, just to get me in trouble. But this time, I can tell it's sincere. She's truly on the verge of tears, and I feel the sudden urge to protect her, reaching for her hands. She breathes, in and out, for what feels like a full minute, all the while holding my gaze and hands. Then she opens her mouth and starts to tell me a story. A story about the night Daniel died. Of her getting wasted at Five Paces. Of someone from the bar calling Daniel to come pick her up, take her home. There are more details, most of them trivial, but I have trouble following them all.

"No," I finally say, letting go of her hands, shaking my head. "That isn't what happened. He was going out to get a burger. That's what he told Mom."

"He lied to Mom. He was just covering for me," Josie says, her face starting to contort in a valiant but unsuccessful attempt not to cry. Tears spill down her cheeks as she continues, "He was on his way to get me."

"But that's just a theory," I say, my heart starting to race. "Right? I mean—how would you know that he was coming to get you? He died before he got there. . . . He *could* have been going to get a burger. Right?"

She doesn't reply or move a muscle, not even to wipe her tears.

"Josie?" I demand. "You don't know that for sure, do you?"

"Yes," she whispers. "I do, actually."

"But how?" I say.

"I can't tell you how," she says.

"Why not?" I say, becoming more frantic and angry.

"Because. I promised someone I wouldn't. . . ."

I kick the blanket off my legs, then stand, pacing in front of the coffee table. "What do you mean you can't tell me how you know that? You drop a bomb like this and then pull some . . . some Woodward and Bernstein *bullshit*?"

Josie covers her face with her hands, mumbling again that she can't, that she promised.

"He was our *brother*, Josie," I say, wishing I hadn't used the past tense, when he will *always* be our brother. "You're telling me crucial details about the night our brother died, and you're worried about a promise you made to someone else? Who was it? Shawna?" I shout.

"No," she says through sobs. "It wasn't Shawna."

"Then who?"

She shakes her head, looking pained and panicked and desperate. And suddenly, just like that, I know who she's protecting.

"Nolan," I whisper, my heart racing, my head spinning. "Nolan called Daniel that night. To come get you."

It is a statement, not a question—and she doesn't deny it.

"So," I say, my voice calm and restrained—the opposite of the way I feel inside, "what you're telling me is that my sister . . . *and* my husband . . . have been keeping this secret from me for fifteen *fucking* years?"

"I didn't know for sure," Josie says, wiping away tears. "Until last weekend."

"I don't believe you. And besides, clearly Nolan did," I say. "Nolan must have known that he called Daniel to come get you. . . ."

"Please don't tell him I told you," she says. "I think he wanted to tell you himself. . . ."

"Fuck. Him." I spit out the words with as much venom as possible, my disbelief morphing into rage. "And fuck you, too."

"Meredith," she says. "Please . . ."

"Talk about a betrayal," I say as Josie begins to bawl and beg. The sound of her gurgling sobs, the sight of her face glistening with snot and tears, only makes me hate her. I pick up one of her boots and throw it as hard as I can. It hits the wall, the heel leaving a black mark. "And what part of 'take off your fucking shoes when you're in the fucking house' don't you get, Josie?"

"I'm *sorry*," she sobs. "I'm *so* sorry."

"For wearing your shoes in the house? Or for not telling me that you and Nolan were responsible for Daniel's death?" I shout.

"God. Don't say that," Josie says, her eyes filled with horror, her lower lip trembling. "*Please* don't say that."

"Well," I say. "Let's look on the bright side. At least this makes my decision to divorce him a little easier."

"Meredith, don't. . . . Don't let that happen to you. . . . You love each other," she says, then launches into a rambling monologue about how this has affected her relationships. That she's been punishing herself for years. Something about Will and their breakup. Something about Gabe.

I cut her off. "Once again," I say. "This is all about you, Josie. All about how Daniel's death affected *you*."

"No," she says. "I just don't want this to have an impact on your marriage, too."

"Too late," I say.

"I'm so sorry. He's so sorry, too. Can't you forgive us?"

"Talk to Daniel about forgiveness, Josie. Talk to God about that."

"I have," she says—which is a neat trick since I'm pretty sure she's an atheist.

"How about Mom and Dad?" I say. "Do they know?"

She shakes her head.

"Think they'll forgive you?" I say. "Think Mom will be okay with this twist in the story?"

"I don't know," she whimpers, her face red and blotchy and streaked with mascara. "I hope she can forgive me. I hope Mom and Dad both can."

"Well, they just might," I say, my voice quivering as I hold back my own tears, determined not to cry until I'm alone. "But I will *never* forgive you, Josie. . . . Not for as long as I live."

chapter twenty-nine

JOSIE

I stay on Ellen's sofa for a long time, nursing then refilling my whiskey, reeling, as I formulate a further plea for forgiveness. I know there is nothing that I can say or do that will change her mind about what I've done—and what I've left undone—for so long. She will only think me more selfish. It crosses my mind that maybe she is right, that this whole trip has been completely self-serving. But then I feel a flash of anger, realizing that there is so often a catch-22 with Meredith; damned if I do, damned if I don't.

I consider calling Nolan, if only to warn him, but worry that might make things worse—that we'll look even more conspiratorial. In fact, I have the feeling Meredith is more upset by the fact that we kept this secret than by what actually happened on that night. I try to imagine how I would feel if I suddenly learned that she and Gabe had been keeping a big secret from me. I can't deny how much it would hurt—and Gabe and I aren't even married.

Then again, what if they were only trying to protect me? Would I give them a pass if that were the case? I tell myself I absolutely would, and nearly awaken Meredith to make this point. After all, wasn't she the one who suggested we not share details of our Sophie dinner with Mom? And wasn't that because she believes the information would only upset her? Isn't that what you do when you love someone? I start to work up some righteous indignation, but can't fully sell myself on the idea. Deep down, I know there's a difference between withholding information about our time with Sophie tonight and lying, even by omission, about the night Daniel died. There is simply no denying that I'm in the wrong.

At some point I doze off. When I awaken, it's still dark outside, just after four o'clock. I decide I have to leave—that I can't face my sister in the morning. So I slip into Ellen's darkened bedroom, where Meredith is softly snoring, and I gather my things, shoving them haphazardly into my suitcase. As I turn to go, I remember the gift I brought for Meredith. Using the flashlight on my phone, I rifle through my bag and find the brand-new, bright-eyed Rabby replacement, its fur still pristine and fluffy. I put it next to her pillow, then whisper goodbye to my sister, somehow understanding that this fight is different from all the others we've had. Although I hope I'm wrong, this one feels final.

A few minutes later, I am in the back of a cab on the way to La Guardia. There is no traffic, and we get there in record time. I pay my fare, then walk into the empty airport. A friendly lady at the Delta check-in counter reassures me that there are plenty of open seats on the 6:00 A.M. flight to Atlanta, and she feels sure I'll get one on standby. "Good luck, dear," she says, giving me a look of pity, probably assuming that anyone who shows up at the airport hours before their scheduled flight is leaving under less than stellar circumstances.

After I make it through security, I head for the restroom, where I brush my teeth and wash my face. Calculating that I have over an hour until they start boarding that first flight to Atlanta, I head to the gate and curl up in a corner. My last thought as I pass out from exhaustion is how disgusting Meredith would think it to sit, let alone sleep, on the airport floor.

I wake up with a whiskey headache, burning eyes, and a stiff neck, but feel a rush of relief when my name is called for the very last standby seat. I take it as an omen, a sign that things can only get better from here.

chapter thirty

MEREDITH

They say you should never go to bed mad, but when it came to my fights with Josie, Mom always enforced the opposite. She'd send us to our respective rooms, insisting that we "get some sleep" because "things always look better in the morning." It was actually pretty sound advice, as we usually woke up and simply pretended that nothing had happened (before finding something new to argue about, of course). Occasionally, we'd even laugh it all off, aligning ourselves against Mom and painting her as an overreactor.

But around four-thirty in the morning, when I awaken and find that sad stuffed rabbit perched on my pillow, I do not feel even a tiny bit better. Instead, I feel considerably worse—just as angry and hurt, but also racked with guilt and worry, certain that my sister will be gone. Sure enough, I get up and look around the apartment, finding no trace of her other than her shampoo on the edge of the bathtub and one of her retro striped tube socks peeking out from under the bed. I search the place one more time, hoping to find a note, if only to get the last word, but there is nothing. I pick up the rabbit and begin to panic, wondering where she could have gone in the middle of the night, whether she could be lying in a ditch somewhere. And although I can't imagine Josie ever harming herself, Lewis's sister does flit through my mind.

So, despite my resolution never to speak to her again, I call her cell. It goes straight to voicemail. I hang up without leaving a message, then get back in bed, still clutching the rabbit. I fall asleep for another couple of hours, then wake up, sweaty and weepy, piecing together a dream about Daniel—the first I've had in a long time, at least the first I can recall. The two of us were waiting on a subway platform together, talking and laughing, and then suddenly he vanished. *Poof.* Gone. For days, Josie, Mom, Dad, and I hung placards, plastering his face all over the city, like the ones posted after September 11. But Daniel never turned up. Of course, it doesn't take an expert to decipher the nightmare, and I can clearly see that it stems from some combination of Josie leaving and Daniel dying, along with the grim thought of Lewis's sister plunging to her death on the subway tracks. I know it was just a dream, but I still start to worry that it is closer to a premonition than a nightmare—and ask myself what I would do if I never saw Josie again. Would I tell my mother about our fight, or would I keep it a secret, history repeating itself?

I get up, pacing frantically all over the apartment, searching for clues that don't exist, before calling Josie a second time. Straight to voicemail again. I then call Delta, thinking and hoping that she simply got on an earlier flight—but they refuse to give out her information. I hang up and call them back, this time pretending to *be* Josie. I get flustered, then busted, then reprimanded about confidentiality. I really start to lose it, then decide to call Gabe—what feels like a last resort.

"Hi," I say, bracing myself when he answers.

"Is everything okay?" he asks, either clueless or in cahoots, both scenarios equally plausible.

I answer the question with a question, asking if he's heard from Josie, determined not to be outwitted by someone I've always viewed as a worthy adversary.

"No," he says. "I thought she was with you this weekend?"

"She was," I say, my hands turning clammy. "We had a fight last night. She left. . . . I thought maybe she got on an earlier flight. . . ."

"Not that I know of," he says, his voice completely flat. "I haven't heard from her."

"Okay," I say. "Will you let me know if—*when* you do?"

He hesitates, and it only takes three seconds for me to be pissed. "So I guess that's a no," I snap. "Never mind."

"Jesus, Mere. Chill *out*," he says.

"Chill out?" I yell into the phone. "She disappeared in the middle of the night, Gabe."

"She's a big girl."

"Yeah. Well, she told me about her big secret," I say, feeling sure Gabe knows everything.

Silence.

"About the night Daniel died?" I press.

"Okay," he says.

"O-*kay*? That's it? That's all you have to say about my sister's role in my brother's death?"

"I think that's a bullshit characterization, Meredith."

"You think it was okay to keep that secret from me?"

"No," he says. "And I'm glad she finally told you."

"Fifteen years late, don't you think?"

"I don't think it's *ever* too late, actually," Gabe says, sounding all sanctimonious and superior and infuriatingly calm. "But that's just me."

"Easy for you to say," I scoff. "Maybe you'd feel differently if it were *your* brother who was killed. And *your* sister had kept a secret from you about the night he died."

"Maybe I would," he says.

For one second, I'm nearly appeased, until he snidely adds, "Then again, Josie didn't keep the secret from *me*, now did she?"

"What is *that* supposed to mean?" I shout into the phone.

"It means exactly what I *said*, Meredith. . . . She told me everything, years ago. She confided in *me*. *Not* you. And I think there's a pretty good reason for that."

My mind races for a retort as he continues, "So maybe you should take a closer look at *yourself* and stop blaming Josie for everything."

"You're a real asshole," I say, my face on fire. "You know that?"

"Yeah," he says. "But I'm the asshole who's always been there for Josie. Which is more than I can say for you."

I hang up on him and throw the phone down, my hands shaking as I collapse onto the sofa and burst into tears. I cry as long and hard as I did when Daniel died, although the grief is obviously a different strain, more layered and complex. At some point, there are no more tears, but I stay put on the sofa, contemplating my life, how I got here. I think of Daniel's accident, of course. And my marriage to Nolan. And those years in between. I think of acting and law school and parental expectations and the home that has always been my home. I think of Josie, how fucked up our relationship is, and consider that maybe Gabe is right. Maybe it *is* my fault. Maybe I resent her because of my own choices. I think of Josie's theory that it's all interrelated, that it all goes back to that night in December, all of our decisions and dreams and mistakes from the past inextricably linked. I consider calling Nolan, then my mother, then Ellen, then Amy, even my father. But I really don't want to talk to any of them, for different reasons, and it strikes me that I've never been so alone.

And it is in this despondent, desperate moment that I think of the one person in the world whom I love without condition. The one part of this tragic story that is beautiful and perfect and un-touched by regret or what-ifs.

"*I am Harper's mother,*" I say aloud, feeling an incredible sense of peace wash over me. Then I stand and start to pack my things, finally ready to go home.

chapter thirty-one

JOSIE

A few hours later, I've landed in Atlanta and collected my bag and car. I drive home on a virtually empty highway, then pull up to my house, relieved not to see Leslie's car in the driveway.

"Hey!" Gabe says, greeting me at the front door in flannel pajama pants and a T-shirt. He looks happy to see me, though not nearly as excited as Revis, who is planting his paws on my shoulders and licking my face.

"Hey, you two," I say, laughing as I hug Revis back.

"I've been calling you," Gabe says, pulling my bag off the porch and rolling it into the foyer.

"Yeah. My phone's dead," I say. "I left my charger in New York. . . ."

"Kiss it goodbye," he says, crossing his arms. "She'll never give that back to you."

I raise my brows. "Meredith told you about our fight?" I ask, thinking that you can't really call it a fight; it was more of a one-sided falling-out.

"Yep. She called this morning, looking for you."

I sigh and tell him that I left when she was still sleeping and got on an earlier flight. "So what did Meredith say?" I ask, sitting cross-legged on the floor with Revis as Gabe takes a kitchen stool.

"She's worried," he says.

I roll my eyes and mutter, "Yeah, right."

"I promised to let her know when you turned up . . . so one of us should probably do that. . . ."

I shrug and tell him to feel free to text her, but that she made it very clear she doesn't want to hear from me ever again.

"Well, she's pretty pissed at me, too. But I'll shoot her a text. . . ." Gabe says, picking his phone up off the counter and starting to thumb-type.

"What's her beef with you?" I ask, rubbing the top of Revis's head, then his throat and belly.

"I kind of went off on her," he says, still typing. "Put her on a little guilt trip of her own . . ."

I perk up a bit, feeling soothed by his loyalty. "And how did you manage to guilt Saint Meredith?"

"I flipped the script on her sanctimony. . . ." he says. "I told her that if she weren't so judgmental, maybe you would have confided in her years ago."

"And?" I ask. "What did she say?"

"Oh, she heard me. . . ."

"But did she back down?"

"A little, maybe." He puts his phone down. "Besides, I'm sure she's *way* more upset at Nolan. . . . I take it you told her that part of the story, too?"

"Yeah," I say, still feeling guilty about including Nolan in my confession, though there was really no other way to tell the truth. "I had to."

"Is he going to be angry with you?"

I shrug, thinking that's the least of our concerns. "I hope not. I'm going to text him what happened. . . . Just give him a heads-up . . . I'm sure he'll understand—and maybe even feel relieved. . . . In any event, I know I did the right thing by telling her."

"You did," Gabe says, nodding. "I'm proud of you."

"Thanks," I say with a big sigh. Then I tell him about our dinner with Sophie, sticking to the facts (that she married, had a son, then got a divorce, and is now in a relationship with a woman). I do not editorialize, wanting to hear his true reaction first.

"Was it cathartic?" he asks, missing the mark—which is rare for him.

I shake my head. "No," I say. "The opposite . . . Meredith and I both expected to see more grief . . . more *longing*. . . . I think part of us, on some level, went into the night actually *wanting* to see a broken woman . . . wanting to hear that his death destroyed her life. . . ." My voice trails off as I silently finish my sentence: *just as it did ours*.

Gabe stares at me for a few seconds, then shakes his head. "Nah. You wouldn't want that," he says. "You just wanted to hear what he meant to her. That he affected her in some profound and lasting way."

I nod, thinking that this time he *is* right—that that really *would* have been enough. "Yeah. True," I say, drawing a deep breath as I stand and take the stool next to his. "So it wasn't cathartic. But I do feel a sense of closure."

"On the Sophie front?"

"Yeah. And also with Meredith . . . I hope she comes around . . . but if she doesn't . . ."

"She will. She always does."

"She might not this time. But either way . . . I did what I had to do. . . . And I feel that I can now move on with my life. I'm ready to have a baby. Right now."

Gabe turns ninety degrees on his stool, as I do the same, our shoulders now squared. "Right now, huh?"

"Yeah." I nod, feeling a rush of adrenaline as I hold his gaze. "Right now. And with *you*, Gabe. I want to have this baby with *you*."

"You do?" he says. His smile is faint, but his eyes are unmistakably happy.

"Yes. I do," I say, overwhelmed with a sense of calm certainty. "If the offer's still good?"

"Yeah." Gabe grins. "I think we're both a little nuts here . . . but yeah, the offer's still good."

"Can you picture it?" I ask him—because I'm finally *really* starting to. Not just motherhood, which I've been imagining in one way or another since I was a little girl playing with dolls, but a permanent partnership with Gabe—and the dark-haired, brown-eyed, brilliant child his genes will likely give me.

"Yes. I can, actually," he says without any hesitation.

"Really?" I say, feeling a little choked up.

He nods. "Yes. You're my best friend, Josie. You're *more* than a best friend. I told you—you're my family."

"You're my family, too," I say. "I just want you to be sure."

"I'm sure," he says. "I'm sure that you're going to drive me crazy. And I'm sure this baby is going to kill my lifestyle. . . . But I've given this a lot of thought—really since the first time you brought it up—and I'm also sure—*very* sure—that this will be the best thing I ever do with my life. That this baby will be everything to me. To both of us."

I break into a big grin, then give him an even bigger hug. As we separate, I tell him he's officially on the hook, no take-backs, and that I'll be calling Dr. Lazarus first thing tomorrow morning.

"So how will this work, exactly?" Sydney asks me the following afternoon as we sit on our usual bench on the playground, supervising the kids during recess. I've just told her about the appointment I booked with Dr. Lazarus for later this week—and my decision to use Gabe's sperm.

"Do you mean the actual procedure?" I ask her.

"Yeah. Will you have to do IVF?"

"No," I say. "Not yet. My ovarian reserve is on the low side, but we decided to try one straightforward round of insemination first. . . ."

"So no fertility drugs?"

"No," I say. "Just an injection of hCG to trigger ovulation beforehand."

"Then what?"

"That's pretty much it. Then we just wait and see what happens. . . ." I say, the weight of my decision sinking in more with every passing hour.

"So no lawyers, either? Like you were going to use with Pete?"

"Correct," I say, getting butterflies hearing Pete's name and thinking about our dinner plans tonight. I push him out of my mind and continue, "They just take the sample from Gabe . . . then wash and process it to basically concentrate the sperm and maximize the chances of conception. . . . Then they just shoot it up there. It's a supereasy procedure." I pat my stomach and smile. "It's like a normal pregnancy . . . minus his penis inside me."

"Oh, yeah. *So* normal." Sydney cracks up just as Edie runs over to our bench, calling my name in deep distress, as she does about twice a week. "Miss Josie! Miss Jo-*sieeee*!"

"What's wrong, sweetie?" I ask, pretending to be more alarmed than I am.

"Wesley called me a 'dumb girl,'" she sobs, tears streaming down her face. "He's *so* mean."

I put my arm around her and tell her what I believe to be true based on months of observation. "Sweetie, Wesley teases you because he *likes* you."

"No, he *hates* me," she insists as I catch Wesley over by the monkey bars, eyeing us with a mischievous smile.

"Trust me. . . . He likes you," I say, picturing the two of them one day dating and telling the story of how they met, back in the first grade in Miss Josie's class. Stranger things have happened.

"And guess what?" I continue in my most excited, I-have-a-big-secret voice.

"What?" she asks, wiping away her tears and looking at me with wide, trusting eyes.

"I like you, too," I whisper in her ear. "A *lot.*"

Edie's tears instantly clear. She gives me a big smile before scampering off, happy again.

"Teacher's *pet,*" Sydney says, elbowing me.

"Guilty," I say, smiling. "She's just so sweet . . . like her mother, actually."

"Too bad her dad sucks," Sydney says.

I shrug, feeling blissfully indifferent to Edie's dad, then say, "I don't know. Will's really not *that* bad. . . . He's just a little lame. . . . I'm glad I'm not married to him."

"*Wow.* You really have made progress," Syd says.

"Yeah. I guess I have," I say, thinking of what a strange but powerful turn my life has taken since the first day of school, back when I feared Edie, despised Will, and pinned all my hopes on some man I might never meet.

A COUPLE OF hours before our reservation at Sotto Sotto, my favorite Italian restaurant in Atlanta, Pete calls me, asking if he can come pick me up. I tell him I appreciate the offer, but that it makes no sense for him to drive all the way to Buckhead when he lives in Inman Park, so near the restaurant. "How about I pick *you* up?" I say.

He starts to protest, insisting that he doesn't mind the driving, but I cut him off and say, "When will you learn you're not dealing with a traditional girl here?"

Pete laughs. "Okay. Good point. Do you want to come early for a drink?"

"Sure," I say. "Seven?"

"Perfect. Eighty-seven Druid Circle . . . just past Krog Street Market."

I scribble the address on a notepad and say, "Got it. See you soon."

"Can't wait," Pete says.

A few minutes past seven, I am standing on the front porch of Pete's charming Craftsman bungalow, ringing his bell. The door swings open immediately, and there he stands, looking cuter than ever.

"Hi," I say, smiling.

"Hi, you." He smiles back at me, then steps aside, holding the door. "You look beautiful."

"Thank you," I say, stepping inside.

He gives me a hug. I can't tell if he's wearing cologne or if it's just soap, but I love his scent.

"You smell nice," I tell him as we separate. "And I like your hair."

"Are you being sarcastic?" he says, running one hand through it, looking endearingly self-conscious. "I actually meant to get a haircut today. . . ."

"No, I *really* like it," I say. "I like a little longer hair on guys. . . ."

"On guys, huh?" Pete says teasingly.

"On *you*," I clarify.

He smiles and thanks me, then leads me to his kitchen, where a very basic plate of cheese, crackers, and green grapes awaits us. "Can I get you something to drink? A glass of wine? A beer?"

"I'd love a beer," I say, sitting at his small round table. I watch him pull two SweetWater beers out of the fridge. He opens them, then pours them into chilled mugs from the freezer. He hands me mine, then sits beside me.

"So how was your day?" he says.

I give him the highlights, as well as a few trivial lowlights, then ask about his day. He reports that it was great, then tells me an inspiring story about one of his favorite clients—a high school tailback recovering from a torn meniscus. As he talks, it occurs to me that I've never seen him in a bad mood.

"So what did you want to talk to me about?" he asks.

I look at him, confused, and he quickly clarifies. "When you were in New York . . . you told me you had something you wanted to talk about?"

"Oh, right," I say, stalling, thinking how long ago that phone call seems. Although part of me wants to tell him everything, right at this moment, with no filter whatsoever, another, greater part of me simply wants to go to dinner with the guy I like.

"It was a couple of different things, actually . . . but we can talk about that stuff later," I say, glancing at my watch. "Should we head out?"

"Sure," he says. "Are you driving?"

"Yep," I say, smiling.

"You opening my car door, too?"

I laugh and say absolutely.

Two HOURS LATER, after a lighthearted, yet still romantic dinner, I pull back up to the curb in front of Pete's house and put my car in park. "Thank you for a wonderful evening. And thank you for dinner," I say.

"It was my pleasure," he says, biting his lower lip as he shoots me a serious glance. "Can you come in for a minute? I promise I won't keep you long—I know you have to get up early."

I hesitate, feeling torn. As much as I want to end the evening on an easy, high note—and delay the inevitable for just a little bit longer—I know this isn't fair to Pete. He deserves the truth. So with a sinking feeling in the pit of my stomach, I nod and say okay, I can come in for a few minutes. We get out of my car and walk back to his front door, our shoulders touching as he unlocks it.

Once inside, he instantly takes me in his arms, and I can't resist the amazing, warm feel of him against me. My heart races with attraction and anticipation as our foreheads touch, then our cheeks and noses. I hold my breath as his lips brush against mine, and he whispers that *this* is our official first kiss, not the one at Johnny's. My heart breaks a little as I think, more likely, that it is our *last*. I make myself pull back and say his name.

"Yes?" he says, staring intently into my eyes.

"Can we sit for a minute? And talk?"

He nods and says of course, then leads me into his living room filled with Packers memorabilia and framed photos of his family—all as happy, wholesome, and midwestern-looking as he. We sit beside each other on the sofa, and he takes my hand.

"So. I *did* want to talk to you about some things," I say, my heart pounding with so many competing, overwhelming emotions.

I can feel him staring at me as I take a deep breath, then tell him that I'm not sure where to begin.

"Start anywhere," he says. "Just *talk* to me. . . ."

And so I do, the words pouring out of me as I tell him everything about my past. I begin at the hardest part, with the night my brother died, then fast-forward to our dinner with Sophie, and my fight with Meredith, then go back and cover the pivotal middle part, when Will caught me in bed with Gabe and broke up with me. Pete listens intently, asking only a few questions of clarification along the way, mostly about the time line. When I'm finished, I take a deep breath, then say, "So. That's the last fifteen years in a nutshell."

He takes my hand in his, holding my gaze. "I'm so sorry, Josie."

"Thank you," I say. "Thanks for listening to all of that . . . *shit.*" I let out a laugh, so that I don't cry.

"It's not *shit*. It's *life,*" he says, finally letting go of my hand, but only so he can put his arm around me. "So what now?" he asks.

I shake my head. "I don't know. . . . The only thing I know for sure is that I am ready to move on with my life. I am ready to be a mother. I want my own family. Not as a do-over, but maybe as a way to heal . . ." I say, wondering if that sounds selfish—if it *is* selfish. "I want to have a baby."

He nods and says he understands.

"And I haven't told you this yet, either—but I got my test results back . . . and unfortunately, my eggs are a little on the low side for my age. . . . So I have to do this. *Now.*"

"I understand," he says again, then swallows. "Did you . . . did you decide on a donor?"

"Yeah," I say, feeling a fresh wave of deep sadness, yet no uncertainty about my decision.

"And?" he asks, with a heartbreakingly hopeful look.

I take a deep breath, then force myself to tell him the rest. "I've decided to have a baby with Gabe," I say.

"Gabe?" he says, looking more than a little surprised. "Are you guys . . . together?"

"No," I say, shaking my head. "Not at all. We'll never be together like that. But he's my best friend, and I know I can always count on him. It's safer . . . less complicated. . . ."

"Less complicated? Really?" he asks, his brow furrowed.

"Well, less complicated than using *you,*" I say, feeling a pang of guilt, hoping that I haven't hurt him—that he doesn't think I'm being cavalier about his feelings, whatever, exactly, they are. "Was that ever even a *real* offer?" I ask, unsure of what I want his answer to be.

"Of course it was," he says, looking into my eyes. "You know it was."

"Thank you, Pete," I say, blinking back tears. "You're an *amazing* person."

"So are you, Josie," he whispers.

We sit in silence for a torturous few seconds, before I tell him I'd better go. He quickly nods, then stands and walks me to the door.

"Good night, Josie," he says when we get there, giving me an awkward little side hug.

"Good night, Pete," I say, then lean up and kiss his cheek, my heart fluttering with wistfulness over what could have, maybe, been.

chapter thirty-two

MEREDITH

After an emotional phone session with Amy on Sunday afternoon, we agree that I should spend a final night or two in New York—that it might be the last chance to really reflect on everything in solitude. So I spend the next forty-eight hours thinking, praying, crying, and replaying the events of the last few days, as well as the last fifteen years.

When I arrive home, late Tuesday afternoon, I find Nolan and Harper in our disastrously messy kitchen, making cookies and listening to "The Little Drummer Boy." Their backs are to me, and for a moment I watch the two of them, undetected. As he lifts her up to preheat the oven, I am mesmerized by the cozy scene set to the rhythm of *pa rum pa pum pums*—so much so that I nearly forget how much I dislike Christmas carols before Thanksgiving. I nearly forget *everything,* in fact, other than the love I feel for my daughter. Then, as Nolan puts her back down, they both turn and see me and my trance is broken. To my enormous relief, Harper's eyes immediately light up, pure joy on her face.

"Mommy!" she shouts, running toward me, falling into my arms, melting me.

"Harper," I say, holding on to her for as long as she'll let me.

Finally, she squirms away, returning to her step stool at the counter, talking a mile a minute, telling me that they're making sugar cookies with red and green sprinkles, as a "practice run" (one of Nolan's expressions) for the batch they'll make for Santa next month. I listen and nod, hanging on her every word, wondering how she could look older after only a week and a half, vowing to never be gone from her this long again. Determined to be more present, patient, grateful. All the while, I avoid eye contact with Nolan, and can feel that he's doing the same with me.

"Oh, Mommy. Guess what?" Harper asks, her trademark preamble.

"What?" I say, walking over to the counter and watching her awkwardly wield a wooden spoon, her tiny arm not strong enough to cut through the still-floury mixture.

"Daddy says we *are* allowed to eat raw cookie dough." Her eyes sparkle with victory.

I start to protest, pointing out the risks of salmonella in raw eggs and batter, the way I always do. But instead I nod and say, "Okay. This once."

"Living on the edge," I hear Nolan mumble.

I finally glance his way, flashing him a tight-lipped smile, my heart twisting with so many competing emotions. "Hi," I say.

"Hi," he says back, smiling back at me just as tensely. "How was your trip? Fun?"

I try to interpret his tone, wondering if it's more flippant or furtive, but can't tell for sure. "The trip was fine . . . but I wouldn't call it *fun*. . . . I missed Harper too much to have fun," I say.

"And you missed Daddy, too?" Harper asks.

I look into her eyes, wondering if she is really this intuitive and insightful—or if the question is simply part of her constant stream of babble.

"Yes. I missed Daddy," I lie, although a very small part of me actually *did* miss him. At least the part of him that is inextricably tied to our daughter.

"Will you help us make cookies?" Harper asks.

"I'd love to," I say, rolling up my sleeves, preparing to wash my hands.

Harper beats me to the punch, pointing at me with her spoon, her face stern. "Wash your hands first, Mommy," she says. "Airplanes are *filthy*."

Out of the corner of my eye, I see Nolan smile. "That's your daughter, all right."

"Yes," I reply on my way to the sink. "She most certainly is."

THREE DOZEN BAKED and decorated cookies later, Nolan and I have barely exchanged as many words, at least not directly with each other. We stick to breezy statements, using Harper as our conduit, such as "Tell Mommy about your visit to the dentist" and "Can you and Daddy guess who came to visit me in New York?"

With the latter question, I stare at Nolan, feeling certain that Josie has already tipped him off and that he knows that *I* now know the truth about the night Daniel died. When he shoots me a remorseful glance, my hunch feels confirmed.

"Aunt Josie," Harper either states or guesses.

I tell her yes, watching Nolan prod at an oversize cookie with a spatula. It has clearly not cooled long enough, but he continues anyway, breaking it. He throws one half in his mouth and finally addresses me directly. "So how did the visit go?" he asks.

"Don't you already know how it went?" I say, my anger bubbling to the surface.

Nolan opens his mouth to reply, then closes it. He might as well have just pleaded the Fifth, and I tell him as much.

"We'll talk in a minute," he says, gesturing toward Harper, now making her way to the family room with cookies in both of her hands.

I shake my head. "Not with Harper awake," I say, thinking that there is no way we can have this conversation without raising our voices. At least I can't.

"My parents are coming to get her," he says, glancing at the clock on the microwave. "In about an hour."

"What?" I say. "Why? I just got home. I want to spend time with her."

"Yeah. Well, you didn't inform us of your itinerary. And I already asked if they would babysit for me."

"So you could do *what*, exactly?" I blurt out, not meaning to sound quite as accusatorial as I do. At least not on this particular topic.

Nolan squints at me. "Um. So I could get a little break, maybe?" His voice is calm, but laced with bitterness. "You know, Meredith . . . I've been a single parent for two weeks here. . . ."

"First of all," I say, crossing my arms, the animosity building. "It's been eleven days—not two weeks. Second of all, I'd be more than happy to take her for the next eleven days. Starting now. Tell your parents we won't be needing them."

"Yeah, we *do* need them, actually. We need to talk. And my parents are going to take Harper while we do," he says with rare and absolute authority.

I stare at him a beat, then shrug. "Fine," I say, letting him win this one, thinking that we might as well go ahead and rip the Band-Aid off our sham marriage. "But I'm putting her to bed tonight."

A short time later, I get in the shower to avoid seeing Nolan's parents, taking my time drying my hair, dressing, putting on makeup. Part of me is stalling, but part of me is going through my usual confidence-building ritual before I walk into any adversarial scenario. One thing's for sure—I am not primping for my husband, and I certainly don't anticipate Nolan's reaction, which is to give me a conspicuous once-over when I walk into the family room.

"You look pretty," he says.

"Thanks," I say, involuntarily softened by the compliment, though the effect lasts only a few seconds. "So Harper's gone?" I confirm.

"Yeah. They just left," he says. "So did you want to go out? Get something to eat, maybe?"

I narrow my eyes, shake my head, and tell him no, I'm not hungry. I hope my implication is clear—*how could you think about food right now?*

"Okay. Just asking," he says. "You typically don't dress like that around the house. . . ."

I wonder if this is a veiled criticism, but I focus on the bigger picture. "We can talk right here," I say, feeling queasy as I sit on the far end of the sofa.

"Okay," he says, staring at me expectantly.

"You wanted to talk. So you go first," I say, ready to hear him out, listen to any and all of his convoluted explanations or attempts to justify a fifteen-year secret.

He nods and takes a deep breath, surprising me with his first words. "I know Josie told you everything . . . and I just want to say that I was wrong."

He stops, waits for me to respond. When I say nothing, he continues, "I was one hundred percent wrong. I should never have kept this from you and your parents. It was as close as you can get to an actual lie without lying."

"It *was* a lie," I say, then literally bite my tongue to keep from unleashing so much more.

"Okay. You're right," he says, nodding, further disarming me. "It *was* a lie. And it was wrong. And I'm so sorry."

I anticipate the *but* before his lips form the word. "But I *swear,* Meredith. I didn't cover that up for *my* sake." His eyes are big, round, and filled with grief.

"Who *did* you lie for, then?" I ask him.

"In the beginning?" he says, dropping his voice. "Mostly Josie . . ."

The answer is a surprising slash to my heart. "You're not married to *Josie*," I say, thinking that I could probably get past the cover-up for the first few years, but not once he and I started dating. After that, his loyalty to me should have trumped all else.

"I know that," he says.

I hesitate, then ask him something I've always, deep down, wondered. "Do you wish you were? Married to Josie?"

"What?" he says, looking genuinely horrified. "Don't be ridiculous, Meredith. Of course I don't want to be married to your sister. Jesus."

"Are you sure?" I say, unable to halt my tangent. "You never liked her? Not even *in the beginning*? You always seemed to have a crush on her . . . or at least she did on you. . . ."

He hesitates just long enough for my stomach to turn. "Okay. Look," he begins. "A long time ago . . . I thought she was hot. . . ."

"When?" I demand.

"When we were in high school and college . . . early on."

"What about on *that* night?" I ask, although I'm not sure why this matters.

"Yeah. On that night, too," he says. "Josie's a pretty girl. Very pretty. But so what? There are lots of pretty girls."

"But you never liked her romantically?" I say.

"No. Absolutely not. I never liked her like *that*. C'mon, Mere. Where is all this coming from?"

"You lied to me for *fifteen* years, Nolan. And now you tell me you did it for Josie's sake. What am I supposed to think? How do you think that makes me feel?"

He runs his hands through his hair and says, "Shitty. I get that. But it wasn't *just* for her sake. It was for your mom and dad, too . . . for your whole family. For *you*, Meredith."

I make a scoffing sound. "How was it for *me?*"

Nolan takes a few deep breaths, then says, "Well, let's see. . . . Just imagine if on the morning after the accident . . . after we talked in my car . . . if I had walked into your house and told your family that Josie was out-of-her-mind wasted the night before—"

"And that *you* called Daniel to come get her," I cut him off, raising my voice, pointing at him. "Don't forget that part."

"I never do. Not for one day," he says, before taking a few deep breaths, collecting himself. "So, I sit you all down and tell you that story—"

"*That story?*" I interrupt again. "It's not a *story,* Nolan. It's what actually *happened.*"

"Okay, Meredith," he says, sounding weary. "Quit being a lawyer and let me finish. Please."

"Fine. Go ahead." I clamp my mouth shut and cross my arms.

"So I tell you all what happened. . . . I tell you that Josie was wasted and I called Daniel to come get her. . . ."

"Okay," I say, thinking that's exactly what he *should* have told us. "And?"

"And what would that have done to your family? How would that have helped anyone?"

I stare at him.

"How would your mom have felt about Josie? Would she have ever been able to truly forgive her? And what about your dad? He just lost his only son and . . ." His voice trails off.

"And *what?*" I say. "Finish your sentence. . . ."

"He just lost his only son," Nolan repeats, "and would inevitably wonder if his alcoholism didn't somehow contribute to Josie's drinking. . . . He'd live with a lifetime of guilt in *addition* to pain. . . . And then there's you and Josie . . . What would the truth have done to your relationship?"

"The same thing it's doing now," I say, staring down at my lap.

"Exactly," he says, as if I've just made his case.

"But what about *us*, Nolan?" I ask. "You and me?"

He stares back at me, seemingly speechless.

"Why did you really marry me, Nolan?" I ask, my heart pounding.

"I already answered that. I told you at Blackberry Farm. . . ."

"Tell me again," I say.

"Because I fell in love with you," he says, too automatically.

I shake my head and say, "I don't believe that, Nolan. I think you liked the *idea* of marrying Daniel's sister. And I think it made you feel less guilty about what happened that night. . . . It helped you make sense of something senseless and horrible—"

He shakes his head and says no, but without any conviction.

"Daniel was like a brother to you," I say. "So you wanted to try to fix things for my family."

"*Our* family," Nolan says. "It's *our* family now."

I tell him that is beside the point.

"No," he says, his voice rising with frustration. "It *is* the point. You're my family, Meredith. You and Harper and your parents and your nutty sister and the baby she's about to bring into this world. You're all my family. And I love *you*—"

I cut him off and shout, "Okay. But are you *in love* with me?"

He groans in frustration, then says, "I don't know, Mere. You make it pretty hard to be sometimes."

I take this as a no, and press onward. "Were you *ever*?"

"Yes," he says, then quickly downgrades his answer. "At least I think so. . . ."

"You *think* so?" I demand.

"Yes. I think so . . . but . . . maybe not," he says, wavering, clearly in anguish. "Maybe you're right. . . ."

I nod, his admission filling me with both intense relief and profound sadness. "That's what I thought," I say.

"But I *do* love you, Meredith," he says, reaching for my hand. I give it to him, then meet his gaze. "And I would do absolutely anything for you and Harper. *Anything.* Isn't that enough?"

I stare at him for a long time, thinking that this is really the crux of our crisis and the question I've been asking myself for years. Is it enough to be partners and parents together? To share the same history and values—and most important, a deep and abiding love for our daughter and family? Can all of that sustain us and overcome the elusive missing piece that I've never been able to quite put my finger on, other than to know it's just *not* there?

I desperately want the answer to be yes, and for a second nearly convince myself that I can will it to be so. But deep down, I know it doesn't work that way, at least not for me. I feel my answer crystallizing in a way it never has before.

"No, Nolan," I finally say, shaking my head. "I'm sorry . . . but I just don't think it is."

chapter thirty-three

JOSIE

It is Thanksgiving Day, and exactly two weeks after Dr. Lazarus shot me up with a vial of Gabe's sperm. It is also the day upon which she told us we could take a pregnancy test and expect reliable results. I wake up and head straight to Gabe's room, finding him shirtless in front of his closet.

"Happy Thanksgiving," I say, grateful that we are spending it together, no matter what our results turn out to be.

"Happy Thanksgiving," he says, eyeing the box of First Response tests in my hand.

"Should we do this now?" I say, holding it up and giving it a little shake. "Or wait until later?"

He shrugs, selecting an unlikely green rugby shirt that he's had since college. "Your call," he says. "I'm ready when you are."

"Maybe we should do it later," I say, waffling. "So we don't ruin Thanksgiving if it's negative?"

"Would that really *ruin* Thanksgiving?" Gabe asks in such a way that I think, not for the first time, that he secretly hopes the test is negative. "I mean—we're just sitting around with my parents and your mom. And we're not going to tell anyone today either way. . . . Isn't that what we decided?"

I nod. "Yeah. That's what we decided . . . but I'll definitely be disappointed. Won't you?" I say, scrutinizing his face.

"A little," he says. "But honestly, I'll be more surprised if you *are* pregnant. What did Dr. Lazarus say we have? A twenty percent chance?"

"Yeah. At best."

"Right," he says. "So if you're not—and you're probably not—we just try again. And maybe she gives you some fertility drugs this time."

Rationally, I know he's completely right. It's just one month, one *try*, albeit a fairly expensive first attempt. I think of all the couples who try for *years* before they get a positive test, going through round after round of IVF, and know that I haven't earned the right to feel anything close to a sense of hopelessness. And yet I still have the feeling that this might be *it* for me. My one and only chance. And that if it doesn't happen this way, right now with Gabe, then it might never happen at all.

When I try to articulate this, I expect Gabe to reassure me—or tell me I'm being melodramatic. But instead he nods, and says, "Yeah. I know what you mean."

"So you feel that way, too?" I ask, my heart sinking.

"A little," he says, sitting next to me on the edge of his bed. "I mean—I think you'll have a baby *eventually* . . . I just don't know that it will be with *me*."

My stomach flutters with disappointment.

"Because of Leslie?" I say. Not because she's been at all difficult or jealous through this whole uncharted, unnatural process. To the contrary, she has handled everything with grace and generosity—which has only made Gabe like and respect her *more*.

But he shakes his head and says no, it has nothing to do with Leslie.

"Then why?" I ask him as I sit on his bed.

He gives me a frank look and says, "Well. Because of Pete."

I shake my head. "No. Pete's cool with it, too. He's really rooting for us," I say, thinking of how supportive he's been over the past few weeks, calling to check on me and even wishing me good luck before my insemination appointment.

Gabe smirks and says, "Give it up, Josie. He likes you. A *lot*."

"I *know* he does," I say. "And I like him. But he agrees that we need to keep things . . . compartmentalized."

"All right," he says. "So what are we waiting for, then?"

"I guess nothing," I say, staring at the box in my lap before slowly removing the cellophane wrapping, pulling out one fortune-telling stick, then squinting down to read the fine-print instructions on the back of the box.

He laughs, slapping the box out of my hands and giving me a little shove off the bed. "C'mon. Like you haven't done this before," he says. "Quit stalling and go find out if you're knocked up."

LESS THAN FIVE minutes later, after I've peed on a stick, carefully capped it, and left it on Gabe's bathroom counter, I walk back into his room and give him a blank stare. He stares back at me, equally expressionless, and takes a guess. "Negative?"

I shake my head.

"Positive?" he says, his voice rising with disbelief.

I shake my head again, then tell him I don't know. "I didn't look. . . . Would you please go check it for me?"

He nods and stands, looking pale, a tough feat with olive skin.

"Wait," I say, reaching out and grabbing his arm. "What do you *want* it to be?"

Gabe swallows, hesitates, and cleverly avoids answering the question. "I want you to have the baby you're meant to have. . . ."

"C'mon. That's a cop-out," I say. "Do you hope it's negative? Or positive?"

He takes a deep breath and says, "Okay . . . I want it to be positive."

"Why?" I ask, my heart racing.

"Why?" he says. "What do you mean *why*? Why would we have done all this if we didn't want it to be positive?"

"So you don't have cold feet?" I ask. "Not even a little bit?"

Gabe shakes his head and says, "I'm nervous, yeah. And it's a little crazy what we're doing here . . . a *lot* crazy. . . . But fuck it . . . at this point, I'm all in." He shrugs and gives me one of his rebellious looks.

"Fuck it?" I say, feeling queasy. "*Fuck* it?"

"You know what I mean. . . ." he says, smiling. "It's too late now."

"But it's *not* too late if it's negative," I say. "You'd be off the hook. . . . We wouldn't have to try again."

"True," he says, nodding, clearly making a big effort to be patient with me. "But if it's positive—"

"How would you feel?" I grill him.

"I don't know, Josie," he says, shaking his head, staring into space. "Happy . . . excited . . . shocked . . . scared shitless . . . a *lot* of things."

"But no regret?"

He shakes his head. "No. No regret."

"Do you promise?"

"I swear," he says, holding up three fingers, even though he was never a Boy Scout.

"Okay," I say, looking at him sideways. "Because, Gabe, I have to tell you something. . . ."

"Yeah?" he asks, squinting back at me with apprehension.

"I actually *did* look at the stick," I confess, my heart beating wildly in my chest.

"And?"

"And it's positive."

"Shut the *hell* up," he says, dashing to the bathroom. He returns one beat later, waving the stick with its unmistakable two bright-pink parallel lines. His eyes are shining and his face is lit with pure happiness, an expression I honestly never expected and have seldom seen him show.

"Holy shit," he says, throwing his arms around me, squeezing me so hard I can't breathe. "We're having a baby."

"Yes," I say, laughing and crying at once. "We're having a baby."

I'M PREGNANT. *I'm pregnant. I'm pregnant.*

For the next several days, I repeat the words in my head, over and over. Gabe and I talk of little else, both of us struggling to digest the magnitude of what we've undertaken. Yet the whole thing continues to feel surreal—and I have the sense that it won't begin to really sink in until I share the news with at least one other person.

In the past, I always imagined telling my family first, then close friends, then the rest of the world around three months. Then again, I also always imagined following the traditional order of things—as in *love, marriage, baby carriage*—and that's clearly all out the window now.

So a few days later, I decide I might as well go *really* unorthodox and tell Pete the news first. In part, it's a pragmatic decision, as we have plans to hang out for the first time in several weeks, and I know he'll likely ask me if I'm pregnant (not that that stopped me from fibbing to Sydney when the subject came up at recess and I told her that I hadn't yet tested). But more important, and for some inexplicable reason, I actually just *want* him to be the first to know.

Out of respect to Gabe, I call and make sure that it's okay with him as I'm driving over to Pete's house.

"Shouldn't we wait for a heartbeat?" he asks.

"I don't think I can wait until then. Besides, I'm sure he's going to ask. . . ."

"Well, it's your call. Whatever you want to do is fine with me. . . ."

"So you haven't told Leslie?"

"Nope."

"Are you *going* to tell her?"

"Well, eventually," he says with a laugh. "It'll be sort of hard to hide it, right?"

I decide not to parse his words or grill him about whether he wishes he *could* hide it from her, and simply tell him that I'll call him later.

"Okay. Later," he says, hanging up way too abruptly.

I roll my eyes, reminding myself that the fact that I'm carrying his baby doesn't mean that he'll suddenly change his personality.

A FEW MINUTES later, I walk into Pete's house. He beams at me and says, "It's so good to see you."

"You, too," I say, telling myself to wait for the right moment to break my news. But before I even remove my jacket, I blurt it out.

"I'm pregnant," I say, getting what I'm pretty sure is my first wave of morning sickness.

He looks at me, startled, a smile frozen on his face. "Are you serious?"

"As a heart attack . . . or an unwed pregnancy," I say, a joke Gabe came up with a few nights ago.

I watch the news sink in, his expression turning glazed, then somber. "*Wow,*" he says. "That was *fast.*"

"Yeah. I know," I reply with a high, nervous laugh. "First try."

"Congrats . . . I'm really happy for you."

"Thanks," I say.

He smiles, then leans in to awkwardly hug me, patting me on the back before helping me out of my jacket, then hanging it in his hall closet. He turns and leads me into his kitchen, as he fires off a quick round of questions. "So, how do you feel? Excited? . . . How's Gabe doing?" His voice is chipper, but something about his face looks strained.

"It's still sort of hard to process," I say, noticing an open bottle of red wine and two glasses on his counter. "But we're both happy. And very grateful."

"Well . . . that's fantastic news. Really fantastic." He pours both glasses, then stops suddenly. "Oh, shit. What am I doing? You can't have this, can you?"

I shake my head, feeling suddenly embarrassed, though I can't put my finger on why.

He merges both glasses into one very full one, then takes a sip, swallows, and smiles. "So what can I get you to drink?"

"Oh, nothing. I'm fine," I say, as we awkwardly stare at each other, and it actually crosses my mind to just say goodbye and gracefully exit.

"Let me at least give you some water," he says, getting a glass from his cabinet, then filling it from the faucet. He stares at it a beat, then pours it out and hands me a bottle of Poland Spring from his refrigerator instead.

"Thanks," I say, untwisting the cap.

"Do you want a glass?"

"No, this is fine."

He gives me a closemouthed smile, nods, then asks when I'm due.

"August third," I say. "According to our calculations . . . but we have an appointment next week to check on all of that."

"So you haven't been to the doctor yet?"

I shake my head.

"So how do you know for sure that you're pregnant?" he asks, sounding a little hopeful, though maybe that part is just in my head.

"About five tests tell me I am." I force a smile.

He smiles back at me, nods, then asks how my parents took the news. "I assume they're excited, too?"

"I haven't told them yet."

"No?"

"Your sister?"

"Nope. Still haven't talked to her since I left New York. . . . You're actually the first person I've told," I say with a nervous laugh, suddenly questioning my judgment.

"Wow, Josie . . . Thank you. That's so nice. . . . I'm really honored," he says. "And touched."

I nod and glance away, mumbling that it's really no big deal.

"Yeah, it *is*," he says kindly, starting to sound like himself again. "And I'm just so *happy* for you. This is what you wanted—and you got it. Good for you." He hugs me again; this time it feels warm and genuine.

"Thank you. I really appreciate that," I say, as we separate. "But there are a couple of drawbacks. . . ." My voice trails off, but I do my best not to look sad.

"Oh?" he replies. "And what are those?"

"Well . . . for one . . . I'm going to get really fat." I laugh.

"*Pregnant*. Not *fat*," he says.

It is the exact right thing to say, and I tell him so.

He smiles and gives me a playful high five. "Gotta love when you say the right thing to a pregnant woman."

I smile.

"So . . . what's the other drawback?"

I take another sip of water, stalling for a few seconds before admitting the truth. How I *really* feel. "Well, I'm a little sad, too."

"About?"

"About *us* . . . I know this will change things between us."

Pete nods, now looking unmistakably sad, too. "Yeah," he says. "I guess it probably will."

My heart sinks, though I am also relieved by his candor. In fact, his complete lack of bullshit might be one of the things I like best about him. So I press onward—and ask him the question I've been wondering since Thanksgiving morning.

"So tell me. If I hadn't gone down this road . . . with Gabe . . . If I weren't pregnant . . . ?" I stop suddenly and shake my head at the futility of what-ifs. "Never mind," I say, shaking my head.

"No. Go on," he insists, holding my gaze. "Please?"

"Okay." I nod, then take a deep breath and finish. "If I weren't having a baby, could you have seen a future for us? I mean—any *possibility* of a future?"

Pete's eyes say it all, even before he nods and utters a very clear yes.

I chew my lower lip, willing myself not to feel regret. Telling myself we could've just as easily broken up in a few months, setting my time line back that much further, bringing me one step closer to my ultimate, inevitable infertility. I also remind myself that this is what I've always wanted—that I'm going to be a mother, and although motherhood is a gift, it is also a sacrifice: the *ultimate* sacrifice. I might as well get used to that now.

"Oh, well," I finally say, forcing a small shrug and smile. "Story of my life."

Several long seconds pass before he clears his throat and says, "But ask me the question a different way."

I hesitate, confused. "What do you mean?"

"Ask me if I can *still* picture a future for us?" he says, his cheeks now flushed.

My heart racing, I ask the question, our eyes locked: "Can you *still* picture a future for us?"

He takes one of my hands in his. "Yeah. I *can*, actually. . . . It's a long shot . . . but I still can."

I shiver, goosebumps rising everywhere—on my arms and legs

and the back of my neck. "Really?" I ask, my insides melting, my voice trembling. "Do you really mean that?"

He nods, looking as earnest as he ever has—which is saying a lot. "Yes, Josie, I *do* mean that. I've been thinking about this a lot. . . . And this baby isn't a deal breaker for me. If anything, it makes me care for you *more*."

I have trouble believing what I've just heard—and yet I do. "Why?" I whisper.

He pauses and frowns, looking deep in thought. "Because it shows me what you're made of," he finally says. "It shows me that you're strong and independent and truly committed to the most beautiful thing a woman can do. . . . I'm blown away. . . ." He smiles. "Blown away, but not going anywhere."

"Even though it could get really messy?" I ask, thinking of how Will used to feel about Gabe. About anything that deviated from his script of how life *should* look.

"Yeah," he says. "Love has a way of working stuff out. Even the messy parts."

"Wait," I say, feeling a smile spread across my face. "Are you saying you *love* me?"

"No," he says, grinning as he takes my other hand. "But I'm not ruling it out. . . . I could definitely see myself loving you . . . loving *both* of you."

For a second I think he means Gabe, then realize that he's talking about the baby.

"That's funny," I say, squeezing his hands and smiling, "because I could definitely see the two of us loving you back."

chapter thirty-four

MEREDITH

"I sn't there another way?" Nolan asks me in early December as we stroll through the botanical garden, enjoying the Festival of Lights with Harper, one of our holiday traditions.

"What do you mean 'another way'?" I say, keeping my eye on Harper, who is about ten yards ahead of us.

"Can't we find a way to be happy? Even though you don't love me?"

I sigh, weary of his self-pitying comments, and say, "Nolan, I *do* love you."

"Okay. Even though you aren't *in* love with me," he replies, as we begin to go around and around in the same futile circles.

You aren't in love with me, either.

Yes, I am.

No, you're not.

But I'm happy with our marriage.

You can't be.

I'm happy enough.

"Happy enough" is not enough.

It is for me; why can't it be for you?

And that's what it has always come back to over the past few weeks, since I returned from New York. The worst of my anger has ebbed, and we've agreed not to make any big decisions until after the holidays, but that question always remains: Is what we have enough?

I think of the recent heart-to-hearts I've had with Ellen, and the several intense sessions in Amy's office. I've even talked to my mom a bit about the subject, though I've yet to admit just how dire things are. We all agree that there is no bright-line litmus test for what works in a marriage, or for what happiness looks like. That it all comes down to the two people inside the relationship.

On the one extreme, there are those rare soul mates, the blissful marriages filled with unwavering passion in which both parties are completely head-over-heels in love. On the other end of the spectrum are the shitty relationships, marked by dysfunction, mean-spiritedness, even abuse—those that are destined to end in divorce or disaster.

In between lies a vast bandwidth of gray-area marriages. Some are arranged by two families, built entirely upon shared values rather than the notion of romantic love. Others have become sexless over the years, morphing into merely high-functioning partnerships, two people committed to their children, or the religious institution of marriage, or the theoretical idea of family and forever. Sometimes people are brought together by loneliness—or default, because nobody else seems to want them.

All of these scenarios can easily be dismissed as pitiful or a version of settling. And for a long time, I subscribed to this notion, too. Now, I'm beginning to see that many different kinds of marriages can work, as long as *both* people are satisfied by the status quo. But it has to be both, not just one, and I'm pretty sure this is what Nolan is trying to say now. Can't I just accept what we have, and who we are together, and find a way to be happy in spite of what we *don't* have? Can't I, just for once, see the glass as half full? Can't I get on board with him, and find a way to make this work?

I watch him take the last sip of his hot chocolate and toss the cup into a garbage can. He then pulls out his phone and calls out to Harper.

"C'mere for a second, honey. Stand right there. In front of that tree," he says, pointing to a huge magnolia strung with thousands of tiny purple and green lights.

Harper happily obliges, posing with a big, toothy grin, then runs ahead again as Nolan checks the image, frowns, puts a filter on it, then shows me his work. "Cool shot, huh?"

"Very cool. Text it to me. I'll Insta it," I say, wishing that life were that easy. Take the flawed image and simply crop it, brighten and saturate it, throw a fancy filter on it. Make it what you want it to be. Then again, I think that *is* the way Nolan approaches life, with his rose-colored glasses.

As if reading my mind, he says, "I know our marriage isn't perfect. I know we have things to work on . . . but we make a really good team, Meredith. Can't we just try a little harder to . . . to get some of that magic?"

I sigh, noticing that he said *get,* and not *recapture,* and tell him I don't think it works like that; either the magic is there or it isn't. "Besides," I say, "isn't that what we've been *doing* for the past seven years?"

Nolan shakes his head and says, "No. It's not at *all* what we've been doing . . . because we weren't being honest with each other."

"*I* was," I say, my defensive instinct kicking in.

"No, you weren't," he says, his face becoming animated. "You weren't truthful in the dugout when you said yes. You weren't honest on our wedding day . . . and even before that, you weren't being true to yourself."

I know he's talking about acting and New York and law school and maybe even moving back to Atlanta and into my childhood home, and I can't deny the charge. So I simply shrug, and tell him maybe he's right.

"But now you know the truth about the night Daniel died," Nolan continues. "And I know the truth about your feelings. . . . Now we *both* know the truth. . . . Isn't that a clean slate?"

"I guess," I say, though I'm not sure what a clean slate really gets us, other than forgiveness and understanding. These are no small matters, but not enough to create *magic*. "But where do we go from here?"

"Well. For one, I've been thinking about our house. . . . I really think we should sell it."

"We can't do that," I say, but I feel a rush of relief just considering the freeing possibility of living somewhere—*anywhere*—else.

"Sure, we can."

"Mom would be devastated. Dad, too."

"They'd get over it," he says. "It's just a *house*. . . . It's just not good for us, living there. . . . Every time I walk by his room . . ."

"I know," I say, sparing him the rest.

"And I think we should consider leaving Atlanta, too. At least for a while. We need an adventure. Just the three of us. We have enough money to do it . . . and I'll always have a job to come back to," he says, talking excitedly.

"Where would we go?" I ask, playing along for a second.

"Anywhere we wanna go," he says. "New York City? You could act again. . . ."

I shake my head and tell him that I think I'm finally over the city—*and* acting.

"Okay, then. Where would you like to live? What do you want to do?"

I tell him I don't know, anything but the law. I've been back at work since the week of Thanksgiving, but I've already made the decision to resign, as I realize that it's a lot easier to say what you *don't* want than what you *do* want.

"Well, let's think about it," he says as we quicken our pace to try to keep up with Harper. "Let's really, *really* think about it. Let's think outside the box . . . like Josie. . . ."

My shoulders immediately tense at the mention of my sister—whom I've yet to communicate with since she left New York in the middle of the night.

"Say what you will about her," Nolan continues. "And I get it . . . she can be a real pain in the ass. But the girl knows how to think outside the box."

"She's selfish," I say, the default tagline I give my sister.

"Is she, though?" he asks. "Or is she just trying to be true to herself? Having a baby alone is really brave."

"She won't go through with it," I say. "She's not that brave."

"Maybe, maybe not. But *we* can be. Let's be brave together, Meredith. Can you just keep an open mind and give it one more, last-ditch try?"

Always before, his idea of trying felt like faking, even lying. Having another baby. Making our parents happy. Going on family vacations to Disney World and the beach, smiling and posing for photos to promptly post for all the world to see. Going through the motions of pretending to be the perfect family. *Daniel's sister and his best friend, brought together by tragedy, yet utterly and totally "meant to be." Hashtag blessed.*

But suddenly now, his idea of trying feels authentic, and I see a small glimmer of possibility.

"Maybe," I say.

He takes my hand, then stops walking, facing me. "Don't say *maybe*. Say *yes*, Meredith. Not for Daniel or your parents or even Harper. But for *us*." He is pleading, *begging*, yet still looks so strong.

I look into his eyes as it occurs to me that we are standing exactly as we did on our wedding day, before our family and friends, promising forever. Yet remarkably, I feel closer to him now, in this crossroad of crisis.

I hesitate, holding my breath, before I finally nod and say yes. It is a soft and shaky yes, filled with apprehension, but it is still a yes, and it is more sincere than my yes in the dugout all those years ago. Then, for the first time in forever, I take *his* hand, rather than the other way around, and we continue on our way, following our little girl along the lit garden path.

chapter thirty-five

JOSIE

It is December 22, what would have been Daniel's fortieth birthday, and I am waiting at the bar at Blue Ridge Grill for Meredith. We have yet to communicate since New York, except to email about plans for tonight, which I spearheaded. At eight o'clock, we will be joined for dinner by our parents, along with Gabe, Nolan, and Harper, but we agreed that the two of us need to talk first and find a way to put aside our differences, at least for the evening.

Determined not to be late, one of Meredith's many pet peeves, I am actually a rare fifteen minutes early, and use the time to mentally prepare for what's to come. Gabe and I plan to tell everyone our news tonight—that we are now eight weeks pregnant. But I start to second-guess myself, worrying that Meredith will accuse me of making this emotional anniversary about myself. It might be a fair point, but for the fact that this has been my only chance to see her—and I fear that it's not going to happen again, at least not anytime soon.

Sitting at the corner of the bar, nursing a club soda with a lime, I keep my eye on the door, spotting my sister the instant she walks in. She sees me right away, too, and acknowledges me with a little wave. I take a deep breath and pray for the best.

"Hi," I say as she approaches me. Her expression is serious, but not angry, and I take this as a good sign.

"Hi," she says, slowly unbuttoning and removing her navy peacoat, then hanging it on the back of the stool. She sits, crosses her legs, then crosses them the other way.

"I was going to order you a drink," I say as the bartender comes to take her order. "But I wasn't sure what you wanted."

She tells me that's okay, giving him a perfunctory smile and ordering a house cabernet.

"We have two," he says, sliding her the cocktail menu on an iPad.

She pushes it back and says, "You choose, please."

Only then does she turn to look at me directly. "So," she says tersely. "How are you, Josie?"

"I'm doing okay," I say, feeling doubly nauseated—both from morning sickness that lasts all day and from the mere thought of the evening that stretches ahead. "And you?"

She sighs again, but says she's fine, too.

"Are you back at work?" I ask her.

She shakes her head. "No. I resigned yesterday, actually."

"*Whoa,*" I say. "Congratulations."

I can tell it was the right thing to say, as she gives me a genuine smile. "Thank you. It was long overdue."

"Have you thought about what you want to do next?" I ask, thinking that my sister could do just about anything she wanted.

"Not yet," she says. "I'll think about that in the new year. . . . For now, I just want to focus on Harper and the holidays."

I nod, smile, and say, "How is Harper?"

"She's great," Meredith says, her expression changing, softening. "She's so excited for Santa. I get a revised list for him every morning."

"I really miss her."

"She misses you, too. A lot."

"May I see her? I was thinking I could take her ice skating at the St. Regis?"

Meredith nods as the bartender brings her wine. "That would be really nice. . . . She'd love that."

I take a deep breath. "So about tonight," I say, my voice rising nervously. "I wanted to talk to you before everyone else got here. . . ."

Meredith takes her first sip of wine, waiting.

"I wanted to talk about what happened in New York," I continue. "Our dinner with Sophie . . . our fight. All of it."

"Okay," she says, taking another sip. Her face is open, but she clearly isn't going to make this easy for me, either.

"Did you tell Mom?" I ask.

"No," she says, shaking her head.

"No, you didn't tell her about Sophie? Or no, you didn't tell her about our fight?"

"No to both," she says.

I nod, resisting the slight urge to subtly point out that she's doing the same thing that Nolan and I did. Trying to spare someone she loves.

Meredith must read me, because she says, "It's only been a few weeks . . . I'm still digesting everything."

"Right," I say, understanding her point, yet also seeing how easily a few weeks can turn into a few years.

She doesn't respond, staring into space, then suddenly looks over at my glass. "What are you drinking?" she asks. "Vodka?"

I swallow, then tell her, "No. It's just a club soda."

She raises her brows and looks at me. "What, are you pregnant?"

I can hardly fathom a less satisfying, more anticlimactic way to convey my news, but the last thing I'm going to do right now is lie to my sister. So I nod and tell her yes, I'm pregnant.

She laughs, then immediately realizes that I'm serious.

"Really?" she says.

"Really," I say, my heart racing. "Eight weeks."

"With Pete?" she asks.

I shake my head and say, "No. With Gabe."

"Gabe?"

"Yeah," I tell her. "We did IUI last month . . . and got lucky."

I watch her process the news, her expression going from shocked to some version of happy. She smiles and leans over to give me a hug, whispering her congratulations.

"Yeah," I say. "We're really excited . . . and scared. . . . We're not taking this lightly at all. . . . It's not a whim, Meredith."

She nods and says she knows. I'm not sure she's convinced, though, so I keep talking, trying to explain my heart to the person who most often misunderstands it.

"For years, I couldn't get over Will and the mistakes I made in that relationship. I wasn't truthful with him . . . just like I wasn't truthful with you."

She stares at me, intently listening.

"I really, really wish I had talked to you sooner," I finish.

"Yeah," she says sadly. "I know. And I believe you."

Her words give me the strength to continue. "If I could go back, I would do things differently. But I can't. . . . None of us can. . . . All we can do is move forward. And that's what I'm trying to do. I want to be a mother. I know it won't be easy, but I'm going to give it my all. Which is why I chose Gabe. . . . He's been a wonderful, true friend to me. He always, always has my back . . . and I think those qualities, that loyalty, will make him an amazing father." I make myself stop rambling.

"I'm happy for you," Meredith says. "And I think you chose right."

This time, I can tell she means it. "Thank you," I say. "Your opinion means so much to me." I smile, then add, "But I thought you didn't like Gabe?"

"Well . . . he's not historically my favorite." She pauses, then smiles. "But then again . . . neither are you."

"Touché," I say, touching my glass to hers.

We grin at each other for a beat, then both glance away. Several long seconds pass before I break our silence, blurting out an apology, trying not to come unhinged. "Meredith, I'm sorry. I'm really, truly, *deeply* sorry."

She blinks, then bites her lip, appearing to be on the verge of tears.

"I'm sorry for drinking too much that night. For not telling you the truth as soon as I suspected it. For not being a better sister."

With this last statement, she looks at me directly in the eye, then says—for the first time *ever*, or at least the first time in my memory— "I'm sorry, too."

"Really?" I say, unable to hide my shock.

"Yes. Really," she says. "That night of the accident . . . remember how we fought?"

I nod and say yes, of course I remember. We fought over a necklace I wanted to borrow from her.

"I should have just given it to you," she says.

I can tell where she's going with this, and I shake my head and tell her it wouldn't have made a difference.

"Maybe not. But maybe it *would* have," she says. "Maybe you would have called *me* to come get you . . . maybe you wouldn't have gotten quite so drunk . . . You tend to drink more when you're pissed off. . . ." Her voice quivers.

I shake my head, adamant. "No. That wasn't it. You and your cheap, ugly necklace had nothing to do with anything. . . ." I say, making a joke to keep her from crying.

"Yes, but neither did you and Nolan . . . You couldn't have possibly known what would happen. . . . I'm sorry I said you were responsible for Daniel's death. . . . You weren't. That was cruel. And it's not true."

I nod, my heart feeling healed, if not absolved. "What about Nolan?" I ask her. "Did you make up?"

"We're working on it," she says. "We're trying . . . but I just don't know. . . ." Her voice trails off as she shakes her head, looking so, *so* sad.

"Because of our lie?" I ask.

"Because of a lot of things. But mostly because I'm not sure we are right for each other. . . . But we're going to try to work things out. *Really* try. For Harper's sake. For *everyone's* sake."

I nod, feeling sure she is now referring to our whole family. I suddenly wonder if that hasn't been part of her burden and resentment over the years. The feeling that she is somehow responsible for keeping us all together.

"I hope you can, Meredith . . . but if you can't? That's okay, too. . . ."

She nods, looking grateful. Bolstered by the feeling that for once, I might be the stronger sister, I keep going. "And no matter what happens," I say, "you chose right, too. You still chose the right father for *your* child."

I turn on my stool and put my arms around her, waiting for her to pull away, relieved when she doesn't. Instead, she raises her head and looks at me with wide eyes. "I know I did, Josie," she says. "Thank you."

We change the subject after that, to lighter topics, pretending that nothing happened, the way we often do after even our biggest rifts. Maybe it's a form of denial. Maybe it's the best way when two people are as different as Meredith and I are. Then again, maybe it's just our odd way of expressing love and forgiveness, which are often one and the same.

As the others arrive, and we are seated—at the same round table by the fireplace where we sat with Daniel and Sophie fifteen years before, to the very hour—I feel certain that this last theory is the correct one. That it all comes down to love. After all, it was love for Daniel that brought Nolan and Meredith together, and love that is making them try again. It is love for my family that makes me want to be a mother. And Gabe's love that has given me the courage to make it happen.

After we order, and our waiter pours champagne for everyone but my dad, Harper, and me, we raise our glasses and toast the memory of Daniel. We share stories about our brother, son, friend. We cry and laugh and cry, until at one point, Meredith puts her hand on mine and whispers, "Go on. Tell them your news. . . ."

And so I do, with Gabe's help, feeling as scared as ever about the uncertain journey ahead, but also at peace. I know by now that you can't control your life, no matter how hard you try. That inevitably people leave and disappoint and die. But there is one constant, one thing you can always count on: that not only does love come first, but in the end, it is the only thing that remains.

ACKNOWLEDGMENTS

More than anything, this book is about family and the sacred sibling bond. From my earliest memories and throughout my life, I have been so fortunate to have Sarah Giffin by my side. There isn't a kinder, more supportive sister anywhere.

I am eternally thankful for my amazing mother, Mary Ann Elgin. She instilled in me not only my love of stories but also my keen interest in relationships, in all their messy glory. I would not be the person or writer I am today without her.

Nancy LeCroy Mohler has painstakingly dissected virtually every line of my eight novels. She was the first to meet Rachel and Darcy back in the fall of 2001 and the last to analyze Josie and Meredith, and I'm so grateful for her true friendship and tireless reads.

I am indebted to my editor, Jennifer Hershey, for her compassion and clear-eyed wisdom, as well as her so generously sharing her own motherhood story with me.

Many thanks, also, to my fabulous team at Random House for their energy, creativity, and professionalism, especially Gina Centrello, Kara Welsh, Kim Hovey, Scott Shannon, Matt Schwartz, Theresa Zoro, Susan Corcoran, Jennifer Garza, Kate Childs, Sanyu Dillon, Debbie Aroff, Kesley Tiffey, Melissa Milsten, Denise Cronin, Toby Ernst, Paolo Pepe, Belina Huey, Loren Noveck, Victoria

Wong, Anne Speyer, Cynthia Lasky, Allyson Pearl, and the entire sales force.

I can't imagine writing a book—or introducing it to my readers—without Stephen Lee. Publicist, reader of every draft, and confidant, Stephen has done it all since I began my journey in publishing.

Enormous thanks to my assistant, Kate Hardie Patterson, for her diligence, loyalty, and extraordinary gift for making everything around her a bit brighter and more beautiful.

I thank my incomparable agent, Theresa Park, for being both nurturing and tough—and for believing in me even when I doubt myself. Thanks also to Emily Sweet, Abby Koons, and the whole Park Literary team, as well as my website designer, Mollie Smith.

I am grateful to my wonderful father and stepmother, Bill and Kristina Giffin; my loving extended family; and all my readers and friends, near and far, old and new. A special thank-you to those in my inner circle who made specific contributions to the birth of this book: Julie Portera, Allyson Jacoutot, Jennifer New, Jeff MacFarland, Martha Arias, Glenn Saks, Lisa Ponder, and Steve Fallon.

And finally, endless gratitude to my inner, *inner* circle: Buddy, Edward, George, and Harriet. You are a daily reminder that love always comes first.

First Comes Love

EMILY GIFFIN

A READER'S GUIDE

A Conversation with Emily Giffin

Random House Reader's Circle: Tell us a little about *First Comes Love.* What is the story about?

Emily Giffin: *First Comes Love* is a story told from the alternating perspectives of two thirty-something sisters, Josie and Meredith, each facing a critical crossroads in her life, while struggling to come to terms with a family tragedy and the secrets that surround it. Sister stories have always been among my favorite in fiction, whether it's the Quimby girls in *Beezus and Ramona,* the March sisters in *Little Women,* or Elinor and Marianne Dashwood in *Sense & Sensibility,* so I was excited to write a story examining this relationship. But beyond the sister bond, this book is also about marriage and motherhood, friendship and family. And of course it's about love—my books are always about love!

RHRC: Did your relationship with your sister provide inspiration for this story?

EG: Inspiration can be a difficult thing to pinpoint, but I definitely draw on all my relationships and experiences when I write. My older sister, Sarah, is my closest friend and my biggest supporter, and I know she says the same about me. But we're also capable of really hurting each other, and sometimes I think that is a function of our closeness. In some ways, the closer you are to someone, the more vulnerable you become. Maybe this is because we show these people our truest selves, or maybe it's a simple matter of being more invested: The stakes are higher the more you care. But that is the contradictory dynamic I wanted to explore in this story. I wanted to talk about women who, despite loving each other and sharing the same family and upbringing, are capable of misunderstanding each other in sometimes critical ways. These misunderstandings come to define Josie and Meredith's relationship, and what they have to overcome in order to reclaim both themselves and their relationship. Fortunately, I can say that my disagreements with my sister have never run so deep, but then again, we have not had to endure a terrible family tragedy. For the Garlands, I think that accident changed everything.

RHRC: How do you think *First Comes Love* is different from your previous novels?

EG: *First Comes Love* deals with the aftermath of loss, and the long-term ripple effect a single tragedy can have on a person and a family. This theme of grief is one I've touched on previously, but never to this extent. In a broader sense, I would say my first seven novels were very much about finding love—that one romantic relationship to fulfill and complete us. And although the title *First Comes Love* would suggest the same, this book is more about finding the courage to live life on our own terms. After all, romantic relationships can often be gravely disappointing. People leave; they disappoint; they die. But we still have other paths to family and fulfillment. *First Comes Love* is about that journey.

RHRC: Do you see yourself as more of a Meredith or a Josie? Did you find yourself taking sides as you wrote the book?

EG: I could probably identify a little more with Meredith, if only because she and I are both married with children (and I used to be a practicing attorney). But I actually found Josie to be more likable through much of the story. As I switched voices, though, I found myself switching sides. I could see both points of view because I dwelled in both their minds. My stories aren't autobiographical, but when I write in the first person, I always find emotional things in common with my protagonist, regardless of how different our lives might be on paper.

RHRC: How do you navigate writing characters who are flawed but still likable, while keeping the reader engaged to the end?

EG: I think there is a difference between being likable and being flawless. Some of the most lovable, wonderful people are the most flawed—and in fact, don't we all sort of resent women who are too perfect? I think creating empathy is the key. Yes, my characters make mistakes and hurt others, but they are good people at heart, and I enjoy the challenge of making readers root for them in spite of their unsympathetic choices. After all, life is about the gray areas. Things are seldom black and white, even when we wish they were or think they should be, and I like exploring that nuanced terrain.

RHRC: How do you approach a character whose actions you don't necessarily agree with?

EG: As a writer, it can be tempting to try and dictate morality or happy endings, but ultimately, I think those stories feel less realistic, nuanced, and compelling. So I do my best to stay true to the characters I've created and really try to determine what *they* would do in certain situations, not what *I* would do or what I *wish* for them to do. In that way, fiction can sometimes feel like motherhood and friendship. We want the best for the people we love, but we can't always control those outcomes. And once again, I think it all comes down to empathy—in both fiction and real life.

RHRC: This is your eighth novel. How has your writing process evolved?

EG: It's actually no different now than when I wrote my first book, which is to say that it's still a very organic, character-driven process. Other than a vague sense of beginning, middle, and end, I generally have no idea where the story is going when I start writing a book. As I get to know the characters and as the relationships between them form, the plot evolves accordingly. It can be a frustrating and inefficient process at times—and sometimes I do wish I had a more outlined, organized approach to writing, but I enjoy being surprised along the way.

RHRC: Will you always write about relationships?

EG: Yes! Relationships are so integral to who we are as people. Ultimately, the sum of our relationships really defines our lives.

RHRC: What sort of research did you have to do for *First Comes Love*?

EG: I never do much research when it comes to underlying emotions—perhaps because I consider myself very naturally empathetic. In other words, I didn't talk to people about losing a sibling or child. But I did have to do some research for Josie's reproductive storyline. I talked to women who conceived with sperm donors and read a lot about the topic. Incidentally, I think I would have chosen this route if I had found myself unmarried at thirty-eight or thirty-nine—so I could really relate to Josie's decision.

RHRC: You don't see a lot of truly platonic male-female friendships in fiction, and the one between Josie and Gabe is such an important part of this book. What made you want to write about that relationship, and how is that different from writing about friendship between two women?

EG: I know a lot of people subscribe to the *When Harry Met Sally* theory that men and women cannot be friends in a purely platonic sense. But I strongly disagree and strive to create realistic male-female friendships in my fiction. It's actually a dynamic I explored in my first book, *Something Borrowed,* with Ethan and Rachel's friendship, and that was one of the very few quibbles I had with the movie adaptation (in which Ethan professes his love to Rachel). As for the differences in a male-female friendship, I really think it depends on the two people, as no two friendships are the same. But if I had to generalize, I would say that male-female friendships tend to be a bit more straightforward, less complicated, and less marked by undercurrents of competitiveness.

RHRC: A lot has been said about how women today feel more pressure than ever to "have it all"—the perfect job, the perfect marriage, the perfect family. Do you agree?

EG: I absolutely agree, and I think that premise shaped the direction of this book. As wonderful as it is for women to have choices, I think in some ways, those choices have added a layer of difficulty to our lives. We put so much pressure on ourselves to be perfect. And I don't think social media is helping the situation, with what I like to call the "hashtag blessed" phenomenon—the beautiful, curated versions of our online lives which often bear little resemblance to reality. Maybe some are bragging; maybe others are simply trying to keep up; maybe some don't even realize they are doing it, but I think it can lead to anxiety and dissatisfaction, something you see reflected in Meredith throughout *First Comes Love*. I think it's important for us to remember that there truly is no such thing as "having it all." There are always compromises we make in our lives, things we inevitably give up to have something else. This is certainly true with both Meredith and Josie. They envied each other but had trouble seeing the things they *did* have. I think that can be a trap for all of us.

RHRC: As you said, many of your books show the start of a romance, when two people are falling in love and finding their way to each other. With Nolan and Meredith, we see a couple in a very different part of the relationship, once they've been together awhile and are struggling to make it work. How is writing about marriage different from writing about dating? Do you prefer one to the other?

EG: Of course marriage is different than dating, just as marriage is different with and without children, if only because the stakes are higher. But all relationships are different, and it's really difficult to compare one to the next. I also think it's impossible to understand what's happening inside another relationship, particularly a marriage. It's so easy to judge from the outside, but only those two people really know what is happening—and sometimes it can feel like a mystery even to them. I do believe that the vast majority of marriages are complicated works in progress and seldom the fairy tale we wish they would be. I think the most successful ones involve communication and forgiveness, and I think we see that with Nolan and Meredith.

RHRC: What do you hope readers will take away from this book?

EG: That's an interesting question. I don't think I ever sit down to write a book with a message in mind, but inevitably one emerges. In *First Comes Love,* I think that message is that you can't perfectly script your life. There will always be bad things that happen to you. But ultimately, we are in control of our lives. We can choose our way and decide to be happy.

RHRC: *First Comes Love* was optioned for a film, meaning we may get to see these characters on the big screen soon. Do you have a dream cast in mind?

EG: Casting has never been my strong suit, perhaps because the characters seem so real and vivid in my mind, and I have a hard time letting those images give way to Hollywood. But I'm thrilled that the book has been optioned by wonderful producers, and look forward to their ideas. And yours! I absolutely love when my readers cast my books, so please send me your suggestions via Instagram (@emilygiffinauthor) and Facebook (Facebook.com/emilygiffinfans)!

RHRC: What's next for you professionally?

EG: I'm involved in several book-to-film projects, including *First Comes Love* and the long-awaited adaption of *Something Blue.* But my real focus is on writing my ninth novel—which will be released in the summer of 2018. I'm in the early stages now, creating a new world and characters, but as always, expect a cameo of a familiar face!

Questions and Topics for Discussion

1. Did you identify more with Josie or Meredith? Why? Did that change over the course of the novel?

2. Josie almost writes off her relationship with Pete because she doesn't feel enough of a spark, but he argues that chemistry can develop over time. Do you agree with him? Do you think the development of the relationship between these two characters felt realistic?

3. Nolan tells Meredith that he initially decided to hide the truth about the night Daniel died because it wouldn't have helped anyone. Would you have done the same in his position? When is keeping such a big secret from a loved one justifiable?

4. Daniel's death is a source of great guilt for many of the characters in this novel. Compare and contrast the different ways that guilt manifests itself in their choices. How do you think Meredith's and Josie's lives might be different if Daniel were still alive?

5. Discuss the theme of motherhood in the novel. What does being a mother mean to Meredith, to Josie, and to Elaine? What does it mean to you?

6. Many of the characters in the novel struggle with the idea that the life they're living doesn't necessarily look like the one they might have imagined or hoped for themselves. Have you ever felt this way? Using examples either from the book or from your own experience, discuss how that feeling can be both a negative and a positive force.

7. What do you think allows Josie to finally get over her feelings for Will, after holding on to them for so many years?

8. Imagine for a moment that your best friend or sister tells you she is having a baby on her own, as Josie decides to. How would you react? What would you say to her? What would you want to hear, if you were the one making that decision?

9. Why do you think Meredith decides not to leave Nolan right away? Would you have made the same choice in her position?

10. At the very end of the book, Josie thinks to herself that love and forgiveness "are often one and the same." Do you agree or disagree with that sentiment? What are some examples of forgiveness being given over the course of the novel?

11. Meredith struggles with the idea of taking time for herself, worrying that both her family and her career won't survive without her. Do you think this is a common fear for women today? What do you think of Amy's argument that "If you end up happier . . . this could really be a gift to Harper in the long run" (page 232)?

12. This novel doesn't end with a "happily ever after"—both Meredith and Josie make their decisions, but the reader doesn't know what the ultimate outcome for each will be. Why do you think the author chose to end the novel where she does? What do you imagine happens next for these characters?

PHOTO: © EMMANUELLE CHOUSSY

EMILY GIFFIN is a graduate of Wake Forest University and the University of Virginia School of Law. After practicing litigation at a Manhattan firm for several years, she moved to London to write full-time. The author of seven *New York Times* bestselling novels, *Something Borrowed, Something Blue, Baby Proof, Love the One You're With, Heart of the Matter, Where We Belong,* and *The One & Only,* she currently lives in Atlanta with her husband and three children.

EmilyGiffin.com
Facebook.com/EmilyGiffinFans
Twitter: @emilygiffin
Instagram: @emilygiffinauthor

ABOUT THE TYPE

This book was set in Sabon, a typeface designed by the well-known German typographer Jan Tschichold (1902–74). Sabon's design is based upon the original letter forms of sixteenth-century French type designer Claude Garamond and was created specifically to be used for three sources: foundry type for hand composition, Linotype, and Monotype. Tschichold named his typeface for the famous Frankfurt typefounder Jacques Sabon (c. 1520–80).